The
Long Way Home

Sabrina Chase

Cover art by Les Petersen

ISBN-13: 978-1-940006-15-4

CONTENTS

Also by Sabrina Chase

Firehearted
The Last Mage Guardian

THE SEQUOYAH TRILOGY:
The Long Way Home
Raven's Children
Queen of Chaos

ACKNOWLEDGMENTS

As always, these books would never see the light of day without the assistance of many people: my splendid and worthwhile critique group STEW, fantastic editor Deb Taber, detail-oriented proofreader Roger Ivie, and countless beta readers. When they are willing to help with an entire trilogy, you *know* they are dedicated.

S. Chase

DEDICATION

To the memory of Captain Carroll "Lex" Lefon, USN(ret) 1961-2012. Officer, gentleman, pilot, raconteur, father. He could fly anything with an engine.

CHAPTER 1
LIFETIME WARRANTY

Moire jigged hard and fast to avoid a spinning chunk of wreckage, hoping the crab fighter chasing her would not dodge in time. Judging from the debris floating about, Fleet was losing the battle–too much of the wreckage was theirs.

She stared as some of that wreckage went by her ship, feeling suddenly cold. It was a piece of fuselage covered with garish abstract swirls of pink, yellow, and electric blue. The colors were still visible under patches and streaks of black from a direct, full-power enemy hit. Jorge's ship. This was not a good day to be a merc. "Dammit, I told you to wait for me!" she whispered, fighting back tears. Jorge was always impatient to get to the fight.

Moire glanced at the communication panel. It showed only one message, the same message for the last fifteen-minutes-going-on-eternity. SAYRES GO WIDE, HUNT/KILL. She never had liked that name; she had to keep reminding herself it was hers. That's what happens when you need a new identity in a hurry. With Jorge dead, she realized with guilty relief, nobody else in the unit would know about it.

The crabs must have killed the wing commander too. The comms went on the blink all the time, but they'd never been out this long before. If the wing commander was down, she was on her own. Wasn't likely the crewcuts would bother contacting her–a merc was just supposed to go get killed instead of one of the crewcuts, they didn't care how.

The crab fighter was still on her tail, and it was beginning to annoy her. *Stupid crab. Why don't you just go home so I don't have to kill you?* It flew close enough for her to see it without the scope. She knew some of the spines on its spiky black surface were guns, but where were the viewports? Might explain why its targeting was so terrible. Fleet should tell them these things. Maybe Fleet didn't know either. They knew surprisingly little about an enemy they'd been fighting for so long. Including why the crabs had attacked humans in the first place.

The crab fighter pulled a sharp turn, flipping in the process. Now it was behind her, to one side. That was one of their favorite maneuvers, and an effective one. The crab fighter fired, the far edge of the spread catching the engine casing. A red pinlight flickered on her display but went out almost immediately. Engine self-repair was one thing about the future she really liked. Too bad *Bon Accord* hadn't...no. She wasn't going to think about that now.

The fighter was following her in an outside circle now. The crabs were good at high-g turns, but she'd noticed they didn't do too many of them together. Moire pulled a sudden curve down and reversed direction. Darkness started to crowd the edges of her vision, but she caught her breath and held it. The trick worked–the darkness receded, and she flipped into another sharp, crazy turn, as hard as she could stand. The other mercs thought she just had a natural talent for high-g maneuvers. She'd never mentioned being a test pilot, and wasn't planning to. It would just raise awkward questions.

Sure enough, the crab fighter didn't follow as cleanly this time. Without any delay Moire flipped up and over, her hand on the firing controls. The fighter sped past her and into a shell round before it could recover. Small fragments of wreckage from the explosion pinged her viewport and fuselage.

More wreckage flew by, some heavy and fast enough to damage her ship, and she pulled away. She remembered the fighter's fin-notch pattern from the beginning of the fight, so they were still working on the first wave. The crab carrier would be disgorging the second wave soon, and there was no way in hell they could withstand it. *Canaveral* was already in bad shape. One of the mercenaries' keel launch bays had been hit, and she'd seen enough damage when she left to tell her Fleet was getting a thorough shellacking.

Someone had to get the carrier. That wouldn't be easy; nobody had made a confirmed hit on a crab carrier although plenty had tried. Even if she went banzai, the carrier's guns were quite accurate. It also had some kind of whacko ship-specific shielding that let the crab fighters go right through, but batted away Fleet ships as if by a giant invisible hand that then held them immobile as they were blasted. She hadn't believed it herself until she saw it in action; it sounded too much like a force field. Which, she had on the best authority, was impossible. Of course her information was eighty years out of date, and she remembered when they thought faster-than-light was impossible too. They were lucky only the carriers seemed to have the shielding.

A large, jagged mass drifted by–enemy wreckage, but too big to be from the fighter she'd just hit. No other hostiles were in the immediate area, so she cruised around it to check it out. It looked like one of the remote-control gun platforms Fleet fighters called dumbos.

The crabs liked to fight defensively. When they showed up, the dumbos were detached from their carriers and deployed around them. Their formidable guns fired almost as quickly as those on the main ship, and if the crabs were forced to leave in a hurry the dumbos were abandoned–and detonated. The few unexploded ones that had been investigated showed no indication of ever being manned.

Something must have triggered the core by accident this time. The dumbo was little more than a gutted shell. A big gutted shell. Big enough for an antique Fleet fighter to fit into, if the pilot was skilled. Moire grinned. A trace of the old what-the-hell feeling returned–what Etienne had called "the mischief." She hadn't felt that for a long time.

It was risky, but safe was for people who had a chance of living to retire. Slow and gentle, she nudged her ship into the dumbo. It took longer than she liked to get in position without damaging it. There was a small hole forward that she considered enlarging, but decided against. She could see enough as it was and the risk of the crabs detecting her alien self inside the dumbo shell was too high. She gave the engines a hefty kick, wincing at the sound of straining metal but not letting up. If this stunt was going to work, it would have to be soon or it was wasted effort.

The Trojan Dumbo drifted toward the carrier. It was hard to judge her position. Was she inside the shield now? Moire bit her lip, frowning. No, she had to be sure. A little bit more. The comm display suddenly flashed random visual junk, then went blank again. She felt a surge of excitement and wrapped her hand around the throttle. Time to find out if she was right.

Reversed engines at full power vibrated through the frame of her fighter. As she cleared the hulk of the dumbo she armed all three remaining missiles. There was no point in being conservative now. She flipped the ship up and around, checking for trouble and targets. The open maw of the fighter sortie port was not far away. That would do for a start. Maybe it would hamper the crabs as much as *Canaveral* had been when its bay got hit. "See how you like it," she muttered, and fired.

She didn't wait to see if the missile had any effect. If she was going to get all three launched she would have to keep going. Number two went amidships, on the general principle that it had to damage *something*, and by then she knew she had their attention. According to her scope, every remaining alien fighter was headed back toward the carrier. And her.

Moire cast about for the last target. By now she was near what seemed to be the bow of the ship. Like most of the alien carriers, the ship had a bulbous protrusion from the main body there: a long, narrow strut with a blob sticking out on the end. It looked like a swizzle stick. It was different enough from the usual spikiness of the crab ships that it must have a purpose. She fired the last missile. It wasn't a clean hit, but the swizzle stick was definitely damaged.

A storm of angry crab fighters suddenly engulfed her. They were doing damage to each other in their eagerness to destroy her, firing without making any effort to avoid their comrades. She spun and turned desperately, using her greater maneuverability as best she could, but she knew she wouldn't last. There were too many of them. She could just give up—but the more crabs she destroyed now, the fewer Fleet would have to deal with later.

A hit, and another. Damage was occurring faster than the self-repair could fix it. Now an engine wasn't responding. At least she hadn't run out of ammo yet. *Any second now.* This was it, she was going to die. Finally.

A blinding flash of light seared her eyes, and her fighter bucked and tossed like it was in a gale force wind. Something slammed into her fighter from behind with a tearing crunch and her tell-board went crimson, but whatever had hit her was hitting the enemy as well. She saw Fleet fighters streaking by, attacking the dazed enemy with ruthless efficiency. There was no sign of the crab carrier.

Soon the only thing moving was drifting wreckage. Lots of wreckage, which she could be considered part of since she had lost engine power. If her tell-board was to be believed the only working system was the running lights. It wasn't fair. She'd done her best to get killed and she couldn't even do *that* right. Fighting a crushing wave of disappointment, Moire started to flip off nonessentials. She was going to have to keep on living a little while longer.

"...hired gun, looks like...merc ship, do you read? Come in, merc!"

She glanced at the console, puzzled. She'd never shut down the comms...and someone was hailing her. "People are trying to sleep around here, flyboy," she responded. "I've had a busy day."

A muffled snort came over the comm. They must be getting close if the signal was that good. She looked about and saw them. Three Fleet directs flew by, then around.

"You look like hell," said the first pilot. "Can you maneuver?"

Moire grimaced and looked at her board. A pinlight flickered red, then stayed yellow. "I've got half of one engine, now. Maybe. Don't wait up."

"We will escort you," said a woman's voice, cool and measured. "After what you did, we will get you back whatever it takes. We owe you."

"Cosign that," the third pilot chimed in. "Yer pretty damn sneaky, merc."

"You don't know the half of it," Moire said under her breath, and she urged her wounded ship into motion.

It took forever to return to *Canaveral.* Moire's fighter could barely move, and there were too many other craft that couldn't move at all. She watched the rescue scows move out and return as her ship crept closer. Damage and destruction everywhere she looked, and frantic calls for assistance on all channels.

Moire slapped the comm switch silent, angry and ashamed for feeling that way. Those people *wanted* to live. It was easy to develop a reputation for fearlessness if you didn't. They didn't know she was really just trying to run away. Run away from the ghosts, and the guilt of still being alive.

One of the Fleet fighters escorting her was flashing its running lights. Moire blinked, then realized she was close enough to *Canaveral* to see the bay doors. Close enough for the override, but she didn't see the indicator on her board. That's probably why they were signaling her.

She sighed and flipped on the comm again. A barrage of voices greeted her.

"Sorry about that. Comms are intermittent," Moire lied, when she could work a word in edgewise. Flight control sounded frantic.

"Sayres, you trying to give us heart attacks? For all we knew you were dead in there. Your ship isn't even broadcasting its ID, never mind life support status. Remote isn't working and you are still moving in under power, if you can call it that. Think you can get yourself in?"

"Bad idea, Control," Moire answered. "I'm lucky to be moving at all." The remote override would have brought the ship in and docked it, if it were working. They didn't like pilots coming in under power on their own. That they had even offered showed how desperate they were.

Mumbled consultations on the other side of the comm.

"How's your air?"

Moire squinted at the panel. It was, of course, flashing red. "No atmosphere recycle. I got thirty minutes on this, then I'll have to go to my shipsuit emergency backup."

A curse, then a sigh. "Sayres, hold your position. We have to figure out a way to get you in. Are you loaded still?"

"Half a belt of cannon shells. No missiles," Moire said, going on memory. That console was completely dead. She slowed her fighter to a standstill.

"Right, that makes it easier. Look, Sayres, we'll get you in as soon as we can. I'm keeping this channel open. Give a yell the *instant* anything changes in there, got that?"

"Got it, Control." Trapped in her own cockpit. Not roomy at the best of times, and she was wearing combat protective gear over her shipsuit.

She watched the cleanup, and the damage control, and her gauges. Just before she was about to switch to the emergency oxygen she heard a metallic clunk on the underside of her fighter, then another. A powered EVA suit rose up in front of her viewport, and the operator raised the center waldo arm. Moire returned the A-OK signal, wondering why they hadn't contacted her. Maybe they had, and the comms were out for real this time.

Her ship started to move forward again. They had attached a line, and she could see other powered EVAs nudging the ship into position. Then she was in the carrier, and then her cockpit was open and many hands were unfastening her harness and pulling her free.

"I'm all right, I'm fine...," Moire snapped. The bay was complete chaos. Mobile robotic cranes were moving craft out of the way so others could be brought in. Where was her unit chief? She had to report in. Moire shook her head, trying to focus. This wasn't the launch bay. She stepped aside to let a woman in a rugged, dented exoskeleton get past. She was carrying a tool with hydraulic fittings big enough to have their own valves.

What did they call those again? Heavy mechanics. She must be in Maintenance, then.

A voice shouted a wordless warning, and she ducked as a thick metal cable went swinging by. The voice added a profane suggestion of where she could go and what she could do when she got there. Leaving would probably be a good idea. They had enough to worry about here without gawking pilots.

Somehow she stumbled out of Maintenance. Mercs weren't supposed to be in that section of the ship, so of course a harassed marine started giving her grief about it. Moire took advantage of the distraction caused by a convoy of wounded to dodge down a side corridor and escape.

Sheesh. You'd think there's a war on.

Emergency lighting only on the lower levels, and smoke obscuring things even more. Closed bulkhead pressure doors more than once made her retrace her route. Some had the "low pressure" warning lights flashing.

Finally she made it to the one still-functioning mercenary launch bay, all the way at the bottom of the ship. It was easy to find a unit chief–they were surrounded by five or more people, all shouting. She found one with only three and reported to him. She wasn't even sure if her unit chief was still alive. Somebody would get it all sorted out.

She made sure she accounted for all of her expended missiles. They were expensive, and Fleet didn't like mercs wasting them. Dimly she noted nobody else seemed to be talking. Maybe she was the last to report. It had taken long enough to get back, and she'd gone all the way out to the crab carrier.

Oh yeah. The crab carrier. Hard to cover *that* up.

"Saw a piece of Jorge's fighter," Moire forced herself to say. "Looks like he got nominated." The chief nodded, respectfully silent. Moire stumbled away, finding a crate against a wall to sit on just before her legs gave out.

She'd blown up a crab carrier, but not quick enough for Jorge.

Suddenly the memories were vivid, strong enough to touch. Standing on a street of what she'd later learned was Brisbane, staring at the security fence, the guard, the no-frills architecture of the facility inside. Military, her instincts said. Something wasn't right, though, and the mind-fogging drugs Toren had used on her hadn't completely worn off or she would have found a less public place to stare and figure it out.

"You want in, *si?*"

Moire spun, almost losing her balance. The man standing in front of her flashed a smile, enhanced by gold filigree tooth covers.

"Uh, yeah," Moire stammered. Her heart was pounding, and lightheadedness made it hard to concentrate. When had she last eaten? If she could get inside, Toren couldn't get her. "Yes, I want in."

The man gave her an appraising look. "Maybe if you want support crew slot, but definitely if pilot."

Huh? "I'm a pilot," Moire said. That much she was sure of. The rest was hazy.

"*Buena Fortuna!*" This made gold-tooth man very happy. "We go inside and talk to Chopper."

Inside. Where it was warm. Moire nodded.

They went past the guard. Her new best friend just said, "New recruit," and the guard waved them by. No salute?

Chopper turned out to be a tall, muscular black woman with fine colored wire braided into her hair, so it stood out in amazing corkscrew shapes. Moire tried not to stare. There were other, even stranger-looking people in the halls. Only a few were wearing uniforms, and nobody saluted anybody. Had the military changed that much while she was gone?

"Pilot, huh?" Chopper gave her a look. "Where'd ya find her, Jorge? So let's see your license. Or chop sheet, we don't care." Moire froze. Jorge started on an involved tale, eventually wheedling Chopper into running a simulator evaluation instead.

The simulator smelled funny, like rancid lemon. It also didn't have the controls she expected. No landing gear. Extra trim jets. One part of her brain woke up as she left the simulator. Vacuum fighters. They weren't testing for atmospheric flight, but for space.

"Seventy-six percent," Chopper said. "Work on your response time and you could get prime rate. Clients pay extra for target efficiency too."

Mercenaries? Space-fighting mercenaries? What the hell was going on?

"Getcher ID and stuff together and be back tonight," Chopper added. "Tabriz got final say, but we ship out in two days so I don't think he's gonna get all picky." She added a comment that Moire didn't understand, even though a few words were in Russian. Jorge responded with something similar, grinning.

This wasn't going to work. A mercenary unit shipping out—to space—in two days. Time to fade out and not come back.

"My lucky day today," Jorge said. "You come back soon? Get you signed up, I get my bonus! Need to get it quick, not much time to spend it."

They passed a room with a huge display on one wall. A crowd of mercenaries were watching it intently, faces serious. It looked like a newscast.

Jorge made a rude noise. "Like those ground-pounders know anything about the war. Don't know why they bother watching, old news by the time it gets here."

War? Who was fighting whom?

"You just ask for me, they let you in," Jorge said. He grinned again. "I gonna wait for you. Get your things quickly, please."

Front door. Armored, she noticed now. And outside it was cold. Outside...outside there were people talking to the guard. She didn't recognize them, but she did recognize the badges they were showing.

Toren.

"Um, Jorge. Look, I have a...problem." He looked at her, some of the cheerfulness in his face replaced by a calculating wariness. "I don't have any belongings. In fact," she swallowed, "I don't have ID. I mean, I don't want to use the ID I–"

"*Comprende, amiga.* You do not say, I do not hear." Jorge scratched his chin. Moire peered out the door, breathing quickly. The Toren people had cleared the guard.

"Can we figure this out somewhere else?" Moire said, hoping her panic did not show in her voice. Hoping Jorge wouldn't give her up as too much effort.

His eyes narrowed. "You don' mind we go off-planet, eh?"

At this point, anything was better than staying and getting caught, so she nodded.

He turned quickly and motioned her to follow. Moire heard the big main door open behind her, and she hurried to keep up.

"I get you fixed up. Gonna cost, too." He must have seen her expression. "When you get paid, *hancha.* You hire in I know I get my money back somehow. But maybe you stay here until I get back, hah?"

"Sure, no problem." Relief made her weak at the knees.

Jorge appeared to have decided the best way to protect his investment was by sticking her in the big room with the display wall, which seemed to be the main off-duty room for the mercenaries. More conversations in the strange, mixed-up language that she couldn't follow completely. She picked up enough Russian to guess Jorge was asking his buddies to keep her there. It became apparent they were also to keep her out of sight of the officers, because whenever one came in sight she was discreetly shifted out of view.

It worked out fine by her, especially when one heavily tattooed mercenary gave her something to eat. She couldn't tell what it was supposed to be, but she was too hungry to care. She saw the Toren people go by, too, sometimes together, sometimes alone. They would peer in the common room, but didn't come in. The mercenaries seemed to treat them with distant civility, but weren't welcoming either. Moire stayed out of sight.

At least she hoped she had. Too many shocks, too close together, made her forget to be careful sometimes. The newscast had mentioned the year: 2115. Eighty years and change since *Bon Accord* had left Beta Centauri.

She'd known that was a risk when the drive went bad. But so long? Anybody who had known her, or of the ship's mission, would be dead by now.

The common room had what passed for a phone directory these days. That was when she figured out she was in Australia. Then, when she did a bit more searching, that Houston no longer seemed to exist in any practical sense.

NASA itself simply wasn't there.

What was she going to do? Even if Etienne hadn't given her that order, she knew she had to report back on Sequoyah. He'd named their ship *Bon Accord* for a reason. They were a good team. Some things didn't need to be said. Sequoyah was too important, and they were willing to die to get that information back.

Jorge finally came back with the fake ID and a story to go with it. It worked enough to get her hired, and that was all she cared about. The mercenary commander, Tabriz, filled her in a little more and confirmed her decision to stay. They were being hired by Norstar Fleet, which seemed to be the main combatant in the war. More importantly, she'd picked up from the newscasts that Fleet was *real* military. Maybe she could find a way to report through them.

The next few months were tough. The training was easy, at least for her. The difficult part was the mercenaries themselves. She stuck by Jorge, and he always had a story for awkward questions. Mostly she kept her mouth shut and tried to figure out what was going on.

Now Jorge was gone, and she had nobody to hide behind. This was going to be bad.

Moire slumped against the wall of the fighter bay, too tired even to think about heading for her bunk. She wouldn't be able to sleep with all the noise going on anyway, and she had to think about what she was going to do. The first mistake she made that got back to Earth would bring Toren down on her.

They must have found *Bon Accord* somehow. They'd put her back together and then they had tried, gently at first, to convince her to tell them what she knew. She wasn't sure what had triggered her suspicions, but when she'd refused, the tactics changed. She'd learned what Toren was, and she was even more determined they would never have Sequoyah.

Toren was, among other things, the main military supplier. She'd thought she would be able to find someone in Fleet to report to, not realizing the mercenaries would be kept so isolated on the ship. Now she wasn't sure she could count on Fleet, if Toren was so heavily involved. They'd find out, they'd find her, and....

No. That was not going to happen. She'd join the crew of *Bon Accord* in oblivion if they did, and take her secrets with her.

Commander Byron Ennis wondered if his commanding officer was deliberately being obtuse. "Yes, but how did she do it?" he asked with determined patience. "She was flying a Vought 6500, hardly top of the line. No special equipment. She still managed to place *three* missiles and nobody else has managed *one!*"

"An interesting question," agreed Shabata. "Go find out." She smiled with cool amusement.

Ennis winced. He'd walked right into that one. "Yes, sir. Does the colonel have any other questions she would like me to ask the mercenaries while I'm there?"

"Look, 'Ron, they may not like you much, but they *really* don't like the rest of us. You deal with them more often, that should take some of the edge off. We need that information." Her dark face was serious and implacable.

She was right, of course, and if he was able to figure out how Sayres had done it, the information would help Fleet *and* his career. He thought for a moment. "Any chance of the captain authorizing a suitable reward? They take their liquor seriously. It might make them less hostile and more talkative."

Shabata nodded, tapping her chin with one finger. "I think that could be arranged." She paused, and said softly, "A whole damn carrier! You'll probably have difficulty shutting them up about it."

Ennis left her office and headed for the mercenary area, surprised that he was able to find an elevator that wasn't on override. Much of the frantic damage assessment and repair had already taken place, but there was still a lot of equipment being moved.

As he descended to the mercenary area, he could feel his tension increasing. Shabata had told him the decision to make him the liaison to the mercenaries had not been hers, and had nothing to do with his background. Even if that was true, he felt the unspoken connection was being made every time he made a report or acted in his official capacity. She understood his situation, but the rest of the command did not—and they considered the mercenaries little better than criminals.

If he were promoted, it would be less of a problem. Promotion was unlikely as long as his superiors were constantly reminded of his origins by his responsibilities, however, and he did not have much time left. If you stayed in the same rank for too long they moved you out of the combat posts and into support.

He found Tabriz in the mercenaries' mess, just above the launch bay level. The room was cramped and awkward, with a cluster of pipes and conduit snaking down from ceiling to floor. He had to climb over it to get to Tabriz in the back of the room. The mercenary commander had a datapad with a remote link and two comms on the scarred plastic table in front of him, and was talking into a third comm to Medical. The bay the crabs hit had been full of fighters ready to take off and casualties were high. That Tabriz was in the mess indicated that his office, near the keel bay, had not been spared either.

Tabriz was not happy to see him, but his frosty expression thawed with the offer of alcoholic refreshment for the mercenaries—and he seemed almost genial when a marine brought down a bottle of real Earth scotch from the captain's personal supply. When Ennis mentioned the other reason he had ventured into merc territory, Tabriz made no objection.

"Ann Sayres, is it?" He turned to a passing mercenary and gave a command. Ennis had learned a little of the mercenary patois, a horrendous mishmash of Russian, Arabic, and a few other languages he couldn't identify. The instructions were to go fetch someone called "Soldier-lass." It wasn't necessarily a compliment.

"That's an unusual name," said Ennis in an offhand manner. He'd learned to be careful about asking questions. The mercenaries did not welcome personal inquiries. "I thought you people didn't care much for Fleet soldiers."

Tabriz gave him a measuring look. "The others in the unit—they call her this. For the way she carries herself, how she keeps her gear. Like a soldier." There was a glimmer of something that might have been amusement in his dark eyes. "You got a name like that too. I hear some crewcuts say you are a...wild horse? They don' seem to like that."

"Mustang. That means I was enlisted before becoming an officer." Yet another reason he was an outsider, and he sometimes wondered if it had been worth it. He'd wanted to prove himself, and thought an officer's rank would stop the whispers. It hadn't.

When Sayres showed up Ennis could see how she had gotten her nickname. Unlike the other mercenaries, she wore no colorful gear or jewelry, no face markings or bodymods. She wore a military-issue shipsuit and plain overgear. Her only concession to merc standards was a red metalmesh flash-scarf—the unit's color—tied to one forearm. Her straight brown hair was cut helmet-seal spec, well above shoulder length. Except for the lack of unit markings, she could have been a Fleet pilot.

"He's come to find out how you did it," said Tabriz when she arrived, jerking his head in Ennis's direction. "Tell him if you want to."

Sayres glanced at him, and Ennis was surprised at the complete lack of elation, of pride, in her expression. She looked sad and bone-tired.

"The others said you want me to do the Black Cup," she said to Tabriz, ignoring Ennis. "They want to do it now, for Kurt."

Tabriz nodded sharply. "Yes, you do it now. Use this," he said, and handed her the bottle of scotch. She took it and left the messroom. A group of mercenaries standing by the entrance, watching the exchange, fell in behind her.

Ennis opened his mouth to object, to delay, but the commander interrupted. "This needs to be done immediately. Kurt Ullman, he might not last very long." The intense black gaze turned to him. "Those *mizake* directs don' like you, but we don' like them so much either. You ain't so bad for a crewcut. You stay for the tattoo, you can talk to her then."

Ennis blinked and nodded, masking his shock with an effort. It was meant as a compliment, but he wasn't sure he was pleased Tabriz considered him non-Fleet enough to be welcome at a mercenary tattoo. It didn't matter. He had work to do, and this would let him do it.

Tabriz got up from the table, snatching one of the comms and clipping it to his belt. He headed for the same door Sayres had used, negotiating the tangle of pipe and conduit with impatient haste. Ennis hesitated. Nobody seemed to be objecting to his presence, so he followed Tabriz.

He threaded his way through the crowded, narrow corridors and down an accessway ladder, ending up at the entrance to the aft keel launch bay. The doors opened as Tabriz strode forward, recognizing his badge ID, and Ennis hurried to enter with him. Technically he should have access, but he didn't remember if he'd pestered the security officer into actually changing the code to include him.

It was like walking into a wall of noise. It took a moment for him to sort out the pandemonium in the launch bay, full of ships and people. At first he thought the mercenaries had not stowed their fighters, then he realized any ships launched from the forward bay had returned here instead. The fighters had a castoff look to them—a mixture of makes and models with traces of the original group markings still visible under the colorful scrawls inflicted on them by the mercenaries.

A group of people wedged its way through the crowd, and he saw in the middle a pneumatic float-pallet with a heavily bandaged man on it. He was attended by two medical orderlies and several mercs, some of whom were also injured. The orderlies were having difficulty maneuvering the float-pallet. One edge was not level with the deck, and it caught on any unevenness in the decking. This close to the hull at the keel the gravitic field was uneven anyway, and this area had not originally been intended for continuous use so it didn't have trim nodes.

The pallet hit another snag, and the orderlies gave it a hard shove. The wounded man—Kurt?—groaned. His face was streaked with soot and blood and blue patches of bloodglue.

"Why isn't he in Medical already?" Ennis asked, unpleasant memories flickering through his mind.

"Medical said they treat him here. They say not much chance they can fix him." Tabriz looked like he was carved out of stone, his face rigid.

"I'll get him up there if I have to carry him myself," Ennis snapped. If Kurt Ullman was going to fight and die like a soldier, he should be given the same medical treatment as one.

Tabriz held up a hand. "A moment. He wishes this." He didn't look quite so angry anymore.

Ann Sayres was standing in the crowd nearby, still holding the bottle of scotch. Another merc came up to her, holding a strange black object, apparently the Black Cup. It looked like a lumpy, short staff with a broad, hollowed-out end. Sayres opened the bottle by the simple expedient of smashing the neck against a nearby elevator housing, and poured some scotch into the hollow.

The mercenaries went completely silent and still. The change was eerie. Sayres took the Black Cup in both hands and went to the launch bay doors, then carefully poured a splash of scotch on the deck before them.

Ennis gasped, astounded that anyone, even...*especially* a mercenary would waste something that valuable and rare.

"For the ones who did not come back today," Tabriz said in a quiet voice.

She went to the pallet, and the wounded man was raised with great care. A blackened hand with only charred stumps remaining where fingers had been reached for the Cup, and Sayres carefully lowered it until it touched his lips. His hand dropped, and then his whole body seemed to collapse in on itself. A shrill alarm started from the pallet, and the orderlies quickly moved it out of the bay, the crowd of mercenaries parting silently before it.

Sayres moved to the clear area in the center, and the other wounded came forward.

"She shares her luck," Tabriz said in answer to his questioning look. "Those who need it most, they go first." When the wounded had all had their sip, the rest formed up in what looked like reverse rank order. When the Cup was emptied, another merc following with the bottle filled it again.

Finally, Sayres worked her way to where they were standing. She looked at Tabriz, but he pointed to Ennis, and she offered the Black Cup to him. He knew it was an honor, knew he could not refuse. He let the tiny dribble of scotch just touch his lips. He'd never tasted the real stuff, just synthetic. Once.

His eyes met hers over the Cup. She seemed quite ordinary to have done such extraordinary things. She was of medium height and medium build, trim and balanced. A few strands of brown hair escaped across her forehead, tangling with straight black eyebrows set over hazel eyes. He saw something in those eyes that bothered him, but she turned away before he figured out what it was.

Tabriz took the Black Cup from Sayres when he was finished. He raised it over his head and stomped his foot. The mercenaries took it up, creating a driving rhythm Ennis could feel in his bones. The beat went on for a moment, then a woman stepped out into the clear center of the launch bay, tall and bronze-skinned with tiger-stripe tattooing framing her face.

She started to dance to the rhythm, a confident, athletic dance, and the others started to clap to the beat and call out. A man joined her after a while, and then Ennis heard the sound of a guitar stick. This was more what he had been expecting, but it didn't seem to mesh with the solemn beginning.

The tiger-stripe woman twirled and dropped, springing up with proud, defiant energy, and then he understood. *I am alive...and while I live, I will fight.*

Ennis finally pulled his mind free of the mesmerizing beat, wondering how long he had been distracted, and feeling guilty. The dancing was becoming more general and less intense, and a crowd of people was clustered around an alcohol tap that had been brought in. It had a flavor dispenser, and it looked like the full-range model: ouzo and sake as well as beer and wine. The captain was *definitely* pleased.

It took him a while to find Ann Sayres. She was seated on a crate, sipping a drink, in the shadow cast by one of the on-deck fighter craft. None of the other mercenaries were nearby.

"Which one is yours?" he asked, looking at the other ships. There were a few Voughts on deck, but he didn't see any 6500s.

Sayres blinked, coming back to the here-and-now, and gave him a disbelieving look. "My ship is a pile of smoking scrap in Maintenance. If they have any sense they'll just melt it down instead of trying to fix it."

"You flew it back."

"I can fly anything with an engine." She sipped her drink moodily, not looking at him, gazing off into the distance again.

Damn arrogant pilot. He tried again. "Was the brain still working when you came in? I want to tap the visual data. This bay isn't linked to the central system, so I can't get it from the general download when you docked."

"Wouldn't have gotten it anyway; they had to tow me in to Maintenance. I don't know about the brain. There were green pinlights last time I looked. Ask them."

"I will." He had known this wouldn't be an easy task, but Sayres was being especially unhelpful. Once again he resolved to bring up the issue of a regular debriefing system for the mercenaries. Command liked to pretend they weren't there, but this was beyond a joke. He'd never been convinced using mercenaries was a good idea to begin with, but Fleet had needed fighter pilots in a hurry and Earth was still resisting the idea of a draft.

"We need to know how you did it," he persisted, suppressing his annoyance. "This is the first real break we've had in the war. What gave you the idea to try the dumbo shell? You could have been trapped in there."

Sayres sighed, and rubbed her face with one hand. She looked exhausted. "There was a lot of debris floating around. I saw this gutted dumbo go by, and thought maybe if I looked like one of them I could get close enough to score a hit. I wasn't sure I could get through the shields that way, it just worked. Must be some kind of passive-active system—there wasn't anything left in the dumbo but the hull. Maybe they key on the profile. Anyway, I had three spears left so I just tossed them anywhere that looked good. Got the sortie bay and the swizzle stick—that thing in the front—for sure. Don't know where the other one went. Then I just hung around waiting for the fighters to come back."

Ennis digested this, nodding, then gave himself a mental shake. Sayres had a real talent for making the impossible seem dull. *She blew up a crab carrier all by herself. Remember that.*

He'd have to hope there was more information in the vid dump from her ship. "We got some information from the carrier wreck," he said. "What was left of it, anyway. We think the...thing you hit was the signal antenna for the dumbos and the other remotes." What was a 'swizzle stick'? Some mercenary slang? "The instant it was disabled they all went dead." There'd been a lot of arguments about that since the start of the war. All the crab carriers made a lot of signal noise, but he hadn't heard of anyone decoding any of it.

"Makes sense," Sayres nodded, beginning to look interested in spite of herself. "I wonder what made it blow up, though. Now that I think about it, I didn't come under fire until the fighters came back. I don't think the carrier has any short-range defense other than the shield."

By now the party was in full swing, and he could barely make out what she was saying. Loud music and voices filled the room; he could even feel the vibrations in the deck plates. "If I get the visuals, I'd like you to take a look and see if there's anything else you notice. Give us a briefing, show us your target points."

"Sure thing." She didn't sound enthusiastic.

He made his way slowly through the chaos filling the launch bay, stopping only to watch a knife dancer with fascinated horror. The man had missed a few times, but he didn't seem to notice the pain or the blood. Ennis was glad Security had insisted on a lockdown for the mercenary levels. The alcohol fumes were rather strong, and he wondered if that had been a good idea.

A niggling feeling that he was missing something crossed his mind. Leaving the launch bay, he hesitated at the elevator station and took the stairs instead. He had some thinking to do, and he was always restless when there was something bothering him.

The alcohol had been his idea—was he worried he'd get blamed if something went wrong? No, he'd only suggested it, others had the approval and the responsibility. The battering of the bottle of scotch? Barbaric, but from a mercenary point of view understandable. They didn't have much use for an empty bottle.

He puzzled his way up to the twelfth level. It was something to do with Sayres—and alcohol. The noise, he had leaned nearer to hear what she was saying, sipping her drink.... On the tenth level, he stopped in his tracks. He'd smelled it when he left, but not when he was talking to her. Sayres had not been drinking alcohol.

Three enlisted came down the stairs, starting at the sight of an officer but recovering quickly and assuming an air of nonchalance after saluting. They presumably had some unsanctioned activity in mind; the stairs were rarely used in this section of the ship. Ennis contented himself with a steely glance and hoped they would think twice about whatever they were planning.

He started up the stairs again. He still had a ways to go to get to officer country. Why wasn't she drinking? She'd looked like she wanted a drink badly. It was available, and she wasn't on duty. *She knew he was going to question her.* She was extremely careful with her answers, and she volunteered little. What was she afraid of giving away?

By the time he reached his quarters he had reluctantly concluded he didn't have enough information. If it was important, he'd figure it out eventually. He remembered what Penderhest had taught him, all those years ago. *Notice everything, forget nothing. You never know when it might be useful.* He wondered what the old man would have thought of how he was putting his advice to use on the other side of the law.

He keyed the door to his quarters and wedged himself in with the ease of long practice. It was tiny, cramped, and annoying but it was all his, and privacy was at a premium on *Canaveral.* If it had been any more comfortable, someone with seniority would have claimed it. Most of the officers at his rank were still sharing cabins.

It was tiny, but it was home. The only home he had. He liked the odd shape of it, the strange nooks created by the intersection of bulkhead and beam. Sitting on the bed with a weary sigh, he pulled down the desk and stared at the screen. He checked the status of his repair requests, then got to work. He had to get the report on Sayres done now—Shabata would want it when he went back on duty in a mere six hours.

He finished the report at last, authenticated it, folded the desk against the wall, and pulled himself upright using the overhead latch. Bracing himself in the proper position, he pulled out the sink and wearily brushed his teeth. The face in the mirror looked like it was looking forward to a visit to the morgue.

He paused, the sono-cleaner industriously polishing a molar. Seeing people who looked like that...long ago. Never long enough. On Fimbul. Why was he thinking about Fimbul? He'd pay money to have that part of his brain removed. Was it remembering Penderhest? Seeing the burned mercenary?

The mystery clicked into place. That look that had bothered him, the expression of weary resignation. Waiting for death. He'd seen it in Sayres's eyes.

CHAPTER 2
NO FRIGATE LIKE A BOOK

"What's gotten into you?" Shabata's voice was sharp. "She's a good pilot. We'd be lucky to have her in the regulars. Why are you trying to make a big mystery out of her as well?" She pushed her datapad away and rested an arm on the table.

Ennis knew the signs. She wasn't going to let it slide. He couldn't blame her for thinking he was overreacting; sometimes he thought so himself. "I don't like mysteries. Not on my watch. I don't like the idea of a mercenary who is that capable on the ship when I don't know why she's here." He tossed a datatab to her, and she caught it midair. He'd been planning to sit on it, but Shabata would need more proof.

"What's this?"

"Vid dump from some of the other fighters. In the thick of the fighting after the carrier blew, there's a clip where Sayres is dodging a crab fighter—and she banks. She's banking a vacuum fighter, Nele! Why? We don't even tell the vacuum crowd about banking. She has to have atmosphere training. And if she's an atmo pilot, what the hell is she doing out in the middle of nowhere getting shot at by the crabs? Even if she's a mass murderer there'd be somebody willing to hire her dirtside. I also checked with some of our fighters. I could only find two that thought they could get their ships in and out of that shell without wrecking them. She's more than just a good pilot."

It wasn't any one thing he had noticed, but a lot of little details. Ennis knew more about the mercenaries than most Fleet officers from having dealt with them so often. Sayres simply did not fit the profile. Her reluctance to talk also made him suspicious. Even if there was a string of hard-core felonies with her name on them, there was no reason not to tell him about something completely unrelated. He knew something about felons, too, and he didn't think she was one of them, either.

He wanted to know why he'd seen that hopeless look in her eyes.

Shabata tapped the datatab on the tabletop. "I still think you are picking up ghosts on your scanner," she said finally. "You haven't told me anything I could take to the captain without getting reamed for wasting his time. Still," she held up a hand to stop his protest, "I agree there's a strange feeling to it. What we need is more information about her."

"It's not easy to come up with believable excuses for hanging around down in bilge class, and she can't come up here."

"Maybe. What were you saying about books earlier?"

"After the briefing I asked if there were any favors we could do for her, and she wanted to know where she could get some books to read. Just trying to get on her good side, if she has one."

Shabata rolled her eyes. "OK, this is what we do. You offer her the whole *library*. If she's anything like you with books, that'll fetch her. The mercenaries don't have access to the data net, right? She'll have to go to the library itself. You have to be with her the whole time she's there, and she gets an escort to and from. That will keep Shaughnassy off my case for security and give you a chance to ask her more questions. Deal?"

"Deal." He knew Shabata was both giving him what he wanted and making sure he'd pay a price for it. She was good at that. If he didn't really care, then he'd drop the whole thing. But he did care. He didn't like mysteries. Not like this.

❦

"Sayres?"

Wake up, idiot. She stood up and hoped the marines hadn't noticed her hesitation. Remembering her alias was the least of her worries. What made her sweat were the things she didn't even know she was doing wrong. Going topship to the library was dangerous. It would bring her too much attention and more opportunities to make mistakes in front of people who would notice, but it could also give her the information she needed to blend in. She was lucky to have gotten away with it as long as she had.

The marines were stolidly silent all the way up in the elevator, to her relief. The library was one level below Medical. She'd heard they had taken Kurt there at the end, but there was not much the medics could do for a man who had been half-carbonized. She was astonished by what they could replace these days, but that had been too much even for them.

The officer who had questioned her about the carrier, Commander Ennis, was waiting for them. Moire felt herself tense. He was far too intelligent for her tastes, and noticed everything. He'd asked some tricky questions in the briefing, too, that made her wonder what he was really trying to find out. Just her dumb luck he was in charge of the mercenary contingent. Her nebulous plans to chat up the marines to find a way to drop Fleet a hint vanished.

"I'll take over from here," he told the marines. They saluted and left. Ennis keyed the door open.

Could she talk to him without making him even more suspicious? She followed him in, watching him as carefully as she could without being noticed. He had a sharp-edged, angular face with a strong jaw and high cheekbones. Attractive, but the only expressions she had seen on it ranged from uncommunicative to uncompromising. He had piercing blue eyes, and his black hair was cut as short as it could be without shaving his head. *Just remember you don't like blue eyes, and you'll be fine.*

"You've been authorized access under my supervision," Ennis said abruptly. "Put in a request for another visit, and I will notify you when I'll be free. This is your reader key," he handed her one of the ubiquitous plastic rectangles with the embedded chip they called datatabs. "All of the main readers and the catalog need it. You won't be able to access any restricted or classified material. Is that clear?"

"Yes." She managed to bite off the "sir" just in time. Mercenaries weren't in the command structure, they were hired help.

That earned her a piercing glance. He looked down at her empty hands. "Don't you have a reader?"

Moire shook her head. She didn't have many personal belongings of any kind. Looking around the tiny library, she saw only large consoles. No racks of books, electronic or otherwise. She should have thought of that. A regular library on a military ship? What a waste of space, when they could just have a central datatap.

Ennis was frowning. "I can't–maybe there's a spare notepad." He went to a storage locker in the far corner and searched the shelves. "Here. It won't hold much, but next time I can loan you my second reader."

That was nice of him. Maybe he was just doing his best to do her a favor, like he'd said. It wasn't his fault he had the social skills of a porcupine.

She took the thing he was holding out to her. The notepad was just a display sheet in a frame, with a few simple controls. She looked with growing dismay at the notepad and the consoles. Somehow the stuff in there got in the notepad, or he wouldn't have given it to her. How ironic. She probably wouldn't have considered the Air Force if the judge hadn't made the military the only real option after they'd found out about her hacking. Now thanks to them and NASA and the sharp end of the theory of relativity, she didn't even know how to download a file.

She sat down at the nearest console and inserted her key. Maybe she could find the instructions without him noticing.

"That isn't a current update–just since our last in-port, ten weeks ago."

Then again, maybe not. Moire took a deep breath and tried to slow her heart rate. Then she understood what he was saying. The index on this reader just showed wireservice news articles.

"How old is the archive?" She tried to keep the interest out of her voice. This could be useful if it went back far enough.

"As much as the allocation is set for." He leaned over her shoulder and tapped one of the controls. "Looks like we've only got three years worth.

Canaveral was commissioned three years ago, so it makes sense."

It would have been nice if it had gone back the full eighty years she needed, but it was better than nothing. She picked up the notepad.

"That reader doesn't port–that's why it's set up for the wires. You can dump articles you want to read later into your mail. The other readers have the library index."

"Strange, keeping a reader dedicated to out-of-date news," she said, trying to cover up her slip.

Ennis was seated at another console now. "They'll read anything that reminds them of home, this far out." There was a thread of harshness in his voice.

"You don't?"

His gaze hardened. "I was born on Fimbul."

"Oh."

It was only momentary, but his eyes widened in astonishment. Moire quickly sat down at an index reader and stared with great energy at the screen. *Stupid, stupid...why can't you keep your mouth shut? Or was it something I didn't say?*

There was a cradle near this reader, and an optic port on a movable arm. The notepad also had an optic port. With a bit of fiddling she got the notepad in the cradle and aligned with the reader port.

Finding something in the index took her even longer. She didn't dare look up the things she wanted to directly–even if Ennis hadn't been there, she knew enough about "benign security" to suspect search queries would be archived somewhere. So she couldn't look up Toren, or *Bon Accord,* or even Fimbul. She settled on history. Nice, safe, dead history.

Her first choice from the list, "The Women's War: Afghanistan 2028-32" was too large for the notepad, so she settled on "The Tragedy of Houston." It was a start. She needed to find out what had happened to NASA.

Small sounds of motion alerted her to Ennis standing behind her chair. "Is that what you usually read?"

"History is a hobby of mine," Moire said dryly.

The transcriber caught another buzzphrase, and Ennis tapped the activate control. His briefing notes took up half the space since he'd taught the program how to remove the captain's unfortunate habit of repeating certain statements, and the screen activity made it look like he was adding comments. Occasionally he did.

The captain continued, "...and now to the main event." *Activate.* "The courier that arrived today came from Far Command. Five days ago, enemy ships were engaged en route to Zamaia. Using the debris camouflage technique, the local battle group completely destroyed the enemy force of two carriers, five heavy battleships, and what appears to have been a troop transport."

Someone whooped, and the room burst into applause. Ennis tried to follow the ramifications of this news. An attack on Zamaia would have been a major disaster. The system was close to the more densely settled areas; the crabs had never come so close before. Fleet had defeated them soundly. This was probably the turning point of the war, if they could keep the advantage.

He said as much to Shabata after the briefing, in the officers' mess. She was not as enthusiastic as he thought she would be.

"Nice theory, 'Ron. Wish it were that simple."

"Why isn't it?"

She sighed. "Politics. We lost a lot of expensive ships—and people—getting to this point. We don't have the resources to go on the offensive now, and it's a long shot to get them. All the decisions are made on Earth, and the people there aren't in danger yet. This victory may even make it harder for us, since they'll argue we don't need any more to do our job."

"But the colonies...."

"Are colonies. Far away, and only a few people on Earth are making themselves wealthy that way. The rest just see the war as taxes and the looming threat of the draft. You of all people should know how much a colony's problems count for back there."

Yes, he knew. The rescue ship had taken over a year to get to Fimbul. He'd just hoped they'd learned their lesson, that things had changed. People still did not like to be reminded about Fimbul. Sometimes, on the bad days, he thought they wished there had been no survivors at all. Shabata was the only person he'd met in his entire career who didn't care where he was from, who treated him as something other than a freak.

No, there was one other. He'd told Ann Sayres, and it had been like waiting for an explosion that never happened.

Shabata poked at the remains of her meal with her chopsticks. "The real problem is personnel, anyway. The capable people who want to leave Earth go for the colonies. We can't get enough people to man the ships we have. It still isn't public knowledge we use mercenaries to fill up the ranks—which is another problem. They can defer our pay, but the mercs are expensive."

Moire waited over a week for her next visit to the library to be approved. Since they hadn't had any fighting, by that time she had almost memorized the book on Houston. At least she had some idea what had happened now. The competition for planets had been violent once the regular colonies started up, and a North Korean splinter government had smuggled in a pocket nuke to take out the space center. The exploration phase had been much more peaceful.

She had to wait with her marine escort for a few minutes before Ennis showed up. As he was keying open the door, an officer with a hard, arrogant face walked by, glancing at Ennis and then at her. "Friend of yours?" he said as he left, his tone cold.

Ennis stiffened, his eyes a blue blaze of fury, but he didn't say anything. Moire didn't dare ask what was going on, but she was quite curious. The officer's contempt seemed directed at Ennis and not her.

He handed her a small personal reader. "Almost forgot this," he said with a brusque tone. It wasn't a recent model, even she could tell that. It didn't matter. It would hold books, and that was all she cared about.

The reader couldn't hold a lot of books, unfortunately, so she mailed herself some news articles as well. Memory storage had gotten gargantuan, but books now had so much extra content: video clips, sidebars, apps, and extra add-ons of all types. They simply took up more room.

A quick glance confirmed that Ennis was engrossed in some research of his own, so she changed consoles and selected the central encyclopedia. Maybe if she started with something like "fibula" and just kept reading, she'd find out what Fimbul was all about.

And there it was. She read quickly, dismay growing with every line. No wonder he'd been surprised by her lack of reaction.

"How did you end up with Tabriz?"

She started, and quickly closed the encyclopedia. Had he seen anything? He was still facing his console. When she didn't say anything, he turned his head and looked at her questioningly.

"The organization his unit belongs to is based in Brisbane," she said, trying to appear calm. "I met up with him there." She turned back to the console, but Ennis wasn't finished.

"What made you choose the mercenaries?"

She'd been desperate, and hungry. "I like to fly," she shrugged. Why did he care?

Ennis looked skeptical. "This is a long way to go for that. You could have stayed on Earth and not gotten shot at."

"You've never dealt with Sydney air traffic. Getting shot at is the least of your worries."

Ennis grinned, a quick flash, and she found herself smiling back. He didn't look nearly so forbidding when he smiled. Almost human, even.

"I've heard stories," he said, nodding. "If you like to fly and don't mind the danger, why didn't you join Fleet?"

"Oh, a buddy was already in the unit." *Some guy I met half an hour earlier, to be precise.* Moire turned back to the console again, hoping he'd take the hint. She should be careful. The more she talked, the more she could make mistakes.

"We're glad you're on board, however you got here," Ennis said. She waited, but he didn't say anything else.

Strange. Why would he want to be so polite to a mercenary? It was possible he was just thanking her for destroying the carrier, but his tolerant attitude was unusual for a Fleet officer. She was half expecting a tirade about only being interested in money, or a lecture on her Duty to Humanity followed by a pitch to enlist.

She didn't dare go back to the encyclopedia now, but she looked through the catalog and picked out her books. Her time limit was almost up by the time she made her selections, so after the books had loaded she took the reader out of the cradle and stood up, stretching.

Ennis was waiting. "How long have you been with this unit?" he asked as they left the library.

"Five months," Moire said, not thinking.

He stopped in his tracks, raising his eyebrows. "You learned how to fly a fighter that well in *five months?*"

Oops. "Tabriz's wasn't the first merc unit I was with," she said quickly, feeling shaky with relief when she saw his suspicious expression clear.

The marines were waiting in the corridor to take her back, and she walked toward them before Ennis could think of any more questions. She was going to have to find another way to contact the command, she decided gloomily in the descending elevator. Ennis was too damned suspicious and she didn't know why. She wasn't sure she could trust him, and she probably only had one chance to get it right.

Moire headed for the mail kiosk as soon as she was back in the mercenary area. The main barracks had a strange, almost prison feel to her, probably because of the metal mesh flooring between the upper and lower levels. It wasn't originally bunk space; it had been converted from a cargo hold. The bunks were stacked like pallets, two deep on each level, the whole assembly bolted together and secured to the beams overhead.

The mail kiosk was at the end of the main barracks corridor on the lower level. Like the bunks, it was a temporary measure for the mercenaries. When the courier ship came in there was usually an immense line of people waiting to read their mail, but the ship had been in for two days and there was only one man seated at the kiosk now, Oscar Rodriguez. He looked extremely unhappy.

"Bad news? Is Corazon all right?" Moire asked, concerned.

He turned at the sound of her voice and tried to smile. "Corazon, she is well. She write to say she have friend, win slot to emigrate to good *colonia*, decide not to go. He give to her instead."

"That's wonderful! So what's wrong? They won't let the kids go too?"

"Children go too. But must pay transport–fifteen thousand eurodollar." He waved his hand at the message on the screen. "I write to say no money here. Maybe borrow some, but not all. She have to pay soon or not go."

"That's too bad. That's a hell of a lot of money to get in a hurry."

"You want send mail, eh?"

Moire waved her hands at him. "I can wait. Let me know when you are done."

He shook his head sadly. "Finished now." He hit the send sequence and pulled his ID from the kiosk slot.

Moire watched him leave, frowning. Oscar was a nice guy who deserved better. All the colonies were desperate for people. The good ones were privately organized with a charter, and all colonists had stake shares in the outcome. Toren's corporate colonies were quite different. Most people wanted to go to the private colonies, but transportation was a problem. Toren also controlled most of the shipping from Earth, and it charged more to colonies it didn't own. Oscar's wife had won a free ticket, but she would have to pay for the children or leave them behind. It must hurt to have to watch this golden opportunity slip through his fingers.

Oscar hadn't asked her if she had the money. She had the whole amount, just barely. Living a low-profile lifestyle was rather cheap, and giving it to him would blow her low profile to flaming bits. Still, there had to be something she could do. He needed the money more than she did, and had a better chance of surviving to enjoy it.

She chewed on her lip and glanced at the kiosk display. The amber "interrupted" light was on. Oscar had been so upset he hadn't shut down properly. That was an opportunity, if she could use it. She couldn't activate the kiosk herself without using her ID, which would clear the screen—and she needed the information. There had to be a way; there was always a way. What did she have to work with?

This kiosk had a vid eye on the inside of one of the doors, allowing the other door to serve as a backdrop. It also had a playback, so live messages home could be previewed and edited before being sent. The question was, could she open the door wide enough to turn on the eye, but close it enough to see the screen? Moire double-checked the buttons on the eye, wiggled her arm and the door into position, and carefully plugged in her ID.

The screen flashed and cleared. Quickly she stopped the vid and played it back as slow as the thing would let her. She smiled. She still had the hacking instinct, even if they'd changed the tech on her. Some of the address was blurred, but it was enough. Sending the money without her name attached took a little more effort. With luck, Oscar's wife would think he found the money by chance and mailed it in a hurry to catch the courier. Hearing voices in the corridor, she pulled her ID out and walked away from the kiosk before someone saw her.

The surviving members of her wing were not present when she reached her bunk—probably at one of the many illegal gambling setups, or trying to make hooch out of potato flakes. She curled up with the reader, feeling satisfied with her efforts. She was glad she could help Oscar and his family. It wouldn't bring back the dead and it wouldn't change things for her, but it was a gesture of defiance against the Universe. And Toren.

The personal reader was a clever device, but short on instructions. Moire cycled through the controls trying to figure it out. When she got the content index it seemed too long. She'd only loaded five books, since it had said there wasn't room for more. The list had eight. The three at the end must have been left from the last time Ennis used it, and the reader hadn't cleared them out for some reason.

Here I was thinking he only read the Officer's Manual of Conduct...*let's see,* Collected Works of Shelley, The Higher Common Sense, *by Abbe Something-French, and* Paradise Lost...*where the hell did he learn to like this stuff?*

The encyclopedia article had given her just enough information about Fimbul to confuse her even more. How anyone could have been born there...the article had used a lot of words like "disaster," "radiation damage," "survivors," and "prison colony."

This was disturbing. If he was smart enough to survive, get out, and develop advanced literary tastes, it was a fair bet he would notice any slip-ups on her part—and he was probably sneaky enough not to show it. She should drop the library visits and learn to play three-deck poker with the other mercenaries.

That might alert him too. She shrugged to herself. Chances were high she would win the Good Target prize in the next fight, and it wasn't easy even for Toren to get information from where they were. The only communication with Earth was by courier ship. The middle of a war was probably the safest place she could be right now, as long as nobody noticed her.

He had undertaken many investigations for the Company, but this one was perhaps the most important. It was important not to cause undue notice that would jeopardize the Long Range Plan, or, worst of all, make anyone outside the Company aware of its existence.

In every investigation he always had to deal with fear, recrimination, worried complaints about imaginary failings—always of someone else. Naturally, employees would feel concern. No one who worked at a Toren high-pri facility could be terminated until an Internal Security investigation had been completed. However, the recommendations of such investigations were always acted on. And employees at a high-pri restricted facility were of necessity more intelligent, observant, and thus capable of deducing that given the nature of their work, Toren might well terminate more than their employment.

Loyalty was usually not a problem at this stage. The potential rewards were too high, and the screening was thorough. He was intelligent and observant himself, and he found he was beginning to suspect the full, audacious extent of the Long Range Plan. He accepted that it would be necessary, on occasion, to kill. Were they not essentially at war? Not the war with the crabs, but an undeclared war that only Toren knew about.

He would never say so, or even think it very often. That would be too dangerous. For him.

He hoped the others of his team were having better luck than their predecessors. It was extremely embarrassing. The subject had managed to escape from the most secure module of the facility, and they had not found any trace of her outside except for a few city surveillance vid shots two streets away. And that had been several months ago.

His superiors had given him a great deal of information about her. He found it unlikely she would have the knowledge or the ability to hide in a city like Brisbane without leaving any trace. Her very...differences...would make that impossible. Someone would have noticed.

The management had grown increasingly frantic the longer the subject remained free. And so his team had been sent for. The best, he had been told, in the company.

Certainly they were the only ones to follow his suggestion. Assume she had left Earth. Work back to find out how, and with whom. But first they had to find proof that their idea was correct. The company wanted results.

"This is the only exit? Are you certain?"

The facility manager nodded her head. "Even the air circulation goes through a scrubber first. There are no other openings in the walls large enough."

The door in question was a type he had not seen before. A large vertical cylinder set in the wall–rotated one way, a clear path through to the outer part of the facility. Rotated the other, a solid wall. No edges to pry, impossible to batter down.

"And the mechanism?"

The manager swallowed. "Badge recognition. The biometrics are all on the other side. We weren't set up to keep people in."

"And how did she obtain a badge?"

"One of the medical staff kept his in his jacket pocket. The jacket was missing." The manager was darting small glances at him, then away, shifting her weight. "She couldn't have done it, though."

Someone had. If not the subject, someone inside. That was what was worrying her. In either case, severe carelessness. "Why not?" He was careful to keep his voice even and gentle. Mildly curious.

"We kept her on a regimen of prolaxane and irenitol. Her recovery from injury was complete at that point. We used dermal implants for ease of reversal of treatment, and to prevent the subject from realizing she was being drugged. She would not have been able to walk from this door to the street exit without collapsing, and the implants last several weeks."

He examined the door again. A tunnel in a cylinder. "Show me."

The manager walked forward, and the door rotated for her. They stepped in.

"It has not closed," he observed, stopping at the far end.

"You're still inside," said the manager. "It won't rotate until the passage is free."

He felt a twitch of excitement. Yes, it was an idea. But how to test it? How would she have done it? The door must sense weight on the floor.

It was an awkward fit for a man of his height, but he managed to brace his back against one wall of the tunnel and his feet against the other. The manager was watching him with concern.

The door rotated. One end of the tunnel now pointed to a bare wall, but the other had an alcove with cable boxes and conduit. He shifted his way down, carefully lowering himself just enough to pick up a tiny white object, almost like a piece of wire. It had something flaky and reddish-brown coating it. Dried blood.

He dropped down and stepped out of the door when it rotated open again. He dropped the dermal implant into the manager's hand.

"I believe she knew she was being drugged," he said.

CHAPTER 3
BETTER STRANGERS

"Maybe they were mad about Zamaia," suggested Pers, moving his arm in the light to admire his new metallic tattoo. "That's the most ships they ever sent, and Chen-Li Run is just a mining camp, really. Hardly anybody there to fight."

"I dunno. Only five days later? Besides, did any crabs survive Zamaia to get the news back?"

"It was going to happen sometime. We have been lucky." Hasan sounded fatalistic.

Moire shifted her head on her arms, wondering if it was worth pulling the sound curtain on her bunk and deciding against it. She wasn't going to get any sleep anyway.

"Yeah, but Chen-Li did not have the fleet ships when the crabs come," Soliyah pointed out. "If we are there, they die." Her dark eyes blazed, then she bent back to her work, scowling. She dripped a little more polymer on the boot seal of the shipsuit she was fixing.

"How they gonna know we ain't there?" somebody wondered. "Them rad-dam crabs got FTL comms, betcha!"

"If they had any kind of communication faster than a courier we'd all be dead by now. Maybe they just got lucky."

Jere's deep, calm voice squashed the thread of hysteria that threatened to emerge. "Can happen. I hear Third Fleet was heading to that section, missed them by twelve hours."

"But if they can hit that close—that colony wasn't that far out, really."

Pers sat up. "I wonder where they will try next. Ignius isn't that far from Zamaia, and they ship a lot there. If the crabs figure that out...."

Moire listened to the heated discussion of the crabs' next target, hoping to learn more. She still didn't know how the war had started, just that it had already been going on when she returned. Nobody knew what the crabs wanted or even what they looked like, although there were plenty of wild stories. They would engage any human ship they encountered, and if damaged and unable to escape, they would destroy themselves rather than be captured. She hadn't heard of any communication with the enemy, so they probably weren't trying to negotiate either.

More interesting to her was that Toren seemed to be calling the shots as far as military spending went, at least for space presence. Their blue T-in-a-circle logo was everywhere. They were the primary supplier for the Fleet: almost all of the big ships came from their yards. Not a complete monopoly, but definitely the biggest player. Strangely, they were resisting any increased tax to let Fleet expand. Why they wouldn't want Fleet buying Toren ships to protect Toren colonies was a real mystery.

Their origins were mysterious too, at least to her. She'd done a little cautious questioning, hoping it was a general enough topic not to raise any suspicion. It seemed to have started as a multinational space technology corporation. Its main presence was in Australia, but it had offices pretty much everywhere in civilized human space. Somehow it had gone from being a contractor for NASA to being NASA's replacement, right around the time Houston got nuked. That part was murky.

She wished she could get to the library. She'd read all the books in the reader she'd gotten when they went into transit two weeks ago. *Canaveral* had been on station for more than three days now and Ennis still hadn't OK'd her request. She needed something to take her mind away, to stop thinking. To stop remembering.

She could have gone on liberty while they were on station, but that was too dangerous. Even the thought of going out just to have fun seemed wrong. Etienne and Michiko and the others couldn't enjoy anything anymore, and besides, she first had to find a way to carry out Etienne's last order.

She should have died with them. Then she wouldn't have to carry this burden all alone.

An itchy shudder vibrated through her bones, faint but recognizable. Moire sat up with a start.

"Hey, what's up, Ace?"

"The drive just engaged. And don't call me Ace."

Soliyah gave her a speculative look. "I am always wondering how you know it is the drive. I don't feel anything."

"Why don't you want to be called Ace? You hit that carrier," said Hasan.

"At that range, it would have taken real skill *not* to hit the carrier," Moire replied, trying not to sound exasperated. "I got lucky, that's all."

Hasan looked skeptical. "Yeah, but...."

Moire heard her commlink buzz with a feeling of relief. The "urgent" light was on, and the textbox just said "ready room." She swung down from her bunk, puzzled. Soliyah and Jere seemed to have gotten the same summons, and the tramp of boots on the metal flooring overhead told her others had as well. Out in the main corridor even more mercs were heading to the ready room. It wasn't a general summons, though. Moire tried to figure out what the common factor was. They couldn't all have gotten in trouble at the same time.

She wasn't the only one who was curious. "How'd I get on the same list as you lowlifes?" asked Andre MacAdam, joining them. Andre was a charming devil with connections to most of the illegal activity in the unit. Moire tried to avoid him as much as she could without being obvious about it. He had copper foil tattoo inlays in his face and arms that went well with his sandy hair and fair skin. She'd heard the inlays were drug-doped. Andre, and the others like him, had convinced her within a few hours of joining that she couldn't trust the mercenaries with her secret.

"You get promoted to lowlife, that's what happen." Soliyah punched him on the arm.

"One pass filter, you guys," cautioned Jere in a taut voice. "Keep it light." He gave the merest twitch of his head toward the main doors. Glancing that direction, Moire saw marines stationed in front—more than usual, and they were inside instead of at their usual position out by the elevator. This was starting to worry her.

There were around twenty mercenaries in the ready room when they came in. Nobody looked happy. Tabriz, up at the front, looked absolutely furious. Moire had never seen him so angry—but he didn't seem to be angry with any of them. Then she saw the Norstar uniforms up front with him. One of them she didn't recognize—a colonel, a woman with dark brown skin and a classically beautiful face. Ennis was standing next to her, and they both had no-expression expressions, looking straight ahead at the wall behind the mercs. There were marines in the room as well.

Everybody was tense and silent. Moire felt a growing disquiet as she started to see a pattern. Most mercenaries came from the unaligned countries, but she didn't see them here. There weren't that many Americans in the unit, but every one of them was in the room. Soliyah, Andre, Pers—Turkey, Canada, and Poland. All Norstar countries. *They couldn't...they can't be that stupid. Are they really going to ask us to volunteer?*

Politics was another topic where she had more questions than answers. Norstar was an alliance of most of the countries with a space presence. Somehow they had created a unified military—Fleet—that was doing all the fighting on the human side. If you squinted and didn't ask awkward questions, Norstar looked a lot like a planetary government.

The colonel said something in a quiet voice to Tabriz. "I called them," he snarled, quite clearly. "*You* tell them."

She looked at him for a moment, then at the assembled mercenaries. "I am Colonel Shabata. I am here to inform you that orders were received stating all Norstar nationals hired for combat support in the war theater are under direct Fleet command and subject to Fleet regulations. The captain has ordered that effective immediately, you are no longer independent contractors. Pilots, as you all are, are given provisional rank as flight officers in the Fleet. The captain expects the provisional rank will be confirmed."

Moire felt her jaw sag. There was a stunned silence for a moment, and then the mercs began to protest. She saw the marines tighten their grips on their weapons, and she tugged Soliyah's sleeve when she started to clench her fists and move forward. Jere just stood there breathing heavily, jaw working. *I was wrong. They* can *be that stupid, and in spades.*

She felt a chill of fear. Now she was in real trouble. Fleet was not going to be as easygoing about background checks as the mercs were, and it would be even harder to avoid notice. When information about her got into the central Fleet information system on Earth, a certain well-known military contractor was going to be on her tail. She had to find a way out. One way or another.

It wouldn't be easy. All the launch bays were locked down when they were on station, even if she could get a ship fueled up without anybody noticing. In combat they were too far away from any station, again assuming she could leave without anybody noticing. Her only chance would be the next liberty. Would it be soon enough, or would Toren be waiting for her there?

Shabata waited for a lull in the uproar, then spoke above it. "Those are the orders." Her voice had finality in it. "How you make use of this opportunity is up to you. As officers you are also able to make use of the training and advancement programs. The Fleet will provide you more advantages than your previous contract."

"How's the pay?" A voice dripping with sarcasm came from the crowd.

Shabata hesitated. "The base pay for a second lieutenant is thirteen thousand ED a year. All on-patrol personnel are on deferred pay, less a one hundred ED allowance. If dependents can be proven, half of the base rate can be paid to them without deferment."

Moire really thought the mercs were going to get violent at this news. They were shouting and yelling; the noise was deafening. That was less than a third of their average pay. Half of 13,000 ED wouldn't support much in any of the Norstar countries. It made the motive clear, though. They'd rather shanghai them than continue to pay them so much money. Or, with the colony raid fresh in their mind, they wanted to hire even more people.

"That's enough!" Shabata shouted. "You'll be escorted to your new quarters now."

If word spread about this in mercenary circles, they wouldn't be able to hire anyone. She wondered if the captain had considered the effect of his plan on the real Fleet officers. They'd always held the mercenaries in contempt. If they were forced to treat them as nominal equals they would be furious.

"I promise you, blood oath, I make complaints to anyone who will listen," said Tabriz. "When this get fixed, I get you back pay too."

Ennis was standing by the door now, with a datapad in his hand. He started to call off names. Slowly, burning with resentment, the mercs came forward. When he called her name, he didn't look at her.

Their new quarters were quite different from the converted cargo bay, and the mercs alternated between being pleasantly surprised at the amenities and angry when they realized how much better the directs had been living. The bunks had real foldout desk consoles and solid sound barriers. That would make the lovers happy, as well as everybody who had to listen to them.

The former mercs were split up among the different fighter wings. Moire was with Jere, Pers, and a few others she didn't recognize. At least the directs weren't there now; she doubted they would be pleased to see their new comrades in arms.

"Hey, target this! They got live links in each bunk! No more waiting for the kiosk." That was Pers for you. He'd find the bright side to anything if you gave him half a minute. "I wonder if we'll get better food up here? I heard they get real fruit sometimes, and bread."

She stared at the provisional commissioning hardcopy. All the important stuff was coded in the badge chip, but they still gave out an actual piece of paper for the commission. Even if the paper was some kind of plastic now, it made her nostalgic. She read it carefully.

"Hey Jere. I thought you said we were all second lieutenants."

"That's what I got. Anybody different?" The others shook their heads. "Why?"

"Mine's a first." She had a sinking feeling as she realized it probably wasn't a mistake. After so many years of careful dodging, she was stuck with a rank that meant she'd have to do something besides fly. It went against all her principles of avoiding responsibility wherever possible. Well, that just gave her even more motivation to find a way out.

"Woohoo, gonna get a whole quarter ED more'n us!"

"Deferred." At least the others didn't seem upset about it. Jere should have gotten it, not her. He had command written all over him, but the directs didn't know that. They *did* know she had blown up a carrier, which was looking like a bigger mistake every minute.

A group had gathered at Pers's bunk, watching him try out the desk communication console. "A message," he said, pleased. "Who could have sent so soon? No, wait...it is saying I have to go to Medical for a physical? I already had this when I join the unit. They keep taking blood samples I won't have any left!"

"So don't go. What are they going to do, discharge us?"

Moire checked her console. She had the same message. One more step toward exposure. She shrugged, feeling fatalistic. They wouldn't let her get away with avoiding the physical, and it would draw too much attention if she tried. Best to go with the crowd. The medics would be so busy and harassed they wouldn't ask so many questions. They'd notice the scars, though. They were hard to miss.

Maybe they could do something about her old hormone implant—of course, then they'd ask why her ovaries had been removed. She shook her head, annoyed with herself. If she lived long enough for it to become a problem, she'd figure something out.

The door opened. Startled, the mercenaries turned to face it. An officer stepped in and looked about the room, nostrils pinched as if he had smelled something unbelievably bad. He reached out with slow deliberation and palmed the door shut.

Moire widened her eyes, breath catching. She remembered him. He was the one who had made the sneering comment to Ennis at the library. She gave the "enemy in sight" signal with the hand not visible from the door and stood at a mercenary version of attention. This guy looked dangerous. He was holding his face so rigid the muscles in his jaw stood out. She would not be surprised if he spat at them.

He looked them over. The other former mercenaries were watching him with narrowed eyes, silent now, picking up the anger in the officer's body language and reacting to it. Ready to fight.

"The captain will have to explain his actions at some point, and don't think those...*provisional* commissions are worth more than used toilet wipes. You aren't officers to *me*. You are scum, and a disgrace to the uniform. Real officers have to *earn* their rank. You wouldn't know about that; all you care about is getting paid. Like any whore would." He came closer, looking at them in turn with unconcealed disgust. "It's different now. You're answerable to *me*. I don't care what you think. You do as you're told. And don't think you'll get loose by acting up. The only way you are going back to your whore buddies is as protein supplements."

Moire saw motion from the corner of her eye. She slammed into Jere just as he launched himself at the officer, fury distorting his face. Jere hit the wall hard, and Moire grabbed his arms while he was regaining his balance. "We prisoner!" she hissed in patois. "Don't say one word updown! He fight hunting, you blind?"

"You must be Sayres." She could read his nametag now; it said Hallin. Major Hallin. "Showing off your new rank?"

"No, sir." Her response seemed to enrage him even further, probably because he couldn't tell her off for disrespect. Jere had himself under control now, and she let go. The others were confused and angry at this turn of events, but they didn't look immediately violence prone. Yet.

"One crab carrier, and you think you're hotter than hell, huh, Sayres?"

"How many you get, crewcut?" She couldn't tell who made the snide comment, but everybody laughed. Everyone except her and Hallin. He let loose with an explosive burst of profanity, and Pers laughed even harder.

"That's it." The major had gone critical, she could see it in his eyes. He pointed to Pers. "I'm going to get rid of all of you, sooner or later, and you're going first." He slammed his hand against the doorplate. "You'll have yourselves and your gear in shape the next time I see you, or you are testing airlocks."

"What gear? What we gotta do with it?"

He bared his teeth in a non-smile. "Ask *her*," he said, indicating Moire. "She knows everything. Right?" The door shut behind him.

The silence was thick and poisonous as the mercs gathered, facing her. "*Sho ebat.* What the hell was that?" asked one in a quiet, angry voice.

"Trouble. He hates us, separately and collectively, and he's going to do everything he can to make us miserable." He was probably good at it, too. From practice.

Jere folded his arms. "So what's wrong with me tossing him around to teach him some manners?"

She shook her head. "He's got all the cards, Jere. They changed the rules."

"You been in Fleet before, ayeh?"

"No." They didn't believe her, she could see it. "Military, yes. But not Fleet." Even as she said it she knew she'd made another goof. Fleet *was* the military now, thanks to Norstar's grand unification. Only banana republics had separate military branches these days.

Well, there went the plan to ask her superior officer for help. At least now she was in the Fleet organization. There had to be *someone* on the ship she could trust; she just had to find them. Quickly.

Pers sat on his bunk looking at his hands, beginning to look worried. He raised his head. "Isn't there anything we can do about him?"

Moire sighed. "Keep a low profile. Hard to do when he's gunning for us, though. Try to be near other crew, especially officers. He'll have to at least pretend to follow the rules when there are witnesses." She shrugged. "Know what the rules are. He'll try to get you on that, and if that doesn't work, he'll try to make you lose your temper. Either way, he wins."

"Wotta lark." A rough-looking guy she didn't know with a lot of bodymods flicked a chewstick at the closed door with an air of contempt. "Bugger this, next port it's party time. I ain't gettin' paid enough for this kind of shafting."

"Got that right, Boggs." The others nodded, grim.

Moire wondered if the ex-mercenaries would even survive to the next in-port. She swore, realizing her plan for escape was in danger. Command must know the commandeered mercs were likely to jump; they probably wouldn't even let them off the ship. Then again, Command wasn't showing a lot of sense right now.

Ennis found an empty Random cube, which was unusual–especially since it was edging on the popular hour for the gym. He took a paddle from the wall rack and went in. He preferred to play solo when he had the chance. When he could concentrate on just the ball and the changing targets, he could forget everything else.

He set the ramp for the time interval high. The first few targets showed up and he hit them with plenty to spare; they hadn't even gone orange. Gradually the time and duration shortened and he had to give it everything he had to hit the target before it went red.

The target appeared on the ceiling, and he took aim for a corner shot. The door communicator buzzed, and he missed.

"Shabata here. Mind if I join you?"

He forced his annoyance away. He'd already lost his concentration, and he had some questions that would be better asked where they would not be overheard. "Sure. Set it for multiple, would you?"

Now the targets had an outer ring of color that didn't change, identifying which player they belonged to. His were green, Shabata took blue.

Shabata was a good player, and set up her shots with efficiency and skill. Ennis took his shot again and hit the target hard.

"Tabriz was right," he said between targets. "Voiding those mercenary contracts is illegal. We are going to regret doing this."

Shabata spun and jumped, smacking the ball with her paddle. "I know," she said, keeping her eyes on the walls for the next target. "But that was the captain's call. He got the orders and passed them on. They need the money to hire more mercs. I hear they are going to put the draft on back home, but it will take time. Time we don't have." She took a savage swing at the ball.

Ennis hit his target on the edge of red, choosing his words with care. "Do you realize we only have a hundred marines on board? Almost as many as the number of converted mercs?" He wasn't going to be the first to say "mutiny." Shabata could figure it out herself. "They don't have any loyalty to us, just their paychecks–and we took those away."

She hit her next few targets in silence, and he wondered if he had said too much. "I have concerns myself," she said in a carefully even tone. "What about that hotshot pilot you were worried about? Is she going to give us trouble?"

"She's getting trouble. Hallin has it in for them. I'm hearing disturbing things from that quarter, and not from the mercs. They are as good as locked down and they haven't even *done* anything yet." Hallin wasn't the only officer giving the converted mercs hell. He was just the most blatant about it.

"Hallin always has a drill up his ass. Especially if anyone's in the spotlight but him. Sayres got interviewed for the *North Star* two days ago; that would be enough to set him off."

The timer buzzed and the targets vanished. Ennis mopped sweat from his forehead and faced Shabata, holding out a hand to stop her from leaving. "I heard about that. The communications officer mentioned it to me, wondering if I knew what it was all about. Sayres refused the interview when she was asked, and then Hallin ordered her to do it. Have you read it yet? It sounds like an interrogation. Name, rank, and serial number. She didn't say much they couldn't get from her ID badge."

"So, she didn't want to and he made her do it because he's a bastard?" she mused, making a thoughtful grimace. "He can't keep it up forever. She may have a rocky patch, but if she's as capable as you say she'll make it through."

What about the rest of them? he wanted to ask, but Shabata had opened the door to the cube and walked out into the crowded gym. They passed a sullen-looking group in new shorts and tees, many with tattoos or bodymods, standing at the Conditioning and Coordination station. Mercs, sent to pass the physical standards.

"The captain is hosting a party to welcome the new officers," Shabata mentioned in a casual voice.

"The new officers we picked up on-station?"

"All the new officers."

He felt a sinking sensation in his stomach that would not go away. "Maybe we should post marines on the major levels. It's a big ship, they might get lost. Wouldn't want that."

Shabata understood. "No, we wouldn't want that."

The captain's party was held the next day, and was not a success. An effort had been made to decorate the officers' mess, but the purple metallic streamers were just the right shade to clash horribly with the dress uniforms they were wearing. Someone had found a source of pastries at the last station, too, which must have been expensive. They all looked slightly different, as if the reprocessor had been having problems. Curious, Ennis tried one. It tasted strange, with different tastes mixed together but still separate.

He looked around the room, feeling depressed. The senior officers were standing around with carefully noncommittal expressions hiding a range of emotions, none of them friendly. The former mercenaries weren't even bothering to hide what they thought of the whole proceeding, and in the middle were the confused new officers, not sure if the icy atmosphere was normal or because of some error on their part.

The ex-mercenaries stood out, too. Ennis knew they hadn't been issued any of the usual kit–the best Stores could come up with were stand-down fatigues at such short notice–but it looked like they had deliberately borrowed the worst-fitting dress uniforms they could find.

Perhaps they were just unused to the entire concept; he knew mercenaries valued their unique look. There was one–Boggs, the tag said–who would never look like anything else. He had stiff, white marled hair and an implausible amount of metal and plastic embedded in his face, along with a snarl of contempt that was echoed in his entire body.

The only one who looked military was Sayres, and her tunic jacket was too short and the trousers too large. She held a glass in one hand, but she wasn't drinking. Again. She was standing near the wall, watching the other mercenaries. Keeping an eye on them?

One of the former mercenaries was drifting toward the door. Sayres gave her a tiny shake of the head. The mercenary grimaced, but moved back. Yes, she was keeping an eye on them, and keeping a bad situation from getting worse.

Shaughnassy intercepted him as he headed toward her, and started chatting. Ennis listened to him with half an ear, keeping an eye on Sayres as the captain came up to her with a new officer, obviously fresh off the mill.

"Lt. Sayres, have you met Lt. Keegan?" Ennis had noticed Captain Hsu circulating about the room earlier, trying to get the disparate groups to mix.

The new lieutenant shook hands, and the captain beamed and wandered off again. An awkward silence descended that the lieutenant clearly did not know what to do with. Ennis felt pity for the kid. He'd been green once himself, a long time ago.

"Where were you commissioned?" Sayres finally asked.

"Dublin." Keegan tried to smile. "I'm...this is my first posting. I just finished University. I never thought they'd send me here," he said with awe.

Very green. A combat posting on a less-than-top-of-the-line ship, and the kid was in heaven. Shaughnassy moved off to the refreshments, but Ennis stayed. Keegan hadn't seen him yet, and he didn't want to cast a senior-officer damper on the conversation by joining in.

Sayres fell silent again. Ennis caught her eye and gave a slight nod toward Keegan, and she took the hint.

"Where are you posted?" she asked.

"Long-drive. I studied gravitics." Keegan leaned closer and spoke in a lower tone. "Who are those other people? They are in officers' uniform but they don't even look like enlisted!" He gave a wry grin. "Those must be those half-assed mercs I heard about. Bet they think they are on top of the world now." Ennis winced. "They aren't *real* officers, are they?"

He moved closer, frowning. This kind of talk needed to get squashed early; they had enough people thinking like that as it was. Sayres looked up as he approached, and nodded acknowledgment. She did not smile.

Ennis looked at Keegan long and hard, until the young lieutenant realized something was wrong and started to sweat. "Until the captain's order, Lt. Sayres was a mercenary. And while a mercenary, she was the first—Fleet or mercenary—to destroy an enemy carrier. You will treat them with the respect due a fellow officer, regardless of your opinion. Is that clear?"

Keegan closed his eyes, looking ill, and nodded. He swallowed hard, white-faced, and stammered an apology. Sayres waved an acknowledgment, and Keegan moved away quickly, stumbling a little.

Sayres just stood there, stone-faced and silent.

"This wasn't my idea," Ennis said bluntly. "Any of it."

"No sir." Her face remained unresponsive.

"It may not have been the best way to do it, but I'm glad you've joined Fleet," he persisted. "Tabriz may pay well, but—"

"I didn't join for the money," she snapped. He stared at her, startled. "I mean, ah, of course the money was important, but there were other...other important considerations. Not that it matters now," she said, lapsing back into silence. Her expression was sad.

Maybe it wasn't the money. The mercenaries were a close group, and fiercely loyal to each other. With Hallin beating them bloody she probably thought she wouldn't find what she'd had before.

"It's not just a uniform," he found himself blurting. "Fleet saved my life. They were the ones who got to Fimbul. And after—they were the only ones who would take me in. I enlisted as soon as I got out of the medical station."

"Nobody would take you because of the disaster?"

"The radiation, the prison—all of it." He clenched his jaw, remembering. The silence was the worst. That, and the loneliness.

"And you wondered why you had tried so hard to stay alive," she said softly.

"Yes." He drew a deep breath, shaken. No one had ever understood before, even when he had explained. *How did she know?* "That's it exactly. Norstar Fleet gave me something to live for. It could change your life too, if you let it."

She gave a short laugh, without humor. "Oh, it already has." She hesitated. "You trust it, then. Fleet."

He nodded.

"What if...you had a problem. A problem you didn't want to tell your superior about," she said carefully, not looking at him.

The problem being, of course, her superior. "It is technically possible to approach that officer's superior," he replied, wishing he had a better answer. "You would want to be very, very sure you had a valid complaint before doing so."

"Of course." She sipped at her drink. She looked depressed, and shifted as if she were thinking of moving away.

"Have you been getting other comments like Keegan's? I'd report him, but I think he learned his lesson."

Sayres gave a shrug, looking unconcerned. "Was it necessary to tell him all that about me?"

"Of course. We have to stop that kind of thinking before it causes any more trouble."

"I meant telling him I was the one who got the carrier."

He looked at her, incredulous. "The whole fleet knows. It's one of our biggest victories in the whole damn war, Sayres!"

"They don't know *who*, just that it got done," she persisted.

He smiled. "After the *North Star* article gets out, everyone will know."

"Who's going to read it off *Canaveral*?"

"The *North Star* is Fleet-wide. They even courier it to Earth for the brass."

Sayres went suddenly white, as if she had been stabbed, and her eyes were wide. "When," she said in a taut, faint voice. "When does it leave for Earth?"

"Already gone." He stared at her, concerned. "Why? What's wrong?

She didn't answer, but took a sudden, deep drink from her glass, leaving it empty. "How long does the courier take to get to Earth from here?"

Ennis thought for a moment. "Twenty days, usually. The courier ships are fast." What was she worried about? A criminal record? "Look, no matter what you've done or who wants you, the captain needs you more. He won't let anybody get to you, at least not until the war's over."

"Oh yes he will," she said, almost in a whisper. "He won't have a choice."

CHAPTER 4
CLOSE YOUR EYES AND THINK OF ENGLAND

Moire sighed deeply and picked up the rifle again. It wasn't a real rifle, of course—some sort of ersatz impact-recoil sim thing—but it was realistic enough that she still couldn't hit the target with it. *Dammitall, I'm a pilot, not an infantry trooper. Why the hell do I have to qualify with a rifle?* It was eerie how Hallin could always find someone's weak spot. She'd never been any good at hand-held weapons.

Sounds of yelling from the boxing/sparring area drifted over, and she spared a glance from her barely wounded target. Pers was getting a reaming from Hallin again. She wished there was something she could do to help, but everything she'd tried had just made it worse. It was only a matter of time before someone exploded.

She squeezed off another shot, good enough for the targeting program to register as a hit, and she began to hope. The next three were misses. It didn't really matter. What else was she going to do, anyway? None of the converted mercs were allowed any personal time. If not on duty or in their bunks, they had to be in the gym until they qualified on whatever Hallin had set them. If they finished one qualification, he found them another. Jere was on his fifth.

Moire smiled to herself. Hallin might have trouble finding things Jere couldn't do. Even money Jere would outperform Hallin; the man was *good*.

She almost wished the crabs would find them. They needed to get back into combat, or there would be serious trouble. Even on duty they had drills and formation sims. Hallin was the worst, but all the converted mercs were getting hammered. She didn't mind the sims herself—virtual reality had gotten quite sophisticated since her training days—but of course Hallin had figured out she liked them and wouldn't let her do them any more. Bastard.

It would all be over soon, one way or another. Only three more weeks before Toren showed up. It might take a few days more to get that stupid *North Star* article in the loop, if she was lucky. Toren had its tentacles all through the military, so its databots would be bound to find it.

Moire ground her teeth, and shot at the target to relieve her annoyance.

Whose bright idea had it been to network everything? It was funny—she could tell a real human being her secrets and have some chance they'd stay that way, but if it ever got on the network.... Even after all the hack attacks, people just didn't learn.

Two hits in a row, a miss, and then another hit. Maybe she should only shoot when she was angry. It seemed to improve her score. Someone approached her and she glanced up, hoping it wasn't Hallin. It was Ennis, in exercise gear and with his short black hair standing up in points from sweat and exertion. *Scenery just got better.* Judging from her reaction, she wasn't dead yet.

"You've been at this for a while," he observed. "You were here when I came in."

"Until I qualify, sir." She stifled a sigh. "Rifles and I just don't get along." Behind him, she saw Andre MacAdam give a wave and the handsign that meant "Follow me." She pretended she hadn't seen it. If Andre wanted to talk to her it was probably about something illegal.

Ennis opened his mouth as if to speak, then shut it with a snap. She guessed he knew what was going on, and he couldn't say anything about it. He didn't look happy. "Well. At least now you can go to the library without an escort." When she didn't reply, he asked, "Can't you?"

"I haven't had time." She indicated the rifle, and he looked even more annoyed. "I should give that reader back to you. I doubt I'll have the chance to use it before the next in-port."

"It's an extra," he said curtly. "Keep it until you get your own."

"Thank you, sir." She hefted the ersatz rifle to her shoulder again. She didn't want Hallin to catch her goofing off. "I have to get back to this or I'll never qualify," she apologized.

Ennis didn't say anything, but he didn't leave either. Then she noticed he was staring at her arm. The loose sleeve of her shirt had pulled up enough for the scars to be visible. She kept forgetting—she'd been wearing shipsuits all the time, which fit snug and had long sleeves. The mercs had assumed she was paranoid about low-g and vacuum leaks and not asked questions, but she knew she would only attract the wrong kind of attention if she wore a shipsuit under her gym kit. She should have worn a bone stress wrap; that was common enough. Too late now.

"Why didn't you have them erased? They look...or is this a mercenary custom?"

She wished she knew how she had gotten them. They were slashed across her forearms in no particular pattern, deep and ugly. She suspected they'd happened when *Bon Accord* was falling apart. If Toren had done it, they would have made sure she remembered. By the time she had found out she could remove them it was too risky to try. That kind of scar would be noticed and remembered by whoever erased them.

She pulled the sleeve down, covering her arm again. "Didn't have the money. It isn't important."

He gave her a high-voltage look, full of skepticism, but he didn't pursue the subject. "Look, Sayres. With my rank level I get personal transmission time on the priority data packets that get sent back with the courier. Since I don't...if you want to send a message home, to your family, anybody you care about...." His words were stumbling awkwardly, and he had color on his high cheekbones.

He meant well, but it felt like he had punched her. She fired, and fired again. Five hits in a row. "I don't have any family, sir. But thank you for the offer." Two misses, then another hit. Her vision blurred with sudden tears as misery washed through her. Never got to say goodbye, didn't even know they were gone until it was too late.

"What do you mean, no family? You don't talk to them?"

"I mean they are dead. Sir." The pain welled up in a sharp burst, and Moire couldn't hold it in anymore. She put the target rifle down and walked away. She left the gym blindly, barely noticing the other mercenaries were no longer there. There were still ten minutes on the clock–Hallin would be on their case, and hers. She didn't care.

All dead. Everyone I loved, everyone I knew. Did you know what would happen if I made it back, Etienne?

Maybe she should take the chance and tell Ennis, since Toren was coming anyway, but what if that didn't work out? She was trapped. If she was going to keep Sequoyah away from them, she needed a final exit.

It would be nice if she could die in a way that made trouble for Hallin, but how? Walking out an airlock was not a comfortable way to go, even if she diddled the safety interlocks successfully. The marines were the only ones with guns, and they had some sort of biometric lock that was keyed to the marine carrying it. Nothing else she could think of was any better. *It would be easier to kill myself if I wasn't so averse to pain.*

Toren wanted her alive, at least until they had sucked her brain dry of information. She didn't have many illusions about what would happen to her after that. They wouldn't leave her loose, free to talk about what they'd done.

Moire stumbled into the group quarters, surprised at how empty it was as she headed to take refuge in her bunk. Then Boggs came in from the lav, wearing only shorts.

Boggs was one of the scariest mercenaries on the ship. She hadn't seen anything to give a reason for this feeling other than his general psychopathic behavior. Not like Soliyah. Everyone knew she was violent, dangerous, and quick-tempered because they'd seen her in action, but Soliyah wouldn't attack without a reason. Moire wasn't sure about Boggs.

"Where the 'ell were you? Come along an' no yap, yer taking a shower."

He grabbed her arm.

Moire pulled back, alarmed. "What's the rush? No offense, Boggs, but I don't want to take a shower with you."

"It's important, bird. Now get in!" He shoved, and she stumbled and slipped on the wet floor.

The shower area was crowded. The rest of the converted mercenaries from her group were there, and a few others. Some were in their skivvies, others in towels and slick with water. They all looked grim and desperate.

"I'm telling you, it won't work!" Jere put as much intensity in his voice as he could without being heard over the running showers. Water flew from his brown, muscled arms as he gestured. "There are too damn many of them, and this is their ship! They know how to use it, use it against us. Even if we can take it we don't know how to run it. What is the point of getting killed for nothing?"

Moire closed her eyes, hoping she wasn't hearing what she thought she was hearing. They must have agreed on the topic of discussion quickly, which wasn't a good sign. Perhaps this wasn't the first meeting.

"We're getting killed for nothing now," one woman pointed out sourly. The others nodded agreement.

"And what are you thinking, then?" Soliyah looked at Moire, eyes burning. The others looked at her too. They didn't seem friendly. "You think like him, eh? Everything...*all right*." Her voice dripped scorn. "That bastard gonna kill Pers, we don't do something. He *said* it. He *doin'* it right now."

Moire glance at Pers, silent and no longer cheerful, standing at the edge of the group. Nothing was visible except for a thin trace of dried blood at the edge of one nostril, but he moved stiffly. It was more serious than she had realized, then. They were angry for a reason. Soliyah continued. "No matter what, we gonna take that *mizake* out. Even if we die...but maybe we won't."

Moire made soothing gestures, hearing motion behind her but not daring to look. They were moving between her and the door. "Jere is right. Why would he lie to you? He's on your side! You won't be able to take the ship, and you and a lot of other people will just die trying. Haven't you noticed the marines? For some reason they like to hang out on this level. Do you really think the command is worried about the crabs doing a boarding action? With the drive engaged?" Now they just looked sullen. "They *know* you are angry. What do you want to bet they already have plans for your attempted takeover?"

"Doesn't matter. We're going to do it. Now are you with us or not?"

She realized with a sinking feeling that they were serious. "No, I'm not with you," she said before she could stop herself. She backed away, but before she got to the door Boggs had grabbed her from behind, one arm across her throat and a knife in his hand. She struggled, but she couldn't get good footing on the wet floor and his grip was too strong. Boggs's skin reeked of chewstick, making her cough.

"How's killing me going to help?" she managed to croak.

"You ain't gonna tell them nothin', bird," he said easily, stroking the curve of her jaw with the knife.

"What can I tell them they don't already know, you homicidal dopesmack?"

Boggs shifted his weight, probably to get a better angle to stab her at. The arm around her neck loosened just enough for her to get a good grip, and she pulled and turned, shifting to one side and stepping backward. Before he could regain his balance, she bent forward with all her strength. It wasn't a clean throw, but Boggs hit hard enough to loosen his grip and she pulled free, scrambling to her feet again.

Her arm was bleeding. She wasn't sure if that was from the knife or scraping it on the shower floor in the clumsy toss, but it wasn't serious. Her situation hadn't improved much. She was away from Boggs and his knife, but there were more people between her and the door now.

"Look. What they are doing to us is wrong, but taking over the ship is wrong too. People will die. Lots of people, and not just directs. What about the rest of the unit? You think this isn't going to affect them?"

"What other choice do we have?" Andre MacAdam hit the shower privacy wall with his fist, then sagged against it. "At least we'll die doing something."

Boggs had retrieved his knife, but he hadn't made a move to attack again. She kept an eye on him, and any of the others who looked like they might take over for him. The sheer frustration of it made her want to scream. They weren't going to stop, and they wouldn't listen, and there was nothing she could do. Why now? She had enough to worry about with Toren.

And why hadn't she let Boggs kill her? That would have solved her problem. *No guarantee he'd kill quickly—I don't think he'd enjoy that quite so much.* Besides, there were other people to consider. People who didn't want to die just now. Including her, it seemed, but she was only delaying the inevitable. Toren was coming to get her, and....

She drew in a sharp breath. Toren was coming. Maybe she could use that. "You just want to get loose, right? If I can get us off the ship, will you swear not to kill anyone?"

"Escape where?" Soliyah asked, folding her arms. "We in drive, yes?"

"Steal a courier ship."

Andre snorted. "Yeah, and then what? Flap our hands? Web ships don't fly themselves." They were paying attention, which was a good sign. They didn't want to get massacred if there was another way out.

"I can fly it," Moire said. "You swear a blood oath nobody gets killed, and I'll fly us out. If you scrag even one dumbass marine, I'll leave you here to rot."

Jere was looking at her with a small smile on his face. "So you're one of those spongehead web pilots, huh? Somehow I'm not surprised. Now this I can go for," he said, turning to the others. "Get off this crate and you've got a chance."

"So how we gonna get a courier? Fill out a requisition? We could be waiting months." Andre shook his head. "Besides, they could use the override and stop us before we go into drive."

Moire swallowed hard. "A courier will be showing up in a few weeks. A civilian one. No override."

"You're sure? How do you know?"

"I'm sure." Seeing the scornful expressions, she added, "That crewcut commander, the liaison? He told me." Andre had seen them talking in the gym, so that should be believable.

Nobody said anything for a moment. Jere said, "Call it."

The mercs slowly gave their handsignal votes, and Moire carefully let out the breath she'd been holding. She'd bought some time, at least.

I don't have any family.

Her voice echoed in his head, resonating, waking old ghosts. A bleak voice, riding on the surface of a sea of pain. What had happened to them? Was that why she wouldn't erase the scars? He didn't believe the cost had prevented her from doing it; it wasn't that expensive, not for just a cosmetic fix.

Ennis scowled. He was getting sentimental. Sayres had been annoyed when he'd pointed out the scars, but she had only gotten upset when he'd mentioned her family. He'd just been trying to help....

Was it worse to never have had a family, or to lose one?

He turned restlessly on his bunk, sleep evading him. Family. He'd longed for one as soon as he was old enough to understand the word. He had early memories of shapes, smells that were comforting, the blurry image of a face. Memories that ended suddenly. Fimbul had been a violent place even before the disaster for the criminals who had been sent there. The criminals who weren't supposed to have children.

He remembered asking Penderhest, when he was old enough to understand something was missing. He'd just finished reading a chapter of *Treasure Island* under the old man's rigorous scrutiny. Every word pronounced correctly, even when he had no understanding of the meaning. Cutlass. Ocean. Tree.

It had been frustrating for him at the time, but now he was grateful. He didn't brand himself a criminal every time he opened his mouth.

They had been sitting in the tiny shelter Penderhest had put together on the surface, almost completely stuffed with plastic bags full of scraps of insulation. It was still cold, even with both of them inside. Cold, but safe. The tunnels had other prisoners.

"Where are my parents?" he'd asked.

Penderhest tucked a scrap of blanket more securely around his head and picked up his cup, which had once been an axle cover. "Long gone, my boy. I'm not even certain I knew them."

"But how did you find me?" The question he should have asked was why the old spy had taken him in. As one of the older prisoners, Penderhest was at a considerable disadvantage, and he'd never been physically dangerous. Taking care of a child in the violent environment of Fimbul would have been a tremendous effort.

"Ah, someone must have asked for my help for a moment, and it became a habit. Or was it you that found me, and would not go away no matter how I growled? It's hard to remember now."

Later he remembered how Penderhest had never looked him in the eyes while he spoke, and how he'd woken late in the night and seen the old man still sitting up, his carefully rationed bottle of vat juice empty in his hands and the lines of his face scribed deeper with pain.

Ennis had not asked Penderhest about his parents again.

He stared at the dull gray surface of the top locker above him, then jerked the blankets free and sat up. He scrubbed his hands over his face, trying to focus. Sleep was impossible when he was this worked up. The only fix was to come up with a plan that would at least give him the illusion of accomplishing something. He needed information.

Now that she was in Fleet he had access to Sayres's records, what little the mercenaries had. Her passport listed her nationality as Australian, born in Woomera in 2045. He didn't believe any of it. He could do some searching in the library to make sure, but deep in his gut he knew looking for information on Ann Sayres would be a waste of time.

Then there was the question of *why*. Why she would have a false identity. Why she was afraid of information getting out about her. All the signs pointed to criminal connections, or maybe former membership in an Armed Action Committee. He remembered her struggle with the rifle and smiled. Not really terrorist material. If she had been trying to avoid notice she wouldn't have been *that* bad.

It wasn't just the things that didn't fit, like the scars. There were little things missing that should have been there. Things she would have no reason to conceal. Like Fimbul. It had meant nothing to her the first time he'd mentioned it–it was just a name. She'd looked it up afterward, though, that was clear.

He'd had that same feeling on Fimbul once, that something was missing and it was important. He'd been on the surface, looking up at the tiny points of light in the ebony sky and panting with the effort of getting oxygen in his lungs from the jury-rigged gas filter. Knowing something was wrong, something in the sky. Missing. He watched until he saw it happen again—a star disappearing, then the star next to it, until an expanse of empty blackness outlined a ship descending to the surface. The first ship to come to Fimbul since the disaster.

He pulled a blanket free from the bunk and draped it around his shoulders, wrapping his arms around his knees. Thinking of Fimbul always made him cold.

Maybe there was a way to find out more about her. They had her full biometrics now from the Fleet physical. It wouldn't take much to convince Shaughnassy they needed to run better security checks on the converted mercs. He could send the biometrics with the next mail courier to check with the Index back on Earth.

He lowered himself back down on the bunk and closed his eyes. A few weeks round-trip for the courier, then a week or so for the Index search. It was frustrating to have to wait so long for information, but he didn't have any choice. Once he got the Index data he would know what he needed to do next.

"You're sure you can fake the log?" Moire knew she was being a pain, but she didn't like trusting someone else to do a hack. These people weren't paranoid enough. You couldn't trust electrons; they'd rat on you first chance they got. They'd ratted on *her* almost a hundred years ago, and the computers were almost AI now.

"Of course," said Markus. "I have only to find the, how you say, interconnect? After the sim is being loaded, then I make it not tell the console. At end connect back, load different sim. No log."

It sounded plausible, but she didn't know enough herself to be sure. Markus seemed convinced. He'd been assigned to help her get sim time because he was one of the few mercs with the know-how to do it. He'd already fudged the schedule to make sure the sim lab would be empty.

The lights were down when they got there, a good sign. Markus overrode the autoswitch to keep it dark and used a small palmlight to read the console.

"Which one are you wanting?"

"There's more than one?"

"See. Harpy 1201, Celeritas, VX-20...."

"Celeritas." Moire moved to the sim units. The lab boasted three full-range models, as well as a bank of limited stations for formation drill. "Put it in this one." She pointed to the full-range unit furthest from the lab entrance.

The open sim units had an unpleasant resemblance to a medieval Iron Maiden–just the size of a human body inside, with space for range of motion but nothing else. The casing was lined with sensors and other electronics, and the video visor dangled free from the top. Most of the sensors and feedback were in the helmet and upper torso section, with special attention for the hands. She stripped down to her shipsuit, and Markus helped her strap in.

He closed the door, and the darkness was absolute. A few moments later the sim visor brightened to an all-white "blank" view, and she felt the sensor array align itself on her body. It was like being hugged by an armadillo.

"*Also*," said Markus's voice in her ear. "You are ready?"

"Let 'er rip," replied Moire.

The image changed. Now she was standing at the "pit," the pilot station of a Celeritas courier ship. She took her place in the deep, wide chair, moving stiffly at first as she got used to the sensor feedback. The viewport confused her, until she realized the web console was also the realspace controls for the ship. A courier didn't have a lot of extra space for duplication, especially if the same person performed both functions side by side. Still, it was strange to have an outside view.

Since this was the first time she had run this sim, she took her time going over the controls. *Little green gods, if I had only had a tenth of this on* Bon Accord.... *A realtime del-cross plot! I could fly this ship through a swarm of black holes!*

If she pointed her finger on a control and twisted the tip on the "surface," the sim would pull up information and specs to display. The important ones hadn't changed that much, which was what she had been counting on.

"All quiet?" she asked.

"No one is coming," said Markus. "Why are you needing this sim? Courier web engine different, *oder?*"

She'd been anticipating a question along those lines, and she suspected Markus wasn't the only one wondering. "We're going to be leaving in a hurry," Moire pointed out. "Good chance they'll shoot at us, too. Faster I can get us lined up and out of realspace the better. I have to know this rig backwards and forwards."

The preflight check had a handy floating display. Thanks to her earlier investigation she did respectably timewise. Then she took a deep breath and started the web sequence.

It took her twenty minutes. *It will never work...they will have boarded us by then. Even if all they have is a can opener.* "How much time do we have?"

"We should have left since two minutes."

"Right, get me out of this. We'll have to come back." Maybe this wasn't going to work after all.

There was a woman sitting at a reader when Ennis entered the library, and when he saw she was wearing stand-down fatigues, as the converted mercenaries all did, he felt relieved. Hallin must have thought the better of his harsh treatment, or maybe Sayres had convinced someone to lean on him.

With a flash of disappointment, he realized the woman had long, dark hair and a slender build. Another of the converted mercenaries, she looked familiar but he didn't recall her name.

She looked up at his approach with an indrawn breath, half rising from her seat to face him, wary and apprehensive.

"Relax, soldier," he said, waving a dismissive hand. "You aren't my responsibility, so I'm not going to waste my time checking up on you. Just don't do anything noticeably stupid, hmm?"

She gave a quick, unconvincing smile. "N—no. Sir." With efficient haste, never completely removing her gaze from him, she pulled out her reader key and grabbed a familiar-looking portable reader. "I finish now."

He stared at the door after she left, scowling. Was she in Hallin's squadron too? He shook his head and turned to the library terminal. It wasn't his job; there was nothing he could do. His mind returned to that conversation he'd had with Sayres at the officer's party, remembering everything that had given him concern. He was even more worried now. Something was definitely wrong.

He quickly skimmed the catalog. He'd already read all the new books he was interested in; he was just looking for something to occupy him during the launch bay repairs when he had to be present but didn't have any duties. He filtered for "classics," selecting a few old favorites, then saw *Paul Clifford* and added it to the list. He hadn't read it in years—what Penderhest had called "a useful model of bad literature." He supposed he still liked to read it to evoke the memory of the old man's voice, dwelling with loving irony on the florid prose as he read. His foster father had loved literature almost as much as he'd loved stealing information.

He seated the reader in the cradle to download. The process was almost instantaneous. This reader had the latest in compression and prediction technology. He'd gotten the reader on Earth before being posted to *Canaveral.* The first and only time he'd been on the planet.

The reader he'd loaned Sayres was not anywhere near as quick, and it had some annoying quirks, like occasionally playing video clips at half speed and no sound, or refusing to recognize the library copy license as valid. He should have warned her about that.

He pulled his key from the terminal and left the library. That other merc—she'd had the same model. He wondered where she had gotten it.

They weren't that common; he'd gotten his from a junk dealer back when he could only afford a used, out-of-style reader.

Swinging by his quarters, he tossed the reader on his bunk and left again. There were marines by the elevator station when he came out. Shabata must have convinced Shaughnassy to post them. Not that there were many people in the corridors, merc or not.

A thought nudged itself forward, and he frowned. So why would a merc have an old reader? They hadn't been allowed in the library until the conversion—Sayres was the first. Why have a reader, then? Even assuming their last in-port station had featured an antique electronics vendor, none of the mercs had been allowed off the ship.

Maybe it *was* his reader. He smiled. There was always more than one way to get something done. Sayres must have arranged for this other merc to go to the library, and that's why she was acting suspicious when he came in. Penderhest would have approved.

When she returned to the sims, Moire experimented and discovered that she could save precious minutes by overriding the safeties and starting the gravitics warmup at the beginning. She'd have to get snappy with the preflight or they would cut in while the ship was still in dock, though. That could get nasty.

The other trick was knowing where to go. The mutineers were meeting to discuss that topic tonight, and since she was the pilot it was a meeting she couldn't avoid. Secretly she had hoped the rest would have given it up by now, but they were more determined than ever.

She wove her way through the mess of cable and pipe in the tunnel on her way to the meeting location, a cross-conduit with more space than the regular tunnel. An unexpected benefit of Hallin's many makework projects had been the discovery of a poorly secured access hatch to the conduit tunnels. It was a tight squeeze, but it provided a safe location when the mutineers needed to meet.

When she got there, Jere was conspicuously absent. He wasn't going with them, and he'd made a point of not knowing their plans after they left the ship. Moire respected his decision, but wondered how safe he would be. The directs couldn't help but be suspicious of him.

Soliyah handed her the reader without comment when she joined the circle, and she scrolled through quickly. The library had useful information in surprising places. It was amazing how detailed the *Cosmographica* articles were. They usually consisted of gorgeous vids and graphics of exotic planets and were low on details, but this one was a "solo web pilot in the Fringe" story. The part she wanted was only a sidebar, but it listed the actual coordinates, mass, and delta-vees of a number of useful stars. It also gave a rough map of human-occupied space so she could get some idea where they were.

"We get to Criminy, ship going anywhere stop soon. Go to Criminy," Soliyah suggested. She took out a knife that she'd managed to hide before it was confiscated and started paring her nails.

Andre nodded. "Yeah, that works. They got bars there, right?"

Moire closed her eyes, trying to remember if she knew where Criminy was. They hadn't used planet names as references when she was flying; they'd used the stellar catalog code of the system's star instead. The star was where the mass was, anyway.

"That's the one at Epsilon Lyrae?" She looked at the map, tilted its axes in the reader to get a shot at the alignment. It was a long way from their current position, and there were not enough stars on the path to help. Mass was the only way to lock on with the drive, and the star they wanted was too distant. "Can't do it."

Boggs leaned forward, breathing hard. "Why the 'ell not? Yer putting too many rules on us, bird. We don't care if you don' like it. You damn' well take us where we want." He gave her a hard shove with his hand.

She grabbed her temper and sat on it. "From our current position it would be a three-leg run for the courier, and it would take well over a week. Not enough supplies, assuming you still want to take everyone who signed on. You want to leave some behind to talk?"

Boggs gave her a cold, dangerous look but said nothing.

"There is this Shipman Point," a voice with a Russian accent said, from the shadows. "It is near here."

"Uh-huh. And it has its own built-in Fleet station, too," George Okabi pointed out, tugging at one of his dreadlocks. "Let's go somewhere else."

"What about Redline?" Cia, a merc from another group, said diffidently.

This one Moire hadn't even heard of. "Is it close?"

Cia shrugged. "Official name is Goldstar or something like that. Ore freighter at our last in-port came from Redline. Crewcut in my group got friendly with one of 'em; she said half the business done there is off-record."

"Yeah, I heard of Redline," said Andre, grinning. "Good place to skip to. And no Fleet."

"I don't want to rot in some skellich mining camp."

"Naw," said a scraggly merc Moire didn't know, "'sides the freighters, there's all sorts a folks showing up. Plenty a ways to get where you want to go, and they all need extra help. Work your way ifn' ya don't wanta pay."

Goldstar was one of the listed destinations in the article. She checked the map, rotating again and again, wishing the reader had better controls for the 3-D map. It was a touchy alignment for a straight shot, there was a large star that could interfere, but she could do it.

After some more discussion, the mutineers took a vote. Redline was the destination.

CHAPTER 5
A RASH AND A ROVING BLADE

Ennis handed off the latest maintenance requests from the mercenary contingent to the crew chief and decided to say hello to Marizio Seung. He hadn't seen him in a few days, mostly because he'd been so busy. Marizio reminded him of the good parts of being enlisted: the camaraderie and the gossip. Marizio found out all kinds of amazing details which even the officers didn't know.

The main fabricator station was staffed by two junior fabtechs engrossed in making what looked like a gravitics shunt. He wanted to ask them why–the fabricator could make just about anything on the ship, but it was usually more cost-effective to stock premade spares–but they looked like they had enough to worry about without a nosy officer bothering them. Maybe they'd run out of spares. There had been enough damage for that to be true.

Where the hell was Seung? Ennis scanned the fab bay again. The clank of something metal dropped on the deck made him turn his head. The plasma forge in the back was dark, and the controls had a red glowtag stuck over the main power switch. He went back. Behind the forge proper, Marizio was kneeling on the deck, half inside the opened base. Ennis wondered if he should come back another time, but then Marizio's head popped out.

"Why don't they just make 'em outta carbon? Save time," he muttered, clutching a blackened component in one hand. His large, round face went blank seeing the officer's uniform unexpectedly in front of him, and then creased with a wide smile when he realized who it was. "Commander Ennis! Hey, guess what? You're in luck. My respected mother sent me a package!"

Yes, his timing was bad. "The medics don't like me to eat your mother's kimchee. Stomach replacements are a lot of work."

Marizio made a scornful noise. "What do they know? They never found anything bad in it, right?"

"Only because it dissolved the probe before they got a reading," Ennis said, trying to keep a straight face. He had a sudden and vivid recollection of the last time Mrs. Seung's homemade confections made an appearance on the ship. Not only had they set off the biohazard scanner and caused a security shutdown of the auxiliary communications deck, but Shaughnassy had asked for a sample as a calibration source and Seung had *not* taken it well.

Evidently this batch was milder, or the scanner had been modified to tolerate it. He hoped it was just the recipe. Anything that caustic should have been screened before it got on the courier.

The old man heaved to his feet, propping the forge access cover against the wall. "It never hurt me one bit–I grew up on the stuff! Makes you tough." He thumped his massive chest.

Ennis grinned. "Maybe that's the problem. If I'd grown up eating it, I might have built up a resistance."

Marizio never could understand why people never tried his mother's kimchee more than once. Then again, Marizio's mother must be at least 130, so maybe it did toughen you up. Marizio himself was almost at mandatory retirement age, and he looked it. The early age-abatement treatments had not been as effective as the current ones. Seung would have been encouraged to retire earlier if he weren't one of the best precision machinists and nanofabricators in Fleet.

Marizio's face fell. "Oh–is it because of that radiation damage you have? I was forgetting." He made a clumsy bow of apology.

Ennis stiffened. "I'm alive. I can't complain." He forced himself to smile. Seung meant well, but it was a painful reminder of reality and the shaky horror of nearly dying. He had taken a lot of radiation damage on Fimbul, despite Penderhest's efforts. If Fleet had shown up a month or two later he might not have survived, except as a wired body in a tank. He'd been lucky. Most of the damage had been repaired when the rescue ships came, or at the medical station afterward. He still had a low-level drug implant and his medical file was immense, but otherwise he was normal. Except people didn't think of him that way. *Take advantage of it. You have an excuse not to eat kimchee.*

Time to change the subject. "Hey Marizio–I thought you said we got some new books on the courier. Or did they leave them behind to make room for the kimchee?"

Seung's worried expression vanished. "Sure, they got some new books; a whole bunch of 'em. I seen the can myself, marked 'Schorzman Foundation', right? They must not've loaded it yet."

Ennis shook his head. "I was just at the library. Nothing new. Of course it probably is at the bottom of the priority list these days."

Marizio got a look on his face like a crafty Buddha. "Lemme see what I can do for ya. Svensen can load the books, and she likes these little *milagros* I make. Sends 'em home to dedicate inna church, just like you're supposed to." He went to a cabinet with many drawers and pulled out a small black object that sparkled, dangling from a short length of filament. It was an exact replica of a crab fighter, down to the tiny spikes and spines.

"You are an artist, Marizio. That's incredible." It was frighteningly realistic. He could feel his pulse increase looking at it. Why would Svensen be interested? He wouldn't want a reminder of the deadly crabs himself; he saw enough of the real thing.

The machinist waved his praise away with a meaty hand. How could something so big do such delicate work?

"Hey, I thought we gonna fix that launch bay for you."

Ennis frowned. "Yes, tomorrow. Why? Don't tell me the replacement beams weren't recast correctly. Again."

"Now, they aren't sure that's what caused the cracks," Marizio said, holding up his hands. "Mendez knows his job. I think the supports got damaged too an' they didn't find it. 'Course when they failed the beam broke again, right?"

"Regardless of whose fault it is, we're still missing a launch bay," Ennis said, gritting his teeth. "So what's the story? Why do you ask? It's still broken."

"I ask 'cause I don't see it on tomorrow's schedule anymore. I thought maybe you moved it."

Marizio was right, it wasn't there. Ennis checked the schedule again, the sinking feeling in his stomach soon giving way to frustrated fury. He *knew* the repairs had been scheduled, and the requisition had been there the last time he'd looked.

It had to be there. They wouldn't just delete it; the repairs were too important. When he finally found it, he swore. Someone had shifted it two days later in the schedule. He pulled the requisition docs, seething. No details, just a "reschedule due to emergency repairs."

He punched the comm for Engineering and got Mackerbee, the commander in charge. "It's Weps," she said in her laconic drawl, cutting him off in mid-rant. "Came in four-five hours ago."

"It took Weapons Systems this long to figure out they had a problem? Look, if we don't get those bay repairs done we won't be able to launch half the merc fighters, and dropout is in two days. If the crabs are waiting for us on the other end we need those fighters!"

"I hear ya, Ennis," she said. "Nothin' I can do. They took all my heavy-mech people, some off other jobs."

Ennis sighed. "How many heavy-mechs do I need?"

"Two. Three's better. Support crew I can manage."

He thanked her and dropped the link, pulled up the master schedule to get the code of the weapons officer in charge, and punched the comm again.

It answered with a warbling wail, then displayed "Priority One override only."

He stared at it for a moment. Priority One meant only the captain or the first officer could get through, which meant the repair probably was a serious emergency. *That, or we got boarded and they are trying to cover it up.*

Marizio was looking concerned. "You got it sorted out, right?"

Ennis shook his head. "Looks like we'll have to do it the hard way. I'm going to find the guy in charge personally." Weapons couldn't possibly need all the heavy-mechanical repair crew for two solid days. What were they doing? Moving the main gravitic node? In flight?

Checking the schedule again, Ennis found the location of the repairs—one of the main hull weapon nacelles—and headed out. He had to wait for the weapons officer to finish issuing instructions to some orange-jumpsuited crew when he got there. The major turned to face him then, and there was no indication of friendliness when Ennis explained his situation.

He didn't need the evidence of the ring to know the weapons officer was Academy; that fact echoed in every movement, inflection of voice, and most particularly the look in his pale, ice-blue eyes that just skirted contempt. If Ennis hadn't outranked him, he wouldn't have stood a chance. It wasn't going well as it was.

"The trim node repairs were extensive. The gravitic changes destroyed the gun alignment."

Ennis gave him a skeptical look. "Any alignment you do while the ship is in drive is dangerous and inaccurate. Do you really think this is the best allocation of resources?"

The major's face became even more rigid. "The extent of the realignment needed is large enough to make the repairs urgent, even in drive. It was only discovered recently."

"I appreciate your position, but the ship needs fighters as well as guns." *Any weapons officer who takes this long to figure out trim node damage will affect the gun alignment ought to be pushing a broom, but let's be polite.* "It takes your people several hours to do a full alignment scan. Hours when you *won't* be using the repair crew. All I'm asking is that you release the crew to me during the alignment. If you can't, I want to hear a really good reason why."

The ice-blue eyes blinked. Ennis was determined to fight it all the way to the captain if he had to, and he hoped it showed.

"Mackerbee needs a—"

"She knows all about it. The support crew is already on standby, so I want you to notify her—and me—the instant those heavy-mechs are available. Got that?"

"Yes sir." He didn't sound enthusiastic, but it would do. The one useful thing about the Academy ringknockers was their high respect for orders and the chain of command, so Ennis felt sure it would be done. Eventually.

The airlock klaxon sounded, and bustle and activity picked up in the corridor. The weapons officer turned back to the airlock, talking urgently on his comm. Ennis considered leaving, then decided to stay. If the heavy-mechs were returning he could make sure they got sent to him in a timely fashion.

Only six people in full EVA gear could fit in the airlock, and the first lot were weapons crew. They conferred with the major as soon as their helmets were off, not even removing their suits. By the time the third group had cycled through it was getting crowded in the corridor, and people were removing gear wherever space was available.

Off to one side he saw someone fumble with the helmet release, then remove it with careful, slow movements. Shocked, Ennis recognized Ann Sayres. He made his way through the confusion to where she stood, growing angrier by the minute.

"You may be a damn good pilot, but you are nothing more than a hazard doing emergency outside weapons repair with no experience! What the hell were you thinking?" It was an effort to keep his voice lowered. "We can't afford to lose people like you. Do you have any idea how dangerous outside repair during drive is?"

She nodded slowly as she popped the seals on her gauntlets, shaking them loose with a little twist and a toss, catching them midair.

"Did you run out of things to keep you occupied? Bored? I'm sure Hallin has a few ideas to fix that."

She lifted her head. Her eyes were bloodshot, lusterless.

"Hallin assigned Pers Kuchinski to the EVA," she said simply.

"And you didn't approve? Sayres, the way it works is your superior officer gets to tell you what to do, and you get to do it. He probably had a reason." None that he could think of offhand, though. Even if the weapons crew needed help in a hurry they would have gone through everybody else on the ship, including Technician Seung, before starting in on the pilots.

Her gaze sharpened and cleared, an angry expression in her strange hazel eyes.

"The only training Pers had was the emergency evac drill every warm body on this ship has gone through," she snapped. "Hallin knows what he's doing, all right, and I'll stop it any way I can. Doesn't anyone care that he tried to endanger the weapons crew with this stunt, not to mention Pers? I have considerable EVA training, but he isn't out to get me. He didn't even ask."

A chill went over him. She was right. If Hallin was deliberately ordering someone who had no training into a dangerous situation, he couldn't ignore it. This was getting to the point where he would have to report it to Shabata or even the captain. Then what she said hit him.

"You have EVA experience? Where did you get that?" She did seem familiar with the gear, removing her gauntlets with the ease of practice. But the mercenaries were just pilots. They didn't do EVA.

She stopped short, then turned and started peeling the EVA suit away.

"My...old unit. We did our own support." She picked up the helmet and gauntlets. The suit dragging from her arm, she wedged her way through the crowd to the storage lockers on the opposite side of the corridor and stowed the gear away with awkward haste. She glanced up and saw him still there, and blurted, "Bendy decks may be harder to build, but at least you don't have to align trim nodes."

Bendy decks?

"Sir."

Ennis turned. The major was standing to one side, disapproval radiating in his rigid stance. "The repair crew you requested is available. Engineering has been notified."

He nodded acknowledgment. When he turned back, Sayres was gone. Ennis stood for a moment, feeling frustration build. What the hell was wrong with her? Any time he asked her questions she deflected, evaded...or simply disappeared. Something else was going on besides Hallin's sadistic command style, and he was no closer to figuring it out. Taking out his comm with a sigh, he alerted Mackerbee to the change in plans.

"Goddamn, Ennis!" She laughed. "Gonna remind myself not to get in your way. What did you do to him? He called just now. Sounded mad enough to chew through the hull."

He felt a reluctant smile tug his mouth. "My lovable personality makes me friends wherever I go. Hey, Mack. You ever hear of bendy decks?"

"Nope. Why, you want some?"

"Just wondered what they were. Never mind. Thanks, Mack."

"For you, no charge. Team should be down at the bay in twenty minutes, ready to go."

That would give him time to get some food before going down to the bay himself. If he kept the pressure on nobody could steal his heavy-mechs for another project.

Ennis could hear Shaughnassy in full rant mode as he entered the officers' mess, and he listened appreciatively as he waited for the reprocessor to make fresh flatbread. Eric Shaughnassy had a talent for a good rant, and it made his own troubles seem easier to bear.

Shaughnassy hadn't slowed down noticeably by the time Ennis had gotten his meal and sat down opposite him. Eric was a mustang, like himself, and Ennis often thought it made him a better security officer—he knew what pranks noncoms could get up to since he'd done most of them himself.

"...and when I checked the motion sensor, it was green! So whatever is setting things off emits IR, but it's invisible and doesn't move." The others chuckled. "It's practically to the point where I just have my taskbot change the date on the report and send it out every goddamn day, not that it ever gets read. Something is wrong–and when I ask for extra people I get shoved to the bottom of the priority list." Ennis realized he must still be talking about the utility accessway detectors that had been tripped recently, apparently at random. Nobody but Shaughnassy seemed worried about it.

"The crabs haven't boarded us once. The threat we worry about is outside the ship, not inside," Shabata pointed out. "That's where the resources are going to go."

"That may change," said Andaluz, the colonel next to her. "You heard about the guy they found beaten to a pulp last watch? He's lucky to still be alive. Seems we have a morale problem we didn't know about."

Everybody looked at Shaughnassy. "No, I don't have any information," he grumped. "That corridor isn't secured–the courier bay at the end is, but not the corridor. Not enough detectors to go around. I put in a request for them. Twice."

Major Yamamoto snorted and shook her head. "I knew pulling those mercs in was a bad idea."

"The guy who was beaten was a converted merc himself. Maybe it was only a merc fight. They are just a bunch of thugs who can fly, anyway."

Ennis clamped his jaw shut, trying to contain his sudden spurt of anger. He could feel the interest at the table diminish. It was only a mercenary. "Who was it?" he asked, when he could trust his voice again.

Andaluz gave him a considering look. "That's right, you deal with those people. Kuchinski. Know him? Is he a troublemaker?"

Pers Kuchinski. There was a sharp sliver of cold in his belly. "He's never caused trouble before," Ennis said carefully. His chrono chirped, reminding him the launch bay repairs would be starting. He would have to get back to this problem later.

He got up, and noticed Hallin sitting two tables over. He was eating, calm and unconcerned.

I know what he's trying to do. Sayres's angry voice echoed in his mind. He began to wonder if she'd been right, and if Hallin had finally succeeded.

❧

The shower timer was only for the water. If you didn't turn it on you could hide out for a while, and she needed to be alone. Moire had been tempted to take refuge in the accessway the mutineers used, but that risked exposing them and this wasn't their problem.

They just wanted to get off the ship. She wanted to get off the ship too, but then she had to find a way to get her information to the right people. Fleet was too dangerous, too closely tied to Toren.

Someone came in, looking at her strangely. She supposed it did seem odd to be standing around the showers fully dressed. She should at least pretend she was going to use them.

The mercs had just had a bin for the underwear packets, and you hoped they had the gender and size you needed. Here in luxurious direct-land they had a dispenser with all those options selectable, if you could figure out how to select them. No buttons, no scrollwheels, no obvious display even. It turned out to have a pressure-sensitive transparent overlay on the metal dispenser itself that only became visible if you poked it in the right place. Even watching the others, it had taken her too long to figure out. Comments had been made. Joking ones, but she'd been noticed.

Just like with her little encounter with Commander Ennis. She'd been tired, but that was no excuse. He wasn't tired, and he'd remember everything she said.

Damn it all to hell, why didn't I tell him everything?

She leaned against the chipped plastic of the shower divider, breathing in the timeless smell of disinfectant and human sweat. Just like the lockers in Houston, now radioactive slag along with the rest of the city.

"Oh yes, sir, I got EVA training with NASA, all the explorer crews were rated." And then he'd remind her that NASA had been defunct for seventy-two years.

Moire pulled off her shipsuit. She wanted to tell him, that was the scary thing. It would be so easy to trust him—and she couldn't think of any reason why she should, except for a very stupid one involving hormones.

Why would she fall for him, anyway? He was dark, brooding, and already suspicious of her. Inscrutable. Military to the core. Nothing at all like Etienne.

Her throat tightened, and she pinched the bridge of her nose in a futile attempt to stop the building tears. She punched the shower valve with a curse and surrendered to the hot, stinging blast of water. Sometimes it seemed like too much effort to keep breathing.

The corrosive mood of depression stayed with her the next day. Word had gotten out about what had happened to Pers, and the consensus of the converted mercs was that she was next on Hallin's list. It should have worried her, but it didn't.

"I'm telling you, you need to be more careful!" This, coming from Andre MacAdam, made her eyes open.

"Why? He seems to be working on us one at a time, should give you plenty of warning before you have to worry."

Andre gave her a look and lowered his voice as they passed a group of directs in the hallway. "I mean, don't say anything that will make them notice, like you did back there. They think you got bacco on you, they will search until they find it. I barely managed to get my load safe through, and I don't appreciate you drawing their attention again!"

Oh. That. She'd made some comment about tobacco, not realizing in the time she'd been gone it had become illegal.

"Besides, I didn't know you used."

"I don't. But I, er, know people who do." Or who had, anyway.

Andre's expression was skeptical as they went in the door to their quarters. A group was gathered, looking somber.

"That's not good. Soliyah must be back from Medical," Andre remarked.

Soliyah was silent, staring up at the ceiling as she lay on her bunk, which was a bad sign. Usually if she was merely annoyed she would yell and curse and throw things–and people–around. The quieter she was, the more likely there was going to be bloodshed. Moire had never seen her so angry before, even the time a merc from another unit had welched on a gambling debt. She'd heard enough about what Soliyah had done to him to confirm her suspicion that it was better not to get on her bad side.

Most of the group was there, but then the squadron was on standby, waiting for a possible scramble once the ship dropped back into realspace. The other former mercenaries in the unit were standing near Soliyah's bunk or sitting in the bunks opposite, faces serious. Even a few of the directs were there–Pers could make friends with anybody.

Moire collapsed on her own bunk and crossed her arms over her head. Things were just going from bad to worse.

Markus shifted in his seat. "So, when is he then coming back?" Soliyah didn't even turn her head.

"Maybe one week, light duty. They have to use two unit bloodglue, his...spleen torn up so bad. Doctor say they got lucky, skull break not so deep, they use sonic-thermal on it." Her voice was distant, unemotional. Probably planning what parts to cut off of Hallin first.

"We'll find out who did it," said one of the directs, clenching her jaw. "I'll keep my ears open, and we'll make the bastard pay."

Soliyah turned to give her a steely look of contempt. "He tell me who."

"Who?"

"Who do you think?" she snarled through bared teeth.

The direct stepped back involuntarily at the hostile intensity in her voice, then turned and left. The others followed, probably having second thoughts about tangling with Hallin.

"If we had evidence we could get him shredded, even if he is a bar-code direct. It's attempted murder. Fleet won't want that to get out."

Moire wasn't so sure about any of that. It was surprising what the military would put up with in wartime, but she was all for encouraging them in less bloodthirsty directions. "Hey, Boggs. Didn't you drop that comm you liberated near there?"

Boggs grinned. "Roight you are, bird. Dunno if the store loop was running then, though."

"So find ou...." The gravity pulse rippled through her and she jumped to her feet, tense and ready to run. "We've dropped," Moire said to the faces turned her way, and they all waited for the scramble. It didn't sound.

"Aww, don't the crabs like us no more?" said Andre, and the tension dropped a notch with strained laughs.

Boggs turned back to his bunk terminal, which Markus had modified for their purposes. Moire nodded to Jere, who took up position in the doorway, effectively blocking access and visibility without being too blatant. Nothing like a closed door to raise suspicion.

Everyone else huddled around the bunk. Boggs tapped the crude interface, cursing under his breath.

"When did he leave–after dinner, right?"

"Yeah, and it would a take him ten minutes to get there, sure."

Soliyah made a short chopping motion with her hand and they subsided, until voices could be heard from the hidden comm.

"You got it! Awwright, that's the–"

"Shaddap!" Boggs looked grim. He pointed to the signal indicator. "That's live."

The mutineers went silent, worried now. All their plans assumed the area was clear unless a ship was actually docking. None of them had run into anyone in all their preparations. Except, of course, for Pers.

The voices were clear now, clear enough to understand.

"...waiting for us? *Canaveral?*"

"Yep. That's what they said. They were waiting."

"And how did civilians get the dropout coordinates?"

"Defense contractors don't think they're civilians, especially not if it's these guys. They think if they built the ship they still own it."

"That's for sure. They had a bunch of 'em on my last post, and you would not believe...."

Moire felt the blood drain from her face, panic and disbelief holding her motionless. Eventually she realized the other mutineers were talking to her.

"What's wrong?" Andre was gripping her shoulder, shaking it.

"We have to leave. Now. On that ship." Part of her marveled at the cool decision, while another part yammered in panic. How had Toren gotten here so fast?

"But we're waiting for...oh." Andre's voice trailed off.

Moire shook her head. "Everything is ready. Let's go."

Soliyah swung down from her bunk. "What we do with Pers? He can't go. We take next ship."

"Those people on that ship are coming for me." She knew in her bones this was true. "If we don't take this ship, now, you won't have a pilot for the next one."

Soliyah scowled. "You don' know they come for you."

"I could be wrong, but I don't think so," said Moire, and held up her comm. The light was blinking, and the message read "Report immediately."

She pressed the "Acknowledge" button, feeling like she had pulled a trigger.

"Why do you do this? You think now it is maybe not them?" said Markus.

"They don't know I know it's them. The longer they think I'll show, the longer we have before it all goes down."

"Goes down where?" asked Boggs, and she groaned inwardly. She was losing her concentration; that was slang from her time, not theirs.

"I figure we have twenty minutes before they realize I'm not coming and send someone to get me, but we have to move *now*. You do what you want. I'm going."

That threat was enough to motivate them. Markus changed into a purloined crew jumpsuit and took the pallet with the gear, disguised as laundry. The rest of the mutineers split up as planned to get stashed equipment and head for the rendezvous point at the courier bay. The comm had been quiet for several minutes, hopefully meaning the crew and passengers had left. Moire waited as long as she could before giving the signal to leave.

"Look bored, look annoyed, just don't look guilty!" Moire reminded them in a whisper. With the ship on alert, people running around wouldn't be noticed as long as they looked like they were on an official errand.

As she went out the door Jere slapped her shoulder and mouthed *Good luck*. She gave him the thumbs-up and a grin that was far more confident than she felt. She hoped he wouldn't get in too much trouble with this. He was still watching as they turned down the corridor.

Ennis was coming the opposite direction. *Don't look guilty, don't look guilty....* "Sayres. I want to talk to you about your comments the other day. There's been a development—"

"We've been ordered to report immediately, sir," she interrupted, thumbing the display on her comm and holding it up as she edged by. The others kept going, obedient to her surreptitious handsignal. "Do you know what it's about? Is the alert canceled?" He shook his head, looking puzzled, and she sketched a salute and hurried off before he could stop her. That had been too close. Ennis had a positive talent for picking the wrong time to get curious.

Down the next cross-corridor, through the bulkhead hatch, left, up the emergency ladder two levels, then right. She'd thought naval carriers were big, back in her day, but these things were huge. Up more emergency ladders. The route had been carefully scouted to risk the minimum number of vids, or anything else that might alert Fleet that something was going on. Some of the vids they couldn't avoid had been hacked, too.

The courier dock was in an awkward place on *Canaveral*, one of the few places on the hull that had enough room for a courier to pull in and yet not interfere with the ship's guns. There were only two routes to it, and both met up at the dock bay corridor. At least it wasn't an enclosed dock, which would have been even more difficult to get out of. They'd had enough trouble jiggering the security on the airlock.

How long had it been? Twenty minutes, thirty? Toren had to know she was running by now. What would they do? How much would they tell Fleet?

The courier docking bay was only a few corridors away, and she dared to hope. It looked empty. Movement out of a cross-corridor made her scramble backward, but it was just Boggs. He had a rifle slung from his shoulder and a smug expression.

"All clear, we got it."

"Where'd you get the rifle?" Moire asked. There were no good answers, and she got the one she was half expecting.

"Couple a' ma-reens don't need 'em now," he said, smiling slowly. He'd probably doped up while waiting for them.

"Great. I hope you didn't hunt them down just for that. What are you going to do if someone shoots at you, beat them over the head with it? They've got locks, remember?"

Boggs tapped one of the metal inserts in his face. "Ain't all jest pretty, bird. I got some what do stuff too." He stroked the gun. "It works for me now."

Oh, delightful. Our own personal sociopath with a loaded, working weapon. Maybe if I ask him nicely he'll shoot me and put me out of my misery.

She could hear noises down the corridor, muffled and unpleasant. "Ah, how bad did you have to hurt those marines, Boggs?"

He shrugged. "That ain't them, that's Hallin."

Moire pushed him aside and raced down the corridor. She took in the scene at a glance as she rounded the corner—two bundles of well-trussed marines in cargo webbing—Soliyah with a knife in her hand, a bloody figure kneeling in front of her that could only be Hallin. His hands were bound behind his back, and something was projecting from his mouth. He was gagging convulsively. The smell of vomit, of blood—she could see his teeth through his cheek as he writhed. Soliyah had slit his face open.

It was insane, she knew it as she did it. Moire grabbed Soliyah's arm and flung her away as hard as she could. In the few tenths of a second that bought her she removed the thing choking Hallin. It was slick and had been jammed in with considerable force. Blood dribbled from his mouth when it came loose. He collapsed on the deck, shuddering with ragged gasps that were half-screams.

"He will make too much noise now. I kill him." Soliyah wasn't even paying attention to her; she was focused on the object of her hatred.

"No." Moire got between Hallin and Soliyah. "That was the deal. No killing, and I fly you out. I keep my promises." She paused, emphasizing her words, hoping to get through Soliyah's bloodlust. "That means if you kill him, I don't fly the ship."

She had her attention now. Soliyah's eyes narrowed. "*Mizake* traitor. I also keep promises. I promise not to leave Pers with this thing."

Andre MacAdam edged toward Soliyah, reaching for the knife, but she slashed at him and he backed away. Nobody else looked willing to try.

"You gonna die for this bastard? You will fly. You have to leave, yes?"

Moire shook her head. "We've been through this before. I'm not going to help you murder. Mutiny is more than enough." They were so close—but she couldn't let this happen. Even if it was Hallin.

Soliyah stared her down, equally determined. "I no leave Hallin with Pers."

There was no time, they had to be looking for her now, and this crazy pig-headed merc was screwing it up for everybody. The trouble was she agreed with her. If they didn't murder Hallin, Hallin would murder Pers. "OK, we take Pers."

A slow smile crept about the corners of Soliyah's mouth. "You can do this?"

Hell no, but it will be fun trying. "You gonna stop poking holes in him?"

She nodded. "We take Pers, he can stay."

Moire swung back to the mercs waiting tensely behind her. "Get in the ship. Strap down and get ready for takeoff. Markus, you do the preflight."

"But I have not—"

"You've seen me do it often enough in the sims," she said, ruthlessly overriding his panicked objection. "Start the gravity warm-up in five minutes, got it?"

She scanned the ranks, thinking. They needed to get Pers out without getting trapped themselves, and she couldn't think how. Somebody had to stay behind for her gradually forming plan to work. She snapped her fingers. "Jere!" As she dug in her pocket for her comm she pointed to the cargo webbing. "Where'd you guys get that? Is there any noise curtain, or something solid? Get me some."

Jere answered the comm, but with hesitation in his voice.

"The package is still going, but we have a job before it leaves," Moire said quickly.

"I don't know...."

"It's in-house, trust me. You'll look good. Just take the port elevator to level twelve, I'll explain there."

He swore and dropped the link. She hoped he'd show; it would get awkward if he didn't.

Two mercs showed up with a swath of thick fabric, ragged on one side. At her direction they dumped the unconscious Hallin on it, and then Moire and Soliyah hurried for the elevator, carrying Hallin slung between them in the fabric.

"Why I go?" Soliyah wanted to know.

"Your job is to get Pers. He won't argue with you." They were probably going to show up on the vids now, but it couldn't be helped. Nobody on the ship was going to sound the alarm over two people being where they shouldn't. She hoped.

To her relief, Jere was waiting in the elevator, worried and impatient. He got one look at what they were carrying and exploded. "Why the hell didn't you just leave? There is no way you are going to—"

Moire hit the close button and then Medical/Override. "Look, we have to get Pers out. The story is you and I found him like this, OK? We think there is some crazy running around whacking people, and Hallin was attacked just like Pers was. Now help me carry him."

"What?"

"It doesn't matter what we say. We say it loud and provide cover so Soliyah can get in without being seen." The level indicator flashed, and she hissed, "Just follow my lead!"

She was shouting even before the door opened, and was gratified by the attention the medics immediately gave her. None of them noticed Soliyah, crouched and hidden behind the trailing fabric. She dodged for cover as soon as they got inside.

Jere began to warm to his role, interrupting in his deep, loud voice whenever the questions began to get awkward. "No, I was in the ready room and she yelled, so I came out to help...I didn't see anybody there, nosir."

How long did it take to find someone in the medical ward? It wasn't that big. A slow-moving orderly was heading for the elevator, and she nearly panicked until she saw a dark head bob out from behind the elevator door. One hand gestured impatiently. She gave Jere a wink, a flicker of an eyelid, and faded back through the confusion.

"Will you look at that cut?" Jere leaned closer, knocking over some equipment on the way. Moire grinned. Man was a natural. He was even flirting with one of the orderlies at the same time.

With Jere's assistance distracting the medics she made it to the elevator without being noticed. The doors closed, and she sighed with relief. Pers was standing, but only just—his face was grey and pinched with pain, and he looked like he would collapse at any moment. His orderly's coat was too small for him.

"We'll have to carry him," she pointed out to Soliyah.

"I don't weigh as much as I used to," Pers whispered.

"We'll get you out of here, anyway," Moire said, trying to cheer him up.

Soliyah put his arm across her shoulder to support him. "I take meds, data clip too. We find medic outside, fix you up." The door opened, and

Moire pulled Pers's other arm over her shoulder. They half lifted, half dragged him out of the elevator.

From the main corridor outside the elevator Moire led the way to the cross-corridor that paralleled the hull. It wasn't that much farther than the direct route, and there was much less chance of meeting anyone.

Moire glanced at the timer she'd set since leaving the courier bay. "We'll have to run. If we don't get there before the courier's gravitics engage it could get ugly fast."

They were in sight of the docking bay corridor when Soliyah stopped short.

"Is ugly now," Soliyah panted, tilting her head. "You hear?"

Now she could. Sounds of a firefight, yelling and shooting. More than one weapon firing too, which meant the alarm had been raised. "I should have taken Boggs's gun away," Moire muttered as they got closer.

Soliyah snorted. "You think you that lucky?"

When they got to the corridor intersection Moire took a quick look at the situation, chewing her lip. The courier bay was straight ahead, but the cross-corridor between them and the bay was held by a handful of marines. Well-trained and accurate marines.

"We run?"

Moire shook her head. "We'd never make it. The line of fire is too clear, and it'd be dicey even without Pers slowing us down. We just need a few seconds."

She scanned the corridor, looking for inspiration, and her gaze snagged on a bright red fire station. They were near the hull, there should be some emergency kits nearby too. She jogged up the corridor, looking around feverishly. It was farther than she thought, but the emergency kit was there. She tore it open and rifled the contents until she found what she wanted. "Emergency Personnel Atmosphere Shelter–Max Occ. 4" was written on the cover.

Moire ran back to Soliyah and Pers, ripping the packet open as she went. When she reached them she pulled the inside tab on the shelter. The tiny gas cylinder activated, expanding the clear plastic shelter but not inflating it completely. Brightly colored graphics, labeled in at least six different languages, scrolled over the plastic with helpful instructions.

"What you do?"

"I've discovered you have a lot more fun if you ignore warning labels," said Moire, dropping the shelter to crack open the fire kit. Opening the fire kit would activate an alarm but by now it probably wouldn't even register, what with all the other alarms going off.

She pulled the hand-sized fire extinguisher loose. She didn't know how they made the canisters so small these days, and it also had the scrolling display tech like the shelter, illustrating proper extinguisher technique. It was small, but it still had the same power as the big ones she'd used many years ago. Fire drills were quite informative—they taught you more than the safety officer realized. Like where all the useful goodies were.

The atmosphere shelter was looking like a limp, wrinkled sausage wrapper now. It had a valve to add extra oxygen, and Moire jiggered the fire extinguisher nozzle to match. It wasn't perfect, but she didn't have time for perfect. Good enough would have to do.

She squeezed the trigger, and the tiny fire extinguisher bucked in her hand. Some of the foam sprayed out of the valve. It had an acrid chemical smell that crawled into her nose and stayed there.

"Get ready to run," she said over her shoulder to Soliyah, wheezing a little from the fumes. The shelter was taut now, and full of opaque foam and vapor. It took up much of the corridor. Nudging it in place just out of sight, she whistled to the mercs and made the "cease fire" handsign. In a few seconds, they complied and she nodded to Soliyah.

"Go!" She shoved the shelter bubble into the corridor intersection. The marines were good. It didn't take them long to figure out something was going on, but it was long enough—especially after a bullet hit the shelter and it burst, spewing extinguisher foam over the entire corridor.

Holding her breath, Moire could hear the marines coughing as she and Soliyah ran with Pers out of the corridor, dodging piles of slippery foam. Bullets whined by them, too close for comfort. *Damn, but they recover fast!*

The mercs had taken cover behind the heavy metal airlock doors, which were pocked and smeared with bullet traces. The other mercs pulled them through and closed the doors, leaving only a crack open for Boggs and his rifle.

Moire hadn't seen any dead bodies on the marines' side, fortunately, but one merc lay sprawled in a pool of blood in the airlock and several more had been hit. She shoved her way through the crowd to the cockpit. It wasn't her concern, and they deserved it for starting the shooting in the first place. As long as none of the marines were killed, she could leave with a reasonably clear conscience.

Markus was sitting in the copilot position when she got there, tapping controls like a drummer. He turned and jumped out of the chair when she entered, saying in a high, cracking voice, "I have done this check, but the indicators they are not exact like you had." He was sweating, eyes wide in his face.

Moire slid into the chair, not bothering with the webbing. "Yeah, yeah, it's a civilian model, right?" She activated the door lockdown mechanism, ignoring the flashing red signal pinlights on the comm console. *You want my scalp, take a number.* More people crowded into the cockpit, carrying Pers wrapped in blankets and padding.

"We want to put him in the copilot, there's no place to strap him in."

"Do it and get out! Secure the hatch, we're leaving!" The ship rocked, tossing people to the floor. Yelling and curses came from the passenger area, and she glanced at the gravitics readout. They were almost at full power. She'd known this was a risk, but she still had to finish the lineup. She looked at the del-cross readout again. It was warped and misaligned, and it took her precious milliseconds to realize it wasn't the courier's engines in trouble. Another, bigger gravitic field had started up, and it was growing stronger.

"*Canaveral* is going into drive!" she yelled. "Hang on!" She toggled the gravitics to active, hearing the groan of the airlock connections as they strained and broke loose. She hoped Boggs had closed the inner door when he left.

The ship was free. Now where the hell was her lineup? The swirl of the artificial gravity was strong so near *Canaveral*. It was instinct and hunch and all the flying she'd ever done rolled into one sense that told her *there*. Just a small swirl in the del-cross river, but it was all she needed.

Je t'aime, Etienne. She engaged the drive.

CHAPTER 6
ONE FOR SORROW

Two months, and no end in sight, Ennis thought bleakly, looking around the dingy atrium in the vain hope that something had changed. Nothing had. The investigation had settled into a routine now, mostly involving waiting on his part. Andris Station had no data feeds in this section so all he could do was make lists on his datapad of things he should have done to prevent the mutiny. That, and try to figure out what the hell had actually happened.

Strange. At the time he had fervently wished for boredom. Now that he had it, it didn't help. He had too much time to remember.

He closed his eyes, fighting the memories away. The chaos and confusion, fear as the startling reports came in and the situation was made clear. It had started with two marines late reporting in from a walkthrough, which he'd only found out much later. Then something involving Hallin and Kuchinski in Medical, but nobody was giving out details.

Alerts started showing up on his commlink. Silent, officer-only alerts, which sent adrenaline coursing through him in chill waves. Rifle fire in the fore section of level twelve. Security reporting vid signal compromised in the area. The sinking feeling in his stomach increased. He felt no surprise when the next alert from Security came directly to him, simply, "ROD Tac Room." Report on the double.

Shaughnassy was standing in the middle of Tactical when Ennis sprinted in the door, glancing at those few of the big displays that had anything on them.

"Well, get a remote in there! We don't have time for you to figure it out!" Shaughnassy yelled into a commlink, then grabbed Ennis's arm and pointed at a display. "Recognize him?"

A blurred, shaky vidloop was playing. Someone, a man, with stiff white hair was aiming a rifle. He fired it, the vid image spun, and then the loop started again.

"Converted merc. Boggs. How the hell is he firing that rifle? Where'd he get it?"

"I'll fill that form when I get to it," Shaughnassy snarled. "Winged the tech sent to find out why the vid inputs are spliced. Notice the doors?

Courier bay. They're trying to get off the ship."

"Who else is with him?"

Shaughnassy wiped his forehead. "Hard to say. Tech said there were at least six. For all I know the whole damn ship is full of them. Found the two marines, alive, but their weapons are gone."

Ennis suspected he could name most of the mutineers. He felt sick. Command had been warned, damn them, and now he was going to have to clean up the mess.

"You'd better lock down the merc sector and guard it. Pull the remaining converted mercs out and isolate them. We don't know how many are still out there or what the plan is."

Shaughnassy shouted the order for the lockdown, looked at his commlink and had a new signal uploaded to a screen. The code at the bottom indicated it was coming from a marine combat vid, and showed the mutineers taking cover behind the heavy bay doors. Ennis thought he saw one take a serious hit.

"I can't do anything else until the situation is under control," he said, looking grim. "Bridge is secure and guarded, but the rest will have to wait. Minake, you got the nose count yet?"

"Incomplete, sir. This is what I have now." Minake tapped a screen. Ennis glanced at the data.

"Do a sort for missing, and display commission date," he said. Minake gave him a briefly puzzled look, then understanding flashed.

It wasn't complete, but the pattern was clear. All but a few had the same date—the date the converted mercs had been changed over.

"Any with that date report in?"

Minake did the search. "One, sir. Jere Anselm. Reported from Medical. Shall I confirm?"

Before he could reply, the blue drive light started flashing.

"What the hell? Where are we going to go?" wondered Ennis.

Shaughnassy grinned. "Doesn't matter—*they* aren't going anywhere, even if they have taken control of the courier. That was smart."

A small shudder in the deckplates made Ennis look up, startled. "What was that?" A direct hit? From who?

"Sir! We have pressure loss in the courier corridor!"

Shaughnassy leaned over the chair, staring at the display. "Get the marines out of there and shut the pressure doors! They must have tried to get loose. We got any working exterior vids there? We must, it's a docking bay," he said, shaking his head.

The dock was empty. Somehow that was the most disturbing thing he had seen in all this. It was the right dock, too. He could see the twisted metal of the airlock interconnects that had been wrenched apart.

He found himself speechless. Distantly, he heard Shaughnassy yelling at someone to drop out, to go back, that the ship was gone.

Gone.

Somehow he convinced Shabata he could help out with the retrieval mission. There was nothing left to find. Days of scanning on the finest resolution, days that blurred into one another. He did remember when it was confirmed Ann Sayers was among the missing. Somehow he had hoped....

Gone.

Command never did tell him what they had concluded, but he knew what he had seen. The biggest pieces of wreckage they had found were from the shredded airlock, back at Nexus 4. A few scraps that might have been from the courier, but not enough. Nothing at all at the point where they'd dropped out, when they had realized the courier was missing.

Were they trapped in webspace? Smeared in a fine, thin layer of atoms across light-years of distance?

Gone.

"Are you all right?"

Ennis dropped back to the here-and-now with a snap. Shabata was standing in front of him, looking concerned. Shaughnassy was just leaving the meeting room where the board was convened.

"Did you have a chance to ask them why I'm still here? I've had work piling up ever since we got here."

She shook her head. "I'm sorry, but they want you available. They don't want to bring Tabriz in on this, for obvious reasons, and you are the one with the most information about the mercenaries."

"I've told them everything I know. Twice." Ennis sighed.

"Look on the bright side," Eric Shaughnassy said, dropping into one of the hard plastic seats nearby. "You have a job to go back to. Hsu would love to have your problems."

Captain Hsu had been relieved of his command as soon as they arrived at Andris Station. Ennis grimaced. In truth, his career prospects were only a little better than Hsu's now. The mutiny had put an end to any hopes of promotion. He hadn't been responsible but his name would always be associated with it, and that was enough combined with all the other strikes against him. The most he could hope for was that they wouldn't have anyone to replace him with when he reached the required promotion cutoff and he could stay in a ship posting. Eventually they would, though, and he'd be stuck in a desk job on some two-level station until they made him retire as Fleet's oldest living commander.

At least he was still in Fleet. He *had* to stay in Fleet. Even a desk job was better than trying to live in the civilian world he had never been a part of.

Shabata had done what she could to help. She had been prompt to point out his early suspicions of Sayres, which made him look as good as anyone could in this mess. He'd reported Sayres's troubling questions about difficulties with commanding officers as well, allowing the board to draw their own conclusions about the mutineer's motivations after they saw what had been done to Hallin.

"I don't understand why we're still here," Ennis complained. "Are they planning to investigate until Hsu's replacement shows up?"

Shaughnassy snorted. "Could be. I wonder what's taking them so long. Are they waiting for Cherenkov to get the requisite time in grade to promote him? There *is* a war on."

They both looked at Shabata, who had more political insight than they did. She shrugged. "They probably want to make sure they pick the right person. Some of this has been figuring out exactly how Hsu screwed up so they can fix it. Mutineers fixed a lot of it all by themselves, really."

"Except the mercenaries are so angry I have to meet Tabriz outside their area," Ennis pointed out. "How are they going to fix that?"

The door to the meeting room opened again, and Misha Cherenkov, former first officer and now the acting captain of *Canaveral,* headed their way.

"Not yet finished," Cherenkov said with weary resignation when he came up to them. "Perhaps soon. I must go back now. You stay, keep me informed."

"Yes, sir." Shabata nodded. Since she was the acting first officer, one or the other of them needed to be on hand for the inquiry board whenever it was in session.

Cherenkov was in the most uncomfortable position of them all. He had all of the responsibility of a real captain but little of the power and the rest of the officers knew his command was temporary. His face had aged visibly since the mutiny.

Ennis was finding it hard to care about the inquiry, the ship, or much of anything else. It was like he was moving through a grey fog; colors were dull, sounds muted. He ought to be furious. It didn't get much worse than a mutiny in time of war, and then there were his destroyed career hopes. He wanted desperately to be busy again, doing anything that didn't involve thinking about what had happened.

Shabata sat down, and Ennis settled himself for more waiting. Nobody felt like talking. He might not have any hope of promotion, but the others had much more to lose. As Security Officer Shaughnassy was in an especially precarious position, since it was his responsibility to prevent things like this from happening. Fortunately he had documented his many requests for increased security as well as his objections to moving the converted mercenaries to the regular units, along with Hsu's dismissive replies. Since the captain had imploded his own career with such thoroughness, Shaughnassy might escape with only a reprimand.

An automatic side door pinged and opened for an old-style vendabot. Was there anything at Andris that wasn't thirty years old?

Shaughnassy shifted restlessly, stretching his long legs in front of him. The ancient vendabot, moving with stately grace through the atrium, was confused by the new obstruction and turned sharply to avoid it. It bumped into the wall, retreated, turned a few degrees, and tried again, repeating the process several times before it could return to its usual route.

"Where did they think they were going, anyway?" Shaughnassy grumbled, returning to the well-worn argument. "They must have had somebody they were going to meet up with at Nexus 4. Maybe somebody in Toren? They were expecting that courier—and we didn't even know it was coming."

It was a valid point, even if Ennis didn't agree with the rest of the theory. The mutineers *had* known the courier was coming, long enough for them to make plans well in advance. He'd been amazed at the sophistication of the modifications they'd made to the courier dock and the vid splices; it must have taken them several days. How could they have found someone to help them so soon after Hsu's well-meaning conversion, though? The mutineers must have acted alone, which meant the most the investigation could do was make recommendations to prevent it from happening again. The mutineers were dead. There was nobody left to punish.

His thoughts kept returning to Sayres's betrayal, like picking at a wound. He'd hoped there would be evidence in the inquiry that she, at least, had been coerced or reluctant, but he'd seen nothing. If there had been a reason—not that he could think of one that would justify what she'd done— he would never know it. And he wanted desperately to remember her without such bitter disappointment.

He'd felt a strange sense of recognition, of understanding when he talked to her. It was that resonance that had first made him curious. Now that she was dead, he would never know why it had been there. He didn't want to think it was because she was a criminal. He'd been fighting that stigma of association ever since Fleet had rescued him from Fimbul, and now a little voice was niggling in his head, *what if it is true?*

The door to the conference room opened and the aide attached to the inquiry came out. "The board is recessing for two hours. It will recommence at eighteen hundred," he announced. "Please remain on-station."

They looked at their chronos, then at each other. "Catch dinner now?" said Shabata. "It's early, but this might be our only chance while the off-base places are open."

"Yes, we can eat protein brick anytime," agreed Shaughnassy. "I heard there's a place that has chicken for reasonable prices. Cultured, of course, but at least it isn't *extruded*."

"I really prefer beef," Shabata grumbled as they headed for the base entrance. "Why haven't they cleaned up that contaminated vat already?"

"It's been cleaned for a while now. They can't get the replacements," Ennis said, waiting for the badge reader to pick up his data at the gate. "Nobody nearby is rated to make base cultures. Tried one shipper from Irukyn-Riu, but they backed out. Too close to the crab war, evidently." He selected a two hour indeterminate return period and tapped "accept." Shabata and Shaughnassy were looking at him in amazement when he turned back to them. "I overheard some of the local enlisted discussing it," he said, raising an eyebrow back at them. "Hot topic around here." Shabata grinned and punched the door button.

Immediately the scenery changed from dull, slightly faded corridors to flashing holosigns in every color. The corridors were wider, more like a regular civilian station.

Andris Station was mostly military, but a significant civilian presence had developed after the base was set up. The off-base section was more lively, full of color and noise and off-duty Fleet personnel. The area nearest the base was especially garish, thick with signs advertising "Friendly Boys and Girls" and a wide spectrum of chemical stimulants.

A group of silent, somber people was gathered around the Seekers data kiosk. There must have been a new upload. Faces and last known ship/location flashed across the screen.

"They ever find anyone that way?" Shaughnassy said, quietly enough the watchers could not hear him.

Shabata glanced over, then away. "Never heard of any, but that's not the point. It makes people feel like they are doing something, and gives them hope. Maybe their loved ones didn't run into a crab scout, and maybe they'll come back. This way, the word is out."

The main causeway was not very crowded at this hour. As they walked, Ennis caught a flash of color ahead. The color, as he feared, was the screaming orange of a press pass, worn by a lanky man with silver hair.

"Oh God. Not another one." The press had scented scandal and had been a constant nuisance. Rumors of mutiny had gotten out, but Fleet was trying desperately to keep them from finding out exactly *who* had mutinied. The orders were strict. Mercenaries were not to be mentioned off base or to civilians.

Shaughnassy grimaced. "He's standing right in front of the restaurant, too. Hell, he's seen us." The man approached them in an unhurried way, giving a friendly nod as he got closer. He was wearing a worn black commando vest over a wrinkled white shirt and black crew pants with scuffed shipboots. It was a ragged ensemble but one that he wore with style. The deep-set eyes, hooded under bushy eyebrows, and a prominent, classical nose gave him the look of a melancholy Julius Caesar.

Ennis glanced at Shabata and blinked in surprise. She was smiling.

"Neville Harrington, what are you doing here? The war is back that way." She pointed.

"Attempting to get closed-mouthed Fleet officers to Tell All," said Harrington with an answering smile. His voice had the clear glaze of an English accent. "This is not my preferred milieu, but credentialed wireservice reporters are somewhat scarce out here. My employers, with touching innocence, deluded themselves into thinking it would make a difference in prying useful information from you lot. And you cannot deny this is news."

Shabata performed the introductions. "Harrington is the closest thing to a war correspondent the wireservices have out in the Fringe," she continued. "I'm not surprised to see him here—I first met him when I was stationed at Shipman Point two years ago, and he's been showing up in the strangest places ever since."

"At the bottom of a mine shaft on Begaty-Horuk, for example," said Harrington. "The Fringe can seem quite small sometimes. You never did tell me what you were doing down there."

"No, I didn't," replied Shabata, unruffled, "and we're not going to tell you what we're doing here. Except having dinner."

"My keen analytical mind had already reached that conclusion," he said. "Would you object to my joining you? I will even promise to refrain from asking nosy questions," he added, as Shaughnassy began to grumble.

Ennis just nodded. Shabata seemed glad to see Harrington, and she was not outgoing by nature. If she thought well of him he was willing to have him along, even if he was a reporter. Harrington and Shabata could chat and he'd have something else to listen to other than speculation about the inquiry. Shaughnassy, outvoted, acquiesced with a shrug.

The restaurant was small, but it boasted real tables and chairs instead of fold-downs and had moderately successful decorations. Like most such places on the station, there was a comm at each table to order and a hatch in the back wall for a simple bot to carry the food. One customer was enjoying a bowl of chili that spiced the air as they walked in, and Ennis suddenly realized how hungry he was.

While Shabata studied the menu display, Shaughnassy ordered the spiciest dish they had. Ennis ordered *arroz con pollo*.

Harrington cocked his head at him. "Every now and then there is something familiar in your accent. Have you lived in England, perhaps?"

"My...foster father was from Cornwall." It was a curt answer, he knew, but anything more would bring up Fimbul. And the fact that Penderhest had been transported for industrial espionage.

Shabata placed her order, followed by Harrington, and the server bot trundled up with table settings and a water carafe. While they waited for their food, Harrington recounted the latest news from Earth–more current than the wireservice accounts any of them had seen, especially since they had been spending all their time with the inquiry.

"You have to be kidding," Shaughnassy said after one tidbit. "They are really trying to get Norstar to allocate colony resources based on nationality?"

Harrington took a sip of water. "Naturally. You can't expect them to do so by taking into account who built them. That would be manifestly unfair to smaller, less space-capable nations," he added gravely.

"I'd be more impressed with that argument if they sorted it out based on how much each country was doing to protect and supply those colonies," Shabata said. "Or would that be considered unfair too?"

Ennis just listened, feeling like an outsider. He knew what nations were in theory, and knew to people from Earth, like Shabata, or from the Inner Systems, like Shaughnassy, it was important. The only distinction he found important out here was Fleet or civilian. The rest seemed to be an artifact of history. Nobody out here cared about nationality. Earth governments were too far away to maintain control. When it was humans against crabs, that sort of thing faded away.

At last the food showed up on the server bot.

"Last time I saw you, you were trying to talk your way onto a patrol ship," said Shabata, taking her plate from the server. "Did you succeed?"

"On the patrol ship, no–but I *did* manage to get on board a cargo ship running in much the same direction, so it worked out in the end. The cargo ship was attacked, you see, and so badly damaged the patrol ship had to come back to evacuate the crew. They were speechless with joy when they saw me again." Harrington tore off a chunk of flatbread, an angelic expression on his face.

Ennis was suddenly reminded of someone else who could recount tales of danger and adventure as mundane events. *Sayres made blowing up a carrier sound like filling out a form.* If the patrol ship had returned to evacuate the crew, they had been in immediate and severe danger. Patrol ships did not have much extra space.

"Sometimes you just can't win," Shaughnassy said, grinning. "But why did you want to go and get shot at? It isn't fun, and sometimes it's permanent. Leave it to the professionals."

"Because there is little information about the war back home, and as I learn more, I find it is mostly inaccurate. People on Earth have a right and a need to know what we have discovered, even if all I do is point out how little that is. Which reminds me–perhaps you can explain something I saw when I was on that cargo ship." He pulled out a datapad from his carrycase and opened it. It was larger than the kind used in the military, with the latest type of display and functionality. It also had multiple pages, something Ennis had never seen before. A custom datapad?

Harrington precariously propped the datapad over the empty dishes and tapped out a search. "Saw these a couple of times. They look slightly different from the official stills released by Fleet to the media, and suspicious person that I am, I wondered why. You see this edge here?"

He pointed to the datapad display. It was not a still shot from a vid, but a line drawing of a crab fighter, done with meticulous skill. Ennis shook his head in amazement. If Harrington had done it while under fire he had iron nerves and an amazing eye for detail.

"If you're thinking of the fins, ask the crabs. They're different for each battle group, sometimes two or three patterns. Probably their version of squadron insignia." Ennis shrugged. "Why did you use a drawing? Didn't you have a vid?"

Harrington swallowed, waving his fork. "No time. Besides, a vid isn't always welcome; Fleet in particular gets rather agitated when I pull one out. Some of the rougher elements in the Fringe feel the same way, strangely enough. At one time I had pretensions of being an artist, but I merely have a draftsman's skill—no art. I use a vid where I can, of course, but for my notes, a quick sketch will often serve just as well, with the advantage of being more discreet."

"Do you have any new doodles?" Shabata asked, eyes wide and innocent.

Harrington gave a deep sigh and looked even more like a melancholy Roman. "If you mean my lamentable habit of making sketches just to pass the time, yes. I suppose you want to look at them, is that it?"

Shabata nodded, amused. "I always do. They give great insight into the strange workings of your mind. Forewarned is forearmed, as you might say."

He gave her a quelling look. "Don't be absurd." He tapped out a command, then flipped the display pages of the datapad. "I keep most of the sketches linked to an archive," he said, handing it to her.

Shabata scrolled through, then handed the datapad to Shaughnassy, who glanced at it in turn. When Ennis got it, he took his time. The sketches in the archive were varied. Anything that caught Harrington's attention had been captured with the same eye for detail as the crab fighter: the exterior of the patrol ship, apparatus for loading cargo, a mining camp viewed from close orbit. A series of sketches of a shipyard documented the construction of what looked like an ore hauler.

He kept going, fascinated. The next section contained sketches of people, mostly the "rougher elements" Harrington had mentioned earlier. Dangerous, probably criminal, lounging at stimulant bars or standing in groups. They had hard, sullen expressions. He wondered why Harrington had sketched them.

One drawing suddenly caught his eye. An ordinary woman, seated on padded rack-bars and holding a sealed drink bulb. Temporary low-g stations used rack-bars a lot; they could be folded against the wall when not used, or pulled out and arranged in any way the user found comfortable. The drink bulb was further evidence of a low-gravity environment.

A sudden wave of cold washed over him, and he stared intently at the sketch. That face—it was partly in shadow. He must be mistaken, seeing what he wanted to see. He'd just been thinking about her, so his mind was searching for the resemblance. It couldn't be her. She was dead.

He heard his voice asking when the drawing had been done. Maybe it was from before Sayres had come on board *Canaveral.*

"Ennis. What's wrong?" Shabata had her hands flat on the table, poised and ready for action, eyes searching his face. Unable to speak, he turned the datapad to her and indicated the display. She stared at it for a moment, puzzled, then her breath hissed out.

Harrington leaned over her shoulder. "Ah yes, the down-and-out spacer. Wasn't that long ago. Just outside of Thuban." He cast an inquisitive glance at Shabata, then Ennis, and his eyebrows rose in interest. "Do tell me what mystery I've stumbled on."

Shaughnassy took a look at the datapad and swore. Shabata shoved her half-finished meal away. "We need to talk to the board."

It was all Ennis could do to keep from peppering Harrington with questions. What was Sayres doing at Thuban? How had she gotten there? It was a system on the far edge of the Fringe. Did Harrington hear anything, know anything about her? Had he seen any of the other mercenaries?

She's alive.

All the way back to the base, that thought echoed through his mind. Shaughnassy was trying to talk to him but Ennis didn't even understand what he was saying. It had to be anger, the anger that had been missing before, that he was feeling so strongly. That's what was making him feel shaky and light-headed.

She looked sad in the drawing. He wondered if she'd been deserted by the others. She should have known better than to trust them.

The guard at the gate refused to let Harrington in at first.

"On my authority," snapped Shabata. "Now move!" The guard visibly withered under her angry glare but stood his ground, at least to the extent of contacting his superior for instructions.

Harrington watched the commotion with an air of relaxed interest. After an involved discussion between Shabata, the guard, and the guard's superior officer via comm, Harrington filled out forms and had a retina scan, then was given a temporary pass.

Once inside, Shaughnassy found the aide and gave him a message for the board. "There's only half an hour before they reconvene anyway, but this way they can't say we didn't tell them," he said, returning to the group.

"Dare I hope to learn anything, or will I merely have the privilege of answering questions?" Harrington asked, intrigued.

"You get to answer questions," said Shabata, "but knowing you, you'll be able to figure out more than we'd like in the process."

"Isn't it curious how that works?" His eyes were bright with amusement.

The board was late in returning. Finally Ennis heard footsteps and voices in the corridor leading to the atrium, and saw the first of the senior officers of the board returning. Two more showed up immediately after, and one of them, Brigadier General Deglett, caught sight of Harrington and his orange press pass.

"What the *hell* do you think you are doing, Shabata?" the general growled.

"He has new information, sir. Important information."

"Important enough to risk your career on, I hope, because that's what you're doing."

Shabata didn't even blink. "They are still alive, sir," she said in a carefully even voice. "He saw one of them."

Deglett looked sharply at her, then at Harrington. "Bring him in."

Ennis found the aide in the back of the room and had him ready to bring up a still of Sayres on the main display. Most of the board had taken their places at the central table, and a legal officer was advising Harrington on what he could and could not say about the proceedings after he was finished. Harrington was listening with an expression of polite agreement that Ennis didn't entirely believe.

One of the board officers wanted to dispense with Harrington altogether, and suggested simply copying the contents of the reporter's datapad.

"Certainly not." Harrington gave her a frosty look, every bit as intimidating as her glare. "I am open to questions and willing to assist your investigation, but I will not permit you to ransack what is in essence privileged information."

"The datapad only contains confirming evidence. It is Mr. Harrington's testimony that is most important," Shabata interposed. Turning to Harrington, she said, "Could you bring up the image you showed us?"

The aide left the room, then returned with an optical link-broadcaster. With some discussion, he and Harrington got it set to accept signal from his datapad and then display it on the main screen.

The senior officers studied the drawing for a few moments. "When did you see this individual?"

"A month ago. At a small refueling station connected with the Garuda Mining company, at Thuban system."

"Never heard of it."

Harrington shrugged. "The station is of recent date. The system is not far from Zet A." Zeta Andromeda was a fairly major freight hub, mostly for mining. It had its own fabrication facilities, so a lot of traffic from the Fringe wound up there.

"Thuban. You are quite certain of the location?"

Merelin, the representative from Fleet Earth, was an older woman who had been called back from retirement at the start of the war and still used the old-style rank of admiral. Her calm, lizardlike face had a skeptical expression. Ennis had noticed, in his occasional appearances before the board, that she rarely said anything, but when she did her few comments showed a phenomenal command of detail. She had caught what the others had missed–if Sayres had been seen there a month ago, somebody had done some rather tricky web piloting since the mutiny to get her there. Zet A was nowhere near Nexus 4.

"I was unable to leave for several days because of lack of transportation, so I had plenty of time to verify the information. If you wish, you may confirm the location with the ship that brought me here. The name was *Sun Bear,* and if you care to pull the posted itinerary you will see the station listed."

More tapping at datapads and low-voiced discussion. General Deglett nodded to the aide, who brought up the image of Sayres on the screen. "We would like you to tell us if this was the same person you saw there."

Harrington looked with interest at the still on the screen, side by side with his sketch. "She was not in uniform when I saw her," he said. His voice was neutral, even though Ennis knew he must have already made a good guess about what was going on. "But she is in all other respects identical."

The board was thorough, having him look at all the mutineers in turn, but he could only identify three, one tentatively. None of the others had been at Thuban.

They must have split up at the earliest opportunity. Smart of them. I wonder where they left the courier?

"Mr. Harrington." Admiral Merelin spoke in her gravelly voice. "Do you know what the individual you saw was doing at the refueling station?"

Harrington rubbed his chin, gazing up at the screen. "From what I could hear, I had the impression she was trying to hire on to a ship. But the captains were coming to her, which implies she is much in demand–an engineer, perhaps, or a web pilot."

The Fleet Earth officer was looking at him. "Commander Ennis. Does she have web piloting certification?"

Merelin had done it again. He sat up, understanding at least *how* the mutineers had escaped. Everyone had assumed the mercenaries did not know how to fly a web-capable ship. But if they had a web pilot....

Ennis had a sudden flash of memory of Sayres sitting in the launch bay of *Canaveral* after blowing up a crab carrier, stating with the unconscious arrogance of competence *I can fly anything with an engine.*

"Not to my knowledge, sir. But it wouldn't surprise me."

CHAPTER 7

THE DOUBTFUL GUEST

"I'm sorry, but it's the captain's orders. Anything you bring on board gets scanned." The crewman at the hatch gave her an apologetic shrug and indicated a thick, open rectangle with a display, a control panel, and an array of pinlights. "Thinks he's still in the Inner Systems, or wants to be, and *I* say anybody who likes being scanned and verified and registered can just *go—*"

"It's all right," Moire said tiredly. "I don't care." Staying alive was just a habit now, and getting harder. She didn't have the protective coverage of the mercenaries anymore, and out here on the Fringe the lack of security and ID meant she wasn't the only one trying to dodge the law. On her own, it was even easier to make mistakes and get noticed. Like right now. The crewman was staring at her.

That box must be the scanner. Moire wondered what it scanned for. She dumped her cheap duffle inside, hoping that was the right thing to do.

"That one is clean. You can put another in now," he said after a moment.

Moire grimaced. "That's all I have."

The crewman's eyes widened. "That's *all?*"

"I had more when I started on *Grubber II,*" Moire added, since he seemed to be waiting for her to say something. "Stuff wandered off on its own. They have some interesting ideas about property rights, that bunch."

The man shook his head and let her pick up the duffel. "You won't have to worry about that on *Shintai.* The captain doesn't like any kind of lawbreaking."

She suspected that had been the only reason he'd signed her on. He'd been ready to pitch a fit about her lack of ID until she'd mentioned she was trying to leave *Grubber* because they were asking her to help them smuggle. Captain Petryk was much more sympathetic then.

"Does he do anything else besides the entry scan?" Moire asked, suddenly worried. She'd heard bits and pieces about the Inner Systems, which appeared to be the planets and stations closer to Earth. "*Shintai* doesn't leave the Fringe, does it?"

The crewman, who introduced himself as Ole, was more than happy to expound. The ship stayed on the Fringe, and speculation among the crew was rife as to why since the captain clearly was fond of rules and regulations. Moire assumed a serious expression and kept nodding, mentally making notes to look up what a "rack roster" was and why everyone had to fill it out weekly. It sounded to her like Petryk just enjoyed enforcing rules without being ordered about in turn, which would explain his fondness for the Fringe. And why he was out a first pilot.

Ole glanced at a wrist-mounted commlink, and his manner suddenly changed and became formal and curt. Shortly afterward Captain Petryk himself appeared at the ship hatch. He gave Moire an unsmiling look.

"So. You share watch when Watanabe on deck. Without experience, that one! And you don' have license. Hope I get one full pilot out of you both," he grumbled, and strode off. Moire raised an eyebrow at Ole, who gave a barely visible shrug. Already this was shaping up to be a fun berth, and she hadn't even found her bunk yet.

Moire picked up her duffel and headed up. She knew she needed to reach the bridge level but after that it got a bit cryptic. As she walked, she examined the interior of the ship. The walls were scuffed and worn, with the occasional dented panel, but all the equipment appeared to be functional, even the safety systems. *Shintai* was a well-maintained ship, which was unusual in the Fringe.

She stopped at what looked like a major corridor intersection and looked around. No signs saying "This Way To Bridge" or anything else useful. There had to be something, or how could the crew find their way around the ship? Leaving trails of breadcrumbs?

A woman came down one of the corridors wearing an unfriendly scowl on her face. She was wearing a stained coverall that looked like she had been sleeping in it. "Who the hell are you? Why are you just standing there, you waiting for a transi-cab or something?"

Moire blinked, taken aback by her hostility. "I'm, ah, Ren Roberts. New pilot. Just trying to find my cabin."

That earned her a look of contempt. "You're standing right next to the map, Fringer. Won't last five minutes if you ever end up someplace civilized." Moire glanced around, still seeing nothing like a map, and the woman gave a long-suffering sigh. "*Here.*" She waved a hand next to an outline of a rectangle Moire had taken as part of the decoration. A diagram of the deck level flickered, then solidified. "Got your key? Figure it out for yourself. I got cargo to load."

The woman hurried off, shaking her head. Moire stared at the map and at the grey plastic thing that was supposed to be her key. The diagram had no labels. It did have a red dot, which she assumed was the eternal symbol for "You Are Here." Moire tried waving the key at the map, but nothing changed. There had to be a way to get her room location out of the thing, or the woman wouldn't have pointed her to it.

She looked more closely. The display vanished, and she waved her hand at it again to bring it up again. Along the bottom was a row of numbers, zero to nine inclusive, and an arrow. She touched one of the numbers, and a new display flashed with the number displayed on it. After a few attempts she managed to get the entire cabin number on the key onto the display, and she touched the arrow.

A blinking green line snaked its way along the map from the red dot to a new location. Well. If it wasn't her cabin, maybe she could find someone more friendly to ask there.

The key worked in the door, and although there were two bunks in the tiny cabin, neither appeared to be used. Moire felt herself relax. Now she had some time alone to figure things out. She found the pull-down desk and with a bit of rummaging around, the duty roster. It was in Russian. Fortunately she still remembered enough from her NASA training to figure it out. If there was a language toggle, she couldn't find it.

According to the schedule, J. Watanabe had the first pilot shift leaving the station. She had the next. The captain's name was nowhere on the schedule. *Both* pilots were on double shifts? What did Petryk do besides read the rulebook?

She spent some more time with the ship maps until she felt she had a good understanding of where everything was, and when hunger made itself felt she headed for the galley.

It was clean and bare, unlike *Grubber's* in every respect. No cheap decorative gewgaws, no erotic holograms, no crusted gunk on the tables. The few off-duty crew there were sullen and not talkative at first. They kept looking at their commlinks for some reason. Then, like a dam bursting, they all started talking. Complaints for the most part, and usually about the captain. No one did more than glance at her. No welcomes, no introductions.

Moire got herself some of the strange processed food that never tasted quite like the stuff it was imitating. She ate her pseudosandwich and drank some ersatz coffee and wondered what was going on. Suspicion of strangers was somewhat understandable out here, but it was almost like the crew knew when it was safe to talk about Petryk, and when it wasn't. Not a good sign.

Shintai undocked a few hours later, and Moire dutifully went to the bridge as ordered. Watanabe was already in the pit setting up for the first leg of the trip. He was a solidly built young man, a little taller than she was, with dark bronze skin and heavy gold hair cut in stiffened layers. He gave Moire a quick, suspicious glance but said nothing.

Fine with her. She didn't feel like talking either. Finding a seat where she could observe the web pilot's pit, she prepared herself for boredom.

The silence persisted until Petryk showed up. The captain surveyed the bridge for a long moment, taking in Moire's position and Watanabe's nervous face turned up to watch him.

"So, what you wait for? Go already!" Petryk snapped.

"Yes sir," Watanabe mumbled, and turned toward the board. The engagement of the drive was not smooth. Moire felt it in the itchy bone-tug that lasted too long, and she saw a bead of sweat on Watanabe's forehead, but Petryk apparently did not notice. He was watching her, and she kept her face carefully neutral.

Petryk stayed for a few more minutes, then left the bridge. Watanabe gave her another quick glance, this time apprehensive.

"New to the ship?" Moire asked.

"I usually do better than that," he said, his face growing darker. "I'm not a trainee, you know. I've been licensed for over a year."

And he was angry and resentful that he'd been issued a babysitter. She couldn't blame him for that.

"Look, I'm only here because the captain ordered me to stand watch with you. I don't know why he did that. Maybe he thinks you need help, or maybe he doesn't trust *me*. Ever think of that?"

Watanabe clearly hadn't, and he didn't look quite as angry as before. "I know I need experience," he said with some difficulty. "But I'm a good pilot!"

"Great. Glad to hear it. That means I can catch up on my sleep. Consider me your personal emergency backup system, OK? I'm not going to breathe down your neck for the fun of it. On the other hand, if you *do* have a problem I'd appreciate it if you'd let me know before the ship blows up."

He cracked a quick grin. "I'll do that."

Moire settled back and propped her feet up on the pit safety rail. "I don't suppose this tub has any books, does it?"

Over the next few days Moire concluded that *Shintai* was not a very literary freighter. Watanabe preferred to create light-mandalas in his spare time, and the rest of the crew had an extensive collection of trid show episodes. If they managed to agree on which one to watch on the only display console, that is. Arguing about trid seemed to replace arguing about the captain.

The first stop was only a transfer point. From the little she could gather without exposing her ignorance too much, a transfer point was like a protostation. It was owned by a company, usually, and wasn't obligated to provide docking unless it was a certifiable life-threatening emergency. Petryk himself had to authenticate before the ship was allowed in. The crew did not get leave and they didn't grumble about it, which told Moire that the transfer point really didn't have anything of interest.

Their next destination was Kerezin, and it was a long, multistage hop. She showed Watanabe how to finesse a lock-in with a slow gravitic rampup, and he, deciding she could be trusted, let her in on the secret involving the captain and the commlinks. Some long-departed, extremely talented member of the crew had installed passive tag readers at crucial locations— and since Petryk always carried his tagged credentials with him, the crew could generally locate him. The tag readers sent status updates that looked like temperature readouts, and if you knew the code you could tell when he had gone by last.

With this information, Moire and Watanabe worked out a system where she would stay in her cabin with a commlink if Petryk was off-scope, and would only take up position on the bridge if the captain was likely to drop in. So far they hadn't been caught, mostly because Petryk was a man of fixed habit.

On Kerezin the crew got a whole ten hours of leave except for the cargo master, Liz Owens. This was the woman who had snapped at her for not knowing about the maps, and Moire was unsurprised by her explosive and profane reaction to this news. During the trip Owens had become progressively more slovenly and smelled of chewstick the entire time. She'd heard Petryk yell at her for it, but it made no impression. Owens had cleaned up a bit in expectation of leave and now she wasn't going to get anything.

Moire gathered the chip with her cut-rate pay and headed for the crew hatch. She was short of clothing, thanks to the light-fingered crew of *Grubber*, and maybe she'd get lucky and find something to read too.

She hadn't been on many stations, even counting Redline where she'd only stayed long enough to dock the courier and find a ship that would let her deadhead out. Kerezin seemed...different. The corridors were narrow, the people in them unfriendly and suspicious. She went past several shops, thinking them closed, until she saw someone using the door annunciator to be let in.

Once in, she suffered a severe shock at hearing the prices. Even secondhand was extortionate, so Moire purchased the absolute minimum. She could survive to the next station at least, which should have a better selection.

She was directed to the barter lot for books. Anybody who wasn't a full-time seller, as well as visiting crew looking for extra money, sold stuff there. Maybe she'd find what she was looking for, maybe not. The shopkeeper was uninterested, since he wasn't going to get any of her money regardless.

Thanking him, Moire followed his directions to the biggest open space she'd seen on Kerezin. It looked like it had been a repair bay at one time, but all the gear and cranes had been stripped out and only mounting brackets and conduit were left on the walls. Someone was playing loud synthe-string music that echoed and clashed.

Only a handful of people, buyers and sellers, were present. Moire stiffened. Across the room was Fretlen, the weaselly purser on *Grubber*. Moire ducked back behind the doorway before he could see her. Were the others there too? She sneaked another look, then started back toward the main area of the station. She really didn't want to run into anybody from that crew, since she'd neglected to tell them she was jumping ship and they were precisely the kind of folks to take it the wrong way. The violent way.

As she walked quickly, darting glances over her shoulder, she wondered how they had found her. Well, they couldn't get on *Shintai*, so all she had to do was get back to the ship without them seeing her. All clear ahead, all clear to the shipdock row and....

Blast. Three of *Grubber*'s crew between her and *Shintai*, chatting with some people she didn't recognize and not looking like they planned on moving anytime soon. And this was the only way from the main part of the station to the dock area.

She looked more carefully. No, there were stairs between every other dock from the lower level. The cargo area. If she could get to the cargo level without being seen, she could go that way.

There wasn't time for a map now. Moire took the first available accessway that went down, mentally rehearsing a story if anybody challenged her. She adopted an aggressive gait and an irritated scowl, as if she had been sent on a bothersome errand. It seemed to work—nobody wanted to talk to her.

She had to go through a door clearly marked "Station Personnel Only," but she finally found the cargo section. It mirrored the dock level in that it was open, the ship hatches connecting directly to it. A web of rail cranes and robot pallet loaders were actively moving cargo.

Moire swung herself up on a pile of crates, hiding in the shadows. It was hard to see everything and be sure none of the *Grubber* crew were there. She would have to move from one concealed place to another.

There was *Shintai*. Moire dodged to another hiding place, and cursed. Right in front of the stairs was a manned station that looked remarkably like the scanner on *Shintai*, only much larger. The people were wearing station uniforms, too. They would not let her just walk on by without questions.

She looked at her chrono. Maybe she could wait until they went on break or something. There were still five hours of the leave left. She shifted her weight, trying to get more comfortable. How much cargo was there left to inspect?

Moire blinked. *Shintai*'s cargo hatch was empty. Completely empty. She didn't see any crew there. Shouldn't someone be watching it? Like, say, the cargo master?

The cargo master who seems to have given herself some time off, Moire thought to herself. She *could* get to the cargo hatch without being seen, if she was careful. Especially if she timed it right and ran behind one of the big pallet haulers as it went by.

Panting, she darted inside the cargo hatch and took cover at the edge of the bulkhead. No shouting, nobody running after her. She waited a moment longer to be sure, then took a deep, relieved breath and opened the interior hold door.

His breathing sounded so loud, so raspy, he was sure they would hear him. He took the end of his shirt and crammed it over his face to hide the sound. Fear and hunger combined in one terrified whole. Where was he? Nothing was the same. The doors had no marks. People were there, but they weren't wearing the right clothes and he couldn't tell if they were Controllers or Created.

If they found him he knew he would be broken. He must have done something very wrong to be here. A spasm of terror shuddered through him and he curled up into a tight ball.

Hunger made him move again. His mouth was dry, too, and it was hard sometimes to stay walking because his knees would buckle. Maybe he was broken now.

A bright flashing light caught his attention, temporarily distracting him from the pain. It was beautiful and red, and he watched it until it occurred to him Controllers might see him. He walked unsteadily past a door with pretty yellow and black stripes around the edges. There was another flashing light on the other side, and on the wall several lights of many colors, not just red. Green and yellow and blue.

A loud clang that he felt in his feet made him jump. The yellow-and-black-striped doorway was closed now. He tried to make it open again but it wouldn't. Then he heard voices coming closer, and without thinking he ran.

The little way he was in opened to a big room. A huge thing, moving, with a big box in front, made him jerk back. He lost his balance and fell. The huge thing kept moving closer, and he huddled closer to the wall. Only it wasn't a wall, not really. It was another big box, and there was a space he could hide in.

Even better, there was a cup with something in it! Round things floated on the surface, and the liquid was brown and smelled strange, but he drank it anyway. It was bitter, but it was better than nothing. He would have drunk more.

People were out in the big space. He watched for a while, confused. What should he do? Could he get back to the training place from here? Still there were no doors with marks.

He saw another person in the big space, but this one was different. She was moving like him, hiding behind things and not letting people see her. Maybe she was Created too. If he followed her maybe she would go to the right place.

She came closer. He drew back, afraid, but she didn't see him. He could see her face clearly now. It made him...confused. It looked like someone he should know, but he couldn't remember. Her eyes were watching everything, and he could see her breathing fast. He must have seen her before and forgotten. How else would he know her face?

She darted away, across the big open space, and he nearly reached out to make her wait for him. Where had she gone? There! All the way on the other side was a big room, and she ran inside and hid. He watched, but she did not come out again.

He had to get to that room where she was. That must be the way back. Back to the safe place.

The good news was she had finally found a book. The bad news was it was originally written in Japanese, the autotranslate function had a curious worldview, and the title translated to something like "Distended Tentacle."

Moire didn't feel she could turn it down, since Watanabe had gone to the effort of finding it for her. He'd also covered for her unscanned and unregistered entrance to the ship, and downplayed her worries about *Grubber* following her.

"The Fringe looks big, but when you add up all the places people actually go it is pretty small. I know some people, if they are trying to meet up, they just pass the word wherever they dock and eventually you find them. Not surprising you saw them."

So she took the book, a cheap framed textsheet, and tried to relax in her bunk.

Moire found her attention drifting in the middle of yet another torrid alien sex scene and skimmed ahead. The aliens seem to be remarkably human, except for the appendages. Somehow she doubted the crabs would be interested in the same things she was in bed, assuming they even used beds.

So where were the crabs? She'd gotten the impression from the rest of the crew that the problems with hiring were due to the danger of the crab war, but there had never been an attack in this area. People were still worried.

She had her own problems. Crabs she could deal with, if she had a ship with guns. She still didn't know who she could trust with her information, and now she had Fleet as well as Toren to watch out for. Hopefully the mercenaries had made good on their plan to sell the courier for extra cash, making it less likely Toren would find out where they'd gone. She hadn't waited around for her share, preferring to get out fast. If Watanabe was right, she might see the mercs around the Fringe again, and that wouldn't be good either.

She needed a plan a little more complicated than "stay alive and hope something happens."

Her commlink made noises, and Moire picked it from the bunk beside her. The first leg from Kerezin was a straight run; Watanabe should be able handle it without any difficulty. Maybe something had come up.

It took a moment to sort out who was talking and what the problem was. It wasn't Watanabe. *A stowaway?* The voices were getting louder and angrier.

Moire swung her legs off the bunk and headed for the door. It sounded like they could use some help, and anything was better than the novel.

She was getting close enough to hear voices. The hatch to cargo hold twenty-three was open—the same one she'd come in through. The bulkhead lights were on, glaringly bright. Underneath one of them a handful of the crew was gathered around a huddled figure on the floor.

He was curled up in a ball, shaking and making small sounds of terror. Two of the crew grabbed him and tried to stand him upright, but his legs kept collapsing underneath him. He kept his arms up around his head, hiding his face.

Moire saw a muscular arm through a rip in one sleeve, and wondered what his problem was. Why was he so frightened? There was a smear of blood on his shirt. Had he fought? None of the crew seemed to be hurt.

He collapsed on the floor again. The hand he held to protect his face was smeared with red, and the fingernails were cracked and chipped, bleeding sluggishly. There was a crate off to one side, unopened but with a corner bent slightly on the cover. It had streaks of blood on it. The carton was marked "Water Filters."

They stood him upright again and pulled his arms away from his head. He was young, perhaps eighteen. It was easier to guess ages at that stage. After a point, the age-abatement drugs made everyone look thirty for years. His face was damp with tears, but his lips were cracked and dry.

"Nuhnuhnuh...," he mumbled, struggling weakly, trying to turn away.

"How did you get in here?" one of the crew wanted to know. "Who let you in?"

Moire turned and left the cargo area, jogging up the corridor to the stairs to the next level, where she knew there was a break station. She grabbed a water bottle, hesitated, then grabbed a second bottle and a drybar.

They were still trying to interrogate the kid when she returned. Liz Owens had joined them, looking disheveled again. She didn't appear to be doped up but her movements were twitchy and restless.

"Stop that," Moire said, pushing people away. "Can't you see he's dehydrated? He can't even talk."

She splashed some water on his face. His eyes snapped open and he snatched the bottle from her hand, draining it in gasping gulps. She opened the drybar wrapper and broke off a piece.

"Try a little of this, now. Take it slow."

Despite her caution he wolfed it down, and stared at the remainder in her hand with longing.

Moire handed him the second bottle. "We'd like to know what you are doing here. How did you get in?"

He emptied the bottle, but not as fast as the first one. His gold-brown eyes were wide, never leaving her face. She thought he hadn't heard, hadn't understood, but then he raised a shaky hand and pointed. "Door."

He was pointing to the exterior cargo hatch.

One of the deckhands snorted. "You expect us to believe that? You ain't even wearing a shipsuit." His tone was skeptical but not as belligerent as it had been earlier.

"He's not reading good input or he would know you don't find water in a box of water filters," Moire pointed out.

"He had to have come from inside," scoffed Owens. "Why even ask him? Of course he's going to lie."

"None of the interior doors were triggered," the steward said, giving Owens a look of dislike. "We only found out he was here because Ole heard him banging the crates around."

"Maybe he got around the locks somehow." Even the cargo master, looking at the stowaway chewing on the remainder of the drybar with ecstasy, seemed to realize that was implausible. "If he did manage to get in when we were docked, he must have had help." She gave Moire a challenging look.

The hatch had been open and unguarded on Kerezin, and Owens knew it. Moire wondered if she should just leave and pretend nothing had happened. A confrontation wouldn't be a good idea when the cargo master was looking around for a scapegoat to cover up her negligence. Now some of the other crew were talking to the stowaway, trying to figure out where he had come from.

Owens stood aside, whispering to the steward. "Just look at them!"

The steward stared at Moire, then at the stowaway. He looked back at Moire, startled.

"I went down the corridor from the pens," insisted the stowaway earnestly. "It's on the other side. There were red lights."

The deckhand scratched his head. "You sure this compartment didn't lose pressure? He ain't makin' any kind o' sense. He can't even lie good."

The steward pulled out his comm, looking grim. "I'm calling the captain."

"Let's not bother him. We can take care of it." Owens was looking worried again.

"He's going to want to know about this," Moire said, and the cargo master subsided, muttering and giving Moire angry glances.

As soon as the captain appeared, visibly in a bad temper, the cargo master lost her reticence.

"The first thing she did was make him more comfortable! She must have known she couldn't get him hired on, with his problems. Well, look at them! Tell me they aren't related!"

Stunned, Moire blinked, then laughed. Then she noticed the crew, including the captain, were looking back at the stowaway, then at her, and slowly nodding their heads. The captain looked apoplectic.

"What you got to say, eh?" he shouted. "I take you in, when you say you got no license but good pilot. I believe you. You think you make a fool of me, eh?" He descended to some idiomatic Russian that Moire hadn't heard since NASA training.

"If the kid looks like me you should feel sorry for him. I've never seen him before in my life, didn't have anything to do with getting him on the ship. If I had, do you think I'd leave him in here without food and water?"

Captain Petryk narrowed his eyes. "He is not relative, you say."

"No!" *No relatives. Not anymore.* She needed to be careful, to calm down. Her pain was making her snappish.

Now the captain was rubbing his head. "How we gonna fix this, eh?"

"Who cares if he is her kid?" a deckhand piped up. "He's a stowaway, we dump him off next port to the authorities."

"I don't think we should let her get away with this," Owens said, frowning. "After all...."

"We had a hard enough time finding her," the steward said, shaking his head. "How long to find a replacement? I want a little more proof than a chance resemblance before I'd get rid of a good pilot."

"We can't prove nothin'. We don't got an ID kit."

Owens sputtered for a bit. "Hey, maybe we do. We got the medical scanner!"

Oh, great. Why are people so fond of getting me in front of diagnostic equipment?

"He could use some fixing," agreed the steward. "But how does that answer the question? They don't do biometrics, it's illegal."

"This one pulls up the closest matching profile it has stored when it does a scan of somebody. So we scan him, save it, then scan her. If it pulls his profile, they're related."

OK, maybe this will work. "Fine by me," Moire said.

They all trooped up to Medical, one of the deckhands assisting the kid, who was still too weak to walk on his own. He submitted to the medical scan without saying a word, his eyes wide with fear.

The cargo master had taken over operation of the equipment. She did something to the controls, but it wasn't the same initial sequence as the first scan.

Moire took the kid's place, and waited impatiently for the scan to finish. It didn't take as long as the kid's, which surprised her. The captain's profanity told her what the result was.

Owens was triumphant. "I told you. She was lying. See? That's his data."

Moire was stunned, then realized what had happened. "Hey, you didn't reset the scanner! Of course it pulled up his scan. It didn't do a new one."

"Of course I reset it." Owens was indignant, but smirking.

Moire kept protesting, but the captain had already lost his temper. "So you want to be together, eh? Family? You stay together, then. But not on my ship!"

Her name was Nooreen Meniran, and all he knew was she was one of the upper management of the Long Range Plan. It was all he needed, or wanted, to know.

"You have another task for my team?" he asked, being polite.

She shook her head. "New information has been received. The subject is still alive, and is no longer...contained. It is the highest priority that she be returned, alive and intact, before she communicates what she knows."

He thought for a moment. "My team is ready to leave immediately. Where was she located?"

Meniran shook her head again. "I stress this is of the *highest* priority. With all due respect to you and your team, skill alone will not be sufficient. We are attaching additional resources to your team. They are also highly trained and dedicated. You will naturally be in charge," she said, with a smile that did not reach her eyes, "and thus responsible for their efficient use."

With an effort he controlled the spurt of anger before it became visible in his expression, and accepted the secure data envelope she gave him before leaving the room. His anger simmered even as he reviewed the information and acknowledged she was correct–the problem was too large for his team to cover with an acceptable level of success.

Well. He would use these extra assets. Information needed to be gathered, and they were certainly capable of doing *that*. But the role of hunters would be reserved for him and his team. He would send these extra agents to Thuban and ports nearby. And one for the Fleet ship. They would gather the information he needed, but the glory of the capture would be his alone.

CHAPTER 8
TRUTH AND FICTION

The comm ID showed Tabriz, which wasn't unusual, but the code was personal, which was. Ennis thumbed the connect, already curious. Since the forced enlistment of the Norstar mercs, the only contact he'd had with the mercenary commander had been direct, official communications demanding legal redress. It had been made abundantly clear to him that Tabriz was unhappy, planning to stay that way, and intent on making Ennis unhappy too. Nothing personal, but he was the Fleet liaison.

"There is problem," Tabriz said, biting each word off. "A money transfer that nobody send."

Ennis didn't understand, and said so. "Somebody got money here?"

"No, no! Money sent from this ship, but not. Rodriguez says this–his wife get, but he not send it. Secure mail go through you guys, I can't help him. So, he worried about it, I say I talk to you, maybe you trace it." He sounded disgusted.

Ennis sighed. "Can you send me the transfer codes and the routing data?" Maybe he could puzzle out the problem from that. Right now nothing was making sense. A mercenary had gotten some unexpected money? No, he'd said it had been *sent* from the ship.

Tabriz made a rude noise. "I can't send you nothin', remember? This only signal link I got with you *affenfressers!* They cut off all the comms down here!" He broke off into a spate of patois that Ennis was glad he couldn't understand.

"I'll come down," he interrupted. Tabriz was so surprised he grunted and closed the connection without saying anything more.

Ennis punched the elevator controls for the mercenary level, mentally readying himself for more verbal abuse. They wouldn't do more than that, he was sure. Reasonably sure. The mercenaries weren't stupid. And if they were, the marines were on permanent guard now.

At least the inquiry was finally over. *Canaveral* was only waiting for the arrival of the new captain and then they would be back in space. Not that he was in a hurry to leave. He'd only just begun to catch up on the backlog of work caused by the inquiry, and with a new captain coming on board it was even more important to look halfway competent. Especially for someone like him. There was a small but measurable chance if he did well, he could escape the promotion deadline.

When he arrived at the lower level his reception was cool. The mercenaries were tense but civil. Tabriz was in his office, looking tired.

"I don't know why Rodriguez bothered, nobody here say they are missing that money," he said, sending a local comm signal to summon the mercenary involved. "That much, they would know. And nobody up there come to say we steal it."

Ennis gritted his teeth at Tabriz's tone, but said nothing. After a few moments a man came into the office, waving a version of a salute in the general direction of Tabriz and Ennis. He had dark hair, an open, leathery face, and three heavy gold earrings in one ear. By merc standards, almost a civilian. He looked worried.

It took some questioning, but finally Ennis appreciated what Oscar Rodriguez was worried about. "Your wife got a message from you, from this ship, but with money you hadn't sent?"

"She get two messages. One I send saying no money, one just with bank code for transfer." Rodriguez scratched his head. "Exactly the amount she need. Of course she think I send it, *comprende?* It not her fault, money was sent to her—they not going to say she stole it? I will pay it back. I *want* to."

"Is it possible somebody else sent the money to her?"

"I ask, but nobody loan me so much. Maybe something go wrong with mail kiosk, it send next message to Corazon by mistake. All I want to know, who I owe money to? Maybe they need it bad."

Ennis knew the mail kiosk had its problems, but he doubted it would misroute things so smoothly. "Did anyone here send money that didn't get received?"

Rodriguez shrugged and looked away. "Nobody say." Of course, it was always possible that the money or the intended destination was illegal and they wouldn't want to draw attention to it. Official attention. Rodriguez was probably worried about that too.

"Did you notice anybody else using the kiosk after you?"

Rodriguez closed his eyes. "Ann Sayres," he said softly. "It was last time I talk to her. How could I forget?"

There was an awkward moment of silence. Tabriz gave Ennis an angry, challenging look. "So. You think maybe she do it? Why not? She's dead. Blame her, she ain't gonna care. Say she did everything." He turned to his desk display and tapped in some commands. "I show you. She have her money in the unit account system. Everything recorded, and I use locked audit system so if you don' believe me...."

His voice trailed off. Ennis glanced at Tabriz, who was staring at the display with his mouth gaping open. After a moment he shook his head with a quick motion and regained his self-control. "*Skolpita.* Here it is.

Fifteen thousand ED bank transfer. Same amount, same day." Tabriz tapped another control. "The account number is the same as the message has. She still have a few hundred left then, but she take all but last fifty one week before the courier come." He leaned back in his chair and spread his hands wide. "So, Abu Miguel. That's who you owe. You going to have hard time paying her back, *tovarich*. Maybe you burn her some ancestor money, eh?"

Ennis craned his neck to get a glimpse of the screen. The text was incomprehensible but numbers were pretty universal. So, Sayres had essentially drained her account one week before the mutiny. Further proof she'd known about the courier ahead of time, not that they needed it.

"Is still a debt." Rodriguez scowled. "I pay back somehow. She help my family, maybe I help hers."

"You know her family?" Ennis blurted before he could stop himself. Both mercenaries looked at him in surprise, and he forced himself to look more relaxed. "She...told me her family was dead," he said, feeling his face heat.

"Could be. She never tell me about any family," Tabriz gestured eloquently. "No kin to notify for funeral, nothing. Everyone have to have will, they join up. She leave everything to the unit. *Everything*."

"Maybe someone else know?" Rodriguez suggested, looking doubtful. "But she not really have friends in unit, except...," his voice faltered, "Jorge. Dead too."

"There must be someone that would know," Ennis snapped. "She can't have just appeared out of nowhere." The parallels to his own life were painful. He had to be careful not to reveal too much by asking questions, though. Sayres's survival and that of the other mutineers was still a closely-guarded secret. Seeing Oscar's face, he added, "If I find anything, I will tell you."

"I don' understand," he said sadly. "How she do something like this, and then...."

Ennis didn't understand either. Whatever reason had moved Sayres to join the mutineers, it certainly hadn't been money. What *had* made her mutiny? Why hadn't she tried to warn anybody? Then again, maybe she had. He'd just assumed she'd been referring to Hallin at the party when she'd made her vague reference to "problems."

"I'm sorry," Ennis said, and stood up. "I wish I could be of more assistance." He felt even gloomier now that he was forced to conclude he'd had the opportunity to stop the whole thing cold. If he'd made an effort to get Sayres to confide in him, and he'd gone to the captain—Ennis sighed. Not much would have changed. Captain Hsu would have refused to believe the mercenaries were angry enough to mutiny until they actually did it.

"Hey. We find out anything 'bout Sayres, we let you know." Tabriz gave him a short, jerky nod. Almost friendly.

"Thanks. I'll do the same."

Tabriz had a few other items to discuss, which Ennis carefully noted down in his datapad and promised to investigate. Some equipment needed and promised but not delivered, two fighters that could not be worked on without access to the datatap that had been shut off after the mutiny, and a merc requesting the chaplain's assistance with the calculation of a holy day.

Finished with that, Ennis waved good-bye and left the offices, trying to shake off his dark mood. Something seemed to have been communicated to the rest of the mercenaries, at least the few he saw in the main bay. They weren't avoiding his glance now, and one even gave him the clenched-fist-over-heart gesture usually reserved for mercs of a different unit. He hesitated, then returned the clenched fist. If he could improve relations to the point where the mercenaries were only mildly annoyed with Fleet it would make a good impression.

The big doors to the main bay were open, but the bay itself was mostly empty—only a few ships and mercenaries scattered about. Now that the keel bay was fixed, all the extra ships that had been stored temporarily were gone. Ennis went in to see if he could find the fighters with the datatap problem and get more information.

The fighters were apparently still in their rack slots below the deck, and it wasn't worth the trouble of getting the deck chief to unrack and ferry them. He'd have to send a mechanic with a solid and detailed authorization chit—maybe he could get Shaughnassy to authorize a brief tap turnon, or a braincube masked to look like the network. Ships were not his specialty, so he wasn't sure exactly what the fighters in question needed. Yet another reason to send someone else down.

As he walked back to the main doors and the elevator, Ennis saw a familiar bulky figure in grimy overalls working with a probe on an exposed engine. There was someone he could ask right now. Marizio Seung looked up as he approached and gave him a nod.

"Going to make them a miniature engine to replace that with?" Ennis asked.

"Yeah, why not?" Seung rubbed his chin thoughtfully. "That'd be cute." He was quite at his ease, nodding to a mercenary who waved and grinned at him as she passed by. Everybody liked Seung. "I shouldn't say it," he said, lowering his voice to a mere rumble, "but these guys are flying ships so old they ought ta be inna museum instead of a war. Good for me, though. I like to work on 'em. Gotta make the parts, see? From scratch. Ain't *nobody* have parts inna warehouse, 'cept salvage. And I hafta read up on 'em too."

"I didn't know you liked old ships."

"Oh yeah, I always go see 'em when I get a chance. I went ta see the old *Constellation,* just before it got mothballed. Thing had a fission reactor, f'real.

Didn't have fusion working right all the time then, so they built a hot-core for variety, I guess." Seung scratched his chin, leaving a trace of dark fluid on his face from his grimy hands. "An' last time I was in Earth orbit, I saw that real old ship they're fixing up for the museum at Tycho base–got a buddy there, he got me in to see it. Thing is so old it got bendy decks."

Bendy decks. Why did that sound familiar? "What's that?"

"They didn't have trim nodes back then, see? The gravitic generators were just too big, too power-hungry. So, they built the ship deck to follow the main node, so wherever you stood, down was, ya know, *down* instead of sideways." Seung's hands sketched a bow-shaped curve. "Bendy. I dunno how they worked in 'em. Makes your head hurt just looking at it."

Now he remembered. Sayres had used the term. "Who uses them now?"

Seung chuckled. "Nobody. They don't even fly 'em in the Fringe. That's why I had to see that one, no matter what. There's maybe one or two others left. Used 'em hard, back then."

This was getting stranger by the minute. How had Sayres gotten so familiar with the mechanics of rare, antique ships? He shook his head, annoyed with himself. It had nothing to do with him, or his job. He started to ask Seung if he knew anything about fighter datatap interfaces when he heard his comm buzz. "The captain has arrived," said Shabata's voice when he picked it up. "Where the hell are you?"

"On my way," he said, moving to the elevators again. It took him a moment to make the connection. The *new* captain. He broke into a run.

Ennis fussed with his collar one more time, then gave up. It was always going to jab him in the chin and he was just going to have to put up with it for as long as the captain wanted. And what did she want? He'd gone through the same initial assessment as every other officer on the ship as soon as she had taken command. Either she had managed to get everyone's current and complete file before she left her last post or she hadn't slept for eight days.

She had made her presence felt the instant she set foot on the ship. He'd heard stories of some tough and cocky types getting reamed with such thoroughness they couldn't speak an hour later. Shabata had met with her personally. All she would say about the meeting was, "Definitely a change in command style," but it was enough for him. He'd known Shabata most of his career, even briefly while he was still enlisted. She didn't need to explain further.

The most important question to him was how this would affect his career prospects. A tough, hard-nosed captain intent on clearing out problems might be tempted to start his reassignment paperwork early. It had been six weeks now since she had assumed command, maybe that was it. She'd made up her mind.

The elevator came to a stop. Ennis gave his sleeve cuffs one last adjustment and forcefully put his appearance and his fears out of his mind. He'd done his best.

"Commander Ennis reporting as ordered," he told the aide outside the offices. He didn't have to wait long. He wasn't sure that was a good sign.

The captain's office was quite different in appearance since the last time he'd been inside, when Hsu was occupying it. Hsu had liked climbing plants and plaques and vid stills of important people. Captain Kushstan had only two decorations: a long, nasty-looking hunting knife hung with its sheath behind her desk, and a rich, ornate rug that shimmered like a gem-encrusted painting on one wall. It was not large, but it didn't have to be.

He tore his eyes away from the glorious color with an effort. The captain was still ostensibly engaged in looking at her desk screen, but he didn't make the mistake of thinking she hadn't noticed. He saw another detail, one he hadn't observed before. She wore the carved iron ring of a *bahriz nahktum*, the famous—or infamous—rebel fighters of the Afghan Women's War. Either she was older than he suspected, or she had fought when she was barely in her teens. He wondered if anybody else had recognized the ring. No one had mentioned it to him if they had.

The captain looked up at him, her deep, hooded eyes shaded in her narrow brown face. She was tall and thin, and that together with the eyes and personality had already earned her the nickname of Cobra.

"I must apologize to you, Commander Ennis," she said, astonishing him so much he almost gasped. "There is no reach of space that politics cannot touch, and like it or not, I must bend to the wishes of Fleet Command. I have done my best to prevent it, and I have failed."

"Sir?" He had no connection to politics, not unless something back on Earth had dredged up the Fimbul disaster. Why would they want him? He hadn't been responsible. And why now?

She leaned back in her chair, tapping her stylus against one finger lightly. "It appears one of the recent mutineers crossed paths with Toren Enterprises before coming on board here. You know it was one of Toren's couriers that was stolen. That courier, it appears, had come to look for her." *On a Fleet ship,* was the unspoken, offended undertone. The captain was extremely annoyed, but not with him.

Her keen glance flashed across his face. "You are not surprised."

"Sayres, sir?"

"So you do know. I was hoping this was all a figment of their narrow imaginations." She was silent for a moment, tapping the stylus again in a thoughtful manner. She was never completely motionless, he noticed, even if the motion was slight.

"She...she seemed to think someone would be coming for her, someone powerful enough to make Fleet listen to them." *And she was afraid. The entire crab fleet couldn't scare her, but she was afraid.*

The captain raised an eyebrow. "I see." She sighed and touched the screen with her stylus. "Toren has sent a representative to investigate this person. He's here on the ship. He wants to talk with you in particular and with anyone else who might know something about her. You are the one Fleet person available who spent any amount of time with her, so you get to take point on this patrol."

Ennis wondered if they'd talked to Hallin. They'd transferred him to an Inner System base for more medical work, so he would have been easier to reach. Then again, he'd been in a foul and unhelpful mood during the investigation, probably exacerbated by the fact that nobody had much sympathy for him.

"Fleet has made it quite clear I am to assist this individual in any way possible," she said abruptly. "We've lost too many ships and they are the only ones who can replace them quickly enough. *You,*" and she pointed the stylus at Ennis, "are to assist him in the same manner. And you will communicate to your superior, in detail, any difficulty this presents in performing your current duties at your previous high standards. Immediately, as they become apparent. Any questions?"

"No, sir." Documentation of the inconvenience was the first step toward removing it as soon as possible. All while being outwardly helpful, of course.

She nodded sharply, then gave him a good long stare. He wondered if he was going to get reamed after all—it had been a much more affable interview than he was expecting. "I looked at your file," she remarked as he started to sweat. She'd seen his rank date for sure, then. This was the kind of attention he didn't need. "A piece of advice, Ennis. People don't forget. There is a point beyond which it is wasted effort trying to blend in. Cobras don't even bother." She waved a hand in a dismissive gesture. The hand with the iron ring.

He dared a small smile. "There are no cobras on Fimbul, sir," he said, and he saw a brief appreciative gleam in her eyes. Her expression, however, remained severe. The situation hadn't really changed, but he felt better about it. The captain would give him a fair chance, and that was the best he could hope for.

She gave him another look. "Very well, Ennis. Dismissed."

Her aide gave him the location where he was to meet the Toren representative, and Ennis headed there directly. It was more work he didn't have time for, but he was curious now. Maybe he could learn why Sayres had been so desperate to leave.

At first he thought the meeting room was empty, although a vid display was set up and a datapad was sitting on the table. Then he saw the man standing at the wall comm, apparently trying to puzzle out the sequence to call. Ennis remembered similar confusion when he'd tried to figure out civilian comm systems on leave.

The man looked up and saw Ennis, smiling with apparent delight. "Ah, there you are. I was just going to call and see where you were. I won't believe you got lost on your own ship!" He laughed, and then stopped abruptly. "I'm Tendo Berens. Toren field rep. I don't suppose the captain told you why I'm here, did she? She doesn't seem the friendly, talkative type, if you know what I mean."

Ennis stared at him, wondering at his tone. *What does he think this is, a cruise ship?* But then, Tendo Berens was so extremely civilian, even for a representative of a military contractor. He was a short, trim person, dressed in formal business attire but with fashionably silver-pointed hair. He almost vibrated with bustling, impatient energy.

Berens waved his hand at the chairs around the table. "Make yourself comfortable–I want to learn everything you know." Ennis took a seat, brushing the vid pointer with his arm. It fell from the table, and Berens made a sudden, quick motion to catch it. Just as suddenly, he pulled his hand back.

Ennis picked up the pointer and replaced it on the table, mildly curious. Berens moved like that a lot, now that he noticed it. Quick and energetic, yet restrained, as if he had to remember not to move too far or too fast.

Berens sat on the table edge nearby, casual and relaxed, but Ennis was sure he'd done it to gain the advantage in height. It was a minor point, and if it made the guy less nervous he was willing to accommodate him. It didn't speak well for Berens's confidence if he felt the need for such tricks, though.

"First, let me give you some background. This mercenary, Ann Sayres? That isn't her real name, and she hasn't been a mercenary for long."

"What is her real name?"

Berens gave him a clear but shallow look, shrugging it away. "It doesn't matter, we'll call her Sayres to keep it simple. We've been chasing her ever since she got into our computing banks and stole some very, very crucial data. I probably shouldn't even tell you that much, that's how sensitive it is."

Sure. If you say so. He'd have to tell Shaughnassy about this. He'd find a contractor lecturing the military about security amusing. The information couldn't have been too sensitive if they told this idiot about it.

"We have to find her and get it back." Now Berens was sounding serious.

Ennis sighed. "Data could be anywhere by now. How long ago did she steal it? She could have copied it and sent it a thousand different places."

"This is special, and not really data," Berens said, lip curling scornfully. "It's unique, like a code key, and it can't be copied. We don't have it anymore and she does. I can't tell you anything more—you'll just have to believe us when we say we need to find her." Berens busied himself with the datapad. "My department head nearly had a meltdown when we first heard she had died. So when we heard she might not be dead after all, it was the highest priority to find her and get that information."

"Fleet wants her badly, too. She was instrumental in a mutiny, and we take that seriously," Ennis pointed out, hoping that was obvious to Berens. He wasn't sure. "Toren may have to wait until we're through with her."

Berens looked at him with an irritating smile, more of a half smirk. "First we have to find her, right? I'm sure Fleet won't mind us asking some questions first. It won't do us much good to wait until after you shoot her." He laughed again, that strange, on-and-off laugh. It was almost like a sound clip he had stored, and accessed when needed. "She probably instigated this mutiny to get away. She's quite resourceful."

"Very resourceful—she used one of your ships to escape from you," Ennis remarked before he could stop himself. Berens's patronizing tone was beginning to irritate him.

Tendo Berens's face had a suddenly frozen expression. The irritating smugness was gone, and there was a tense pause. "Yes." His voice was flat. "*I* would not have..." he seemed to recollect who he was talking to, and the smooth veneer returned to his face and voice. "Believe me, the person in charge of that effort is no longer working for Toren."

"Did she steal this...whatsis to sell to a person or group? You might have better luck investigating from that end. We don't have much to go on ourselves."

Berens ignored him. "Now, I have the evidence from the board of inquiry—I've been going over it the last few days, and I have some questions."

Don't we all. Ennis bit back a comment, knowing it would expose his resentment. Of course this civilian contractor was given access to all the evidence, when people like himself had "no need to know." Well, now he had access to Berens. If he played it right, he'd have a chance to look at it too.

He thought about it as Berens kept talking, nodding in the automatic serious-paying-attention mode that he'd learned in countless briefings. He wasn't going to find out anything except by accident—Berens was making it clear his purpose was to be useful, a tool or a resource. He would have to make his opportunities. Berens didn't seem to think much of his intelligence; he could use that to his advantage.

Berens got up off the table and moved to the datapad, and Ennis returned to the business at hand.

"Let's start with this—it's an audio clip, made when they were in the process of stealing the ship."

"No video?"

Berens shrugged. "It was from one of the marines they captured—he was tied up, but tried to work his comm to get help. He succeeded only in turning on the record mode. It wasn't a good recording either, but we ran it through the computers and got something useful out of it eventually."

The replay at first had only faint voices, then a high-pitched, intermittent sound he at first thought was an artifact of the processing. Gradually he realized it was muffled screaming. Hallin. Then thumping sounds, one loud. Voices that were clearer.

...kill him....

...keep promises...you kill him, I don't fly....

He recognized the last voice with a jolt. Sayres's, ragged with tension and fear. She was bargaining for Hallin's life. *I'll bet the bastard never mentioned that.*

The audio playback stopped. Berens was looking at him with a question in his eyes.

"She was the one who flew the ship?" he said, knowing he had to say something to explain his surprise. Berens wouldn't know how much he already had learned from the inquiry. "She never told us she was a web pilot." He was pleased with the tone of indignation he managed to create.

Berens was amused. "Oh yes, she's a good one. How Toren first noticed her, in fact." A twitch, and the smug air of secret knowledge was suppressed. "Now this person she's defending—Major Hallin—is he a friend of hers?"

The laugh was out before he could stop it. "No, not a friend."

"Lover, then? She must have had some reason to stop them from killing him."

"He was making her life miserable. I don't know why she would defend him." Except for her basic decency. She might have hated his guts, but she hadn't been out to kill him.

Berens's theory that Sayres had been the instigator of the mutiny, that it had been created just to help her escape, didn't make sense. The mutiny would have happened without her, as anyone on the ship could have told him if he had bothered to ask. No, he realized, Sayres had wanted to leave so desperately that she had bargained with the mutineers, and what she had offered was her piloting. In return, nobody was killed. The recording was proof. Hallin was the only one who had come close, and she had stopped it by reminding them of their agreement.

He shouldn't be feeling so relieved, he told himself firmly. She hadn't stopped the mutiny or warned Fleet. But if she had refused to help them, if they hadn't been able to leave *Canaveral,* there would have been a bloodbath. The mutineers were as desperate as she was and much less concerned about killing. If he had been in her place, what would he have done?

Ennis shifted in his seat, feeling uncomfortable. Berens restarted the audio playback. The dialogue was choppy and hard to follow, but he heard the name Pers more than once. Then the voices faded away, distant, and all he could hear were sounds of movement. He leaned closer, trying to hear more.

The vid pointer rolled off the table again. This time Berens caught it absently as he continued to talk. Ennis felt a vague sense of unease, but couldn't tell what had alerted him.

"That's all the useful stuff from that." Berens waved a hand. "The marine got rescued before they came back to the courier bay." He sounded annoyed. Berens had never named the marine, Ennis noticed, or considered him as anything other than a means to obtain information. Naturally he would not consider his life of any importance. Ennis gritted his teeth. Berens consulted his datapad again. "This other mercenary, the one she rescued from medical. What do you know about him?"

Ennis shrugged, shaking his head. Now was a good time to play dumb. He had only heard scraps of rumor about this, nothing official, and he couldn't tell what was real and what was speculation. It all sounded incredible.

"Sayres and some others took this Hallin guy, who was all cut up, to the medical section where Kuchinski was," Berens explained. "They made enough of a distraction for Kuchinski to get out. What about him? That was a risky move. He must be important, or she wouldn't have bothered. Would they stay together after the escape?"

"I don't know. She didn't seem that involved with any of the mercenaries." Even the mercenaries had noticed, and that told him Sayres had been hiding for some time. From Toren? Even then?

Berens gave an exaggerated sigh, looking at him as if disappointed. "Somebody must know. These mercenaries—I understand they are all in a separate section below, right? What about getting me down to talk to them?"

That would certainly solve their problem. Berens and his attitude would not be well-received downstairs. Ennis sighed and tried to convince him this would not work. He did *not* want to get stuck in another investigation, this time for murder. "These are not nice people, Berens. A number of them have criminal backgrounds. I only deal with them when I have to, and I make a point of not asking nosy questions."

"You are supposed to be helping me, Commander Ennis." Gone was the cheerful, energetic expression. He sounded snappish and irritable.

"I'm telling you the truth. It may not be helpful, but it's all I have."

Berens flicked the back of his finger on the cover of the datapad. "This isn't enough. I need more information. I don't care how you get it. They are mercenaries; it should be easy to bribe them." His face was closed, implacable.

Ennis had a sudden sense of familiarity, and his muscles tensed. He'd been in a situation like this before. A dangerous situation, judging from the instinctive rush of adrenaline. What was dangerous about a smarmy, idiotic field representative?

I don't think that's what he really is. Berens was playing a part, and he'd done a good job. But he hadn't known he'd be dealing with someone who had faced the dark corridors of Fimbul and their dangerous inhabitants on a daily basis, where instantly sensing a threat was a necessary survival skill.

The image flashed before his eyes, a harsh, terrifying memory. Suddenly he knew what had made him suspicious. When Berens had caught the vid pointer, he had instinctively flipped it in his hand and held it like a knife. His stance had shifted as well, in a way only another knife-fighter would recognize. Some things you never forgot.

Ennis scratched his head, acting the part of an out-of-his-depth soldier and playing for time. He had to be careful not to reveal what he knew, or even that he suspected something.

He could authorize a visit by Berens, but it would be better if he visited the mercenaries himself. He didn't want Berens riling them up again just when he'd gotten them calmed down. The captain had ordered him to assist in any way possible, and to document the inconvenience of said assistance. This could be made *very* inconvenient, and he might learn something in the process. Berens would only hear what he told him. "I'll try. But I can't promise anything."

The smiling veneer was back. "Of course not. Now...were any of her personal belongings left behind?"

It went on like that for some time. Finally Ennis escaped to his quarters with relief, feeling wrung out. Berens was amazing. How one human being could talk so much...and he'd had to be careful to maintain his stolid front. *It takes a lot of effort to appear stupid. I had no idea.* The more he saw of Berens, the more he was convinced the man was extremely dangerous. Which made him wonder why Toren had sent him here. If all they planned to do was ask questions they wouldn't need someone like that. Which implied that Toren, and Berens, were ready to use force to get what they wanted.

He keyed open the door and wedged himself in, going by habit. He didn't see the partially open locker door until after he'd scraped his shin on it. He didn't have enough energy to swear.

An entire day, wasted. He looked at his chrono. Nine hours spent in the same room with Tendo Berens. How the guy found the energy was a mystery. He could get started on the dump file for the captain, anyway. There would be plenty of evidence that Toren was placing an undue burden on *Canaveral* and him. The sooner they got rid of Berens the better.

Pulling out his comm, he left a personal message for Eric Shaughnassy to contact him. As a friend and a fellow officer he owed the Security Officer a warning even if all he had were vague and insubstantial instincts. Eric knew his background and would respect those instincts, especially if the safety of the ship and crew were at risk.

Ennis unfastened his shirt and dropped it on the bunk. He sat down beside it intending to pull down the desk, but as soon as he sat down fatigue hit him, like running into a wall. He ran his hands over his head, trying to wake up. His hair was getting long; he needed to cut it or the curl would start to show again. It always looked messy that way. Unprofessional. He sighed and grabbed the shirt to stuff in the laundry bin, then remembered to pull out his card folder from the front pocket.

He hesitated, then opened it. The hardcopy of Harrington's sketch was tucked behind his Grade D-6 vehicle operator's license. He'd asked for the sketch on impulse after the reporter had finished giving his evidence to the board. Harrington hadn't even asked why. Maybe he thought Ennis just liked his artwork and was flattered. He wasn't sure why he had asked for it himself.

He cupped the small piece of printout in his hands. What had she been thinking about, sitting slumped in a desolate refueling station on the edge of the Fringe? Her posture was weary, but the spare lines of Harrington's stylus had caught the stubborn line of her jaw. He wished the shadows had not hidden her eyes.

Berens should have made up a better story. She wouldn't steal anything. Sayres didn't give a damn about money—she'd given almost everything she had to Oscar Rodriguez's wife, a woman she'd never met.

There was no excuse for the mutiny, but Toren had no reason to care about it. And Fleet had no reason to help Toren clean up the consequences of their sloppy internal security.

He might never know the truth. Sayres was out on the Fringe, a resourceful web pilot—the only thing Berens had said that he agreed with. They might never find her.

Ennis carefully tucked the sketch back in his card folder.

CHAPTER 9
MAMMA KNOWS BEST

Petryk threw them off the ship at Bone. Moire knew he would have liked to have done it earlier, but Bone was the next scheduled stop. Not even for revenge would he spend extra money or deviate from his schedule. He certainly wasn't about to let her avoid her shift, or the extra duty of watching Watanabe. Only now he also showed up on the bridge, making conversation impossible. She'd made a few attempts to argue with him, all disastrous.

"I wish you'd let me say something," Watanabe whispered when Petryk visited the head after the last of these. "I know you got in through the cargo hold, so that guy could have too."

"Not worth it," Moire whispered back. "He'd just get mad at you too." Watanabe looked like he would have argued more, but the captain returned and they both fell silent.

She knew the cargo master had rigged the machine. If that woman put as much energy into her real work as she did into her plots and schemes, she wouldn't need them. None of the other crew would speak up for Moire now, thanks to her, and the captain wouldn't listen to them if they did. He'd made up his mind. It was annoying, but she'd reached the conclusion she wasn't going to find what she needed on *Shintai* anyway.

From Ole she found out the full extent of the captain's malice. "He ain't gonna pay you," he said, leaning against the doorframe of her cabin.

Moire shrugged, packing her gear yet again. "That's OK. I can find a job soon enough on any station."

Ole's eyes widened. "Didn't you know? Bone isn't a station. It's a planet. Just mining and stuff. Hardly anybody comes here."

"Terrific." Nothing she could do about it now. "What's he doing with the stowaway?"

"Sending him with you, of course," Ole grinned. "Dunno why he's acting so gear-sprung about it. Point of pride with the other captains now, getting a real stowaway." He made a face, imitating Petryk's staccato voice. "'So high standards, my crew! Wanted on my ship that bad, knew I would not hire!' That sorta thing. I heard of maybe two other stowaways ever.

Pretty much any ship will hire ya to do *something* if ya want to get on it bad enough."

Under Ole's friendly escort Moire headed for the main cargo hatch. Watanabe was watching from the door to the bridge, pale and angry. Moire just shook her head minutely at him and kept going.

"So how am I getting down to this planet?" she asked. *Shintai* didn't have any landing capability that she knew of.

"We offload to an unmanned orbiting platform. That's all they got here. Definitely Fringe, hey? Shuttle comes for the cargo, I guess they take you down too."

Petryk was there, as well as the stowaway escorted by two of the crew, and the ship's medic. The medic handed her a textsheet with an apologetic mumble Moire didn't understand. Something to do with the kid?

She wondered where they had been keeping him. He looked a lot better than the last time she'd seen him, but still scared. The cargo had already been moved so there was nothing to wait for. One of the crew gave the stowaway a shove, and she headed for the door. Petryk watched them leave, grim-faced. Moire shifted her half-filled duffel on her shoulder. *I don't know if it will do any good coming from me now, but...,* "You don't need to worry about Watanabe, Captain," she said. "He's a good and careful pilot."

Petryk said nothing. A muscle twitched in his cheek, then he gave a grudging nod.

The stowaway was looking at the station beyond the hatch entrance with a puzzled look on his face.

"Come on, let's go." When he didn't move, she took a grip on his arm and tugged. He followed without resistance.

Her first impression of the orbital platform was it was just another cargo bay. Crates, boxes, even a few plastic cartons with the Remote Space Mail logo and blinking red security pinlight. Air, which was good, and a little gravity but not a full g. That meant the platform had its own power of some kind. Also good.

The hatch closed behind them with a clang of finality, and she heard the connections disengage. Now they really were on their own. The stowaway looked around, his face revealing bewilderment, then he saw one of the station viewports. He wandered over and touched it hesitantly.

"There's something inside," he said, so quietly she barely heard him. He scrambled away when she walked over to take a look. Viewports? Wasn't that a bit of a safety issue in a cargo dump?

A large curved surface with a barely visible skin of atmosphere took up most of the view. Low orbit, another worry. If it wasn't manned...maybe they could adjust the orbital altitude remotely. Tech *had* improved since her day, she had to remember that. The planetary surface looked fairly uniform, more like what she remembered of Mars. Before it became a suburb of

Earth. A frosting of something-or-other on the poles and a gradually shaded darker belt around the equator. No obvious bodies of liquid, or cities. She really hoped someone down there knew they were here and was coming to get them. It looked abandoned.

"It's called a planet, kid. We're the ones inside." He stared at her with wide, apprehensive eyes, but didn't say anything. Something was wrong here. Was he mentally deficient? Recent head injury, maybe?

Moire looked at the textsheet the ship medic had handed her when they left. Results of a full medical scan; she was assuming it was for the stowaway. No name was listed. The diagnosis was thermal stress and dehydration. No head injuries mentioned, and in fact he seemed to otherwise be in phenomenal health. At the bottom, however, was a long list headed "anomalous system elements detected."

That must be their polite way of saying "drug scan." It didn't make any sense. If she was reading it right, it was saying the kid had trace amounts of personality depressants and significant levels of synthetic hormones, but no recreational or mind-impairing substances. None of this was good news. Somebody had clearly doped him up, but why?

She gave him another, more careful look. He'd cleaned up well. Muscular, matching her first impression in the cargo hold, and tall. His dark, heavy hair looked like it had been hacked rather than cut, but maybe that was the style these days. Yet for all his size and strength, his face had the look of a child, an open look of wonder and fear. He had pale skin that probably had never seen a sun, and gold-brown eyes that almost, but didn't quite, slant.

Oh yeah. Looks a lot like me. She stared at him, trying to see any resemblance. Maybe it was the eyebrows. His were straight too. Unusual enough that people would notice and ignore all the things that were different. He might be a distant relative, but it was unlikely. All her cousins were on her mother's side and tended to the slender and blond. And Moire's stored ovaries had been nuked along with the city of Houston, assuming they hadn't been tossed out years before.

"Are we going to be broken?" he asked in a hushed voice, inching closer. He'd evidently decided she wasn't completely dangerous.

What was that supposed to mean? "We are going to wait for the shuttle and hope the station doesn't have a leak. They weren't expecting us." Looking around, she could tell Bone's sorry excuse for an orbital platform had seen better days. The fact that they didn't rate a manned station was a bad sign too. Proof that Ole hadn't been telling tales. Bone didn't get a lot of traffic, and that was going to make getting out again much harder.

"Oh." He seemed confused but reassured. Moire started to prowl the cargo space, hoping to find a comm panel, emergency gear, or even a head. How long did they expect people to wait up here?

The ceiling had long booms for the cargo cranes, and associated harnesses and gear for moving crates. She'd seen that in action unloading *Shintai,* so it appeared to be standard in the Fringe. From Owens's complaints, it was also old-fashioned–Inner Systems had cargobots, or some kind of automated setup that didn't even require a human to unload a ship.

The far wall had some dingy animated safety posters with gender-obscure humanoids showing correct operational procedure for equipment that no longer seemed to be present. There was also a control station. The original controls had been removed and a smaller console cleverly inserted in their place. The job had been neatly done, but it did not inspire Moire with confidence. Especially since some of the display readouts had been taped over or relabeled in paintpen. One even read "Comes" but she hesitated to power it on. What if the wiring was as good as the spelling and she accidentally opened the main vent?

She looked back. The stowaway was following her. He stayed just beyond arms reach, but was watching her as if he was expecting something.

"You got a name, kid?" Whatever his problems, it looked like they were stuck with each other for a while.

"Name?" He hunched down against the wall, staring at her.

"Yes, name. What people say when they want your attention."

He held up his wrist just enough for her to see a grey-green plastic cuff fastened on it. "It makes a noise you can feel," he said, and a grimace flashed over his face. She didn't see a latch. Was it fastened on permanently? Maybe he'd escaped from some institution.

She sighed and found a semicomfortable crate to sit on. "What about when you were young–growing up? What did your parents call you?"

He shook his head, looking confused. *Oh boy. This is starting to get weird.* "Let me guess. You don't have ID either." Not that she had any right to point fingers in that department, but she *did* have a name. Several, in fact. She kept having to make up new ones, so why not for him, too? "OK, here's what we do. Real people have names, right? So your name is...Alan. If somebody says, 'Hey, Alan,' they are talking to you."

"Alan." He mouthed the name as if it might break. "But...I am not a real person. I'm Created."

"What does that mean?" He ducked his head as if to avoid the irritation in her voice. "Look, kid–Alan. I'm not angry with you. Have a seat. Who knows when that shuttle pilot is going to show up." She patted the crate next to her. "Who told you you weren't a real person?" She tried to keep her voice calm.

"The Controllers," he whispered, not looking at her. He was tense, hunched as if expecting a blow.

He refused to say anything more, his expression more and more miserable each time she asked, and finally she just gave up. Moire resumed her tour of the cargo bay. No water, no food, no emergency station, and most definitely no bathroom facilities. If you needed it, Bone's station planners expected you to bring your own.

She looked at her chrono. An hour and change since *Shintai* had dumped them. She hoped the shuttle would get there soon. What if the air recyclers weren't rated to handle two people on their own?

Something clicked, then whirred in the walls of the station. Alan jumped up and looked everywhere, eyes wide and breathing fast. Seeing the indicator pinlights changing on the control panel, Moire went to check it out. "Automatic docking controls," she said. "Looks like the shuttle is here."

More clanking, then a thump that shuddered through the entire station. When the hatch finally opened, a weather-beaten face framed in rough, streaky-blonde hair peered out. "Anybody home?" the woman said cheerfully. "All ashore that's going ashore!"

She pulled herself into the station just as Moire approached the hatch. Nobody else was in the shuttle, yet another indication of Bone's lack of standard procedures. The pilot was tall and whipcord lean, dressed in multiple layers of disparate clothing over a much-patched shipsuit. She took a look at Moire and Alan and grinned.

"So there you are. Here I am thinking I didn't hear right, *two* passengers? Nobody downstairs is expecting anyone, and we just don't seem to get tourists. There's the action committees, of course, but they usually have their own ships." She paused, gave them a searching look. "You did want to land on Bone, right? Don't have a choice now," she continued, not even waiting for an answer to her question, "unless you want to wait for the next ship, and Lord knows when that will be."

Alan was staring at her in slack-jawed wonder. All the time the pilot had been talking she had been moving the overhead boom extension from inside the station through the hatch, latching the end into place in the shuttle cargo bay.

"It's a different room again," Alan said, pointing to the open hatch. Moire hoped the pilot hadn't heard. The last thing they needed was awkward questions neither of them could answer. Even if it wasn't her problem, anything that got her noticed was bad at this point.

"Let's give her a hand with all these crates. The sooner we are out of this tin can the happier I'll be." If she could keep the kid too busy to make his weird comments that would be good, too. Moire found the cargo straps and hooks for the boom. Shipping on the cargo freighter had also taught her about the need for the fore-and-aft rigging for the crates for transfer across unequal gravity fields, which was definitely the case here.

The pilot reappeared to guide the first of the crates Moire had attached to the powered boom. "Now there isn't much excitement here, but you folks don't look the type anyway, no offense—we used to have a joyboy, but he retired, so to speak, and Mammachandra don't hold with strong drink or brain scramblers. If you have to have a wild time and your pathogen file is up to date, you could try Bobo's. There's windcart races on the Flats every month—that's local month, twenty standard days—unless a storm comes up...."

Alan went to attach a crate to the boom. The crate was not as high as the others, and the hook didn't reach. He thought for a moment, then reached under the crate and tipped it up until the grommet hole reached the hook. Moire could tell from the way his muscles moved the crate was heavy, even in the reduced gravity of the station.

Moire glanced quickly at the pilot, who was temporarily speechless with astonishment.

"That's one way to do it," the pilot said dryly, recovering, "but for ordinary folks we have the length adjuster." She pulled the tab on the hook line to show him how to lengthen the strap. "Maybe you need the exercise." She grinned and gave him a friendly pat on the arm as she left. "Just how strong do you aim to be, anyway?"

Alan glanced down at his arm, then back at the pilot, reaching up a hand to where she had touched him. He looked both frightened and pleased. When he saw Moire looking at him, he ducked his head and went back to work.

He quickly got the hang of loading the crates and guiding them across the gravity gap into the shuttle, and it wasn't long until the pilot grabbed the lone mailbag and tossed it by hand into the shuttle. It sailed slow and even until it came to the hatch entry, where it curved down in the stronger field and dropped just inside.

Alan was looking about for more crates, frowning in disappointment. He seemed to like moving them.

The pilot dusted off her hands. "I'm forgetting my manners, not that I have many to forget. I'm Lorai Grimaldi." She said it with a lilt and a flourish.

"Ren Roberts," said Moire, using her latest alias. She offered her hand and got a hearty handshake in return. "And this is Alan."

"Well, Alan," said Lorai, giving him a good lookover, "You do your mother proud."

Moire opened her mouth to object, then thought the better of it. Nobody seemed to even consider the possibility that they *weren't* related, and she couldn't just leave him all on his own, at least not right now. He was even more out of place and helpless than she was. He might even be good camouflage for a while—neither Fleet nor Toren were looking for a family on the run.

Passenger accommodations were jumpseats welded in the cargo bay.

"You can strap yourselves in," Lorai added as she made her way to the pilot's compartment, her tone indicating that was a matter of personal preference. "Shouldn't be long. One thing good about a dying planet is you don't have so much atmosphere to slog through." She shut the door to the compartment.

Now there was a good example of why talkative people were so useful. Moire always appreciated them. It was easy to hold up her end of the conversation without exposing her ignorance, and she could learn many useful things in the process. Alan was looking quizzically at the harness straps on his seat so she reached across to help, then clipped her own harness in place.

She hadn't realized Bone was dying. The glimpses she'd caught from the station platform still showed what looked like vegetation in the equatorial regions. She wondered how long it would last.

The shuttle disconnected from the station with a clank and a thud, and sudden acceleration pushed Moire back in her seat. Alan looked concerned, gripping the webbing of the harness.

"Still think it's a room?"

He shook his head, breathing fast. "It's...moving."

"We have to get down to the planet. Remember that round thing you saw from the viewport? That is a really big place. The station where we were floats around it." He looked at her, trembling, then covered his face with his arms like he had on *Shintai*. The shuttle was already starting to get bumpy; they must be hitting the top of the atmosphere. If she didn't give him something else to think about he would panic. "Alan."

He had pulled his legs up and wrapped his arms around them, making a faint keening noise. Under the ragged hair, one eye peeked out at her.

"We're going to play a game with the people here, OK?" From what she'd seen of him so far, she figured this would be the best way of reaching him. "We're going to see how long we can fool them in to thinking we are normal—that means they don't look at us funny, or ask us where we are from really, or why we said something. Watch what I do, and try to do the same thing. Don't talk much unless people talk to you first. If you have a question, ask so only I can hear you. Think you can do that?"

Alan nodded, looking interested. The noise was getting louder, the shuttle shuddering and bouncing from side to side, and she shouted, "Just follow me." *And if we don't survive the landing, never mind.*

A final bump, stronger than the others, shuddered through the shuttle followed by a stretch of quiet. "We're down," Moire said to the kid. He slowly uncurled himself, his eyes wide with fear. *I don't know if we landed or crashed, but who cares?*

Alan pulled at his webbing, growing more and more frantic when he couldn't get it off.

"Stop that." He froze. Maybe she'd been a little stern, there. "Remember how you put it on?" As a hint, she grasped the front buckle and undid her own. Alan gave a quick, convulsive swallow and tugged at his own buckle. The rest of the webbing he managed on his own, growing more confident as he went. He wasn't like anything she'd ever encountered. He'd remembered how the webbing went as soon as he'd stopped panicking, and she was pretty sure he'd never seen it before. Weren't mentally deficient people slow to learn? He'd picked up cargo handling quickly, too.

The hatch to the cargo area opened with a blast of icy air, carrying the strange smells of a different world—dry and slightly musty, like leaf mold. Lorai bounded in, rubbing and beating her gloved hands together.

"Welcome to Bone, folks! We're at Waylands, and this here's the depot. You can get everywhere from here, assuming you want to go anywhere else. We've even got sealed tunnels connecting most of the town, so you don't have to have an oxygen booster—good thing for you, huh?" She grinned. "Pressure's OK, but we don't have enough oxygen this far north. There's places in the equator zone where it's high enough, least that's what they say," she added, shrugging.

Moire looked around the shabby, prefab depot. Another shuttle was parked inside, even more dilapidated than the one they'd come in on. Someone had painted "All-Planet Delivery Services" on the side.

Alan had followed her out of the shuttle. He started shivering violently, his hands tucked under his arms, but he didn't say anything. Moire was cold enough herself, but the kid was only wearing a lightweight fabric shirt and pants. She dropped the duffel from her shoulder and rooted around the few possessions she had. The flash scarf was useless for warmth—it was metalmesh, intended to be worn outside a pressure suit for identification. She did have a soft downtime shirt, but it wasn't very heavy.

She looked at the shirt, then Alan. It also would never fit him. She sighed, and shrugged out of her wrap jacket. Offering it to him, she then pulled on the downtime shirt. It wasn't nearly warm enough, and what had been a wrap jacket for her barely closed in front for Alan; the sleeves came to just below his elbows. He was still shivering. They had to do better than that.

"That all you brought with you?" Lorai was standing nearby, watching the process with a growing crease between her eyebrows. She cleared her throat. "Er...the captain said you would be making your own arrangements. It's two hundred ED transport for the both of you." She looked away, no longer cheerful.

Moire winced. That was steep, very steep, but the Fringe was expensive. "He didn't mention it. Of course, we weren't on the best of terms so it might have slipped his mind." She took out her paychips. It was so cold she had to warm them with her breath to get the value display to come up. Barely enough.

She handed Lorai three chips. "It's five ED off. Can I trade this for the difference? I don't have a changer." She offered the red flash scarf. Now she was broke. "How often do ships show up here?"

"We got one or two that show up pretty regular—two, three times a year. Other than that, who knows? Could be five in a week, could be one a month."

Petryk had probably known that, damn his black heart. How was she going to stay alive? Piloting was the only thing she knew how to do.

"I hope there's work here," Moire said, sighing.

"That bad?"

"We can manage dinner, but breakfast looks iffy." She had the kid to worry about, too. It wasn't fair. Running away was supposed to let you *avoid* problems, not add to them.

Lorai looked at the chips in her hand for a moment, rubbing them to see the values. She picked out one and dropped it into Moire's hand. It was a chip with 45 ED on it. "You owe me the rest, OK? I'll keep this as a reminder." She took the scarf. "I need money for fuel, or I'd let more of it ride," she said apologetically.

"I...I don't know when I'd be able to get it. Maybe you should take it now." It was a generous gesture, but if Toren or Fleet found her....

Lorai waved the money away. "Nah, you're good for it. I'm not worried—where are ya gonna go that I won't know about? I don't doubt you'll find work, but you'll need something more to wear or you won't live to morning. Say, you folks ought to boost off to Mammachandra's before they close up. She'll take care of you." She pointed at the main door off the depot, on the opposite wall to the bay doors. "Down the big tunnel about half a kilometer, then take a right at the Blue tunnel. First big door on the left. They got a sign," she said, raising her voice as Moire left.

Moire looked back to make sure that Alan was following. It was noticeably warmer in the tunnel than the depot and the air was not so thin, but it was still quite cold. The tunnel was rough, looking like it had been cut out of the rock with some kind of thick spray foam coating the walls. Glowtubes, arched to match the roof, were mounted at regular intervals. They passed other tunnel entrances, labeled by color. Blue tunnel was bigger than most; it seemed to be the equivalent of Main Street. It even had metal decking on the ground.

She found Mammachandra's without any trouble. The display over the door read alternately "Chandrashekar's Restaurant" and "Everything Store," and the wear on the decking at the entrance indicated this was a popular destination. No sign of any of the other inhabitants. It seemed to be late, local time.

The big main doors opened to an atrium, with one bigger, solid door beyond it that stood ajar. Beyond that was a large room crowded with crates and boxes, display racks holding every kind of device or supply anyone could want. Clothing, electronic sensors, and things Moire couldn't identify hung from the walls, the ceiling supports, and any available surface.

An archway off to one side led to the restaurant section. Tables were scattered thickly over the floor, and a dark-haired woman was putting away the fold-downs that were bolted to the walls.

"The kitchen it is closed now. It is only reheated food I can make for you," the woman said, wrestling with a sticky fold-down. It finally gave way with a protesting *skreek* and she stood up, looking at them for the first time. "Now yours are faces I have not seen here before. You came with the shuttle, yes? You are the two the ship left?" She was slender and dignified, with Indian features and a gentle lilt to her voice.

Moire was impressed. News traveled fast on Bone, even in the dead of night. "Yes. Lorai said you would be able to help us."

"Are you wanting food? You can eat, I will see how I help you."

Moire looked at the wall where prices had been paintpenned. Simple protein brick with plain sauce, 5 ED. Fancy sauce was 2 ED extra. The other options ranged up from there, including a real chicken egg, cooked any way you liked, for a mere 20 ED (payment requested in advance.) She calculated her remaining resources. With Lorai's loan, she had almost 100 ED. At these prices that wouldn't last them long, and they still needed to find a place to sleep.

She debated not eating anything, but the kid was looking peaky. She remembered the explorers' survival training. You burned a lot of calories in cold environments, and chances were they were going to be cold tonight.

"We'll both have the plain brick-and-sauce," she said. "Hot." The woman nodded and vanished into the back kitchen area.

Moire took a seat at one of the tables. After hesitating for a moment, Alan joined her, glancing at her as if to see if she disapproved. He was still shivering. The woman returned with two plates and a small cup of milky tea. She put the plates before them, then took a seat at the table with the cup of tea in her hand. "Now eat, and tell me what difficulties you are having."

Alan poked at the slab of processed protein with his fork, took a bite, then dug in with happy sounds of enjoyment. Moire stared at him, surprised. Brick-and-sauce was the cheapest food on the Fringe. It provided the nutrients you needed to live, but it was not a gourmet delight. She took a bite herself. Either the woman had given them the fancy sauce by mistake, or she always used spices as a matter of course. It wasn't half bad.

Moire introduced herself and Alan, using her most recent alias. "We were kicked off *Shintai*," she said bluntly. "We don't have much money and most of that I still owe Lorai. So we need gear, a place to sleep, and work."

"I am Mahari Chandrashekar," the woman said, bowing her head politely. She sipped her tea for a moment, thinking. "We have new clothing here, very good. But you are not having much money, and you will need many warm things." She got up. "I have this that might help."

She went to the corner of the restaurant where a counter blocked off an area and reemerged with a large, tattered plastifiber box. "Here are left things that no one has come back for. You take what you need; for tonight, for next day, however long you need you take."

Alan had finished his meal and was alternately making designs with the sauce and licking it off of his fingers. Moire frowned at him, and he cringed, tucking his hands under his arms. *Somebody hurt this kid. He's twice as big as I am and he's terrified of me.*

Well, that was going to stop. "Never mind that. Let's see if we can't get you a bit warmer," she said, keeping her voice calm and soothing. She rooted through the lost and found box. It was a strange mix. She didn't want to speculate on how the shipsuit liner had gotten there.

Moire found hats and gloves for both of them. She got her wrap jacket back, and Alan assembled a motley collection of shirts and a thin, ragged coat. At least he wasn't shivering anymore.

Mammachandra was frowning. "No place you can stay will be awake now. I am thinking you must stay here tonight. In the morning we can talk, find a better place." She picked up their plates. "Come with me."

She led them through the kitchen and back to a narrow corridor. Past a door with a heavy metal bar was another corridor, and a small room with empty crates and boxes. Mammachandra disappeared for a moment, then came back burdened with a double armload of what looked like stiff, heavy blankets.

"Storm baffles," she said, puffing as she laid them down. "For the doors that must be opened."

She left, and Moire started assembling the storm baffles into something resembling a bed on top of two wide crates. She didn't blame Mammachandra for sticking them here—they were unknown, admittedly broke strangers, and this way there was a locked door between them and anything worth stealing. It would have been nice if the storage room had a heater, though.

Sleep did not come easily. The packing crates had too many reinforcing ribs and other lumps, and were cold in the bargain. It didn't bother the kid. He fell asleep almost immediately and remained undisturbed as Moire tossed and turned.

Too many problems. She should leave the kid somewhere. He needed professional help, help she couldn't give. People were bound to notice his strangeness. It would be difficult to leave him here, unless she left for good and didn't come back. Bone might be useful to her, though. Few ships meant few means of escape, but it also meant news didn't travel off-planet very fast. She could hide out here for a few weeks, maybe. Find out who would listen to her without turning her in.

She'd have to stay with the kid, though. Moire chewed her lip, thinking. She needed a good story, one that would cover anything he might let slip, and he knew even less than she did. Where could someone grow up that ignorant?

Her thoughts drifted, examining and discarding ideas as they came, not noticing when she finally crossed the boundary of sleep.

She dreamed of Etienne. Dreamed that he was still alive, holding her and looking at her with that teasing glint in his eye. She woke with a fierce burst of joy, thinking none of it had happened. *Bon Accord* was still intact, he and all the others were alive. Then she remembered where she was, and the misery was almost more than she could stand.

Maybe she'd gone numb, because she couldn't even feel the cold anymore. She shifted, then came fully awake. Alan was snugged up close against her, one arm draped over her body and his face in the hollow of her shoulder. She hadn't even noticed, with the heavy weight of the blankets—or maybe she had. Maybe that's what had triggered her dream. Nobody had held her since the accident.

Noises came from outside the storage room, banging and clanking. They were probably what woke her in the first place. She gritted her teeth and pulled away the blanket, gasping at the cold. It probably would be a bad idea for someone to see her and the kid wrapped around each other like that. The Fringe was a wild place but they thought he was her son.

Alan blinked sleepily at her as she struggled with the blanket and his arm, making no attempt to either hold on or shift away from her. He seemed completely unembarrassed. For all she could see, he didn't even think it deserved comment that he'd been holding her all night. *Weird, weird, weird.* Nobody could be that oblivious—could they?

"Still don't remember how you got on *Shintai?*" she asked, teeth chattering.

"I was in that room that wasn't there again," he said, as if that were a clear answer. He raised a tentative hand to her chin. "How do you make it move like that? Were you trained?" He moved his own jaw up and down, experimentally.

His earlier terror had evaporated. She was glad about that, even if it meant he was more talkative and likely to say something that would get them both the wrong kind of attention. "Let's see what trouble we can get in today," she said, moving stiffly to the door of the storage area. The cold of the handle radiated even through her gloves. When she opened it, the corridor beyond was empty. The banging noises were coming through the door to the kitchen area. She hoped Mammachandra had unlocked it; she was hungry.

"WrrrrAAAAh!"

She started back, looking about wildly, and didn't see anything at first. Then she looked down. Her first impression was of a lump of ragged, slightly green fur with intervals of scales. As she sorted it out, she saw the creature had a head, a thick tail, and a strange assortment of appendages. It wasn't even as high as her knee, low and compact. She backed away, looking for a weapon. Alan was behind her, craning his head over her shoulders. At least he wasn't screaming.

The creature approached, more of a flowing slide than a walk. "RarRARrarrar." Maybe she could kick it. She heard the heavy tromp of boots down the other corridor, and the creature turned and undulated toward the sound, disappearing around the corner. More of the creature's strange noises, and then a man appeared, cradling the whatsis in his arms.

"So there you are. You have survived the night, yes?" He had pale blue eyes that almost disappeared when he smiled, and a salt-and-pepper beard. "I am Jens Turing, and I introduce to you Munchausen. So called because it is mostly unbelievable," he said, scratching what was probably the thing's head.

"What is it?" Moire watched with fascination as the creature extruded some small, fingerlike tips which it used to grasp the edge of Jens's heavy outer coat. It started to chew on it with tiny little teeth in multiple rows, like a rasp.

"These are neryas, yes? You have not seen one before? This is their planet, poor things, so they are quite good at surviving. Maybe not so good at looking nice, but they eat any pest that tries to get in. Many people here have one for that reason."

So this was an honest-to-god extraterrestrial life form. Somehow she'd thought they would look less mangy. Munchausen also had the general air of being designed by a committee, and three surprisingly mobile eyes.

They moved toward the door to the kitchen, where good smells were filtering through. Jens rescued his coat from Munchausen with an exasperated sound, giving him a chunk of what looked like copper pipe to chew on. Mammachandra was busy in the kitchen, holding a commlink to one ear while she expertly moved pots from thermal ovens and readied plates. Jens dumped Munchausen on the floor and gave her a kiss.

"You did not tell me how you find these people, my dear."

"You were anyhow half asleep. How do you even remember?" Mammachandra smiled at him. "Talaveras is calling. He says there is a big storm, and it is coming up the usual way. Already it has hit the outpost, and it is reaching him in minutes."

"So." Jens nodded. "I go and make the broadcast, then. I think they eat with us this morning, OK? This way I will hear everything. Else you will ask them all the questions and forget to tell me what they say."

Mammachandra clucked and waved her hand in exasperation and Jens left, the crinkles about his eyes deepening with amusement. Since Mammachandra was still talking on the commlink to the distant Talaveras, Moire followed Jens. Just off the main doors between the kitchen and the restaurant was a small room she hadn't noticed last night. It was crammed with communication equipment, and a much-amended map of the planet was pinned to one wall.

Jens picked up a headset and busied himself at the console. "All-system, this is Turing at Waylands. Sweeper storm coming from Talaveras Station, reported oh-five-two-five. Please send response signal." He repeated the message. On the map, one of the handwritten names suddenly had an active green pinlight next to it. A few seconds later, two more lit up.

"I do this myself," Jens said, indicating the map. "Also it picks up emergency signal, and the light is red then. Now we see that everyone knows. Maybe something wrong if no answer, someone go and look for them at that place."

Now that she looked, she could see the thin cabling that ran up to the edge of the map. It looked like Mammachandra's was the nerve center of Bone. "You folks look after each other."

"But of course," he shrugged. "Who else is here?"

Breakfast was not lavish, but since it was free Moire was not going to object. It was hot, too; another important consideration. She wondered why Jens and Mammachandra were being so friendly to two complete strangers, but from their comments Moire realized visitors were rare. And as the communications system indicated, the people of Bone were in the habit of looking out for each other.

The table held a pot of synthetic coffee, a pitcher of chalkwater, and a plate of cinnamon-dusted flatbread. Alan, of course, ate like he'd never had anything better. He didn't like the chalkwater, but she made him drink some anyway. Calcium was hard to come by in any other form, and between light-g planets and temporary stations it was easy to lose bone mass.

Some of the ideas she'd come up with before she'd fallen asleep had come together in a fairly believable story. Surely there were some people nowadays who still weren't fond of technology? It was a pity she hadn't been able to get anything useful out of Alan, though. That would have made the story better, and easier for him to remember.

"We only came here because Captain Petryk wasn't mad enough to throw us out an airlock," Moire replied when they asked her. "I was crewing on *Shintai,* and Alan had stowed away on the ship. The captain thought I had something to do with it and he was furious. He'd have every right to be mad if it was true, but I didn't even know Alan was looking for me. I, um, never really saw much of him before now. I wish I'd known he wanted to leave...he's spent almost all his life on a strict, isolated colony that has strange ideas about using technology, or he would have known how to send me a message. Anyway, the captain got rid of us the first chance he got and here we are."

Jens carefully set his coffee mug down and got up. He walked once around the room, and then sat back down again, breathing heavily. He was evidently trying to hold on to his temper. Mammachandra's face was as immobile as stone. Jens brought his hand flat on the table with a bang, making Alan jump. "*Ach,* now you are on Bone. Better here than with that *scheissekopf* Petryk, eh?"

Mammachandra nodded. "We deal often with this man, and this is not the first time we see him act in this way. Let us talk of other things. We need to find work for you, yes? It is good there is this storm, many people will be coming and will stay, you can talk to them perhaps. What is it you can do?"

This was addressed to Alan, who froze, then stammered incoherently for a few words before Moire interrupted. "He doesn't know much modern tech, since he only left the colony recently. But he's strong, and he can learn." *I hope.*

"And yourself?"

"I'm a pilot."

Mammachandra opened her eyes wide, choking on her sip of coffee and coughing. "Lorai Grimaldi has not hired you already? Or has she not told you she is needing the pilots for her ship?"

"She didn't mention it, but...."

Jens was quietly chuckling. "And you did not have a chance to say, is that not right? No, Lorai is known for this. For you all is well, then. She is long looking for someone to fly her other shuttle."

Other people were coming into the restaurant now, and Mammachandra rose to greet them. Jens finished his coffee. "For the young one it is more difficult. Everyone is needing help, but it is assumed you can do certain things, you understand? I make this suggestion. I do the mechanical repair, and I can make use of someone with strength. It will be enough to provide him food, and perhaps he can learn something then that he can do." He got up from the table, collecting the plates. "Now, let us see if there is someone with a room for you."

⚓

The Beast was flying fairly well for a change, but Moire didn't relax her vigilance. It was the mechanical equivalent of a balky mule and could act up at a moment's notice, which made it a constant struggle even after weeks of practice. She spared a glance for the beacon locator. Of course Bone didn't have any location satellites; that would be considered an expensive luxury.

Besides, the beacons worked pretty well. It was a good thing she'd actually done it before, though, even if she'd been flying a petrochemical-fueled, propeller-driven, fixed-wing airplane at the time.

Her dropoff was located in the Dead Zone this time, and she was looking forward to seeing it. Bone didn't have much in the way of continents or large bodies of water–it hardly had any water at all, which was part of its problem–so the largest divisions were made in terms of the Zones. The Belt around the equator was the narrow band of remaining life. On either side of the Belt were the Dead Zones. They held the remains from whatever disaster had killed off most of the planet's fauna and plant life. Everything else, to the poles, was Clear Zone–colder than the Dead Zone, but without the debris. Waylands was on the edge of the north Clear Zone.

When she had signed up to be an explorer she hadn't thought she'd be doing her planetary surveys by means of a delivery service. It was still fascinating. She really wanted to take a look at the Belt, but it was too dangerous for her. Lorai had mentioned that the local law enforcement concentrated its attention there.

"Why is that?" Moire had asked. "Jens said hardly anybody goes there, except the xenobiologists."

"Ah, we got these busybody action committees. Come in two flavors here. There's the ones that think the great die-off was caused by us showing up. Never mind it's been going on hundreds of years, before we even left Earth. The other set of leaky gaskets figure since everything on Bone is dying, there's no reason not to destroy everything right now and avoid the wait."

"Wonderful. Hard to know which set of idiots to root for."

Lorai grinned. "Ain't that the truth. Mostly we just point them in the right direction and let them go kill each other in the Belt, but sometimes they don't get the hint. Had some problems with them threatening people at the outposts. That map of Jens's isn't just for weather, ya know." Lorai patted her holstered gun. Moire had noticed a number of people on Bone went armed, and now she knew why.

This dropoff was well clear of the danger area. Moire activated the commlink and announced her arrival, but only got the autoresponder signal in return. That happened a lot. Even when they heard the signal, people were disinclined to chat. She closed in on the beacon and circled, looking for a clearing to land in. This couldn't be the first time these folks had gotten a delivery. Had Lorai dumped it off the side while hovering? She circled again, and this time saw a bare patch off to one side of the habitat, with a thick wall of dead brush separating it from the building.

The Beast settled down in the empty area, protesting, and promptly tilted as soon as the supports took the full weight. The stupid number three hydraulic must be acting up. Again. Since nobody was bounding out to greet her she went to the tool locker for a sonic adjuster. Pulling up the face mask on her hood, she pinched the valve for the oxygen booster and opened the hatch.

It was warmer than Waylands outside, but still below freezing. Moire crunched her way through the frit to the hydraulic housing. She'd have to remember to check the intakes before leaving, too. Frit was a mixture of sand and ice crystals, and it formed concrete-like encrustations on anything warm.

It was too bad her cargo was too heavy for her to move herself; otherwise she could just leave it and go. Lorai had sent a message before she'd left, announcing the ETA and cargo, so somebody should be around and waiting. She finished messing about with the hydraulic and put the tool away, and still nobody had shown up. She'd give them a while longer and then go look for them. Now she had time to investigate.

Moire walked around the clearing. The more she looked at the jagged debris piled high about her, the creepier it seemed, like standing in an old battlefield. The bare plant branches and stumps had streaks of mineral color running through them, and they were twisted in tortured shapes. She didn't know if that was how they grew normally or if it was a side effect of death.

She looked closer, fascinated. On the ground, half covered in frit, were strands of fiber loosely gathered in bundles. Interspersed with the fibers was a long pile of translucent, interlocking plates, ranging in size from a few square centimeters to tiny, barely visible flakes. The pile ended in a lumpy bundle, and then she saw the teeth. Tiny little teeth in multiple rows, like she'd seen on Munchausen the nerya. It was a skeleton. Traces of desiccated flesh and hide were still attached to it. Decay was slow in the dry, oxygen-light atmosphere, and scavengers were few.

Bone had almost gotten it right. Just a little closer to its star, just a little more massive—maybe it would have worked. But not this time. Bone would have life for only a little while longer. Planets with life were rare, and extremely valuable.

Would she ever get back to Sequoyah and explore it, too?

"Ey, you jest going t' stand there?"

She turned quickly, startled. A huge, rough-looking man with hands on hips was watching her, probably amused, from what she could see of his face past the hood and the oxygen booster.

"I thought you were ignoring me, you took so long to show up. You wanted to put on clean shoes, right?"

He laughed delightedly, turning up his frit-encrusted boots to admire them. "Yep! Hey, yer name's Roberts, innit?"

The way news got around on this planet.... "That's me."

He cocked his head, three hundred pounds of delicate curiosity. "Any relation to Andy Roberts, lives on Criminy?"

"I don't think so," Moire answered, heading for the shuttle cargo hatch. She really needed to pick better aliases. If she wasn't careful she could end up getting invited to a family reunion. "Don't know anybody on Criminy. Friend of yours?"

It worked. She got the whole history of her dropoff, who called himself Grigs, and his good buddy Andy Roberts. She found the crate with the repaired oxygen condenser while he talked, and between the two of them they got it moved out of the shuttle cargo bay and out to the edge of the clearing. Grigs waved good-bye as she got back in the shuttle, looking disappointed at the short conversation.

She thought about Grigs as she flew back to Waylands. Lorai hadn't told him her name; she had been there when Lorai had sent the message. If some half-wild prospector in the North Dead Zone had heard of her, it was a safe bet the rest of the planet had too. She'd stayed on Bone too long. If she couldn't get back into space soon, Toren would find her. And this time they would make sure she had no opportunity to escape.

She should leave anyway. Bone had very little information, at least not the kind she needed. The closest thing to a library she'd found were the old issues of *Cosmographica* that Mammachandra rented out. Lots of pretty pictures, but no advice on where to report new planets. Everybody was thinking about the war with the crabs now, not exploration.

What was she going to do about Alan? Abandoning him would be cruel, but he was better off on Bone than on *Shintai,* at any rate. He wouldn't fare well if Toren found him with her, either. It would be best if she just left.

It was later than she'd planned for, and the light was fading when she reached Waylands. She could see the tunnel lights as she came in. They were really more like trenches, not full tunnels like she had thought earlier. They had roof slabs of rough-fused silica that let light in during the day, and at night the glowtubes shone through faintly, just enough for a dark-adapted eye to see.

The depot doors slid open at her signal, and she set the shuttle down. Lorai was there, loading some cargo for an early morning flight. "Well, if it isn't Redshift Roberts. Nobody shoot at you?"

"No. Why do you ask?"

"They've been having some trouble out that way. Didn't think it had reached where you were going, but when you were late I started to worry."

That explained why her dropoff had taken so long to show up. He'd been checking her out first, making sure she wasn't hostile.

She shut down the shuttle. Working for Lorai wasn't bad. She'd managed to pay off her debt in the few weeks they'd been here, and she and the kid were able to rent a tiny room above the power generator building. The noise was annoying at times, but it was always warm. There was even something left over after food, if she was careful.

Thinking about it made her realize she was starving. She'd been flying all day: fourteen hours. She headed down the tunnel to Mammachandra's. She should tell her to ask the ships coming in if they needed a pilot.

CHAPTER 10
MEMENTO MORI

"You need to get down here, Ennis. I can't tell you why." Shaughnassy was curt and unapologetic.

Ennis felt his hands clench reflexively. "Look, in case you forgot, I still have that guy from Toren hanging from my neck like a bloody albatross and I only just got rid of him for today. So I am *not in the mood* for this, Eric!" He took a breath and tried to calm down. Shaughnassy was a friend, but he was also a senior officer. Yelling at him would not help his situation.

There was a pause. "I've had to deal with him too. I understand. I'm asking you to see this yourself because otherwise you won't believe me. The Index data came in."

It took him a moment to remember. Sayres's Index data, which he had requested months ago. Before the mutiny. "On my way," he said, and closed the connection.

When Ennis got to Security he was not greeted with the usual complaining banter.

"Shut the door," Shaughnassy said, grim and unsmiling. As soon as it was closed he started the snoop-sweep device on his desk, and he didn't look away from the readout until the first scan completed.

"Eric, what the hell?" Ennis had never seen the Security Officer act like this before.

Shaughnassy looked at him, his eyes haunted. "I don't know what to make of this, and that's a fact. She's not in the Index." Ennis just gaped at him. He heard the words, but they didn't make any sense. "I didn't want to send any of this on the network, that's another reason I wanted you in here. I double-checked the file. Same gene-code as her medical records. I even made Medical match all the files, *all* of them, to make sure there hadn't been a switch. That's how annoying I've been lately, and don't think they didn't tell me about it. Not only is she not in there, when they couldn't find her they got authorization to do a root-and-branch, and that came up empty too. Seems to be a family trait, not being in the Index," he growled.

"That's impossible."

Shaughnassy waved his hands in agitation. "I know. Do you think I'm being this twitchy for the fun of it? If she'd been an independent aboriginal, or one of the technophobe religious nuts, maybe it could happen, but she's clearly not either."

"Did you get anything back on the other mercs?"

He rolled his eyes. "Where to start? More warrants than you can shake a stick at, of course. Best of all, a genuine, accept-no-substitutes AAC wirechopper. Boggs, remember him? Used to be with the Liverpool Cell. His warrant list is longer than all the rest put together."

"God." There had been an action committee bomb technician on board *Canaveral*, and nobody had known. "At least we don't have him anymore."

"Yes, and PolEurope wants to know what we did with all the bodies. According to them he leaves them about like candy wrappers. He got kicked out of the cell because he was more interested in killing than furthering the movement, if you can believe it."

Maybe they owed Sayres a favor for getting these people off the ship. "She had family once, but she told me they were dead."

"Who?"

Ennis grimaced. Shaughnassy was not as fixated as he was. "Sayres. She said they were all dead, and I don't think she was lying. When did the Index get generated?"

"I keep forgetting you grew up on that chunk of ice instead of a real planet. They finished the baseline in 2034."

They both calculated mentally. "If her parents died when she was three, and she somehow had access to the alpha-class age-abatement treatments when they first came out—maybe it's possible *they* wouldn't be in there," conceded Shaughnassy. "But it doesn't explain *her*."

"What's bothering you? You think she's a clone?" It was illegal to clone and he'd read considerable discussion in the popular press about it, but he'd never heard of any documented cases.

Shaughnassy gave him a look of dripping scorn. "What do you take me for? If she was a clone of someone, they'd be in the Index and we'd find them. She *isn't in the Index* and *everybody* is in the Index. I don't know what I'm worried about, I just think I should be," he said, slumping in his chair and glowering.

Shaughnassy's instincts were those of a good Security Officer. The Index had been created for precisely this reason; security. If Sayres had somehow circumvented it, others could too. "And when do we get this information? Exactly too late to be of any use!"

"The more I learn about her, the less she makes sense," Ennis said. "A web pilot who takes a job with vacuum fighter mercs? Who isn't in the Index, and has done EVA?" *And had never heard of Fimbul,* he added silently. She was impossible.

Shaughnassy fiddled with the picture frame on his desk, then glanced up at Ennis. "You gonna tell Berens?"

"He's got better access than we do, he probably already knows. He hasn't asked me." *And I don't know if I'd tell him if he did.* "About Berens–I know you think I'm obsessed, but he's starting to worry me. Arroyo told me he tried to use an unrestricted datatap. Claimed he mistook it for one of the public ones, but he only did it when he thought Arroyo wasn't in the room."

"Yeah, I know. You are obsessed, but not delusional. And no offense, but I believe you when you tell me someone's a cutter. So in the regular performance of my duties I set up a surveillance node on him and the tracking badge he is required to wear at all times. Said node," Shaughnassy said, pointing his stylus at Ennis in a good imitation of the captain's style, "I may at my discretion make available to those with need for that information."

"Thanks, Eric," Ennis said, stifling a grin. "Vid too?"

"Yes, vid too," Shaughnassy sighed. "At least wherever I have my precious, rare, never-supplemented vids *available.* Can you believe even after our little incident they *still* won't authorize any more internal detectors? I'm just going to send my complaint to FarCom directly, marked to the attention of the next board of inquiry concerning *Canaveral.* It will save time."

Ennis took the offered node activation key and awaited events. Berens was quiet for the next two days, and Ennis began to wonder if he had been imagining things. He still kept the surveillance node active on his screen if he could maintain security on it, which usually meant only in his quarters. Everything else was too public.

Another long night of writing. Ennis finished another report and started in on the next, sparing a glance for the vid link in the upper corner of his desk display. It was showing a long shot of the corridor where Tendo Berens's cabin was located.

He'd given Berens a report earlier that day, and his suspicions were now back at full power. Berens had reacted quite calmly to the sparse information Ennis had gleaned from the mercenaries, much more calmly than he'd been expecting.

Berens was a driven, capable individual who hadn't achieved his goal, and all of a sudden he had changed his approach. He still was making requests to speak to various people and complained about lack of access, but he wasn't pushing with the same driving intensity for direct contact with the mercenaries. Ennis didn't think for a moment he'd really given up.

The activity monitor bleeped, and he looked up at the vid link again. Berens's door was opening. That was OK; he was allowed limited solo mobility, mostly on that level. Then he looked at a separate handheld display and nodded to himself. The security chip in Berens's visitor ID wasn't moving, and Berens was.

"He's left his badge behind," he told Shaughnassy on his commlink as he headed out from his quarters.

"Mmm. We can get him on that, if nothing else."

"Let's give him some time. Maybe he'll do something worse. Where's he headed?"

Shaughnassy was silent for a moment. "Access to stairs—no doors opening that level. Wait, elevator being called, should be able to see that. Yep, it's him. So where does he want to go…huh. Down, big surprise…but only to level fourteen. Oh, he has to avoid the marines at the elevators on sixteen, so he's going to exit above and get down some other way. Think he'll try the stairs?"

"Might. What elevator bank did he use?"

"Bow. He's down…head for Central, I'll use the override and get you there faster."

An elevator was waiting at the Central bank as he ran up, and he hit the close button. "I'm in Central Delta, Eric."

"All the way down?"

"No, same level he used. I have to find out where he's headed. I'm going to shut off audio when I'm there, OK?"

The elevator dropped, the level numbers blurring with speed. It slowed, and stopped on level 14. The textbox on Ennis's commlink said, "Hallway is clear. Good luck." The door opened, and he moved out. He jogged cautiously down the main corridor, heading for the bow. Berens must be somewhere on this level still.

How had Berens gotten so familiar with the ship? He'd known exactly where he'd wanted to go and the best way to do it. Then he snarled silently. *Don't be such an idiot.* Toren had built *Canaveral.* Berens probably had the plans.

That changed everything. Berens would know about the accessway hatches—but he'd read the transcripts of the inquiry, so he'd know they were secured now. So, how else could he get where he needed to go without detection?

He was thinking so hard he almost missed it. A thin, grey cable that blended with the bulkhead, dangling from the hull inspection hatch. *Of course. The hull space.*

The hull had multiple bulwarks for extra protection in case of a breach. The bulwarks matched the interior levels exactly except at the bow, which was separate and sectored over several levels because of the complex shape. If Berens got to the thin space between the inner and outer hull, he could get to the lowest level and exit where the mercenaries were without anybody knowing. Especially if he had advanced intelligence tech, like the safety lock override that was currently attached to the lock of the hull hatch.

Ennis thought for a second of calling in Shaughnassy and his crew–this was escalating fast. He didn't even have a sidearm. But if Berens was this determined, it might be the only chance to stop him before he caused any real problems. Hopefully he wasn't anticipating being followed. Ennis eased open the hull hatch just enough to get past and quickly slipped inside. It was dark. If Berens had seen the momentary flash of light when the door opened, he was in trouble.

Ennis could feel his heart hammering. It was too much like the tunnels on Fimbul, where he'd come close to being killed on more than one occasion. The gangs had prowled them looking for those desperate enough to take the risk. He had survived, though, and now he was the hunter. He knew what to do.

He made his way down by feel, following the rungs that descended along the inner hull surface. As his eyes adapted he could see more: beams and struts that filled the space between the hull at sharp angles, a test cable that drooped from above and went off into the gloom, a forgotten metal-protected glove lying forlorn on a winch housing. He almost picked it up, thinking it might be useful, then remembered where he was. There was dust all over it. It could have been there for years and he really didn't need any more radiation exposure.

A thin line of light led him to the hatch where Berens must have exited the hull space. The same grey cable override was attached to the lock, and now he could see the tiny green pinlight on the sensor head. He hung on the rungs and eased the door open a little more, slow and careful. It appeared to be a storage area, strangely shaped because of its location near the hull and the bow. An array of pipes ran along one wall.

Berens was sitting on a drum of solvent near the hatch, close enough for Ennis to see the smears of dust on his clothing from his trip between the hulls. He was punching something into what looked like a comm, except that it was three times the size of a regular one. He finished whatever he was doing, then waited, staring at the screen. Ennis took a hint from this and tapped out a text message to Shaughnassy as quietly as possible, waiting until Berens stood up and moved to the door to actually send it.

He shifted his weight to ease open the hatch, trying to decide on a good location in the storage room where he could get closer and still stay hidden, when he heard voices–a deep, male voice, then Berens. The deep-voiced man first sounded suspicious, then angry.

"What are you doing here? They didn't let you...."

Berens's reply was inaudible, followed by sounds of a scuffle and a meaty thud. A pause, and then Ennis heard a *thwip,* followed by another thud, larger than the first. Berens appeared in the doorway, stooped under the weight of a big, dark-skinned mercenary. He struggled to get the man into the storage area, then closed the door. Berens's face had an ugly bruise forming on the jaw.

Ennis wished he had been the one to punch Berens. The more he found out, the more he felt sympathy for Sayres and resentment against Toren. She wouldn't have run if they hadn't been chasing her. What were they after her for? What could possibly be so important that Berens needed to run covert operations inside a Fleet ship in time of war?

Berens dragged the man across to the pipes and propped him up, tying his arms and legs to the pipes with strips of memory plastic.

Ennis could just make out the mercenary's face through the crack in the hatch. He recognized him—one of the few converted who hadn't mutinied: he'd questioned him for his report to Berens. Jere Anselm.

Once the mercenary had been bound to his satisfaction, Berens went to the closed door and attached a small device that flashed a red pinlight until Berens connected it to a second, smaller device on the wall.

Berens turned back, and Ennis drew in a sharp breath. All of the odd mannerisms were gone, and in their place was the cold, ruthless efficiency he'd caught only a glimpse of before. Had Berens killed Anselm? Then why tie him up?

Berens pulled a small gun from his pocket and made some adjustments to it. It looked strange; translucent and oddly proportioned, not like a standard weapon. He must have assembled it on ship: he wouldn't have been able to smuggle it on board intact. At least he hoped not. Shaughnassy was not going to be happy regardless.

This was getting bad. He had to get out of the hull space and across the room to reach Berens to stop him, and there was no way he could make it without getting shot. Berens was too far away and the space he'd have to cross didn't have enough cover.

Berens put the gun away and took out a medical injector, placing a handful of small cartridges on a crate nearby. Selecting a cartridge, he put it in the injector and placed it on the side of Anselm's neck. The mercenary's eyes bulged, and he moaned as the drug took effect. Berens took another cartridge, a different color this time, and injected that as well. Now the mercenary was hanging limply, his jaw slack and eyes half open.

Berens shoved his thumb hard against the underside of Anselm's chin. "Keep your head up. You're going to answer all the questions I ask, got that? And you're going to tell me the truth, whether you want to or not, so don't even bother trying to fight it. Did you know Ann Sayres?"

"Yes." Anselm was slurring but intelligible.

"Did she tell you where she'd traveled? Mention any planets?" It seemed to take a while for the question to percolate through to the man's drugged brain. Berens slapped him, hard. "Where did she say she'd been?"

"Didn't. Didn't say much." A thin line of blood dripped from his mouth.

"Did she have anything with her that looked unusual, objects that were different or strange?"

Anselm just looked at him, making a wheezy, moaning noise of confusion. Berens punched him, once, twice. *Where the hell is Shaughnassy?*

Ennis knew he had to take the chance, or Anselm was going to get killed. Berens seemed to be completely engaged in his interrogation process. Ennis climbed up a few rungs, then pushed the hatch door open slowly. Hanging from the rung just above the hatch, he eased himself in a quick, fluid motion to the floor.

No gunshots, no sounds of surprise. Penderhest had taught him that one; he was glad he hadn't forgotten how to do it. Ennis rolled over silently and risked a glance. Berens was still facing his prisoner.

"Did she ever mention Sequoyah?" Anselm shook his head. "Ever hear the name Moire Cameron?" Another shake of the head. "Where is Sayres now?"

Anselm laughed. It sounded odd coming from his swollen, bleeding lips. "Flying patrols in hell. She tried...."

This answer seemed to take Berens aback. He must have forgotten everyone outside the inquiry still thought she was dead. "Where was she planning to go?" he finally asked.

"They didn't tell me. Wouldn't tell me. Gonna stay...."

"Where do you think they were going?"

"Follow the red line...." Anselm was sounding more vacant now, his voice fainter.

Ennis crept, low and stealthy, behind a rack pallet. He still wasn't close enough to rush Berens, and the crates between him and his target were too low. He couldn't get closer without him noticing.

Berens asked a few more questions, but now Anselm was making no sense at all. Finally Berens turned away, jaw working. "Goddammit, you don't know anything, you worthless piece of shit. You made me do all this work for nothing. You've got it coming, and you won't be a loss to anybody."

He reached in his pocket. Ennis felt for one of the long metal pipes on the rack pallet, bracing himself to attack, but Berens didn't take out the gun. Instead he pulled out a thin black cylinder with a thicker red top. Incendiary. Berens was going to kill Anselm and get rid of any evidence of the interrogation in the bargain.

Berens made a muttered sound of exasperation and moved to the door, which still had the grey sensors attached to it. As he went by the rack Ennis rose up and struck him hard on the back of the head with the pipe.

Berens dropped and lay still on the floor.

CHAPTER 11
SIMPLE GIFTS

There were only a few people in the restaurant area when Moire came in. Jens was sitting with some acquaintances, but he came over to chat with her.

"Today Alan is using the line welder by himself," he said. "He is doing well. Still he does not say much."

"He's not talkative, no." Alan rarely spoke at all, except to her. Even she had a hard time getting him to answer questions.

"I am thinking...he is quick to learn the work, and he has the skill for it. I would like to take him as apprentice. But now Mahari is saying you ask for ships that will hire. You are planning to leave?"

"If I can. Haven't had much luck with that." Only two ships had shown up since she'd arrived on Bone.

"*Caspian* is needing crew, I know. You did not ask them?"

"Captain said they go to the Inner Systems sometimes. I like staying on the Fringe." She didn't dare go anywhere else. Too much of a chance somebody somewhere would recognize her, and her lack of ID would be more of a problem.

"Ah, well, we are glad to have you both as long as you can stay. Perhaps you will still be here when Anja comes to visit. It would be good for her to have someone her age to talk to." Jens got up and returned to his friends.

Moire had heard a lot about young Anja Parvati, the pride of her parents, currently studying medicine with a traveling doctor who circled the Fringe. It was disconcerting sometimes how Mammachandra and Jens thought she was a proud parent, too. Jens certainly was assuming Alan would go with her when she left.

As she was finishing her meal, Alan himself appeared and silently sat down beside her.

"It's late. Why didn't you go back to the room?" Moire asked.

For a moment she thought he wouldn't answer. "It's empty," Alan said, his voice so soft she could barely hear it. "Nobody is there saying things." He looked at her. "I hear noises and think they are bad. When you are there too, I hear them and they aren't bad. Why?"

Moire blinked. That was the longest speech he'd ever made, and he'd even asked a question. She heard something clink against the surface of the table as he laid his arms on it, and she glanced down. He had an opaline chain wrapped around his wrist, the kind of thing she'd usually seen for attaching small pieces of gear to a belt or harness. Ornamental.

"Where did you get that?" Moire asked, a sinking sensation in her stomach. Alan didn't have any money. Maybe somebody gave it to him.

He pointed to the store. "It has lots of them."

Moire closed her eyes briefly, feeling ill. She glanced over at Jens. He was talking to Mammachandra, and she was laughing. Neither of them were looking her direction.

"You can't take stuff without paying for it!" she hissed through clenched teeth. "It doesn't belong to you!"

Alan just looked at her, puzzled. "I saw people take things from there."

From the corner of her eye, she saw Jens get up to help Mammachandra clear some tables. When their backs were turned, she got up hurriedly and pulled Alan into the store.

"They paid for what they took. With money. We have to put that back before anybody notices or we'll be in trouble." She started unwrapping the chain from his wrist. Alan just stood there, confused but unresisting. "Did you take anything else?"

He pulled out a handful of flashy, cheap plastic gizmos, and two more chains. Judging from his choices he liked bright colors. Moire took his treasures and started putting them back where they belonged.

"Don't take anything from the store again without permission, OK? Mammachandra would be very angry with you."

Alan watched her with sad eyes as the pile in her hand diminished. "But why?"

This was really starting to worry her. Even a three-year-old understood the concept of personal property. Looking at his wide gaze, she saw only honest puzzlement.

"Just...please don't do it. All right?" He nodded.

Moire searched through the store, looking for all the places he'd taken something. Alan wasn't standing by her when she finished replacing the chains. She looked about, finally finding him near the back. Behind a small counter was a display cabinet with some of the more valuable merchandise, and on top was what appeared to be a kind of shrine with a statue. It had an everlight in an open brass bowl in front, and smaller lights around it. The statue was a bronze-colored stone, a strange Indian figure with an elephant head. She assumed it was a god; she didn't know which one. It must have cost a lot to ship something heavy like that. They hadn't packed it well, though. One of the elephant's tusks was broken off.

Alan was staring at it, fascinated. "Why are there the white things on strings?" he asked when she came up. All about the head of the statue, hanging from the roof, were what she would have called small paper airplanes. Now they were probably made of plastic printout and nobody but her remembered airplanes.

"I don't know. Decorations, maybe?"

She nudged Alan out of the store with a feeling of relief. Jens and his friends waved to them both as they left. She waved back. Alan lifted his hand tentatively then snatched it down again. He was definitely making progress. He used to just stare.

The tunnels didn't seem as cold as they did at first, or maybe she was getting used to it. Their room was on the other side of Waylands from Mammachandra's, all the way to Red tunnel. Alan walked silently beside her.

"Is it OK to just look in the store?" he asked finally.

Poor kid. He was just trying to understand. "Sure." He didn't even seem resentful that she'd taken all the pretty things away from him. She felt in her pocket. Lorai had returned the red metalmesh scarf when she'd paid off her debt, and she'd been carrying it around ever since. "Here. This is mine, and I'm giving it to you. You can keep it. It's yours." Maybe she could teach him this way.

Alan stopped and took the scarf carefully in both hands, as if he was afraid it would break. "I don't have to pay?"

Moire grinned, feeling relieved. He had been listening after all. "Nope. I paid for it a long time ago, and you don't have to pay me because it's a gift."

He held it up to the light, and then waved it about experimentally. "It is better than the things in the store," he said, twisting it into a knot, then hanging it about his neck and playing with the ends. He sounded much more cheerful, and Moire felt a weight lift off her. He didn't have much to be cheerful about.

Someone was going to have to work on explaining things to him when she left. He seemed to listen to her and at least try to understand. It was good he was getting along with Jens. Maybe he'd learn to trust him, too.

"Come on, kid, let's go home. I'm tired," Moire said gruffly.

They turned down Red tunnel. Even this late there were people standing around or heading for Bobo's. Bobo's location in the Red tunnel was quite appropriate. Bone's one former sex worker had retired but there were plenty of freelance amateurs, and they congregated here. The desperate and broke stood about in the tunnel itself–Bobo's was expensive, and he required you to buy something to stay long enough to find a "hitch" for the night.

She quickened her steps. If she didn't make eye contact, sometimes they got the hint and left her alone. Most of them recognized her by now and knew she wasn't a player. If it hadn't been so dark she might have been tempted to try the outside route instead of the tunnels, but it was too dangerous if you couldn't see where you were going.

The door to Bobo's cycled open as they passed it, spilling out sounds of loud music and conversation. Alan, distracted, turned his head to look. Moire grabbed his arm and pulled him along.

"You want to go in, doncha doll?" One of the standabouts, a large woman in a miner's coverall, moved to block their way. Her teeth were discolored from chewstick. "I'll take ya, if yer momma won't."

Alan hunched in on himself, moving so Moire was between him and the miner.

"He's not interested," Moire said, trying to edge around her, but the woman shoved her back.

"He can speak for himself. What's it to you, anyway?" Alan's face was flushed and he looked uncomfortable, but he still didn't say anything. "Aw, he's shy. Lookit that. You just need a little push, right? You'll like it fine ifn' a try it. Come on, doll."

Alan still didn't move, didn't look up from staring at the ground. The miner was looking angry now, and some of the other standabouts were making comments. It appeared this woman had been trying for a hitch without success for some time. "That's a pretty scarf ya got there, doll. Betcha wouldn't want ta lose it, huh?" The miner snatched it from his neck and dangled it in front of his face. "Come and get it!"

The woman backed toward the door to Bobo's, but she didn't get far.

"No! It is mine!" Alan yelled. He struck her hard in the face, a clumsy blow but effective, and snatched the scarf and ran. Moire followed him, swearing under her breath. The miner was sagging against the tunnel wall, moaning and holding her bloody face.

Damn, that kid is quick. Fortunately the tunnels didn't give him many places to run to. She'd seen him run past the power plant entrance, so he hadn't gone to their room. Moire turned her head, listening. Nobody was following. The miner must have decided against pursuit, and nobody else seemed to care.

He'd never yelled like that before. There had been a look of pure terror on his face when he ran. What had he been afraid of? He'd taken the scarf back, and even though the miner was pushy she hadn't actually attacked him.

Well. I think he understands personal property now.

The first side tunnel had only closed doors, and she could see all the way to the end. Nothing. It was just a hunch, but she suspected Alan was too upset to think of opening doors to get away. The second side tunnel looked empty at first, but when she investigated it had a cross branch with some construction equipment stacked about, apparently to extend the tunnel farther. She moved to the pile of crates in the far end. It was in shadow. She thought she heard suppressed sobbing.

"Hey. Alan." The sobbing stopped. "It's me. Moire." *Oops.* "Are you planning on staying there all night?"

The air was frigid here. She could feel her eyelashes starting to freeze together. A sniff, and faint sound of movement behind the crates. Moire perched on a stabilizer strut on one of the excavating devices, ignoring the numbing cold of the metal radiating through her clothing. She was tired, she was cold, and she didn't know what to do to help him. How did you reach somebody so far removed from normal?

"I don't want to go back." His voice was tight and shaky.

She let out a breath, feeling relieved. At least he was talking now. "Back where? We need to go back to our room, or we'll freeze here. And I forbid you to go to Bobo's."

Another small sound, a soggy laugh or a sob. "They'll break me if I go back. Created don't ever hit Controllers. They break you, right then."

"Kid, I don't even know where these Controllers of yours hang out. How can I send you there?"

Another scuffling sound, and she could see the edge of his face and one hand. The red flash scarf was crumpled in it, clutched tightly.

"Kid. Alan. Are these Controllers looking for you? I'll take your word for it they are bad people, but who are they?" The hand holding the scarf was shaking, but he said nothing. "How did you get away from them, if they didn't want you to go?"

"I heard a voice like my nenner," he said, soft and strained, as if the words were being pulled from him. "When I finished growing they took me from my group for training. I was a special project, they said. The others stayed with their nenners, but if you were a special they took you away. I thought I heard her. I didn't go far, I didn't mean to be wrong...but I got lost. And the Controllers came, so I hid. I tried to go back, but nothing looked the same. And the door wasn't open anymore, and there wasn't any food, and...and I saw you and thought you knew the way back, but then the other door was closed and the angry people found me."

Moire tried to puzzle it out. Filtered through Alan's limited understanding, it sounded like he was somewhere and got on a ship without knowing it. Probably more than one. *Shintai* had only stopped at stations and places like Bone, and she didn't think any of them were likely origins for someone like Alan.

The others stayed.... "How many Created were there, the place where you were before?"

His shadow shrugged. "Lots. I heard a Controller say they were generating five hundred that year."

She shivered, suddenly feeling even colder. Five hundred, all like Alan. How the hell could anybody hide something like that?

Alan eventually crawled out from behind the crates, but he was still terrified. When they finally got to their room he refused to sleep in the hammock.

"It's too far," he said, curling up on the floor next to her. The room only had one bunk, which was too short for him so she didn't feel guilty about taking it herself. He usually didn't mind the hammock, even after she got him to stop swinging in it.

Moire got up off the bunk. "The floor is too cold. Come on, get up. I'm tired, Alan. Let's get some sleep." She grabbed his arm and heaved with all her strength. He didn't budge. OK, force was out. "Guess I'll take the hammock, then."

His eyes widened. "No! This is your place." He patted the bunk.

"You aren't sleeping on the floor, OK? So either get in the bunk or the hammock, and do it now."

"I have to be close," he pleaded. "In the dark I could be alone, and that's for being bad."

He was upset about something, she just didn't know what. She was so tired....

"Kid, I'm sorry but there just isn't room. You didn't mind it before, did you?" He just looked at her, clutching his blanket. Maybe there was a sneaky way around this. "Get in the bunk, kid. Move all the way in."

"But...."

"I'll be there too."

He got up then. Somehow he managed to contort himself to fit in the small space, leaving barely enough room for Moire beside him. It was a good thing she wasn't planning on staying long. He fell asleep almost at once, and as soon as his breathing slowed she sat up.

The hand tucked underneath his head still clutched the red metalmesh scarf. *Just tell me who these people are, kid. I'm already mad at them.* This was the most he'd ever said about them. She'd tried several times before to find out how he'd gotten on *Shintai,* or where he had grown up, but nothing would shut him up faster. And then he would have nightmares....

She had to leave him here. Jens could take care of him, teach him a trade. She'd have to warn Jens about his peculiarities, about never leaving him alone. He couldn't be punching people every time something went wrong. Funny thing was, he didn't know how strong he was. He had been acting purely from fear, not aggression, when he'd hit the miner.

Alan twitched in his sleep, making faint noises deep in his throat. Another nightmare. The plastic cuff on his arm was visible. That was another thing he never talked about, except for that one time on the station platform. He would never let her touch it. She noticed for the first time there was writing on it. Carefully, trying not to wake him, she adjusted his arm so she could read it.

Cadmus Batch 0712-09-8870-02. Below that was the label "Unit Activation" and a date, approximately eight years ago. She couldn't see any way to take it off.

Poor kid. She pulled the blanket up further and tucked it about him, then got up and collapsed in the hammock.

Moire tried to stay close to Waylands as much as possible after the incident with the miner, even confiding in Lorai to the extent that Alan had had a violent run-in and she wanted to keep an eye on him.

Lorai waved it off. "Aah, that's just youth for ya. Sure there's fights, but nobody takes it personal around here. Kinda surprised anybody'd wanna ping his scope, just from the size of him. He'll be all right."

Moire bit back the reply that it wasn't Alan's health she was worried about. He was strong enough to kill someone without meaning to. Instead, she took most of the meager savings she'd accumulated and invested in a personal commlink for him. She made sure he saw the whole process of the transaction, too, and he was suitably impressed. He was also completely engrossed by her demonstration of the commlink in action.

"So, you think you understand it now?"

He nodded, looking serious. "I make the screen wake up, and then I find the code that means you, and then I push this, and it finds you. How does it do that?"

"I, er, I'll tell you later." Much later, if she had any say in the matter. He was full of questions now, as if they had been bottled up all this time. "I have to make a delivery to a mining camp now, and I won't be back until late. Call me if anything bothers you, OK?"

The flood of questions stopped, and he clutched the commlink to his chest. "OK," he said reluctantly.

As she left the depot she wondered if she should have taught him how to take incoming calls, but that had seemed a bit complex on top of everything else. Besides, he called her at the earliest opportunity. Knowing that the commlink actually worked appeared to calm him down enough that she made it to the mining camp without getting another call.

The shuttle was full of cargo and the camp had more to send back to Waylands, so she grabbed the mailbag and some of the smaller boxes before signaling the unloaders to go to work on the heavy crates and equipment. The sooner everything got delivered, the sooner she could head back. Sprinting across the landing pad against a strong, sand-enriched wind, she cycled through the main door of the habitat into the welcome warmth. Damn, but Bone was cold!

"Hey, Ren!" Moire looked up from shaking the sand out of her oxygen booster and hood. The camp manager, a talkative Chinese-Latina named Esperanza Li, was waving at her. "Nice weather for the races, huh? Who's your favorite?"

Oh yeah. Windcart races. "Kalmirov," Moire said, dredging a name up at random from conversations overheard at Mammachandra's.

"You like him?" Esper widened her eyes, and grinned. "I mean for racing, *chica!* Looks don't win! How long's he been your favorite, eh? Tell me more."

Moire laughed and quickly looked at the label on the top package. "Oh, Gip's finally got his delivery. Here's the mail, Esper. I'll go take this to him personally." She gave the camp manager a determinedly cheerful smile and escaped. Everybody wanted to talk to her on trips like these. Camp people didn't get out much. Unfortunately, they liked to gossip and she was doing her damnedest to stay off the chat circuit, so Esper was doomed to disappointment.

Moire wandered the circular hallway of the habitat as slowly as she could, to waste time. Gip Farouz's living and working quarters were too close to the camp office for that to help, though. He did the mineral assays and other testing, so the location made sense for him.

He answered the door himself and his gentle, leathery face creased instantly with a smile.

"Ah, you have brought it at last!" He took the package with care and slowly stepped aside. "Please, come and join me. You may find this interesting yourself, with your travels."

Moire reluctantly followed Gip inside. One of the miners had told her Gip was over ninety years old, even though he didn't look it. Age-abatement tech made things difficult for her to judge. Hearing that, she had worried he might possibly recognize her, until she reflected a ten-year-old boy probably hadn't been paying a lot of attention to news reports about missing exploration ships.

"For this, I will make tea. You have time, yes?" he inquired.

Moire hesitated. "I'll have to go when they finish loading," she said, looking around at the amazing clutter that filled Gip's quarters. A plastic grid was fastened to one wall and filled with dusty mineral samples, carefully labeled. A small glass-fronted case with an atmospheric readout inside contained a handful of actual, physical paper books. She stared at them, unsettled by the strange familiarity.

Gip searched through a crammed cupboard and brought out a small metal tin. Moving with slow but steady movements, he set up a self-heating pot and carefully measured out the dried leaves. *Real* tea, not artificial concentrate. Out here that would be an expensive luxury, and an honor.

"You've been on Bone a while?" Moire asked, picking her way through the cramped space to what looked like a place to sit. Gip was a tiny, slender man and could get around easily, but she felt like a accident waiting to happen. Sitting down would be safer.

He turned his head away from the pot and the lines around his eyes deepened. "I was on the first ship that came to this place, after the ship of exploration, of course. And its name...oh, for the memory of youth! It was *Buckeye*, the name of the ship I came on. Only I remain of those who remember; I have been here the longest of any." Gip nodded with simple pride. He carefully poured out the tea into two small glasses in metal holders.

The scent of mint wafted from the glass as he handed it to her. Gip set his tea down on the only clear space Moire could see in the entire room, the floor, and with a grunt of effort reached for his parcel.

"The day I heard one could travel to other worlds, I wished to go," he said with a conspiratorial smile. "How I envied the explorers!"

Oops. Moire took a quick sip of her tea, hoping it hid her reaction. And her face. Maybe his vision wasn't as good as it used to be, or he really didn't recognize her.

"Ahhh." Gip reached down into the packing material and, with a look of great satisfaction, pulled out what looked like a blackened piece of scrap metal in a plastic container. "A friend has sent this, knowing of my interest. He believes it to be a fragment of a crab ship!"

Moire choked and coughed, desperately trying to keep from spilling the rest of her tea. "Why send it to you?"

"Oh, I have long been interested in them!" Gip turned stiffly in his seat, indicating a data terminal that Moire saw was completely covered in datatab racks. "It is my desire to understand. To find intelligent life, and then find it so violent to us—it is a dream destroyed. So I collect everything I can about them, and if I am granted wisdom perhaps I can learn why. If I were a younger man I would go to see myself, but I cannot travel as I once did, and they have never come near Bone," he added, shaking his head. "But you, you have perhaps come nearer?"

She hoped her face revealed nothing, while in her mind the vivid image of the crab carrier flashed before her eyes. "Most people go out of their way to avoid the crabs," she said carefully. "I haven't heard of them showing any interest in talking to us, just killing us if they can." Maybe she could learn something from Gip Farouz, if he was such a devoted crab researcher. But he just sighed and shook his head sadly, from which she concluded he hadn't come across any peaceful crabs either.

"People are afraid—they no longer seek new places," he said. "It is not good for us to live like this. To be human is to learn. A way must be found to end this war."

"No argument here," Moire said, "I wish we knew why they—" Her commlink chirped. Alan, wanting to know if she was done yet.

"My son," she explained to Gip. "He worries if I'm late."

Gip gave her a gentle smile, his hands placed together before his chest. "Ah. You have a son. This is good—he will be a comfort in your old age.

And in the fullness of time what comes to us all will not remove your kindness from the world, for he will still be with us, *inshallah.*"

She never knew how to respond to such things, so she just nodded uncomfortably. "I should check and see if they are done with the loading."

Gip rose with an effort. "Wait but a moment more." He went to the back and she heard banging and heavy objects being moved. He returned with a small, battered box.

"Take what you will," he said imperiously, holding it out to her. "I have no son or daughter, and I am old. These are pieces of my history. Let them travel with you for a time."

Moire opened the box reluctantly. The box had an assortment of small objects, some valuable only to someone who knew their stories. A pink pearl the size of her thumbnail, carved like a rose. A crumpled brass cartridge casing. A crudely carved wooden chain of three links. Had that come all the way from Earth?

Something flashed blue and red at the bottom, and her heart skipped a beat. It couldn't be. She pulled it out, balancing it on her fingertips as if it were as fragile as a butterfly. The enamel was cracked and broken at one corner where the metal had bent and the fastener in back was missing, but the rest was intact. The red shockwave delta, the field of blue, and the white letters. *NASA.*

"This was given to me by one who first discovered this world. He thought no one would remember the explorers, and it made his heart sad. He returned when he was very old, to see Bone once again before he died, and I spoke with him."

"What was his name?" Her voice cracked.

"Francisco Delaguarez."

Cisco. I am holding Cisco's pin in my hand, and he has died of old age. "I will remember." She felt a tear slide down her cheek. Cisco had waited for months for a post on an exploration ship, growing increasingly frustrated and despondent as the few slots were gradually filled. When he was picked for one of the last positions still open he had literally bounced off the walls of the barracks in sheer joy. How could someone like that be dead? *Why didn't you wait for me, Cisco?*

Gip Farouz closed her fingers around the pin. "Do not weep. I, too, remember. Teach your son, and they will live in memory again."

CHAPTER 12
THE HIGH COST OF ENLIGHTENMENT

"What the hell were you doing? Reading the manual?" Ennis fumed. "Do you realize that mental deviant was going to kill Anselm and start a fire in a storage area full of flammables?"

"I know it seems like forever, but if you look at the clock it was less than five minutes from the time I got your message," Shaughnassy said in a soothing voice. "Next time, be more specific than 'a storage area on the sixteenth level.' There are at least seven. Or take a locator chip. Besides, what was the rush? You handled it beautifully." He stepped back as Ennis approached. "Now, don't spoil your good impression with the captain by striking a fellow officer. She's quite pleased with you, you know."

Everyone on the ship was quite pleased, with the possible exception of himself. Not only had Tendo Berens been caught red-handed circumventing security, compromising the safety and integrity of a Fleet ship, and smuggling a gun, it was virtually impossible now for Toren to send anybody else to take his place.

"I really ought to thank them for all of the clever gadgets he left around," Shaughnassy continued, rubbing his hands gleefully. "Much easier than putting in a requisition."

"They'll want them back," Ennis said, feeling uneasy.

The Security Officer laughed. "They're going to have to ask for them specifically then, and they're in enough trouble already."

They were called in to the captain's office at that point. Ennis let Shaughnassy do most of the talking, confining his part to an unvarnished description of his actions in intercepting Berens.

Captain Kushstan heard them attentively, her long fingers twisting her carved iron ring.

"Good work," she said when they had finished. Coming from her, that was high praise. "I will make sure you both get the credit for this."

No. Ennis felt a sudden, sharp chill of fear. "Sir, I...I would prefer my name not be mentioned."

The captain went completely motionless, one eyebrow raised. Shaughnassy sputtered. "Are you *crazy?*" He remembered where he was and collected himself. "This is *not a good career move,*" he whispered to Ennis, rolling his eyes for emphasis.

He knew that. He was almost as surprised as they were. Shaughnassy knew how close he was to the cutoff date for promotion, and this might actually make a difference.

Something was extremely wrong. He was remembering things, feeling instincts he'd tried to forget for years. Perhaps it was climbing through the dark hull space that had triggered a sudden memory of a booby trap one of the Fimbul gangs had set in the tunnels. He still didn't know why that one rung of the ladder had looked wrong, but the instinct had been so strong the muscles in his arm had locked when he had tried to reach for it. This felt the same. It wasn't a conscious process of thought, he was simply bone-sure if Toren knew he was involved his life would be in danger.

Berens didn't know who had stopped him and he wanted it to stay that way. Even if it meant losing his last chance at promotion.

The captain gave him a dark, brooding look. "Are you certain, Commander Ennis?" He nodded, not sure of his voice. "Very well. If you change your mind before the next courier arrives, let me know." She fiddled with her stylus, looking at her desk screen, then leaned back. "There was some news on the last one that might interest you. Major Hallin commanded this ex-mercenary Berens was so curious about, correct?" Ennis nodded again. "It appears Major Hallin died in an accident shortly after his arrival at the Beta Centauri medical station." Her hooded eyes flicked back and forth, observing them. "I would offer my condolences, but it appears the major made himself almost universally disliked on this ship."

Shaughnassy was looking somber after they left the captain. "I'd like to know more about that accident," he said after a long silence.

It was suspicious, he had to agree. Jere Anselm had known Sayres, and Berens had tried to kill him and make it look accidental. Hallin's death was rather...convenient.

"Maybe I should take my name out too," Shaughnassy said.

Ennis took a deep breath. "Maybe you should."

Even when the courier came and went, and *Canaveral* had stopped to offload Tendo Berens, it wasn't enough to quiet his jangling nerves. Waiting for the enemy was always a bad idea, whether now against the crabs or then, on Fimbul. He needed to know more for his own survival if nothing else. He had more clues now, if he could piece them together.

Ennis sat at the library console, wondering why he was so reluctant to begin. Tendo Berens wasn't even in the same sector anymore. He'd been sent off on a military courier from the station the day after *Canaveral* had dropped him off. He hadn't even needed to ask Shaughnassy to do a security sweep after he'd left, either. It was as safe now as it was ever going to be.

Knowledge is power. He took a deep breath.

Searching for Index anomalies only produced a huge listing of parentage lawsuits and other legal messes that had come out of the Index when it first appeared. No missing people. He went through everything he could think of, following cross links and random connections until his eyes felt rough and dry from staring at the console display so long. He had to try something else.

He'd put everything he'd heard from Berens's interrogation into his datapad's sound-parser. Now he fed the phrases, one by one, into the console.

The cross-link search tried everything at once, then broke it down into smaller and smaller groupings. He hadn't expected much from the highest-order search, especially with the limited data available in the ship's library.

The first term that had any real results was "sequoyah." But the cross links didn't make any sense. Giant trees? Cherokee alphabet?

The other terms came up with similar nonsense, but he looked doggedly at everything.

Moy'rah [Moira, Moire, Mayra...] + Kah'mron [Kameron, Camera on, Cemmerin, Cameron...]. Search result: 100% match. Source: "Straight on 'til morning—the first explorers of space." Source type: book.

He looked at his chrono, and swore. How many hours had he wasted on this?

The book was old, and he was distracted by the chapter descriptions. How the early exploration ships had mapped the gravitational lines, for example. He'd never thought about it, but it made sense. Somebody had to find out the hard way where the lines were, and how to use them. Another chapter was headed "Not Yet Returned." A number of the early ships never made it back. The first gravitational generators were notoriously unreliable, and the power sources not much better. It looked fascinating. He'd have to check the book out later and read it for pleasure.

But not now. He called up the index, and there it was. *Moire Cameron.* It was crosslinked to an image caption.

The book was full of ancient 2-D stills. Was it a still if it had never been part of a video clip? Photographs, they called them then. People had the same look in all of them, whether from the clothing or the hairstyles, he couldn't tell. He'd have to tell Seung about this book. Lots of old ships.

Ennis raised his eyebrows, surprised. The still that the index entry linked to showed one of the lost exploration crews. They were posed in front of the shuttle that would take them on the first leg of their trip to Luna station. It looked like it had been intended as an official, formal picture, but the crew was relaxed and grinning, arms about each other with easy camaraderie.

In the center of the group was Ann Sayres.

Somehow he managed to leave the library, fighting the instinct to run.

There was nowhere to run to, not on *Canaveral*. The best he could do was hope it was only his imagination, but without much conviction. Ennis shut the door to his quarters, feeling numb. Then he locked it, leaning against it, gripping the reader tightly. With an effort he stood and moved to the bunk, opening the reader again and selecting the exploration book. The picture was still there, still real.

He closed his eyes, feeling the cold in his fingertips, remembering to breathe. He looked again; she was still there. Smiling as if she'd just heard a particularly funny joke. It wasn't a chance resemblance; it was her. The way she stood, the strands of hair that escaped and scattered themselves across her forehead, the quirk of the lips.

Unchanged. The photograph was dated almost eighty years ago, and she looked exactly the same as the last time he had seen her. They hadn't had age-abatement technology back then. The picture was impossible. She wasn't in the Index either, and that was impossible too. It was as if she had simply stepped from the past to the present.

He stared at the picture, hoping to calm the chaos in his mind. He needed facts, not speculation. The caption read, "The crew of NASA XS-312, unofficial name *Bon Accord*. The ship never returned from its fifteenth mission. Last contact was August 18, 2028, as it left Beta Centauri station. No trace of the ship was ever discovered."

He counted down the faces, unsurprised when the woman he knew as Ann Sayres was listed as "Moire Cameron, pilot (USAF)." It was all coming together too fast. Ann Sayres was Moire Cameron, who had been lost on an exploration flight over eighty years ago. Toren was hunting her, and nobody else knew she had survived.

How *had* she survived? He shook his head, irritated. A good question, but not the one he needed to ask. Why was Toren hunting her so desperately? *Think. This is important.*

He discarded the idea she had stolen anything from Toren; it was more likely the other way around. They wanted something from her, something only she had. She'd been part of an exploration mission. What if they'd found something important? What would be so important Toren would be willing to kill to get it?

He looked again at the picture of the crew of *Bon Accord,* studying it hungrily, searching for any clue. The man who had one arm about Moire's shoulder, looking at her rather than the camera. "Etienne Larochelle, commander (RCAF)." He remembered Moire's sad expression in Harrington's sketch, and doubted Larochelle had survived.

He shut off the reader. He could stay quiet and hope nobody noticed. Delete the book from his reader, maybe even remove any trace of his reading it in the library. Nobody knew what he'd figured out from Berens's comments. But as long as Toren thought someone, anyone on *Canaveral* had the information they were seeking, something like Berens's attack would happen again. He didn't have a choice. His silence would put Fleet in danger.

Maybe, if Fleet moved fast enough, they could stay one step ahead.

CHAPTER 13
ALARUMS AND EXCURSIONS

Moire took a big swig of chalkwater before she realized what she was doing. She shuddered as she swallowed. *God, this stuff is awful.* It still tasted like the stuff NASA had inflicted on them. *You'd think they would have found a way to fix that by now.*

There wasn't much to do except sit in Mammachandra's at the moment. The troublesome hydraulic on the Beast had given out so completely she was grounded until Jens fixed it. He and Alan were working on it now. She'd thought about staying to help, but there wasn't much she could do without getting in the way, and she didn't feel like talking. The pin that Farouz had given her weighed her shirt pocket down like lead.

The last time she had seen Cisco he'd been so new he squeaked. He'd managed to find a planet, though. Looked like he'd turned out well. If she'd only gotten here earlier–Cisco would have helped her. Now she just had another ghost reminding her of her responsibilities.

She rested her face in her hands. It wasn't fair. She was just the pilot. They'd left her–*all* of them–and now she had to do it alone. It was the team that had made it possible and she didn't have the team anymore. Etienne was in charge; he made the decisions, she flew the ship. It was easier that way. She'd never liked making decisions for other people.

He had expected her to report the discovery of Sequoyah. They all had. That was why they'd stayed at their posts until they collapsed, why he'd ordered her to not to help them. Fly the ship. Get the information back.

Damn Cisco and his stupid pin. The memories were too strong, too painful, and she didn't have enough money to get drunk.

Something bumped against her leg. She glanced down. Munchausen was glaring at her, its three eyes all focused on her in a tight bunch. "MrmrmrYAAAh. RAAAAAH." It dug at her foot with one of its appendages. There was only one thing that would make the nerya so insistent and looking under the table, she found it.

"Here's your copper pipe, OK? Now stop eating my foot." Munchausen grabbed the pipe and changed in shape from long and cylindrical to more like a squashed beachball. Its peculiar, three-part mouth opened to start chewing on the pipe, already ragged from this treatment. "Damned if I know why you want it so bad," she muttered.

"They need the copper." The man sitting at the table next to her smiled apologetically at her startled expression. She'd been so caught up in her thoughts she hadn't even noticed he was there. "I'm David Eng. I haven't seen you around before."

"I haven't been on Bone long."

"No, I think I would have noticed you," he said with a cheerful grin. He didn't look like any of the locals, although he was wearing a gun. His clothing didn't look warm enough for Waylands, and his wiry, dark red hair was worn longer than was customary on Bone. He turned his chair to face her. Munchausen moved its eyes to keep one on each of them, but kept on with the serious business of copper ingestion.

"I'm working down in the Belt, studying the neryas and the other local life-forms. I'm a xenobiologist." That would explain the gun, then. For a moment she had been afraid he was the local law enforcement. "What brings you to Bone?" he asked.

Moire shrugged. "It just happened to be on the way." This guy was far too friendly and curious. If he really wanted to know, he could ask Mammachandra. She didn't see any reason to encourage his curiosity by giving him answers herself. *But enough about me. Let's talk about you.* "Why do they need copper?"

"It's almost like salt is for us. They use it for some of the adaptive processes in their metabolism. Copper is not easy to find here, so they have developed a taste for it." He pointed to one of the lumps visible in Munchausen's grubby fur. "This one is old, and it hangs around humans a lot. Probably eats quite a bit it can't process. They migrate toxic or dangerously indigestible things from their digestive array to the skin. Sort of do-it-yourself armor—if it was bad for them, it would be bad for anything trying to eat them, right? This one has more cysts than usual in the wild and a correspondingly increased appetite for copper."

"What would eat a nerya?" Moire looked at it skeptically.

"Now? Nothing. The predators have died out. The only reason they're still around is they are the most efficient scavengers I've ever come across, and I've been to most of the bio-positive planets. They are tough, too. It's almost impossible to poison them."

"So what have you studied beside neryas?"

He hesitated. "I can't say I *studied* them much, but...you know the aliens that we're fighting?"

Not you too. "The *crabs?*" The front lines were on the other side of human space, but there was no avoiding the crabs on Bone.

Eng smiled in a deprecating way. He moved his chair closer. "As much as I could. The ones that were still alive when we got there were badly injured and we didn't know what to do to fix them. Toren decided they wanted to ship everything back for the big experts back home when the last one died, so us field types lost out. Then I got sent here. This isn't a bad posting–don't have to wear a suit, for one thing."

Moire concentrated on picking up her chalkwater in a calm, unhurried way. Running screaming from the room would probably attract attention. "You work for Toren?" *Please say no.*

"They're the ones with the money for xenobiology," he said, a trace of defensiveness in his voice. "And they let me pursue whatever I find interesting."

"That's good." They seemed to tell him where to go, though. Toren must check in with him now and then, get reports. "How long have you been here?"

"Almost seven months now. Time flies when you're getting shot at." He grinned. "Say–have you seen the Crystal Maze yet?"

"No. What's that?"

"Condensed ocean, we think. It's an area full of giant crystals in a low depression, maybe three hundred kilometers from here. Beautiful. Would you like to go see it? I've got my ship here. I came for supplies, but I'm not heading back until tomorrow."

"I'm waiting for some repairs. As soon as they're finished, I have to get back to work." She gave an apologetic shrug. "Thanks for the offer, though." She got up, fighting the urge to back away, to run.

"Maybe some other time. I come up every few weeks, you know. If your repairs get delayed, find me, OK?"

"Sure thing." Her smile felt rigid. *When hell freezes over.*

She'd just made it to the door when he called out, "Wait! What's your name?" She hurried out, and when she turned down the tunnel to the shuttle depot she broke into a run.

She felt safer inside, but colder. Moire paced about, rubbing her arms and trying to stay warm until Jens and Alan finished the repairs. She couldn't help glancing at the doors now and then, but they stayed closed. Alan saw her do it and looked puzzled, but he didn't say anything. Playing the Game. Sometimes he was better at avoiding notice than she was. If you never said anything, you didn't say something wrong.

She watched him work, his expression serious as he followed Jens's instructions with careful precision. He seemed to know what he was doing, even remembering to don safety gear when needed. She could almost imagine he was normal.

Lorai came in from her last run. There was a whoosh as the bay doors opened, bringing in the dead, dusty smell of outside on a wave of cold. Moire wondered again why the depot didn't use any airlocks or anything to keep the oxygen in. Maybe it was too expensive–the doors didn't stay open long, so they didn't lose that much. The pressure on both sides was the same.

As they were cleaning up from the repairs, the wall comm made its annoying squawk. Lorai groaned and slowly walked over to it. "Never lets up, does it. So why aren't I rich?"

Mammachandra was on the other end. "Lorai? It is *Ayesha* that is signaling. They have cargo, one trip will be sufficient. Is Ren also there?"

Moire went up to the wall comm. "Yep, right here."

"I tell them there is a pilot seeking work off-planet, and they very much wish to talk to you. Come speak with them. They are only going about the Fringe, as you are wanting."

Lorai rolled her eyes, leaning against the wall with one hand. "Dunno, you might want to think twice before signing on with that bunch. People call it 'OhShit' 'cause parts of it keep falling off. Makes that thing look dependable," she said, hooking a thumb at the Beast.

"It is true," Jens nodded, looping some cable neatly and slinging it over his shoulder. "You hear how they call for the shuttle? They are no longer permitted to use the station for their unloading. They have this difficulty staying in even orbit."

"Yeah, I remember that. Used six months of adjustment fuel just getting the damn thing back on track one time. Kinda pretty when all that debris hit the atmosphere, though," Lorai said, grinning.

Mammachandra clicked her tongue in disapproval on the comm. "*Ayesha* has been falling apart this same way for many years."

Lorai snorted. "Any time in a ship that runs that light is too long." She glanced at Moire. "Captain has Type III Renchett's. They use the trim nodes up and *reversed;* practically free-fall in there. I like my bones the way they are, thank you. And the crew!" She shook her head. "Strangest bunch I ever seen. Must be hard finding anybody willing to work on a ship like that."

"Are you wanting to talk to them?" asked Mammachandra. "Otherwise I will tell them not to bother."

"Yeah, I'll talk to them. On my way."

Moire headed for the door. It sounded bad, but this might be her best chance of getting off the planet. She was discovering how hard that was, and now with her curious Toren-funded xenobiologist poking around she didn't dare take the chance he would mention her to someone. *Ayesha* traveled around the Fringe; she could find a less dangerous job on another ship without too much trouble.

Alan was standing in front of her. She could tell from his quick, shallow breathing he was agitated and trying to hide it. Moire glance quickly back at the open area of the depot. Jens and Lorai were talking, not paying much attention to either of them.

"What is it?" she said, softly.

His face twisted, then he regained control. "You aren't...you have to stay *here*. You can't go away."

She hadn't told him about planning to leave. She felt a twinge of guilt looking at the frightened expression in his gold-brown eyes and had to avoid his gaze, wondering if that had been a good idea. Alan was running too, but not from the same people. Bone would be a better place for him. He wasn't a stranger anymore, and Jens and Mammachandra would look after him.

"I have to go. You don't have to come with me," she said, trying to sound encouraging. "You like working for Jens, don't you? It wouldn't be good for you on that ship, and I–"

"No." He jerked the word out harshly. "I want to go too. With you."

She tried to move past him, but he wouldn't budge. This was not going well. "Look, kid, it'll be just like a long trip." Only she wouldn't come back. "You can handle that, right?" Why was he acting like this?

"Why can't I come?" He was looking stubborn. And unconvinced.

"They may not have room for you. Or work you can do. Don't you like it here?"

"You could ask them," he said, as if he hadn't even heard her question. "If they have work can I come?"

"If they don't, will you stay here, um...until I get back?" Moire countered, hoping he wouldn't ask the obvious question. She hadn't expected this much resistance. She should leave him now, before he became even more attached to her–but she didn't want to cause an uproar. She still needed to get away with the minimum amount of notice. If *Ayesha* hired him, she would just have to find a way to part company somewhere else.

Alan thought for a moment, then nodded unhappily. Moire nudged him toward the door, and this time he moved. "Let's go see if they're agreeable."

She entered Mammachandra's carefully, shielding herself from view with Alan's bulk, but David Eng was not there. She heaved a sigh of relief.

They crowded into the communications room, where Mammachandra was already seated in front of the vid comm. "The tea is selling well. You have brought more, yes?"

The woman on the comm nodded. She had a brooding, sulky face and dark hair. "We got some new types, too. Put a sample in, if ya like."

Mammachandra glanced up. "Here is the pilot I am telling you of. The captain is there still?"

The woman flicked her eyes to Moire, surprised. "You *want* to.... Stay there! I'll go get the captain." She flashed off the screen. The audio pickup had what sounded like shouting in the distance.

After a few minutes, a new face came into view. He moved slowly, settling himself before the vid with care. Moire could see something was wrong with him. The skin on his face sagged and bulged in odd places. His eyes held an expression that was both gentle and sad. "I'm Captain Davies. Beaufort Davies. I hear you're looking for a pilot's berth."

"Yes sir." Moire felt Alan scrunching closer to her in the tiny communications room.

"Well, Roberts, we are looking for a pilot. You've been doing ground transport here, who'd you fly web for?"

"Before coming here I was first pilot on *Shintai,* and before that I was flying *Grubber II.*" Neither of whom would give a good reference, but that was the wonderful thing about the lack of faster-than-light communications. Davies wasn't going to wait to check up on her.

Captain Davies nodded. "OK, here's the deal. We run light, I suppose you know that. We'll take you on trial, half pay, and the next half on signed contract. Crew shares in the cargo profit."

"Sounds good to me." Alan tugged on her sleeve, contorting his face with an urgent, silent message. She held up a hand to stop him. "One question. My son wants to come along. He can work for his transport, if you have anything he could do...."

Davies waved a hand. "That him there? Of course he can come. We can use him, and we'll pay him too."

It had been worth a try. Maybe it wouldn't be too bad. She was kind of getting used to having him around. It was nice to know somebody who knew even less about life nowadays than she did, and it was damn lonely being a desperate fugitive sometimes. "Great. I believe we have a deal, Captain."

Davies gave a slow, gentle smile. "I'll be seeing you on board shortly, then." He closed the connection, just as Moire remembered one last detail. Transportation.

She swore as she turned away from the vid comm. "How am I going to get to the ship? I don't have two hundred ED saved up." Mammachandra was silent, looking thoughtful. "Maybe he won't leave right away—or I could ask him for a loan, but he doesn't even know me."

Mammachandra patted her shoulder. "It is of no matter. We are knowing you. The money is there."

"I can't borrow from you!" Moire protested. "Who knows if I'll ever get back here?"

"It is anyhow not my money," Mammachandra answered, her face serene. "It is the god's. You wish to go, yes?" Moire nodded, confused. "Come, then. I will show you who will help you."

She led Moire to the store section, Alan following close behind. Mammachandra went all the way to the back and stopped before the shrine with the elephant-headed statue.

"Lord Ganesh, he protects and guides the traveler. It is not always safe to travel the Fringe, there are dangerous people there and of course now there is war as well. Some who do not worship Ganesh still are thinking it is lucky to give to him–but they give as promises to pay, you see?" She tapped one of the white folded shapes that hung about the statue. "If they come back from a dangerous trip, they pay. But it is not my money. When I can, I give to help. When you are able, help some other traveler in need, and the debt is repaid."

She stood before the statue and chanted a soft, singsong prayer in a language Moire didn't recognize, lighting a tiny matchstick of incense. She bowed with easy grace, then unlocked a cabinet underneath the statue and brought out a carved sandalwood box. Setting it before the statue, she bowed again and opened the box. Gathering the paychips inside in her hand, she turned and put them firmly in Moire's palm.

Moire checked the values, adding up the total. Somebody must have been extremely superstitious–one was for fifty ED. "Here's the extra," she said, trying to hand the chips back.

"No. You will have other needs–your son does not have a shipsuit, yes? It is essential that he have one for this ship, or he will be ill. Take. Ganesh is also known to value the love of parent and child."

And since she'd have to buy it from the Everything Store, Mammachandra wasn't going to lose out either. Moire squashed that thought firmly, knowing that without her help she wouldn't have anything. No reason Mammachandra shouldn't benefit from her charity.

Alan was standing close beside her. He'd never let her get more than a step away from him since she'd mentioned leaving, still afraid that he'd be left behind. *He's not my son, dammit. I found him in a cargo hold.* But her irritation faded as he looked at her with a lost and bewildered expression in his eyes, an expression that went oddly with his strength and size.

He'd argued with her. That was a first. He'd been afraid, but more afraid of her leaving him.

Moire sighed. "All right. Let's get you some gear."

Lorai was already prepping the shuttle when Alan and Moire arrived in the depot.

"Before I forget...." Moire handed her the remaining chips, still covered with the thick smell of sandalwood. Lorai took them with visible reluctance.

"Where'm I gonna find another pilot, Roberts? Now I have to do all the flying and I'm not getting any younger. G'wan, get stowed," she said, waving her hand at the shuttle. Alan left off tugging at the tight neck of his new shipsuit and went inside. Moire would have followed but Lorai grabbed her elbow to stop her. "You gonna tell me what you're running from?" she asked, giving Moire a stern look.

"What makes you think I'm running?"

Lorai snorted. "I seen you fly. Nothing scares you–you flew the Beast without breaking a sweat. Now you are jumping on a self-propelled slow explosion just so you can get off the planet as fast as you can. If somebody is bothering you why didn't you come to us? It's not that damn miner, is it?" There was hurt in her voice, and Moire struggled with her conscience and the need to explain.

"It isn't anybody here on Bone–other people, looking for me, and it would be better for everyone if I leave before they get here." Lorai looked mulish and unconvinced. Moire interrupted her next attempt at argument. "It's trouble I don't want to bring on you, OK? You have all been good to me, do you think I'd let that happen?"

She'd started to like Bone, and the people. She'd had to leave *Canaveral* just when things were looking up too. This was starting to become a trend. At least there was a small chance she could come back to Bone. Fleet was forever off-limits. She could imagine the look of contempt on Ennis's face if she ever encountered him again.

Moire shook herself, trying to dispel the sudden gloom she felt. She should warn Lorai about Toren, but knowledge itself was dangerous. "If anybody comes asking for me, just tell them I left and you didn't talk to me much."

Lorai looked at her without saying anything for a moment. "These people got names?"

"There's a list. You don't want to know it."

Lorai shrugged. "All right, Roberts, have it your way. Who'm I kidding? You're wasted on suborbital hops and mail runs. Maybe you'll be able to keep the *OhShit* intact–but it'll be a challenge, even for you."

Alan handled the trip up much better than she had expected, possibly because she took the time to drill him on the basic safety features of his shipsuit and he didn't have time to panic. When they got to the ship, the hatch connection took two tries before it sealed.

"Still sure you want to crew on this disaster?" Lorai asked.

Moire gritted her teeth and nodded. "I don't have better options."

"Goddamn." Lorai rubbed her chin. "These bad guys what are chasing you, they are gonna keep chasing you? Think they'll be able to find you after this?"

"Mammachandra has probably already told half the planet I'm on the ship. They'll know."

Lorai's face twisted. "Here." She pulled the gun from her gunbelt. "Might need this. Noticed you didn't carry one dirtside, was gonna suggest it with trouble spreading from the Belt. Don't like the speed, was getting a better one anyway."

It wasn't a very convincing lie. The gun was old, but Moire had seen the care Lorai took with it. "You've never seen me shoot. I'd be more of a danger to myself than the enemy, trust me."

At a loss, Lorai looked at the gun, then Moire, then jammed it back in the holster. She grabbed Moire and gave her a crushing hug, then released her just as suddenly and pointed at Alan. "You take good care of your momma, you hear? Don't let anybody hurt her."

He nodded, serious. Moire felt at her sore ribs and decided none of them were cracked.

A knocking noise came from the hatch door. "All right, already!" Lorai undogged the latch and swung the door open. "Watch the gradient, now, it's nasty."

The gravitational gradient was like walking through glue, and then they were through. Waving good-bye to Lorai, they stepped inside the ship.

CHAPTER 14
A SENSE OF GRAVITY

The corridor off of the hatch area was dimly lit, the flooring uneven. A cable or flexible pipe, Moire couldn't tell which, had come loose from its bundle and dangled from the ceiling. *I hope this wasn't a mistake.* Besides the usual hot metal and old-refrigerator smell of a working ship, she could just detect a hint of the exotic, like woodsmoke or incense.

Her duffel felt like nothing in the marginal gravity of *Ayesha*. Alan had a comical expression on his face, walking on his toes like he was afraid he would fly away.

The woman who met them at the hatch was the same one she'd seen on the vid comm. She kept looking back at them, as if she was afraid they were going to leave. She was small and wiry, with dark, kink-curled hair tied back loosely with a wooden clip. Out here wood, or any other kind of real, organic material meant money–which didn't match the shabby, broken-down feel of the ship. Maybe it had been a gift.

Some crew came down the corridor from the other direction with small float-pallets for the cargo. There was hardly enough gravity to make the float-pallets useful. Moire recalled Lorai's disappointment at her leaving and smiled ruefully. Maybe they'd be lucky and Toren would never find out she'd been on Bone.

"I am not staying down all the way," whispered Alan. He was breathing fast.

"It's OK. It's just low gravity here. You feel all right?" He thought for a moment, then nodded. "Remember the Game," she whispered back and pointed to the woman leading the way. He clapped a hand over his mouth, a stricken expression in his eyes.

After going up a few levels, the woman stopped outside a doorway. "Steward's office," she said. "He'll get ya set up."

A grizzled head poked out. "Yolanda, what are you...oh, there you are," he said, catching sight of Moire and Alan. "Found us all right, I take it. Is the offload going to take long?" Moire looked back, but the woman named Yolanda had left. He grumbled something under his breath, then shrugged and waved them in. "Don't take it personal. She's like that with new people. Guilty conscience, if you ask me. I'm Harvey Felden, steward. I'll take care of you; anything you need just let me know. Usually I'm busy with supplies at a port, but we don't get anything from Bone so I can help you now."

He was thin and hunched, and Moire suspected the grey in his hair wasn't cosmetic. The fine lines on his face and other physical indications of age meant that he must be at least seventy, or had missed out on the age-abatement treatments. He was definitely the oldest she'd seen in any crew.

Besides the usual screen and desk, the office had a bank of atmosphere content monitors, labeled for the different decks. He rummaged through a desk drawer, finally unearthing a bundle of the narrow plastic rectangles that were used as keys. "I'll show you the cabin first. Can't get you your own too," he said to Alan, "but there's plenty of space in the crew bunk area."

Alan shifted restlessly. "Any reason he can't share mine?" Moire hastened to ask, before he could say anything. Even if he could be convinced to try it, she wanted to be able to keep an eye on him.

"There's only the one bunk—it's the captain's cabin, but he doesn't use it. I suppose we could hang a temporary," he said, scratching his head. "That going to be good enough?"

"That'll be fine." Felden didn't seem to think it an out-of-the-way request, and she relaxed a little.

"I'll do that, then. And it's only fair to warn you that her high-and-mightiness will want to check you out. Madele Fortin—she's in charge of the galley, *and* the medical department. Damn nosy...can't leave you alone for a minute. Always poking you for something or other. I figure anything going to kill me will show up in time for me to find *her*, but no, she's got to have *tests*. That's the real health hazard, if you ask me."

Tests? Moire started worrying again. She was just going to have to dodge them as best she could. If the medic was also the cook, she was probably pretty busy.

Felden went past them and down the corridor. "Cabin's this way."

They went down three levels, past battered and scraped doors and utility cable runs that were missing their covers—and from the looks of things, the covers had been missing for some time. Moire wondered how old the ship was.

"Whatever you do, don't mess with that," he said, pointing to a small utility door on the way. Someone had marked in red paintpen "Danger—wiretrap. Not to open ever." "This ship used to belong to a part-time smuggler, at least that's the story I was told. Keep finding stuff in the oddest places, and that one's booby-trapped. We haven't found a way to disarm it yet."

Even better. Built-in bombs. Just in case you forgot your own.

"We run two-by-ten shifts, since we don't have enough crew for shorter rotation. Main meals are on the schedule, help yourself to the drybars and anything in the snackbox otherwise. Food isn't bad," he admitted grudgingly, "though it would probably be better if *she* wasn't involved. Putting all kinds of medical goop in it, if we only knew. Here you are," he said, stopping in front of a door lettered "Captain" in faded yellow paint. He inserted the keytab in the lock.

For a shipboard cabin, it was spacious. Besides the bunk, one corner had a separate, permanent built-in desk, and another door led to a head with a tiny shower. "Don't get too excited, it don't work," added Harvey. "The shower, that is. I *think* the head is still working, least nobody told me if it isn't."

"The captain doesn't use this cabin?" Moire asked, wondering why.

"He's got the bridge office fitted up, since he stays there most all the time anyway." He scratched his chin. "Let's see—we can fasten the temporary to that wall, or hang it crosswise. Takes up a lot of space, but you can take it down if it gets in the way. I'll get that next. So what group gets you, young man? Got any engineering training?"

Alan glanced at her, looking for hints. She shook her head minutely.

"There's always cargo handling. If you don't speak up Montero will start asking; they always need crew for the repair shifts."

Alan perked up. "I have done repair," he said softly. "I can use a line welder."

Moire blinked, astonished. The kid actually volunteered information, to a virtual stranger. A definite improvement. He'd been changing quite a bit, now that she thought about it.

Harvey cocked his head to one side. "Sure you want to do that? We'll keep you busy. All right, I'll take you down to Montero. He'll be so happy he might actually talk. Say, the two of you should get along just fine. You don't have much to say either, do you?" He gave Alan a friendly pat on the arm. Alan started, wide-eyed. "Not to worry, we got enough jabbering on this ship to go around."

He handed a keytab each to Alan and Moire. "Now, how about a quick tour of the ship on the way to Maintenance?"

Moire dropped her duffel on the bunk. "Am I going to be wanted on deck soon?"

"Captain's resting. Not leaving for a while yet," Harvey said curtly. His expression was almost surly, then changed to one of sadness. "He's been working too hard—has to do all the web piloting, see? He just can't do that anymore. We're all real glad you showed up." He snapped his fingers. "Before I forget, first mate will probably want to see you. Should have the contracts ready."

He led them through more corridors to a cluttered, messy office. The first mate was a woman with a round face and lank blonde hair that had been pattern-dyed. She glanced up at Moire, then aside. In that brief moment Moire was surprised to see a glimpse of recognition and some other, stronger emotion. She wasn't sure what it all meant, but she didn't think the first mate was happy to see them.

"So you are the new pilot. I'm Ilyana Ramutis. Been a while since we had a family on board—I don't count the couples. I'll need to see your ID."

"No ID."

"No?" She didn't look surprised.

"Left the last ship in a hurry, that's why we were stuck on Bone. Didn't get to take much with us."

Ramutis rolled her eyes, sighing. "Least you could do is come up with a story that isn't worn out." She shoved an open plastifoam box that still had some moldy food in it from her desk onto the floor, followed by a crushed drink bulb and some dusty textsheets. She pulled a keyholder out of a pocket and opened a metal locker, taking out a flat oblong object. She unfolded it on the newly cleaned desktop. "If you don't have ID I need retina scans for the insurance. Then you can sign the short-term contracts. If you decide to stay on, we'll have the full-term contracts." Ramutis gave her a challenging stare, as if she doubted that would happen.

She could refuse the retina scan, but what would that get her? They'd probably just dump her on Bone again, if Lorai hadn't left already. If they were desperate for a pilot they might not, but it would still draw attention. She nudged Alan to go first, and he did, stiff and uncertain.

"Do you wait for the insurance to get them before you do the long-term contracts?" Moire asked.

Ramutis shrugged, her gaze becoming evasive. "We get new people all the time. Too expensive to keep shipping the data back. They let us keep it in a secure data vault on Zet A, with the same company that handles our funds and other accounts. If anything happens we'd send it in then."

In other words, they never sent it and it never got in the network. That should be safe enough. She took her turn at the retina scanner. The contracts were short, boilerplate text, but at least they were contracts. Few ships on the Fringe bothered with such trivia. She picked up the stylus and signed hers, and Ramutis changed the readout from her pilot's contract to one for a general crewmember. Moire handed Alan the stylus, suddenly wondering if he knew how to sign his name.

He didn't. Ramutis raised her eyebrows at the scrawl he produced while Moire tried to look unconcerned. She had to teach that kid a few things, or he was going to get them in real trouble some day. She wasn't even sure if he could read.

As he was finishing, a look of fierce concentration on his face as he gripped the stylus, a comm signal sounded. "Bring Roberts to the bridge when you're finished," said the voice, which Moire recognized as the captain's. "I'd like to go over a few things before we leave."

"I'll take her up," Ramutis said. She closed the connection and punched another code. A few moments later a young woman showed up. She gaped when she saw Alan, then gave him a blinding smile. "Tenna, take him to Montero. He'll be joining the repair crew."

Tenna bounced with excitement. "I didn't know there were guys like him on Bone! They must keep it a secret or something. Come on," she said to Alan, who was looking uncertain. "What's your name?" Alan looked back at Moire and she nodded reassuringly. Tenna could be heard asking more questions as they left. It looked like Alan had found a new friend. She'd have to keep an eye on him. From what she'd seen he wouldn't know how to handle that kind of interaction, and he got difficult when he was confused. Then again, maybe Tenna would motivate him to learn how to behave with people.

Moire followed Ramutis up to the bridge. Here, at least, things seemed to be in fairly good repair. The captain was standing before the pilot's pit, and he turned when they came in.

"Roberts. A pleasure." He shook hands, but Moire could barely feel any pressure from his grasp.

His head was completely hairless and his skin was unnaturally clear, showing fine veins on the surface. His entire body was puffy and awkward-looking and there was a faint sour smell around him, like vinegar. He wasn't wearing a shipsuit, just a loose, wraparound tunic and baggy trousers. His forearms were wrapped in clear support webbing. On one ear, almost enclosing the entire edge, was what looked to be a simple gold ornament. She'd seen them around the Fringe earlier: captain's earring. More communication device than jewelry, although some were quite ornate.

"I have the watch, Ramutis."

"You have the watch, Captain," she acknowledged, and left.

Davies turned to Moire. "Don't take this the wrong way, Roberts, but I'd like to see you do a dry run. *Ayesha*'s a touchy ship, and then we've made some changes of our own from the standard setup. The controls are rather sensitive."

He indicated the pit and the pilot's chair with a courtly gesture, and Moire took her seat. It wasn't as fancy as the courier, that was for certain. There was a blanked-off section of the console where the del-cross display should be. *You're getting soft, Cameron. You flew quite well without one for years. That courier spoiled you.*

"We've got the black book in the display overhead," Davies added. "Why don't you set up for the next leg to Pykko."

The black book display had been added as an afterthought, on a jury-rigged boom that could be moved with controls on the console. The console also had the search entry, and Moire punched in the name Pykko. She wondered if it still had data from the exploration teams in there, or if more accurate readings had been done since then.

The display popped up the star's coordinates and associated data, and she started setting up the system. Data entry wasn't so bad, although it took her longer with all the corrections she had to make because of the sensitive settings. This much was the easy part–anybody who knew what the readouts were for could enter the data. She raised an eyebrow. Pykko had a huge delta-vee–that would make things interesting for a lineup, and it was a good test for an unknown pilot. You'd really have to know what you were doing to find it.

There was a listed gravitational anomaly, but it was weak and not in their direct path. They shouldn't even notice it.

Now she had to do the lineup, and without the main drive engaged. At least this ship had dual "legs"–the pilot's term for the gravity sensor feeds. The extra sensitivity helped here.

She noodled her way around, feeling for the elusive nudge that would locate the star, keeping an eye on the readouts.

There. She latched the thumb switches on the legs, then looked at the chrono. She lost all sense of time when she was searching; it was a zenlike state.

She reached for the hold-steady switch.

"No! Don't ever use that," Davies said, alarm on his usually placid face.

"It will drift if I don't," Moire said, puzzled.

"It's worse with the hold-steady on. The gravitics don't stay uniform. With the hold-steady, the bubble builds up a resonance and in a short time you're bouncing all over. You have to stay live the whole way."

Moire swore under her breath. No wonder *Ayesha* was having trouble finding pilots. She was going to have to keep her hand on the leg the entire shift.

"You take her up for real, once we finish with the cargo. I'll stay on the bridge this time, but I reckon you have the feel for her." He moved slowly to the wall comm. "Menehune, how's the offload progressing?"

"Almost done, Captain," came Yolanda's voice.

"Signal me when the shuttle is undocked and out of range. We're ready to go." He took his seat in the wide, reclining chair alongside the pit. It adjusted itself as he settled in with a sigh. It wasn't long before he opened his eyes again, one hand moving toward the ear with the comm device. "All ship, secure. Drive engaging." He nodded to Moire. "Let's go, Roberts."

It took every ounce of her concentration to fly *Ayesha*. It kept drifting off true in a way that reminded her horribly of the last flight of *Bon Accord*. That accounted for at least half of the tension in her muscles. She didn't even think to look at the chrono until her shift was nearly over.

After the first few hours Davies had fallen asleep in his chair, seeing she knew what to do. Midway through her shift a gofer had brought her food and a drink bulb. She'd nearly choked when the bulb turned out to be coffee. *Real* coffee. She'd almost forgotten what it tasted like. She hadn't even seen it offered at Mammachandra's.

Moire stumbled wearily down the corridor to the galley. She was starving, exhausted, and twitchy with the terrible memories that had come flooding back. *Nobody died this time. Remember that.*

The galley wasn't large, especially with people already there. She looked for Alan, but he wasn't present. She hoped nothing was wrong. Someone moved toward her, and it almost seemed like a moving wall. The woman wasn't fat, simply *big.*

"So, I imagine you are hungry. What would you like? We've got gumbo, and linguine with fixings all ready, and I can make you something else if you want. I'm Madele Fortin, by the way." From her appearance, Fortin was almost as old as Harvey Felden.

"Gumbo sounds good," Moire ventured, her mouth watering at the appetizing smells in the air. Everyone in the galley swiveled around to take a look at her. She waved, and tried to give a cheerful smile. There were two young-looking kids, Tenna being one of them; a man with soft brown skin and long, straight black hair, and another man with a droopy mustache, a wide, friendly grin, and flashing dark eyes.

"Do join us," said the mustached one. "You look like you will fall over with tiredness and that will never do. Madele will make us leave so she can fix you up right here," and he pounded the table. Moire sat down. "I am Fariq al-Salah, but you may call me Freddie because you have a friendly face. How we are fortunate! She is a pilot, and lovely too!"

"Don't frighten her off with what you think is charm, Freddie," the older man said dryly. "She's only just got here. I'm Gren Forrest, chief engineer," he said to Moire. "And this is Tenna, and Michel." Tenna giggled, while the young man Michel ducked his head shyly.

She was beginning to see why Lorai had made such disparaging comments about *Ayesha*'s crew. The captain was slowly dying, the first mate had a permanent, nonspecific grudge against the Universe, and the rest were mostly very young or very old. Gren Forrest seemed all right, though, and Freddie. Maybe she just hadn't discovered what made them special yet.

Madele returned with a huge bowl of gumbo, covered with a slab of bread. "Here you are. If you want more just say so. Hope the meal I sent up was enough—didn't know what you liked, and of course Harvey would never think to ask something like that." She rolled her eyes and took a seat nearby.

The gumbo was delicious: thick and rich with the flavor of tomatoes and garlic, and some kind of meat. Moire wondered where the meat had come from—it certainly tasted real. Then she took a quick bite of bread, eyes watering in pain. Madele had a heavy hand with the hot pepper.

"You need to get that junk out of the workshop," Gren said to Freddie, continuing their earlier discussion interrupted by her appearance. "You can hardly move in there. What if it falls on somebody? Just because it's low gravity doesn't mean it won't do damage."

"It isn't junk!" Freddie protested, sounding hurt. "It could be useful. It all has parts we might need some day. Save us a lot of money, eh?"

Gren groaned, putting his face in his hands. "We have enough money to buy anything that might be found in that pile. What we *don't* have is space!"

Madele nodded. "This ship makes a good profit," she explained, looking at Moire. "Mostly we run luxury goods all over the Fringe; it's high-margin cargo. Also we take basic supplies to places that aren't on the regular routes yet."

Moire heard this with skepticism. "If the ship is doing so well, why don't you fix the gravitics?"

"They'd have to be completely replaced," Gren answered, temporarily abandoning his argument with Freddie. "This ship is too old and beat-up to take that kind of repair; we probably wouldn't even get out of the dock. Only real answer is to get a new ship, and that's too expensive even for us right now." He took a sip of his coffee. "Gravitics are an aggravation, aren't they? How much of the shift did you fly?"

Moire frowned. "The whole thing, of course."

He choked, and coughed. "What, the startup too?" She nodded. "Now that's a first. Usually takes a new pilot a few shifts to get the hang of it."

"It wasn't the easiest ship I've flown, I'll say that." She mopped up the last traces of gumbo with a piece of bread. With food, she felt almost restored.

"Now you've had your meal, I want to take care of the rest of you," Madele said firmly. "If you keep an eye on your mineral balance and make sure to use the exercise equipment, you can keep your bone loss to an acceptable level."

Ah. The tests. Not the kind she'd been worried about. They'd be a good idea if she was planning to stay for more than a month, which she wasn't.

"Can it wait until I've had some sleep?" Moire asked. "It's been a long day, and I still don't know how my son's doing."

"Of course," Madele said, concerned. "Your son went up earlier. Didn't say much, but he seemed fine."

Sounds like Alan, all right. Nobody had funny expressions on their faces, either, so he must have passed muster. She felt a rush of relief.

"I'll see you all later, then," Moire said, and left the galley as they waved. Sleep was her goal now. If she timed it right, she could visit the medic just before her shift started tomorrow. That would keep questions to a minimum.

"There is one thing, however." Madele had followed her out of the galley, and was speaking in a kind of hoarse whisper. "Your son's medical scan was, oh, a little strange. I'd like you to take a look, just to see if...."

Unable to escape, Moire was borne along on a gentle, irresistible wave of speech to what appeared to be the medical station. Madele fussed at a display for a moment, then pointed. "It's synthetic, but why does he need it? I couldn't find anything that had ever been wrong with him."

The diagnostic had pulled up the hormones again. What Moire noticed, however, was that something was missing from the first scan she'd seen: the personality depressants. That explained a lot.

"I'll ask him if he knows," she said. Catching Madele's expression of surprise, she added, "I haven't been around much until recently. It's a long story." It would be a long story as soon as she made it up, that is.

She excused herself and headed back to her cabin. Alan was already sprawled in his hammock, one arm dangling loose. He stirred when Moire stumbled on the decking in the uneven light and struggled to sit up, looking alarmed.

"Just me," she said. He subsided with a drowsy smile.

"I tried to play the Game," he murmured, "but they ask so many questions...."

Uh oh. "What questions? What did they say?" Alan didn't reply. He'd fallen asleep again.

Moire sat down on her bunk with a groan. If he hadn't been thrown out an airlock, it could wait.

❧

I could get used to this, thought Moire as she poured her daily allotment of coffee into a bulb. After three weeks she found herself depending on it. Maybe it was all part of a devious plot to keep her on the ship; there was no way she could afford a regular coffee habit on her own. It had to be incredibly expensive, but on a ship that specialized in carrying expensive luxury goods—and out on the Fringe, luxury focused mainly on food—it wasn't as expensive as it could be.

"How can you drink that?" Alan asked, making a face. "It makes my tongue shrivel up."

Moire grinned. "I suppose it is an acquired taste. You don't have to drink it if you don't like it." He appeared relieved, and her grin widened. Sometimes she could almost imagine he was trying to make a joke.

Alan had adjusted well to *Ayesha*. It might have been the drugs wearing off, or Tenna's cheerful chatter, but he seemed happier even than on Bone. *I wonder if we'll ever go back there.* She should send a message to Lorai, if she could figure out a way that wouldn't leave a trail. They must have something like postcards still. "Ship still intact. Family well. Regards to Ganesh." They would know who it was from.

Alan left a few minutes later to start his shift. Since they were in realspace now, approaching Fivemoons, she was enjoying the luxury of a down cycle. The first mate had the responsibility of docking to the station.

"So what's wrong with that kid?" Gregor Jadrich, the assistant engineer, jerked his head at the door Alan had left by.

"Is something the matter?" she asked.

"He's slow. He doesn't know things any two-year-old would. He walked halfway across the ship to deliver a message when there was a wall comm right next to him." There was resentment in his voice, confirming Moire's assignment of Jadrich to the Bad Attitude section of the crew.

"Walking's good exercise. And he works hard. That's good exercise too," commented Harvey, looking sourly at Jadrich. His expression said *You should try it sometime.* "Haven't heard Montero complain about young Alan being slow."

Jadrich made a rude noise. "Would he notice?"

"He grew up in a low-tech colony," Moire said. "He doesn't know about a lot of things." She felt herself tensing. What else had they noticed about Alan?

"What were you doing in one of those?" Harvey wanted to know. "I don't believe you'd fit in too well."

She was going to have to put some more work in on this alibi. It was showing signs of strain. "I wasn't there. His father...I hadn't seen Alan until a month ago. He found me, in fact. I didn't even know where he was before then."

Jadrich got up, giving her a disbelieving look. "That still doesn't explain why he's so slow. You sure his gestation tank got enough oxygen?" he said as he left.

His what?

"I don't know what Gregor's problem is," Harvey commented. "I was feeling quite chipper when I came in—had plans for my first few days in port, looking forward to having a good time. Now I wonder why I even woke up today. What's it to him if your boy doesn't know everything? Alan's not working in Engineering." He rubbed his chin, glancing at the door with a speculative look. "I'll bet he's peeved because Tenna can't even see him if Alan's around. Thought he was hot stuff, Gregor did, but it don't take a full-spectrum scope to see young Alan has him beat."

"Thanks." Moire took a gulp of her now-tepid coffee. "Have there been any problems I'm not hearing about?"

"Tenna lives in fear that he'll leave this port, but I don't think that's what you had in mind. No, nothing I've heard of that isn't explained by what you just told us. He's not reading things well," Harvey said, hesitantly. "Manuals and the like. Least that's what Montero was telling me."

At least he *could* read. Moire nodded. "I'll work on that. Anything else?"

Harvey shook his head. "Montero isn't complaining—he just noticed. So, the two of you have plans for the port? Or do you split up?"

"We'll be staying on the ship." Fivemoons was only one jump from Redline, and she didn't want to risk meeting up with any of her former comrades in the mercenaries or the Fleet personnel who were doubtless chasing them. This was only the second port since she'd come on board, too. *Ayesha* had a few more regular stops, and then it was doing a "wild run" all over the Fringe, wherever anyone needed cargo shipped. That would be much harder to trace, and would be a better time to leave.

"You're sure? You didn't leave the ship at Pykko, either. We'll be here three days at least."

"I'm too beat to party, and I'm broke. Besides—"

"What's wrong? They got a doc here, I heard, if you don't want Madele," Harvey interrupted, looking concerned. "You shoulda told her, though, she ain't *that* bad, I mean, she's gotta look after the captain and he's still alive."

She was going to have to compile a list of words she couldn't use anymore. Harvey was starting to look offended on Madele Fortin's behalf.

"There's nothing wrong with me, really," she said hastily. "I just mean...um, I'm just not feeling up to it. Alan isn't ready for Fivemoons. I've heard it's a wild place."

Harvey pursed his lips. "Could be, could be. I've seen wilder myself."

After the crew had left the ship Moire found Alan and they went exploring.

"Is it still the Game?" Alan wanted to know.

"Nobody here but us," Moire answered. "No Game for now. Why?"

She found herself being towed down the corridor to the Maintenance section, Alan talking nonstop the entire way. "Why do people have two names? And I saw on Carlos's wall both his names but there were others with it too! And why does he make humming noises when he works? And...."

Moire did her best to answer all his pent-up questions, and she was hazily aware from what he was asking that he was quite observant. And curious. Inside Maintenance a whole new universe of questions opened up that she was much less qualified to answer.

"What does he use it on?" she said, staring at the thing on the wall. It looked like an old-fashioned milkshake mixer, only without the stirring thing.

Alan shrugged. "All sorts of things. A sandwich, once."

Moire prodded the whatsis, hoping for clues. No labels, of course. One section of silver trim turned out to be some kind of switch. A faint blue-purple light shone out from the top, followed by the scent of ozone. "Hmm. Maybe a sterilizer? I'm not sure."

She also was unable to come up with a satisfactory answers for a collection of clear plastic teardrops on a string, each with a preserved flower inside; a strange vidloop in a cube showing a woman in an extremely thin–and tight–white shipsuit writhing and giggling on a black surface; or a little Jesus statuette holding an ankh as if he were warding off vampires. It had been carefully placed on the narrow sill of a viewport, facing out of the ship. Montero was worried about something out there, apparently.

Eventually Alan noticed the pattern. "Why don't you know? The others do."

She could see disaster looming in the distance. "I'll try to find out, OK?" Moire smiled brightly, looking about desperately for something to distract him with. He was damn persistent when he was curious.

She finally resorted to bribing him with his favorite snack, lemon-flavored starch puffs. They tasted like freeze-dried soapsuds to her, but he loved them. Sitting in the galley she heard the faint sound of a hatch slamming, then footsteps and voices growing louder until Tenna and Michel entered the galley. They were carrying their recent purchases from the station.

"There you are, Alan! You should have come with us," Tenna said, dumping her share on the table. "Look! They had a place with trid show copies! New ones, too, at least ones I hadn't seen yet. They had *Galloway*, and *Star Hunter*, and all my favorites."

"We are going to set up the trid viewer now, if you want to watch," Michel said. Alan nodded enthusiastically. Moire smiled, feeling relieved. They'd be engrossed for hours now, and Alan would probably forget his earlier question. She decided to spend some time on the exercise equipment.

It was another sign of Davies's consideration for the crew that the ship had high-quality exercise gear. Not only was it expensive, it was permanently set up near the holds, taking up valuable space that could have been used for cargo.

The first mate came down the accessway a few minutes later, stopping when she saw Moire but continuing after glaring at her. Ramutis silently set up the resistance boxing equipment while Moire continued with the tension "weights."

"You always gotta wear that same damn shipsuit? Go get another one," Ramutis said suddenly. She seemed almost angry. Moire didn't know what the problem was, but then Ramutis often acted like that. The only person she hadn't seen her yell at was the captain.

What was the problem with her shipsuit, anyway? It was plain black, which was unusual. Most people favored bright colors and designs, but the military never had been big on style. *Military. That must be what she's asking. She thinks I used to be in Fleet.* She needed to find a way to stop Ramutis from making any kind of connection between her and Fleet, even the wrong one.

"Hey, surplus is cheap. At least that's what the guy selling them said they were. Might have been the old five-finger discount, but how could I tell?" It was mostly true; she'd gotten it from one of the mercenaries when she'd joined the unit in Brisbane.

Ramutis looked up, an arrested expression in her eyes. After a moment she gave a grudging nod and seemed to relax. "Don't see them often, except for Fleet. Ugly, but real functional. Kind of like Fleet itself." She punched and jabbed with fierce energy, her teeth bared in a snarl. "How do you like the ship?" she asked, when she stopped for a moment.

"I think the gravitic drive is possessed, but other than that it isn't bad."

Ramutis stared out at nothing, then started punching again. Angrily. "Should be able to fly web myself," she gasped. "First mate's job to do what the captain does, but I can't. Davies hired me anyway. Wanted me for realspace if his vision acted up. Sometimes he's almost blind." She lashed out savagely. "My watch, he'd sleep on the bridge. I'd yell if the readouts drifted. Engines were real bad once, had to drop out midway so he could rest."

Moire shuddered. On this ship, she'd be afraid they would never start up again. Stuck in the middle of nowhere with no way to send a signal except by sublight communications. They'd be dead by the time anyone heard it—and out on the Fringe, even if someone did hear it there was no guarantee they would be friendly.

After their conversation Ramutis was less hostile, but Moire didn't see much of her again until their next stop two weeks later. She knew why, now. Somebody had to be on the bridge to check on Davies.

"Ready up there, Ramutis?" Moire watched the readouts carefully. Just one tick more....

"Whenever you are, Roberts," came the first mate's voice from the comm. Ramutis was on the realspace deck, waiting for dropout.

"Dropout commencing." Moire disengaged the drive, shaking her head at the slow, dragging ripple she felt in her bones. They'd lose at least two hours on the clock for that—what web pilots called "Einstein's Revenge." The longer a ship spent in that relativistic region the more obvious the time differential.

She'd had more than her fair share of that, thanks to *Bon Accord*. Moire wondered if that was why she was so sensitive to changes in the drive field. Nobody else seemed to feel it as much as she did.

At last the readout showed zero gravity bubble. "First Mate, you have the conn. Gravitics are disengaged."

"I have the conn," responded Ramutis. "Right on the money, Roberts. Station is hailing. Should be about four hours to dock."

"Good job," Davies said in his soft, drawling voice. He was standing on the pit stairs, his eyes on the readout. He'd heard the whole exchange on his captain's earring. "Ramutis, I'll be going ashore when we get there. Have Harvey send someone to help me out."

"Yes, Captain," the first mate said quickly.

Davies turned with great weariness and took a careful step up. He'd been acting even more tired lately; Moire hoped his illness was not responsible. He took another step and stumbled, falling awkwardly, instinctively trying to break his fall with both arms. He collapsed on the stairs, groaning and then crying out sharply as his arms began to spasm and flail. Moire flung herself out of the chair and tried to hold him still. His eyes were bulging, sounds from his mouth seemed to be an attempt to communicate but she couldn't understand what he was trying to say.

"Ramutis! The captain's hurt himself. He can't talk." Moire scrambled for the comm, searching the list for Madele Fortin's code.

"There's a small container on a cord around his neck," Ramutis said urgently. "Open it and put one of the red tabs in his mouth, and hurry! He can break his bones if his muscles spasm too long."

Moire fumbled with the container, spilling the contents in her haste: a handful of small red squares, thick and soft to the touch. When she put one in the captain's mouth he bit down hard. A shudder went through his body, and he sagged limply on the stairs. Moire searched for a pulse, but he was so puffy with fluid she couldn't find it. He did seem to be breathing.

After what seemed like hours but was probably only a few minutes Madele Fortin burst on the bridge with Tenna in tow.

"What happened? Did he have a seizure?" She grabbed the kit bag from Tenna's nerveless hands and opened it, rummaging through the contents.

"He fell," Moire said, feeling helpless and frustrated. She didn't even know what was wrong. "Ramutis told me to give him one of these, and the spasms stopped." She held out the red squares.

"Solverlactin," Madele said absently, looking at the readout of one of her diagnostic devices. "Voluntary muscle relaxant. Very strong, very quick. That was good. It looks like no bones broke this time."

"This has happened before?"

Madele nodded. "A sudden motion—or a blow—can start the spasms. He takes another drug to prevent strong spasms like these, but it is expensive and hard to get. He was going ashore to get more. We need to hurry. Solverlactin only lasts for an hour or so, and it is risky to take too many doses." She shook her head. "At this stage of his disease, there are few drugs that are safe to give him."

"Will he recover?'

Madele looked at the captain, sadly, then turned back to Moire. "As much as he was before this, yes. It is not the first time."

Nooreen Meniran added a touch more opacity to the model and considered the effect. Storm clouds were always the hardest to get right, which was why she had chosen them. They seemed...appropriate. So much of their appearance was subtle and beyond awareness, and yet the human subconscious remembered the ancestral time when storms were feared and detected the slightest mistake.

Lighting would create the full effect–that, and the correct formula for the aerogel. She considered the model and was satisfied. Starting the build sequence, she stared out the window at the view of Irukyn-Riu's stonelands and felt her anger returning. Only now it did not blind her with its fury. She had been right to focus on her atmospheric art until she could think clearly again, for matters were so desperate now any mistake could be fatal. Fatal for the company, fatal for her.

So. Berens had been discovered, and in such a way Fleet could not help but be suspicious. The board would ask her how this would impact the Long Range Plan, and she would have to admit that they would only be safe until Fleet had developed resources to replace Toren with. They could delay, undermine, sabotage. There were certain governments that owed Toren favors and could be induced to object to any competitors–but that was perhaps even more dangerous than not doing anything. If Fleet was convinced Toren was actively working against them they might even stage a direct takeover of the company.

Fleet *would* replace them eventually no matter what they did. She would have to recommend that the schedule of the Long Range Plan be accelerated as much as possible. That much would not be a shock to the board; they had already considered it to account for the sudden and inexplicable improvement in Fleet's ability to fight the crabs. The carefully maintained balance in the war was in danger.

That, fortunately, was not her responsibility. She had to find Moire Cameron and extract her information. Strangely, it appeared Cameron had not confided in anyone on board the ship. Hallin had not responded at all to any of the keyphrases, nor had their admittedly limited surveillance picked up those terms in Fleet's communications. At least she would not have to clean up *there*.

She would have to send out more teams. Every one she could get from the company. Alert every Toren employee with sufficient clearance to look for her. She would also need to ask the board to raise the engagement protocol for the agents. It was more dangerous to shrink back from necessary killing, and requiring clearance from the board took too much time.

The fabricator beeped and the pressure vessel walls lifted up with a faint whoosh of air. Her aerogel atmosphere sculpture had turned out well: the dark, brooding storm clouds looked as if they would unleash lightning at any moment.

She frowned. There was still something missing from her analysis. Berens had not been the best agent the company had, but he was still extremely competent. How had Fleet been able to detect him and stop him so efficiently? Had they been suspicious from the beginning?

Meniran knuckled her forehead with a groan, trying to will away the incipient headache. She could not simply hope that Fleet had gotten lucky, or that it was an unimportant issue. Nothing could be left to chance. Only Fleet could stop the Long Range Plan. They would have to infiltrate Fleet.

It had seemed like a good idea to wait for the next staff meeting, but now Ennis wondered if he should try to talk to the captain some other time. The news she had for them was entirely bad. The crabs had launched another major attack in a different sector, and while the defenses had held, the cost was high. As one of the handful of surviving carriers *Canaveral* was going to be extremely busy.

His original reason to intercept her at the meeting was to prevent his request from showing up in any schedule, since by now his paranoia was in full swing. After considering Captain Kushstan's probable reaction if something else happened and he hadn't warned her, he decided to follow his original plan.

"What is it?" she growled.

Ennis brought up the image on his datapad. "I did some research on my own, sir. After the incident with Berens." He put the datapad in front of her.

"And this is...oh." She paused, her glance flicking over the display. "Are you sure this hasn't been fabricated?"

Ennis looked about the meeting room. Everyone had left except the captain's aide, and Kushstan tilted her head at him to go.

"I only found it because of what I overheard Berens saying when he was interrogating that mercenary. This is the only reference I found, and the book has been in the library for the last two years. That's a pretty subtle plant, sir."

"I see. Curious, but why do I need to know this, Commander Ennis?"

There was a strong hint of why-are-you-wasting-my-time, and he hastened to add, "She was an explorer. I think she found something Toren wants badly. Maybe they won't send someone openly like they did with Berens, but they were willing to take some serious risks because they thought there might be some information here. They are going to try again."

The captain was playing with her stylus again, but in a way that made Ennis think she wished it were a knife. "I don't need these stupid games going on in the middle of a *real* war." The muscles in her jaw tightened. She closed her eyes for a moment, then sighed. "Come to my office in two hours."

Ennis spent the time trying to decide what the captain's priorities would be, caught between her responsibilities to the ship and Fleet, and Fleet's dependence on Toren. They had to do something, but what?

When he entered her office he saw the strange-looking translucent gun Tendo Berens had carried on her desk. "Scan-resistant," she said, seeing his surprised reaction to its presence. "From what Shaughnassy has managed to find out, the mechanism isn't that special otherwise. Standard power cells, takes standard ammo, but it can also use almost anything else that fits in the chamber. It can also do a short-range power blast."

The captain shifted her gaze from the gun to him. "Take it." He hesitated, then picked it up. It felt smooth and light in his hand. "Have a seat." She had a weary expression on her face. With a visible effort, she shook it off. "Do you know why you have that gun?"

"Because Berens was interested in me from the beginning. Because we can't be sure they won't figure out I, or somebody else on this ship, knows what they are really after."

"Partly." Her face was grim. "You are to carry that gun at all times—take it to the head, the shower, everywhere. You will also put together a report, on a closed, secure system, of all the information you have. You will make only three copies of this report. One you will carry with you at all times, one you will give to me, and one you will give to Colonel Shaughnassy with instructions to conceal it in a place neither you nor I know about. You will finish this report in time for the next courier, which is expected in four days. You will take this report, and the sealed report I will give you, to Fleet Far Command, and there await further orders. These orders, and the existence of the report, are classified. Is that clear?"

"Yes, sir." His thoughts had gone fuzzy with shock. The captain had decided to dilute the risk by informing her superiors as secretly as possible, but he wished she had picked someone else to deliver the information to FarCom. He knew that one reason for sending him, besides his knowledge of the situation, was to get him off her ship so Toren would be less likely to show up. At least she'd given him the gun.

She gave him a somber look. "And Ennis. Watch your back."

"We have visual feed on channel four thirty-five" the courier pilot announced over the ship comm, shortly after dropping out of webspace. "If you haven't seen FarCom before, it's worth a look."

Ennis suspected the pilot was used to carrying upper brass, who liked these little courtesies. He picked up the courier's output on his datapad. At first he didn't see the channel listed, but then he remembered the datapad was still set to *Canaveral*'s broadcast settings. He did a local rescan to find the channel.

It wasn't long before Far Command came into view. It was immense; similar in scale to a small moon but nowhere close to symmetrical, it bristled with sensor and signal arrays, weapons clusters, and launch bays. It also had a number of ancillary facilities tacked on—two massive repair docks, and what appeared to be detachable supply pods. Ennis suspected they would have to be removed if FarCom changed location, since they weren't really part of the main ship. FarCom was technically a supercarrier and capable of web travel.

As they got closer Ennis could see a lot of ship activity around Far Command, more than the expected support ships of the supercarrier group. There was another courier coming in as well. Was it usually this busy?

The courier glided closer to the exterior docking area, and Ennis shut down the visual link. Assembling his gear, he made sure his reader was handy in preparation for yet another bracing round of bureaucracy. At the center of things, FarCom was bound to be the worst he'd ever experienced.

The two contingents from the couriers mixed in the dock area, chatting as mutual acquaintances found each other. Ennis overheard the name "Congu" and perked up his ears. That was where the last battle had been.

"We lost the entire first wave," said a major, looking grim-faced. Ennis didn't recognize him; he had been on the other courier.

"The whole thing?" said his friend. "What the hell happened?"

The major shook his head. "We don't know. They were all fitted with the camouflage just like before. Same crab wreckage that had worked the last few times. They must have figured it out, because it didn't make a damn bit of difference. It was a slaughter."

"So that's why the pullback. When are we going to ever get a break in this war?"

"It's more than a pullback. We can't defend that sector anymore. Allende's people have been tasked with evacuating anybody who is still out there. News is going to spread all over the Fringe that we can't protect them."

The friend snorted. "You need to get out more. The Fringe is already jumpy as hell. Every station I go to they got those kiosks of missing people, notice that? Hundreds of ships going missing. *We* know most of them are probably drive failures from poorly maintained ships, but no, they are convinced they are all crab kills. Even out at Criminy where there's never been a crab sighting!"

Ennis headed for the station entry, thinking hard. So that's why there was so much activity here. Maybe they were planning to move. FarCom's present position was quite close to the front lines of the war, and with the current reversal of fortune in the most recent fighting it probably would be in preparation if not execution.

The latest news put Fleet right back where it was before—thrashing about to find the enemy, and getting roughed up when it did since there was no way to know how many they would find. The only consolation was the crabs were having just as much of a problem finding them. Crab detection technology apparently wasn't any better than theirs, and a system-by-system search would take hundreds of years.

He handed his order tab and ID chip to one of the enlisted at the entry desk, who scanned it briefly and then issued him a temporary badge. He turned away, affixing the badge. One of his fellow passengers, a colonel, was going through the same routine and starting to steam.

"They already know I'm here, the courier sent the data as soon as we dropped out. What's causing the delay? I have important business here. Is this off-prime cycle?"

"It is currently prime cycle, sir," said the wooden-faced enlisted at the desk. "Off-prime does not begin for four hours. If you are expected you should not have long to wait. I'm sorry, sir, but I don't have the authority to let you in."

The argument continued. Ennis left for the waiting area, which had a bank of autovends, some mail and data kiosks, and rows and rows of empty chairs. He didn't know why the colonel was throwing her weight around. FarCom hadn't had much time to process the information the courier had sent before docking. He, on the other hand, could be waiting for hours. Nobody was expecting him.

In one corner was a sign reading "Observation deck," with text flickering beneath. He went up to read it. The sign informed him that the observation deck would be closed when FarCom was in drive, during radiation events, or at any other time the Safety Officer deemed it necessary. There were no other notices, so it was a fair bet it was open.

He went up. Even if FarCom was suddenly stricken with efficiency before he returned, they could find him with the tracking badge he was wearing. The door was of the max-seal variety, like an outside hatch but without the airlock fittings. When he opened it, he could see why.

The observation deck was a platform surrounded by a clear bubble, with wings of heavy shielding folded back against the hull. A radiation meter was mounted on the wall but it was hardly ticking over. The bubble was on the lee side of FarCom, away from the system's sun.

Ennis stood motionless at the center of the bubble, willing his mind to only focus on the present. He always liked looking at the stars. He'd learned that on Fimbul, to keep his mind away from the terror and the cold. When he'd mentioned it afterward he'd learned there were those who found the starfield cold and intimidating. On Fimbul if you couldn't see the stars you were in the tunnels, and in danger. Stars meant safety.

Up to one side, at the edge of some dark protrusion of FarCom, was a dull red nebula. It glowed, round and ragged, like a drop of blood diffusing in black water. He'd heard of the Helix nebula, seen vid stills, but it still took his breath away to see the real thing. The shreds of hot gas, delicate and immense, were shaded in color and intensity like the petals of a glowing flower.

He wished stars meant safety now. He saw his grim expression reflected in the surface of the bubble and tried to relax the tension in his muscles. New ships always made him react this way. He hated transfers, the unsettled feeling of having to prove himself to another group of strangers.

This wasn't an ordinary transfer, though. He knew there was very little chance he would ever get back to *Canaveral*. He just wished he could be certain they would send him to another ship–any ship. Maybe the threatening approach of the crabs would make Fleet reconsider. He still had a little time left before the cutoff, and he wanted desperately to hold off the inevitable.

Then what? Even the desk job would some day come to an end. Where would he go? Fleet was all he knew. He couldn't go back to Fimbul. Penderhest, the only family he'd ever had, had been dead for many years. The few friends he had were all in Fleet. He wished there was a place he could return to, where he would know what he was without a uniform.

They called his name a few minutes after he came down from the observation area, as he stood before the autovend trying to decide among the assortment of unappetizing choices. Two marines were waiting by the door. The soldier at the entry gave him a temporary billeting tab, which if nothing else meant he had escaped from the autovend as his only source of food.

Following his escort, Ennis saw the red-hashed border indicating the security scan section of the corridor ahead. He held his breath when he crossed the boundary, but no alarms sounded. He walked on, feeling extremely conscious of the gun he carried. Even when he crossed the far edge of the scan area, there was no indication it had been detected. The captain's orders had been explicit and detailed in the report, so he was covered in the event there was a problem. He wondered how scan-resistant it really was–it had to be good to get past *Canaveral*'s security, but he hoped FarCom's was better.

It hadn't taken them long at all to call him. The angry colonel was still waiting even though she had been expected. That meant someone was very interested in what Ennis had brought, and it made him worried.

The marines brought him to an office door. One of them punched the annunciator. No voice answered, but a green pinlight lit up and the door opened. Ennis stepped in, at first thinking the lights were off. Then he notice a low, soft golden glow coming from several small, self-powered glowballs scattered throughout the room. They were tucked into shelves, stuck to the walls, and scattered in the corners like phosphorescent mushrooms. He'd seen restaurants decorated like that but never a military office. There was also the slightly brighter glow of a tubelight just above a desk screen.

As his eyes adjusted to the dim light, he realized the office was crowded with material. Data cases lined the walls, covering every available surface except for the desktop and the single chair facing it. On the other side of the desk was a man.

"Commander Ennis. Please have a seat." From the little he could see, the man had short, bristly hair, with skin taut over the bones of his face. The voice and the air of assurance all indicated a senior officer, but Ennis didn't see any rank insignia. "I am Pol Namur. Will you join me?" He indicated the cast-iron teapot, flanked by two small, rough-glazed bowls.

Ennis nodded, feeling numb with shock. Even he had heard of Namur, mostly in the form of whispered rumors. Namur was in charge of the least known of the intelligence groups, officially named Special Measures but more often referred to as Umbra. Every group in Intelligence was trying to get information on the crabs, but Umbra had produced most of it. He tried and failed to think of any reason Umbra would be interested in his report, which was completely crab-free.

Namur poured the tea. Ennis picked up his bowl and sipped. The tea was smoky in flavor, unexpected.

"We are civilized warriors here, at least to the point of drinking tea. And since you woke me up, you will have to indulge my weakness." Namur's eyes glinted in the gloom.

Ennis supposed some of his surprise must have shown, because Namur curled the corners of his mouth in a ghost of a smile. "Within these walls, formality is given less importance. It has its place, but here it can impede our hunt for the truth."

"This was important enough to wake you up?" Despite what Namur had said, Ennis felt strange speaking so casually to him. Once an officer, always an officer.

Umbra also occupied a strange niche in Fleet. Neither fully military nor fully civilian, it operated under its own rules. Ennis recalled hearing that Namur had been at least a brigadier general once. Had he resigned to accept the position with Umbra, or had there been some other reason forcing him to leave Fleet Command? Namur didn't seem old enough for retirement.

"Ordinarily, no. We already had the information about the Toren operative running amok; that arrived a few days ago. My rude awakening came about because I left a databot running for the name of a ship," he said, leaning back and sipping his tea, "a ship mentioned in your report. I have only skimmed it, mind you, but the other content would place you under my jurisdiction anyway and I decided to indulge my curiosity since I was already awake. You'll need to adjust your cycles to match while you're here, you know. I run off-prime." Ennis nodded, still confused. "This is not the first evidence of Toren's curiously misplaced priorities. You are to be commended for preventing any loss of life. We have not always been so fortunate in these incidents."

His voice kept its gentle, even tone but there was a dangerous edge underneath.

"We will discuss that later. Now, this ship I mentioned. Two years ago the station at Beta Centauri got a distress call. Patchy, incomplete, didn't have the ship data encoded in the background transmission—just a straight, uncompressed call for help. Beta C is an old port, almost as old as Earth, and they sometimes get time-delayed distress calls from years ago. This one was different. They sent a rescue ship when they discovered the signal triangulated to a position *inside* the system, but by the time they arrived nothing was there. Searching produced only fragments of wreckage. The theory developed that the signal transmitter for a damaged ship had made it through long enough to send the signal, but the ship itself had not.

"I was not convinced," Namur added, pouring more tea. "Suspicious circumstances—not the least of which being a Toren ship in the area that left hastily just before the rescue ship arrived—were plentiful. I set a databot to alert me, high priority, if any of the things I'd noticed came up again. The name of the ship from the transmission was one of them."

Of course. *"Bon Accord?"* Ennis really wanted to know why the head of Umbra thought a strange distress signal deserved a high priority alert. Curiosity alone would not have been enough.

Namur's eyes were hooded, hidden in the shadows. "Even so. Now, what can you tell me about it?"

Namur's office was still lit with the misty golden glowballs when Ennis returned at Namur's main shift time. He decided that was the way the head of Umbra liked it. It made the office walls seem nebulous and indistinct, the dim spheres of light barely revealing objects seen in the distance.

"You have led a most interesting life," Namur said as he came in. That was probably the most polite way Ennis had ever heard his dubious past described. "I congratulate you. It was gratifying to find an answer to a puzzle, even if it only leads to another puzzle."

"You mean, why Toren wants to find her?"

Namur leaned back, steepling his long fingers before his face. "That is a part of it, yes, although I believe we can narrow down the possibilities. We know Toren has a great deal of interest in potential sites for new colonies." He gestured to the desk screen. "I think it is more than that, however. They are so interested they are willing to commit violence, repeatedly. She must have found a planet that is quite valuable indeed. I would also like to know how Toren found the ship in the first place, and how Captain Moire Cameron got away from them. But that's incidental to the matter at hand."

"Captain?" Ennis asked, not sure he had heard correctly.

"A rank that predates the armed forces unification, roughly equivalent to the rank you hold yourself. Cameron was an Air Force pilot before going on loan to NASA, the government agency in charge of space exploration at the time. We don't know much more about her after she transferred. Toren took over NASA's function—and records—a few years after *Bon Accord* vanished, so we can't look her up without alerting them. Her military record shows some rough spots in the beginning. There are cryptic references to a 'deferred legal judgment,' and an irate complaint from her commanding officer about the service being used as a juvenile detention facility, so it seems Cameron had some brushes with the law. However, after the rough start her record is exemplary. Combat tour completed, tail end of the Korean Breakout conflict. Six months test pilot stint, and then NASA."

Namur leaned forward, looking at Ennis directly. "Officially, Cameron is of little importance beyond the mutiny. She only interests us to the degree that Toren is causing problems in their attempts to get at her. But you need to know what she is—extremely capable and resourceful."

Ennis sensed he was not being told the entire story, but he was surprised the head of Umbra was telling him anything. Namur had gotten up in the middle of his sleep cycle to find out more, and he didn't think it was because of the possibility of a new colony planet. Something was seriously wrong, and it seemed to involve Toren. "Why do I need to know any more than I do now?"

Namur smiled, the taut skin drawing even tighter over his face. "To perform your future duties. I have made the recommendation that you be transferred to Intelligence. To Umbra."

Ennis froze, stunned and disbelieving. His worst fear had come true. Namur clearly expected his recommendation to be acted on immediately, and Ennis didn't think anyone would argue about a slow-grade officer if Umbra wanted him. He tried not to let his bitter disappointment show. At least he was still technically in Fleet. He hoped. They wouldn't discharge him as part of the transfer, would they?

Namur looked at his screen. "We'll get you some training and try to get a better reading on that gun you have. Toren has some nasty tricks up its sleeve–that's one of the best scan-resistant guns we've come across. Detector at the entrance didn't pick it up. Worrisome. Anyway, we'll send you out to look for *Canaveral* mutineers–not that I think it is worth pursuing, but it makes a convincing cover. Unofficially you will be looking for Cameron, and you will bring her back alive if at all possible. It is only fair to warn you we will be discreetly leaking your movements to Toren once you leave FarCom," he added, glancing at Ennis. "You are to draw their attention, frankly, away from and off of our ships."

Yes, something was definitely going on. He should be glad he could still serve Fleet, even if his new job title was Bait. "Understandable," Ennis said, grimacing. "Personally inconvenient, but understandable. I hope this training will cover defensive measures as well?"

"But of course, Commander Ennis. And I fear you will have plenty of opportunity for practice."

CHAPTER 16
CONTACT WITH THE ENEMY

The wall comm in her cabin sounded, and Moire switched it on.

"Schedule says you're going ashore in a bit," Harvey said.

"Yes. Is there a problem?"

"No, everything's fine. Just wanted to remind you to take a commlink with you, just in case."

She patted her pocket. "Got it right here. How's the captain doing?"

"They're letting him out today. He'll rest better in the ship; the station gravity is too heavy for him like he is. He wanted me to thank you for what you did, and the crew does too."

"I just did what Ramutis told me to," Moire said, feeling uncomfortable. *If I were really doing you a favor, I'd tell you to stop flying on this ship. It's a death trap.*

"If you hadn't, he could have died. Well, have a good time on station, but not *too* good, OK? Angelos law can be bought but they're real expensive."

She laughed. "Alan will keep me out of trouble," she said, and closed the connection.

Alan bounded to his feet. "Are we going now?"

"All set?" she asked. Alan nodded. She went for the door, then stopped. "Nah, let's be careful." She went to her locker and pulled out the hood from Bone. Removing the oxygen booster pad, she put it on. It wasn't a perfect disguise, but it wouldn't attract too much attention, either.

They left the ship by the personnel door, off to one side of the cargo area. Yolanda was supervising a local dock crew unloading an array of crates. This was a major stop; one whole bay was being emptied. Alan watched with interest. He was much more confident now, but he still didn't like Moire leaving him for long periods.

"Michel tells me the game he has cost ten ED. I have more than that, right?" Alan asked. Moire had heard all about the game, in mind-numbing detail. Michel had allowed Alan to play it occasionally, which was nice of him. It had done wonders for Alan's social skills. He certainly talked a lot more, at least to her.

"Yep. Is that what you want to get?"

He nodded. "I can figure it out by myself then. When you play, there are not-real people but they talk to you as if they were real. Every time you play they say the same thing, that's how I knew they weren't real." He seemed proud of this discovery.

Moire wanted to see what the hiring situation was like for pilots on this station, since this was the first real opportunity she'd had to look for another job. She felt slightly guilty about leaving the crew of *Ayesha* in the lurch, but they would be better off if she did. It was only a matter of time before the captain could no longer function at all.

By following the flow of people leaving the shipping area, they found the main commercial part of the station. Just outside the shipping section was a kiosk for advertisements.

"Let me check this first." Alan sighed, and his shoulders sagged. She waited her turn at one of the terminals, watching the varied people go by. Her patchwork style of clothing was hardly noticeable here, although there weren't many wearing hoods. The station was rather warm for it. She wasn't the only one wearing military surplus, though. There was a scruffy-looking silver-haired man with a Roman nose wearing a black field vest, walking idly by as if he were waiting for someone. Their glances crossed, and she turned away quickly. He looked slightly familiar. She racked her brain, trying to remember where she might have seen him.

Not Fleet. She'd remember that. Maybe it was just a resemblance. She risked another glance. The man had walked away, looking both ways at the main causeway of the station as if deciding where to go next. She shrugged to herself. *There must be a few people who aren't out to get me.*

A terminal opened up, and she took her place. There were plenty of jobs listed for pilots, but they were all for routes that were Inner System, closer to Earth. She frowned. Who was doing the Fringe flying, then? When she'd looked after dumping the mercenaries there had been jobs. What had happened?

She wasn't going to find out here. Maybe she could find the local equivalent of a newspaper or something. People still had to get their information somehow. "All right, let's go shopping." Alan perked up. "I wonder where we find something like that game?"

It was nice to get off the ship and not be in immediate danger. The only trouble was she didn't recognize a lot of what she saw, and Alan was looking at everything with wide eyes that told her he was just as bemused as she was.

The holographic ads and shop signs, gently drifting as if there were a breeze in the station, were fairly easy to figure out. A large display screen near the entrance to Angelos security showed vid clips and rotating, full-figure images of people. At first she thought it was another ad and was trying to puzzle out what was being sold, and then she read the text underneath. *Felony-D, murder.* That image was replaced by another, a thuggish-looking woman. *Felony-D, data trespass, enslavement.*

Moire drew in a sharp breath and moved quickly away, keeping her head tilted down so the hood shadowed as much of her face as possible. Wanted posters. Was she being shown like that in every station on the Fringe? What was a felony-D?

Fortunately nobody but her seemed to be paying attention to the display. A crowd was gathered farther down the main station corridor, where a sign overhead read "NewsService!" in letters that exploded in silver rain and then reformed.

"'New Upload Today: Many Leaving Outer Colonies,'" read Alan. "What does that mean?"

Moire shook her head, not wanting to get into an explanation in public. There were three kiosk stations, all busy, and Moire saw the crowd was watching the changing header screen which seemed to have headlines as a teaser. There was her newspaper equivalent. People were using readers and textsheets to apparently get the latest copy of whatever it was.

"We'll come back and see," she said. "It's too busy now. I wonder where they sell games around here?"

It took a lot of searching but they finally found Alan's game in an export shop. The price was considerably more than 10 ED, and it was only a datatab.

"Huh. Says it works on a standard reader," Moire commented, scrolling through the packaging text. "We should get you a reader anyway, and some books. You need to work on your reading, kid."

Alan scowled. "Carlos Montero already has manuals."

"Books, kid. Books. Not manuals. Books are fun to read. They tell stories. Like a game that you play in your head." Alan felt at his face, looking confused. "Not like that. Never mind, you'll understand when you try it. I hope."

Books were even more difficult to find than the game. They walked through most of the commercial section of the station, occasionally seeing crew from *Ayesha*. She thought she saw Yolanda Menehune near the seedier area, where the roughs and toughs hung out. She was surprised to see Gregor Jadrich there too. Nasty as he was, he didn't seem that type. He was deep in conversation with a woman with enough bodymods to be a mercenary. As Moire watched, the woman glanced around and pulled him after her into the bad section. He didn't seem unwilling, so it was his own damn fault if something happened to him.

Moire found a restaurant when Alan started to get hungry. She was glad to sit down for a while; the station's full gravity was taking a long time to adjust to.

"This is more like what Mammachandra gave," Alan said, munching. "The food on the ship tastes different."

"Madele is a good cook," Moire said. She also used better ingredients, which probably cost ten times more.

The restaurant they were in had an open front, and they were seated close enough to the causeway for Moire to see the shop signs. One Stop Euphoria, which seemed to specialize in alcohol, legal drugs, and sex paraphernalia; Carneva's, a real non-cultured meat restaurant, very tony décor outside, including the bouncer/maître d'; Hot Shots, which was either a radical clothing shop or an escort service, she couldn't tell which. Maybe it was both. She almost missed the tiny, old-fashioned static sign posted on the corner of a cross-corridor that looked like a utility niche: Ex Libris.

She pulled out a credit chip and put it in the table slot, grimacing when she saw the total. She punched "accept" and took it out. "I think I see another possibility," she said to Alan.

Ex Libris was the tiniest store she had ever been in. There wasn't even room to step inside; they had to stand in the corridor. All it had was a small display case overhead with a selection of readers, and a terminal. An ancient, wizened man with a wispy beard who looked like he had stepped out of a Chinese painting of venerable sages was sitting beside the terminal. His colorful knit hat with small pompoms hanging from strings around the edge detracted only slightly from this image.

Looking at the readers, she had a sudden rush of memory of the library on *Canaveral* and Ennis loaning her his extra. She hoped he got it back after all the excitement wore off. Going to the library had been one of the few pleasures she'd had since Toren had found her. She'd even enjoyed talking to Ennis. *Get over it. After what you did, I doubt he wants to be friends anymore.*

She picked the cheapest reader available. "I want to get some books, too."

The ancient Chinese sage pointed to the terminal. "You get one free with this," he said, indicating the reader. "One volume, anything but Top Ten."

Which was all very well, because she had no idea what the current books were like. All of the titles she recognized were in the "Classics" section on the terminal anyway. She scrolled through, hoping for inspiration, while Alan watched over her shoulder. She picked out a good-sized picture dictionary, so she wouldn't have to explain every other line. It might be good for her, too. After more thought, she decided on children's books for the rest. She wouldn't have to tell him that's what they were, and he was rather childlike in his understanding.

The Jungle Book seemed like a good choice, since he was almost feral himself. Illustrations were an extra charge, but she included them. Some Roald Dahl followed, and *Huckleberry Finn*. She tried to find another of her old favorites from her childhood, but all she could remember was the title had something to do with dogs, and there was a talking earwig. A fuzzy search on "talking earwig" produced a book on garden pests.

She snapped her fingers. *The Secret Garden.* That was another good one.

"Excellent choice," said a voice behind her. She spun, startled, her eyes widening farther when she recognized the silver-haired man in the black vest. "I do beg your pardon," he said, stepping back and holding up his hands. "It was rude of me to be so inquisitive."

For a confused moment she thought his accent was Australian, but then she realized it was more subtle. English. He was watching her with an air of mild concern. She sensed Alan move up beside her, and the man's gaze shifted and changed, a flicker of shock and astonishment passing over his face in an instant.

Oh, damn. She glanced at Alan, but he seemed unconcerned. The man in the black vest was leaning against the wall in a relaxed attitude, arms crossed, but his eyes kept flicking back to Alan.

"I don't know if you've read any of Burnett's adult fiction, but if not, refrain. Appalling melodrama and sticky-sweet in the bargain."

Maybe he wasn't a Controller, then—or maybe he was fiendishly subtle and after them both. *To sell us to the Mole People, no doubt. Paranoia takes too much work.*

She tried a smile. "Sorry. I'll be finished in just a second."

He made a dismissive gesture. "Please take your time. Choosing books should be savored."

She wanted to get away, now. "I'll take those," Moire said to the owner, and handed him her credit chip. He peered, blinking, at the terminal screen, then entered a value on a small personal changer that already had a chip in it. He showed it to her, and she nodded. After processing the payment, he entered a code at the terminal, and then five colored datatabs in succession.

Moire could feel her shoulder muscles tensing as the owner slowly assembled the books and reader in a single package. She turned to go, expecting the man in the black vest would call out or try to stop them, but he didn't.

"How often do you get newswire updates?" she heard him asking the store owner.

She took Alan's arm and walked quickly away, glancing back now and then to see if the man was following them. There was no sign of him, and she relaxed.

"Let's go back to the ship now," she said to Alan. "I've had enough fun for one day."

Moire looked around the crowded galley and decided to stand instead of wedging into the tiny space next to Madele Fortin. "Is the captain coming down to join us?"

"Nah, he'll comm in. Always does. Besides, where you planning on putting him?" Harvey Felden wanted to know. "*She*'s taking up all the extra space," he added, giving Madele a look.

Madele sniffed. "I don't know why you bother showing up, Harvey. I know what you'll say. Too expensive, not enough supplies–if it was up to you we'd never leave port." She was setting up a vid comm on the table in front of her.

Ramutis, on the other side, studied her datapad. "Any other requests? Roberts, you or your son got any ports of interest? Can't guarantee we'll make it, but you can ask."

We can request stops? Moire shrugged. "Nope, nothing for us."

Ramutis nodded. "Makes it easy. Tenna, it doesn't look like we'll get close enough to Chancy to stop there. Maybe next time." Tenna looked disappointed.

The captain's face appeared on the vid screen. "Everybody present, Ramutis?"

"Everybody present, Captain. I just finished the request list."

Davies nodded, his eyes glancing off screen. "Yes, I see it. The jobs we have received are just about the same as last time, except Zen End and Rockwall aren't on it. Anybody know why?"

Yolanda Menehune leaned forward. "Yeah. Ubring's ship is going there regular now. So they're shipping with her."

Everyone digested this news for a moment. "She's welcome to 'em," Gren said gloomily. "Maybe she didn't notice there've been five ships in the last year gone missing around there. I know they say it could be the crabs, but I doubt it. Trouble with large profits is sometimes people want to take them from you."

"We have large profits too, and nobody's tried to take them," Madele pointed out.

"Only because nobody knows where we're going to be, including us," muttered Gren.

"But are we going to Kulvar?" Freddie wanted to know. "It's Yolanda's favorite. Her cargo sells so well there, and the port master hasn't been sober for years!"

"Haul and stow, Freddie," Yolanda said sourly. "You want to do your own shopping?"

"Ooh, that's where you got arrested, wasn't it," said Carlos Montero to Gren, showing interest in the proceedings for the first time. Moire hadn't seen much of Montero; he tended to putter around the repair shop and rarely came to the higher levels. When he did he seemed to be operating in a fog. That was probably why he didn't mind Alan, which was a good thing.

Gren snorted. "Don't be ridiculous; nobody gets arrested on Kulvar. Shot, maybe, but not arrested. You're thinking of Cullen. Extremely law-and-order there." He shook his head in disapproval. Moire wondered what the engineer had done to get arrested. He didn't seem the type, unless you could get arrested for being constantly grumpy.

"Are you sure it wasn't Kulvar? I remember with vividness the trouble we had leaving once, and the lovely Yolanda beating someone over the head with a piece of pipe to get the hatch closed," Freddy added.

"That was Chaim Efer's trouble. Got himself shot up and we had to work double shifts until he got patched up and rested. I'm glad he left; always starting fights, he was." Harvey Felden shook his head.

"If we could get back to the dull routine of work?" Ramutis said with a growl.

On the vid screen Davies waved a hand as if to calm her down. He didn't seem too upset. "There's a new one on the list, too, but I've never heard of it. Cherubim Camp. They want to ship some crates rated sensitive/fragile."

"It's a new mining camp," said Gregor Jadrich immediately. "Just getting started up."

Davies nodded thoughtfully, but looked skeptical. "Long way for a few crates. Won't make much over cost."

"I don't like the coordinates," one of the cargo handlers said with a scowl. "That's too close to the crabs."

"The route is, but not the destination," Davies pointed out. "And there hasn't been any recent activity that I've heard of. They can't get us in drive."

"The camp's going to be big," Jadrich added. "Might want to check it out, think about adding it to our regular route. We shouldn't let Ubring get them all."

"That's a point," agreed Davies. "And it's on the way past Chancey, so if we go Tenna can get her visit home, but it's a stretch. Call a vote, Ramutis."

The only determined vote against was from Felden, who complained about supply costs for the trip. Moire voted in favor, as did the crab-complainer, reluctantly. It looked like she was stuck on *Ayesha* for a while, and a new camp would be hard for her various hunters to find. If the Fringe folk didn't know about it, Fleet and Toren definitely wouldn't.

"Great. Now I gotta re-rig a cargo hold," Yolanda said after the vote. "Sensitive/fragile, and crates to boot. What a hissing leak." She looked even more sullen than usual.

"I can help you set it up," offered Jadrich.

Felden, standing next to Moire, whispered in her ear, "I don't know what drug he's taking but we ought ta take up a collection and get him some more. He hasn't bit anyone for hours!"

"He volunteered for work, too," Moire whispered back. "If he keeps this up people might think he's human."

"Thank you everyone," Davies said. "We have our schedule now. As soon as we get the cargo in and stowed we'll be off." His image vanished from the vid.

The "wild run," as they called it, was hard work but interesting. Many of the camps treated the crew like long-lost family when they showed up. Now they were finally on their way to Cherubim.

Tenna had been excited enough when Davies had agreed they'd be going to her home, and now that they were only one stop away she was almost bouncing off the galley walls. Moire ate and watched her chatter away, amazed at her energy. She would have left, but she was waiting for Yolanda to make the day's coffee.

"...and my *next*-oldest sister, she's been saving up to gestate an embryo just like on Earth. She can't take the time to do it herself, besides, who would want to? It must be horrible. There's a new gestation facility on Pykko, she wants to do it there. Easier to get to."

"Whaddya looking for?" Yolanda looked up from the technically advanced combination coffee grinder/brewer/pot to glare at Montero. He had been holding open the door to a storage locker in the galley and staring at it blankly for some time.

Moire had been wondering the same thing, watching him commune with the storage locker with his usual bemused expression.

"I can't find my large multigrip," he said absently, waving one hand in an abbreviated description of the tool in question.

Yolanda stopped, took a breath, and tried again. "So why try the condiments cupboard?" she asked, looking like she was afraid to hear the answer.

"I already looked in all the places it should be," he answered, with Mad Hatter logic.

Yolanda gripped her tight-curled hair as if she were going to pull it out. "Ancestors guide me...," she moaned.

"Where did you use it last?" Moire asked, trying not to grin. She got up and poured out her share of the coffee.

"Michel borrowed it to set the tension braces for that special cargo," Montero said, rubbing his head. "He brought back all the other tools, but not that one. Maybe he used it somewhere else. It's a good multigrip," he added seriously.

Yolanda picked up her drink bulb and shrugged. "I'll go up and check. He probably didn't look everywhere. Should check on those damn crates anyway." Montero smiled sleepily and wandered out of the galley, glancing from side to side for the missing multigrip as he went.

Tenna hadn't stopped talking. Moire nodded over her coffee, fighting the horrible suspicion she was going to get introduced to every single member of Tenna's growing family. She shuddered, hoping she wasn't getting all this history in preparation as potential mother-in-law.

The short hops they were doing now were just as tiring as the long runs, since greater precision was needed with timing the dropout. She'd overshot two, Davies one. The vagaries of *Ayesha*'s drives were even more apparent in quick bursts. *Maybe it's the rampup that's causing the trouble. I should ask Gren to run a Marshall plot of the main drive, that would show it....*

"Are you going to gestate any more kids?" Tenna asked, and Moire choked on her coffee.

"One's enough for me," she said with feeling.

"You could afford it right now, at least when you get your payout at the end of the route," Tenna pointed out enviously. "Pilots get a lot, and Ramutis said we did really good this time."

"I don't know if I get–"

Yolanda stalked into the galley, breathing heavily through her nose. "We been suckered, damn their microscopic seal-compromised hearts. Delicate equipment, my grey hair! They're shipping empty crates!"

Moire turned, feeling uneasy. "What do you mean, empty crates?"

"I was just making sure their precious cargo was OK. When I was looking for Montero's stupid multigrip, I saw one of the lids was undogged. I thought hey, better make sure nobody diddled with it, right? Damn crate is empty, except for some empty wrappers and other trash. They're going to claim we stole it and...."

Moire felt a sudden stab of fear in her gut. She got up and stuck her head out in the corridor. It was quiet. She went back in and straight for the comm. They were headed to an unknown camp, and Tenna had just pointed out they were at the end of the run–lots of untraceable cash, instead of cargo to get rid of. She'd wondered how anybody could have attacked a ship in drive when Gren had mentioned the missing ships earlier. Now she thought she knew.

Yolanda was staring at her. "What the hell?"

"Ever consider the possibility those crates weren't empty when we loaded them?" Moire said grimly, punching the comm.

"I told 'em we needed that scanner fixed." Yolanda started to swear in a language she didn't recognize.

"Gren here," said the voice on the comm. "What's up?"

"Lock up your area," Moire snapped. "I think we've been infiltrated. Yolanda just found the crates for Cherubim open and empty."

Silence, then a distant clang heard through the comm. "Shut the emergency doors. I'm putting the reactor on manual override only, this console. Roberts, you have to get to the bridge before they do. They've probably got people waiting for us at the dropout."

Well. At least she hadn't been imagining things. "We got any weapons on board?"

"Captain's office. Lockbox keyed to him and Ramutis. Find Montero if you can; he knows his way around the ship, ways they won't know. Get moving–I'll contact the others."

"You by yourself there?" It was only a suspicion, but her guess was the pirates had some inside help.

"Yes. And I'm going to keep it that way." That was good. One less thing to worry about.

"Roberts out." She punched the comm again, this time for Montero, as she rummaged through the kitchen for weapons. The display flashed as it rerouted to a remote, the usual response since Montero was rarely in one place. It connected, but there was no sound except for a rhythmic, keening noise.

"Montero? Are you there?"

"She's bleeding, bleeding...what do I do? Oh God...Ren, someone shot Madele!" he sobbed.

Confirmation that she really didn't want. "Carlos. Look around her. Do you see her kit?"

"Uhh...yes!" he gasped.

"Open it and find the bloodglue packet. It's blue." At least it should be, if first aid was the same as on military ships. "Where is she hit?"

Carlos choked. "Chest. It's bad, Ren."

Moire grimaced. "Do the best you can. Where are you?"

"Level four. I didn't see anyone! Who could have done this?"

There just wasn't enough time–they could already be on the bridge. She could ask him if he knew a shortcut, but for all she knew the pirates had hacked the communications system already. "Find a safe place for both of you, out of sight. I'll send help as soon as I can." She cut the connection and turned back to Yolanda, standing guard at the door to the galley. Tenna was whimpering softly with fright in a corner nearby.

Moire heard the sound of running feet, and Alan burst in the door, his eyes wide.

"Someone is screaming!" he gasped. "Up there!" He pointed in the direction of the stairs to the next level.

"Did you see anyone on the way here?" Moire asked. He shook his head. She looked about quickly. "OK, everybody grab a knife. We're going to have to do this the hard way."

The next level was quiet when they went up the stairs, but a trail of blood showed trouble had preceded them. How many did they have to deal with?

"Yolanda. How big were those crates?" Moire whispered as they went.

"If they had more than two apiece, they were really good friends. For five days." So, maybe eight. Not counting any of the crew who were in on it. She peered cautiously around a corner. Harvey Felden, carrying a heavy wrench in one hand and a piece of metal rod in the other, was running down the corridor toward them. If those were the only weapons he had, he wasn't one of the pirates. Besides, he looked terrified.

"Psst! Harvey!" He started, then hobbled toward them.

"I'm going to have a word with that—"

"Oh, shut up already," snarled Yolanda. The hand with the knife was shaking.

"Quiet." Moire started to run up the corridor. Gunfire, up ahead. Maybe the others had gotten to the bridge, and the captain had opened the weapons locker. Or maybe the bad guys had gotten there first.

Alan shouted, and she spun around. A stranger was standing in a cross-corridor—one of the pirates. Moire saw the rifle in the woman's hand and ducked instinctively as the bullets smacked into the wall beside her, sending splinters of metal that stung and cut. Alan screamed and launched himself at the pirate, flailing and swiping at the gun. Taken by surprise, the woman lost her grip on the weapon and it fell to the floor.

The pirate backed up, pulling out a smaller handgun. Alan scooped up the fallen weapon and fired in one smooth motion. More shouting, from the corridor ahead, and three more armed strangers appeared. Alan fired again, three shots. Three very accurate shots.

Moire stared at the dead pirates, frozen with shock. *How'd he do that?* She put up a hand to the hot stickiness on her face, and it came away wet and red. A scalp wound, messy but not fatal. Alan didn't know that, though. He was running past the crumpled body of the woman in the corridor, crying.

"Don't be broken! Don't!" He grabbed her and almost knocked her off her feet. He was staring in horror at her face.

"I'll be OK, kid. I just don't look good right now." She glanced down at the first pirate, feeling dizzy. She recognized her now. The woman who had been with Gregor at Angelos.

"This low-tech colony he's from don't mind guns? They sure taught him how to shoot," said Harvey, in a dry voice. He had a point. The pirates had all been shot in the same location, like target dummies. This hadn't been the first time Alan had picked up a gun.

Moire avoided Harvey Felden's questioning look by stooping to take the pistol from the pirate's hand. "OK, people. Grab a weapon and let's take back our ship."

CHAPTER 17
LUX AETERNA

Alan was moving through the corridors like a trained soldier: hugging the wall, checking intersections before entering them, always with his gun pointed ahead. Moire resolutely refused to think about what that meant. She had to get the ship secure.

She looked at the handgun she held and grimaced. Someone in this crowd had to be able to hit what they aimed at, and it wasn't going to be her. From what she'd seen the others might even be worse. Except for Yolanda–but she was so twitchy she'd probably shoot anything that moved.

Her handgun was more to intimidate the enemy, and she could do that without using it. Especially if she had Alan to back her up.

The ship was quiet, and had been ever since the firefight. They moved quickly up the next set of stairs, cautious and silent. Moire peeked around the corner to the entrance to the bridge, which had a small set of steps. Ramutis was sprawled halfway down them, blood pooled about her and smeared down the side of the wall.

"She's hurt bad!" Harvey gasped and moved for the stairs. Moire grabbed his arm and pulled him back.

"Part of her head is missing. Hurt isn't the word." Moire watched the opening to the bridge carefully. Harvey had spoken quietly enough the pirates might not have heard him. She thought she could see motion on the bridge, and she could hear voices, but nobody came out to investigate.

She considered the first mate's body, wondering what had happened, and what Ramutis had been trying to do. She'd been killed on the stairs, that was clear, and facing her attackers. Defending the bridge. Why? To buy time for the captain to open the weapons locker?

It didn't seem to have worked. She crouched down, thinking furiously, and the others gathered about her. "We have to get them out of there," Moire whispered. "If we go shooting up the bridge now, in drive...."

"Right," said Yolanda. "This ship doesn't need any help falling apart."

Moire took a deep breath. "Get ready. And please don't shoot me, OK?" She stuffed the handgun in a side pocket, hoping the bulge wasn't too recognizable, and scrubbed the blood off her face with one sleeve. Her scalp was still bleeding, but it only had to look normal for a few seconds.

Staying close to the corner for a quick retreat, Moire stood and stepped away from the wall. Nodding to the others still in hiding, she raised her voice. "Ramutis! What happened?"

Hasty steps from the bridge, and an armed figure appeared in the entrance. Moire gaped at him, spreading her empty hands in the air, then spun around and ran as noisily as she could, yelling. She heard the sharp crack of a gun as she went around the corner, and the sound of a bullet hitting the far wall.

Alan was already taking aim. He got the first pirate who took the bait, Yolanda the second. A third pirate took up a position inside the bridge entrance, the muzzle of her rifle protruding. Alan soon made her retreat to a more secure location. Moire was pretty sure he'd wounded her.

After that, no motion was visible from the bridge entrance. Harvey gripped his weapon close, looking desperate. "We are going to be dropping out soon, aren't we?" he whispered, his voice shaking.

"You're assuming the captain is at the controls, and cooperating."

"One of them might know how to do it," he persisted. Moire doubted that very much. One of the surviving pirates might have a little web piloting, but flying *Ayesha* was an entirely different matter. Still, the pirates might *think* they knew how, and that was dangerous too.

The minutes stretched on. An increasingly insistent, annoying beeping noise was coming from the bridge now. Moire looked at Harvey, puzzled, but he just shrugged. She could hear shouting now, the voices angry and desperate.

She put a hand over her stomach, feeling the rhythmic pulses she had thought were from nausea, or shock. *That's not me—that's the drive.* "We've got to take the bridge!" Moire yelled, and waved the others on. "The drive's unstable!"

The pirates must have set the hold-steady when they took over the bridge. She ran for the steps, but Alan was ahead of her. She should have told him to stay behind...and what would that have done? They could still all die if they didn't stop the drive.

Alan was shooting as he ran, Yolanda beside him. Moire followed them in, running blindly for the pilot's pit. She stumbled over a body and fell down the stairs, grabbing the railing just in time to stop her fall. She heard more firing as she scrambled up and grabbed the legs, disengaging the hold-steady. As soon as she did, the legs jerked violently out of her hands.

With all her strength she could not pull them back. What the hell had they locked on to? There weren't any black holes in this sector, but that's what it felt like. The oscillations were getting worse. She didn't have a real star to aim for, and the ship was getting damaged.

She changed her tactics and tried to center on the unknown gravity node, attempting to steady the drive. The ship shuddered. Motion on a monitor caught her eye, and she swore. The coupling readout, the closest thing to a speed indicator in webspace they had, was ratcheting at unreal values–and climbing.

A heavy pulse of gravity buckled her knees, followed by a wave of weightlessness. Another gravity pulse, heavier than the first, and then the weightlessness that followed remained. Moire felt the collapse of the gravity bubble internally, sharp and hard, and she looked at the coupling readout. Zero.

Well, that solves that problem. She pulled herself to the edge of the pit, looking up. Alan and Yolanda were floating by the captain's chair. Nobody was shooting. Alan had caught a stray bullet along one forearm, but the wound didn't look serious.

Captain Davies was still in his chair. He'd been tied down tightly with plastic webbing. His eyes were open, staring, and Moire could see no sign he was breathing. Blood formed a cloud about his mouth, more blood down the front of his shirt. Yolanda cried angrily, trying to untie Davies with one hand while hanging onto the chair with the other.

Tenna screamed, curled up in a ball and floating. "There's no air, there's no air!"

"We gotta get to the lifeboat!" Harvey was pale and sweating, arms and legs thrashing vainly. "They musta set off that contact bomb!"

"We just lost gravity!" Moire shouted. *Probably not something they encounter that often these days.* "Calm down, everybody. Look at the board, Harvey. The hull is intact." She pulled herself up from the pit, clutching the rail. "Tenna, are you hurt? Any more hit? How many were up here?"

Alan was much more calm than the other three, but he had a puzzled expression on his face. "I think they are all.... Where is down?" He flailed, losing his grip on the chair and sailing away slowly. Moire twisted and snagged one of his legs, pulling him down beside her.

"Down is broken," she said, "Hold on to something, or you'll float." She looked about. Two more pirates up here, the woman who had shot at the door and another man. The body she had stumbled over getting to the pit was drifting underfoot, and she nudged it over. "Gregor. Somehow I'm not surprised."

Yolanda cursed, viciously. "You see? You see what they did? They tied the captain down and beat him, and the seizures killed him. They didn't even know. He couldn't have told them anything if he wanted to."

Moire pushed off for the far wall, scrabbling for purchase when she hit it. There wasn't much to hold on to near the wall comm, and she had to punch the code for Engineering quite gently to avoid pushing herself away.

"Gren, we've got the bridge. Ramutis and Davies are dead. Do you have any good news for me?"

"What the hell were you doing, Roberts?" Gren nearly screamed.

"Trying to blow us up?"

"I had to stabilize before dropping out," Moire snapped. "There was some kind of gravitational anomaly that snagged the alignment. I couldn't move anything, then the gravity went apeshit and died. What's the status?"

Gren was cursing, with a hysterical edge to his voice. "I can't get a response from the trim nodes. Nothing. Main node gives a precursor pulse but it's tiny, all out of whack, and it won't build to drive level no matter what I do."

"Never mind the trim. Find out what's wrong with the main node. Is the engine stable?"

"OK for now." His voice calmed as he took a deep breath. "It was touch and go there when the nodes went, but it's holding level. I'll look at the nodes." He closed the connection, and Moire turned. Tenna was trying and failing to control her retching. Moire didn't know if it was the weightlessness or the bodies bothering her. The metallic smell of blood filled the air.

"Somebody needs to go find Montero and Fortin," she said. "And see if anybody else is hurt. Tenna, did Madele give you any medic training?" Tenna shook her head, looking miserable. *Damn. Why did they have to shoot our only medic?* "All right, you stay here and watch the door. The rest of you search the ship and get help to Fortin."

"Why? What's wrong?" Harvey was looking pale.

"Madele was shot," Moire said shortly. "Montero is with her, and has her medical kit." Harvey spun away, grabbing at any available surface to propel himself toward the door.

"Why can't you go too?" Yolanda wanted to know. "We don't know we got 'em all. What are you gonna do here?"

Moire turned back to the pit instrumentation. "I have to figure out where the hell we are."

She didn't mention that it might not matter. If Gren couldn't get the gravity nodes active again, there was nothing they could do but wait and run out of supplies.

It took a long time to search the ship, since everyone was having trouble moving around. It took her a long time to figure out where they were, and when she finally did she stared at the coordinates in disbelief, the sinking feeling in her gut mixing with her astonishment at how fast they had traveled. That had to be a speed record—but since they were stuck in the middle of nowhere nobody was going to hear about it.

Through it all she heard the rest of the crew as they searched the ship. They'd found Madele Fortin, still alive. One of the cargo handlers had been found dead in the hold where the pirates' crates had been stowed. Michel had been shot and left for dead, but only had a broken arm and a graze on his head. A few even came to clean up the bridge, which was a little too full of floating blood and bodies. Eventually the entire ship was searched, and people started gathering in the galley. She decided to join them and break the news gently.

In zero-g the galley was not nearly so crowded, and there were fewer of them. Harvey Felden was in the medical bay watching over Madele Fortin, who was still clinging grimly to life. She had regained consciousness long enough to give some directions on her own care.

That was the one bright spot in the whole disaster. Looking at the crew, Moire could see they thought it was only a matter of time before they were all dead, Madele included. The loss of the captain had shaken them badly. Montero was still weeping, shaking his head, and rubbing his eyes as if trying to wake up from a nightmare.

Moire nodded at Gren, who cleared his throat. "I'm afraid it's bad, people. It may have just been coincidence, or something the oscillations caused, but the trim nodes failed catastrophically in drive. They're fused—I can't even get diagnostic feedback. It looks like the failure combined with the oscillations did something to the main node. There's a precursor pulse but it's so out of synch I can't do anything with it."

"What do you think the problem is?" Moire asked.

Gren shrugged. "If we're lucky, it's just the sustaining feedback circuit, but I doubt that's the only thing wrong. I'd have to go outside the hull and move some major components if it isn't, and we don't have the people or the equipment to do it." He looked away, his face working with emotion.

This was not looking very hopeful. She wanted to remind them things could be worse before she hit them with the rest of it, or they'd give up completely. "OK, that's our drive status. Good news is Gren has the engine reactor going, so we have power and realspace mobility. And the hull is intact." They were staring at her now, daring her to make them hope. She took a deep breath and plunged ahead. "When the drive went unstable, we picked up a link to a gravitational anomaly. It pulled us off course. *Way* off course. We are now in the region of Lambda Velorum, and as far as I can tell, at least fifty light-years away from anyone who cares."

She didn't mention the crabs and hoped nobody else would either. For all she knew it was perfectly safe, but few humans ever came this way. The lack of G-type stars had made it a low priority in exploration, which was one reason it had taken her so long to find out where they were.

The others took the news numbly, only their eyes showing the shock.

"I've got the distress signal on just in case, but our only real hope is getting that node going again." She took a look at the crew. Alan seemed to be handling it the best, probably because he didn't understand what was going on. The rest had expressions that ranged from despondent to suicidal. *Gotta do something about that fast, or we may as well blow up the ship now and avoid the wait.* "Who is senior on the ship now?"

Gren slowly raised his head. "I am." He gave her a long, gloomy look. "What do you want me to do? We aren't going to survive this. It doesn't matter who's in charge."

"I've seen worse." She closed her eyes briefly, forcing away the memory of *what* she'd seen.

"Really." His expression was skeptical, and Moire gritted her teeth.

Loosening the seal at one wrist, she pulled up the stiff fabric of her shipsuit to show the scars on her arm. "Yes. Really." She'd worry about the wrong people hearing about them if they got back to a port. "We've got air. The ship's in one piece. I didn't even have that when I got these." *But I did have a working gravity node.* Well, they were just going to have to fix it somehow. She wasn't going to let this crew die if she could help it. Once was enough.

"You think we can get back?" Michel asked, a thread of hope in his voice.

"We have a better chance if we do something instead of sitting on our hands waiting to die," she said bluntly.

"So what would you do, then?" Gren asked.

"Find out what's really wrong with the node. Then go through all the equipment we have—the cargo, Freddie's junk, anything—and see if we can't jigger a fix. It only has to last to the nearest settlement."

Gren nodded, looking thoughtful. "Any objections to the captain's plan?" he asked finally, looking at the rest of the crew.

Now wait a minute.... "Hey! You can't do that, *you're* the senior—"

"Yes, I am." He was looking pleased with himself. "That means I get to decide what's in the best interest of the ship and crew. I've got experience with gravitics, so I fix them. You've got experience surviving."

"But...," Moire spluttered, then noticed some of the crew were actually grinning. A bit shakily, but they were grinning. She did *not* want to be stuck with the responsibility. Besides, Gren knew the ship, the people, and he wasn't eighty years out of date.

"We should do this properly, yes? For the luck, and with respect for Captain Davies," said Freddie. "All in favor of Captain Roberts?" He raised his hand, and the rest of the crew followed. Alan looked to one side, then the other, and raised his hand too.

"Double pay, since you're captain and pilot," Yolanda pointed out. "But you can't spend it until you get us to a port. How's that for motivation?" Someone laughed.

I don't know why, but it seems to cheer them up. Moire sighed. "All right, but only until we're out of this, OK?" So they wanted her to be captain, did they? Time to start her regime by handing out orders. "Somebody help Michel get to the medical bay."

"But I want to help," Michel protested.

He could barely get around now with only one working arm, and he couldn't do much more than that, but everybody needed to be busy with something.

"You will. First tell Harvey you'll be watching Madele, and then you are going to find the manual for the medical scanner and start reading. Got that?" He nodded vigorously. "Yolanda, I want you and Harvey listing supplies. Everything in the whole damn ship. Freddie, help them out with your stuff. Tenna, get some rope or cargo webbing and start running it along the corridors so people have something to grab on to. The rest of you report to Gren. I'll be on the bridge figuring out where we want to go." Ah, the power of delegation. She looked around. "Everybody got that? OK, get moving."

Moire waited for a moment to let the crowd sort itself out, not wanting to be kicked. She heard Gren tell Montero and some others to start moving some equipment, and then he swam awkwardly over to her. "Some things I need to show you on the bridge," was all he would say.

She launched herself out of the galley and headed up. The stairs were easy; they had railings. The long corridor to the bridge was bare, though, and took some work. Unlike the rest of the crew, she had lots of practice with zero-g maneuvering.

Moire launched herself at an angle with a gentle push, slowly rotating herself as she drifted forward. Her feet were beneath her when she approached the far wall, and she pushed off again toward the other wall, again at an angle. A few more tacks and she was able to grab the edge of the bridge doorway.

Gren followed, grunting when he hit the wall hard. The bridge had been cleaned, but Davies's body was still in his chair.

"What should we do about him?" The pirates had been cycled out of the ship disposal system, but Moire supposed they would want to treat the captain differently.

"Poor Beaufort," Gren said softly, his rough brown face twisting with sorrow. "He didn't deserve to go like that." He shook his head, struggling to regain his composure. His long black hair floated in waves about his head. "Store him in a refrigeration unit, I suppose. He's got family. But first...." He made his way with awkward, flailing movements to the chair. Grimacing with distaste, he removed the captain's earring.

He really was determined to make her captain. "Ah, Gren—that's not necessary."

"Yes it is," he said shortly. "Where'd he keep the control...right, the leg pocket. Here. You'll need these to open the safe."

Moire took the earring and a metal band with reluctance. "Why do I need to open the safe?"

"Some of the holds are secured, and he kept the keys there. We'll probably have to do a main system restart if we retune the node. Need the ship code for that."

The earring was made of small, flexible sections, with the communications electronics built into a thicker segment in the back. It was a master commlink. The metal band Gren had given her was made of flat square plates, and each had some kind of interface setting or display. It had fasteners so it could be worn as a bracelet. Davies hadn't worn it that way, but he'd avoided wearing anything that constricted him with the exception of the earring. Now she knew why he wore that.

Gren moved to the bridge office. "Bring it here, I'll show you how the safe works."

The office had a lived-in feel, especially now that all the little pieces were starting to drift from their original places. One corner had a net of cargo webbing covered with a piece of thick, soft padding. A blanket was neatly folded on top of a wide pillow.

The safe had a hand-shaped indentation with touchplates at the tips of the fingers. It also had a retina scan.

"Aren't we going to need him to...."

Gren shook his head. "With his condition biometrics didn't work too well. He had the safe modified. It recognizes the person wearing the captain's earring and touching the plate. Sends low-level voltage signals. There's a pressure code, too." Moire put the earring on, and Gren demonstrated how to use the touchpad to set the code.

The faceplate of the safe clicked, pushed out, and then rotated up and in. The interior held datatabs and textsheets and a sheaf of hardcopy. A pullout rack held a range of plastic keytabs, each labeled with the number of a hold. Moire took them out. "Give these to Harvey. He'll need them."

"We've got the manifests."

"We didn't have pirates listed on the manifest, did we? I want him to open the crates."

Gren nodded. "Good point. I'll tell him. You'll probably want to set the main channel to auto," he said, pointing to the control bracelet.

This was more than she'd expected. As far as he was concerned she really was the captain, and it made her uncomfortable. Moire hesitated, looking at him. "You didn't need me to open the safe," she said finally.

"Someone else needs to know how," Gren answered.

"That's a lot of trust for someone you haven't known that long," Moire said.

He looked at her with his usual dour expression. "On this ship we get a lot of people coming through. You learn to read them after a while. You're a strange one, Roberts, and your son, too—but there isn't anyone on this ship that doesn't have secrets. What's important is what you do here. You've saved us before, that's all we care about. Just keep doing that, all right?"

Gren left, and Moire went to shut the safe again. The key tray wouldn't go in all the way, and she shifted some of the contents to make more room. A flash of familiar color caught her eye—purple-blue edging, on a textcard. She picked it up. A Fleet document? Here? Textcards were used for things like licenses, or registration, that had to be kept separate for some reason. Who on the ship had a connection to Fleet?

She scrolled up the header, feeling suddenly cold as she read. *"Ilyana Ramutis. Dishonorable discharge...cowardice under fire...."* Now things that had puzzled her started to make sense. Ramutis reacting so strongly to her Fleet shipsuit and her suicidal stand defending the bridge. Refuting the charge.

She didn't have to worry about Ramutis reporting her now. Moire tucked the discharge underneath, out of view, and shut the safe. Ramutis must have given it to Davies to keep secure after showing him. Gren had been right about Ramutis, anyway. Nobody else had even mentioned it, so she presumed Davies had kept her secret. So would she.

She pushed off carefully to the pilot's pit. Trouble was, the black book didn't keep a record of a place's population. It did, however, have an additional realspace section with approach planes and station configurations. Going to a mining outpost wouldn't help much. They'd still be on limited supplies since the outposts wouldn't have enough extra, and ships didn't show up that frequently. They needed to find something a little bigger if they could, but as close as possible. There wasn't anything close enough for a single run with one pilot, though. If they got the nodes up, they'd have to last for a while.

It was tedious work—looking up the nearest points, referencing back to see if they had a station. She heard the sound of someone approaching and looked up with relief, glad of the distraction.

Alan's head appeared over the rail of the pit. He pulled himself down beside her, using the stair edges. He looked troubled.

"Shouldn't you be with Montero and Gren?"

Alan shook his head, and his rough-cut hair swirled. "Gren is doing something all by himself. He told us to go rest and he would call us when he finished." He wrapped one arm about a post and the other about his knees. "I don't like the Game anymore," he said, his voice wavering. "It isn't working. I want...I don't want them to be angry with me."

Moire stared at him, astonished. His expression was worried, lurking fear and apprehension in his eyes. "Why would they be angry with you? What makes you think that?"

"They look at me sometimes, and they talk soft so I can't hear. Is it because I took the gun without paying? I tried to give it back, but she wouldn't take it because she is broken."

He'd used that term before. "Dead, Alan. Not broken. Dead." He was hiding his face now, shaking. Moire felt a cold chill run over her. What *was* he? "Nobody is angry with you, Alan. You saved our lives. That was a very brave thing you did, grabbing that gun. When we get gravity back I should show you how to do some hand-to-hand fighting, though. You're good with a rifle, but–"

"It's not the same!" he burst out, anguished. "It doesn't change back! They aren't getting up again, they are staying broken!"

"What should they do?" Moire asked carefully. Afraid of the answer.

He looked at her, perplexed. "Sometimes they aren't there, when you come out of the box. Like Michel's game. Sometimes they are real, and when the training is over they get back up again."

"Would this be the special training you mentioned?" Alan froze, then slowly nodded. Moire felt ill. Some warped person had trained Alan to kill using simulations, but hadn't taught him the difference between the sims and reality. Alan hadn't realized what he was doing when he shot the pirates.

She closed her eyes, breathing deeply until she thought she could control her voice. "Alan. This is going to be a little complicated, all right? The people who were fighting us were trying to kill us. Make us dead. We stopped them by making them dead instead. They were real people, just like you and me. Now that they are dead, they won't get up again. Ever. Just like Captain Davies won't get up again."

Alan shot a horrified glance up at the captain's chair. "But he wasn't...."

"He was quite sick. They hit him, and that was enough."

Now he was crying. "Everything is so different," he whispered. Moire pushed out of the chair and drifted beside him. Holding onto the railing with one hand, she put her other arm around him.

He started violently, eyes wide.

"What's wrong? Are you hurt?"

"They don't...the Controllers don't let us...." He looked away.

"There are no Controllers on this ship," Moire said flatly. "I won't allow any, either, and I'm the captain now." She put her arm around him again, slowly and gently. He didn't pull away this time, but she could feel his tension.

"Did the Controllers say why you were doing the special training?"

He wiped at his face, roughly. "I finished growing early. So they could start me then, and not wait until I was seven."

Moire felt like she had been punched. *Dear God, they were doing this when he was a child. Finished growing? Before he was seven?*

"Alan." He glanced up. "How old are you?" He was silent, hunched. She could feel him shaking.

"Before I...before I saw you, they said, 'Eight years. He will be ready for use soon.'"

Someday, if she survived, she was going to get extremely angry at someone. Violently angry. But she couldn't do that now, it would only frighten Alan. *Eight years.* That was the date on his arm cuff, the one she hadn't thought was real. That was the answer to the puzzle. He acted like a child because he was one. A child in an adult body. A child who knew how to kill like a professional but didn't understand death.

Someone is going to regret this.

So many questions. Who had done this, and for what purpose? How had they done it? Eight years old, and fully grown at seven. The questions would have to wait. Alan was hurting *now.*

He was making suppressed keening noises, straining with the effort to silence himself. Moire held him tighter, worried. He twisted suddenly and buried his face in her shoulder, wrapping both arms around her with all his strength. Moire gasped for air, ribs aching, as he sobbed.

She concentrated on keeping them both anchored, wishing more than anything in the world that she knew how to comfort him. She didn't know the words to say, so she just held him until he quieted.

They sat together, silent, for some time. Then Alan shifted, looking up at her with his reddened, damp face. "Will there be more pirates?"

He didn't seem worried, just curious. "I don't think so. Nobody knows where we are."

"Good. If I have to help Gren I can't be with you."

Moire smiled, shaky with relief. "You have to be with me if there are pirates?"

Alan reached up and touched her head where she had been wounded. "Lorai said not to let anyone hurt you," he said simply, as if no other explanation was needed. "So if there are pirates, you tell me."

She managed to persuade Alan to sleep in the captain's hammock, promising to wake him when she was done, and dug back into her work.

Finally Moire finished her search of the black book, noting down the few candidates on a datapad she'd found in the captain's desk. The closest was over a week's flight with a direct lock and stable drives. That was Gren's problem. If he could fix the node, she would fly it. Somehow.

She hadn't heard anything but a few exchanges on the earring, so it sounded like not much progress had been made. She should check on the others, maybe get something to eat. Now that she thought about it, she was starving. When had she last eaten?

She floated by the signals position on her way out. She grabbed the chair to stop herself. Remembering Alan's worry about pirates, she snorted. They should be so lucky–she'd be willing to fight them if they had a working ship she could steal. Still, why not see if there were any signals out there?

The board took her a few minutes to figure out, but it had enough similarities to the fighter communications panel that she got it eventually.

Nothing on the main channels. She keyed in some of the military frequencies using the compression sequences she remembered–nothing there either.

She checked the distress broadcast; it was still running. On a whim, she turned the reception to the distress band. The communications deck automatically filtered out their own signal, but she still heard something–a faint but unmistakable voice.

"...esteran Pride, location...ese respond. Wester...ide...coordinate...ond."

She activated the locator on the communication panel display. When she saw the coordinates Moire fumbled at the control bracelet. She could use the captain's earring to call out, if she could figure out how. Struggling with the bracelet, she entered Harvey's code. She didn't want to bother Gren if he was in the middle of fixing the nodes, and Montero would just frustrate her with his fogginess.

"Can you get to the bridge?" she asked when Harvey answered. "I'm picking up a distress signal, and it's right ahead of us."

CHAPTER 18
OTHER DUTIES AS ASSIGNED

Ennis didn't see much of Namur after the second meeting. A junior aide went through an exhaustive debriefing, and then handed him off to the specialists. Some of the training was exactly what he had expected–encrypting transmissions, signal surveillance, personal close-quarters combat. The rest was more specialized. A detailed description of all the different activities Toren was involved with took an entire day, and those were the legal ones. He doubted Tendo Berens was involved with any of them.

The personal combat training was grueling, but Ennis didn't complain. He wanted as much as he could get before they sent him out again. "Commando fighting without the toys," was what his instructor called it. He was pleased to find that he had not forgotten everything he learned on Fimbul. There were some dirty fighting techniques even the instructor didn't know.

At the end of one intense session he found Master Gunnery Sergeant Inahosa Hsa-Li waiting for him. She was holding the scan-resistant gun in the palm of one broad, capable hand. Namur had taken it for examination, turning it over to Hsa-Li as one of the best weapons experts FarCom had.

She didn't look happy. "Next time capture the user manual too, OK? This has too many features and no labels."

"Sorry, Gunny. He must have swallowed it," he said, deadpan. "I hadn't been to spy school then. Were there any surprises?"

"It would have been nice to know that selecting the energy blast means an automatic switch to hairtrigger settings *before* I tried it," she said with a repressive glance. "I'm sure the deck needed resurfacing, but it also took out some of the signal cable in the conduit below."

"Anything important?"

"Just the decompression alarm interlocks for the emergency doors," she said with careful restraint. "I doubt anybody noticed, it was only prime-cycle lunch time."

Ennis fought to keep from grinning. "I thought the weapons range has reinforced decking for just that purpose."

Hsa-Li gave him a withering look. "It did, Commander Ennis. Note the use of the past tense. It turns out to have different energy settings," she continued. "Not just one. You get more than one shot if it isn't set to maximum power."

Ennis turned it over in his hands, sobered by the implications. That was an impressive amount of energy from such a small weapon. It could take out a section of hull, or an airlock door. "Why doesn't it have biometric security? You'd think they'd want to make sure nobody could use it but them."

Hsa-Li glanced about the now-empty practice room and lowered her voice. "Think about it, Commander. You're a spy now too, like it or not. A biolock is traceable back to the owner and as good as an admission of guilt if the gun is used. This," she said, hefting the translucent gun, "is anonymous. It even has a coating–fingerprints, skin flakes, nothing sticks. A real top-end weapon. It may be unique, custom-designed for the operative you took it from. I've never seen anything like it before."

This was not good news. If Master Gunnery Sergeant Hsa-Li hadn't seen it before, it was probably because it hadn't existed.

"This may be more trouble than it's worth, Gunny. Don't you have something less experimental I can use instead?"

Hsa-Li cocked her head, giving him a steady, considering look. "If Namur thinks you need it, you do. He knows his business." Coming from her, that was high praise indeed–and unexpected from someone military speaking of civilian intelligence. Perhaps working for Namur wouldn't be so bad. "Now would the commander like to hear what else I've learned about this gun, or would he prefer to figure it out for himself?"

He knew it was getting close to the end when Namur's aide set up an isolated system, put in a restricted datacube containing the less publicly-known activity of Toren, then sat down and watched him. Ennis set a filter for locations in and around the Fringe. Umbra had been interested in Toren's activities for many years, and there was a lot to sort through.

The report on the crab scout ship that had been captured distracted him for a moment, especially the notation that Toren had taken over investigation of the ship and remains of the crew. *Keep your mind on your work. That can't have anything to do with Cameron.* It was not the only instance where Toren had involved itself with crab-related information. There was also a disturbing list of independent transports and small colonies that had been bought out, intimidated, or just plain taken over by Toren.

The reports usually mentioned locations well on the trading and mining routes, names he was somewhat familiar with. Except for one, a few lines about a suspicious amount of medical equipment being transported by

Toren to Kerezin. He looked it up. Kerezin was almost the farthest human outpost, and tiny. "100 crates. Contents labeled 'biogeneration vessels, food grade' but are in fact gestation tanks," read the report. That was *extremely* strange. Maybe someone had just gotten a code wrong–the ship he'd been posted to before *Canaveral* had gotten a crate of landscaping equipment because someone had transposed two digits. Toren must not be immune from administrative brain seizures either.

All he'd really learned was Toren had a presence in the Fringe, more than he'd thought. His suspicious side wondered why there was no mention of any information Toren had gathered from all that crab material after they'd taken over. Maybe that just hadn't been included in the file. He hoped so, anyway. He'd have to question their motives otherwise.

He reported one last time to Pol Namur's office. When Namur greeted him, Ennis sensed a subtle tension in his voice–his face remained in shadow, unreadable. Then he saw the snoop-sweep device. It was so out of place he almost didn't recognize it. The head of Umbra, in the heart of FarCom, felt the need to run a snoop-sweep. It was extremely disturbing.

"Now begins the...interesting time," Namur said softly. "The dangerous time. You might say you have not had enough preparation, and you would be correct. The one advantage we have over our opponent is surprise, and if we wait, that advantage will be lost. This is my advice to you–always keep them off balance. You have shown an aptitude for quick assessment and action. That is the best weapon you have."

"And the gun?" Ennis still felt reluctant to carry it.

Namur smiled, a slight curve of his thin lips. "Simply knowing that you have it will unsettle them. I suggest revealing that information only *in extremis*. For your own safety, I thought it best you should have it. I do not know the full extent of Toren's detection technology, but they made that gun to evade it. That has been the eternal dilemma of weapons–they can be turned against their makers." He placed a textcard and a datatab on the desk before Ennis. "These orders authorize you to investigate and track down the mutineers. In the event you need additional assistance, you are empowered to request it from the nearest Fleet post. This," he tapped the textcard, "permits you to travel on any regular courier. If you need to travel to a location the couriers do not go, there are funds available. I am afraid you are mostly on your own for this, Commander Ennis. While the mutiny investigation would permit additional personnel, the risk to your other mission is too great."

Ennis nodded, keeping his face carefully blank. Namur had probably already arranged for someone to follow him. He was after something too important to permit a barely-trained intelligence officer to handle alone. "How soon will Toren find out about my itinerary?"

Namur chuckled. "I imagine someone will be indiscreet...oh, perhaps a day after you leave FarCom. It then depends on how alert their agents are." He tapped at his desk console, inserted a datatab, tapped again, then took the datatab out and handed it to Ennis. "I had inquiries made at Thuban about all ships leaving after our mysterious friend was sighted. It was not always possible to determine if they had a new pilot aboard."

Inserting the tab in his datapad, Ennis scanned the listed data. There weren't that many ships, since Thuban was so remote. What ship would Cameron be most likely to take? One that wouldn't advertise a new pilot. One that wouldn't go anywhere near a Fleet station. He flagged four ships, then removed one that had returned to Thuban.

"So, where do you intend to start?" Namur asked, with an expression of polite interest.

"Wherever I can get to first," he replied, showing Namur his list.

Namur raised his eyebrows. "Rather distant, aren't they?"

"She will be wanting to avoid notice if she can."

Namur was silent for a moment, studying the list, then turned to the desk console. "There are no direct couriers, of course. But Sandero is not far from two on your list. From there you should be able to arrange transportation." He extended his hand.

For the first time, Ennis noticed the prosthetic bioplastic webbing extending along the back of his hand and disappearing under his sleeve. Namur had been wounded so badly they could not reconstruct, requiring implants and the control webbing to restore the use of his arm. Ennis grasped the offered hand. "Good luck. And remember–they will move quickly once they know."

It was a long trip to Sandero, and well before he arrived Ennis decided that any Fleet posting, even with Umbra, was better than the alternative. He was more determined than ever to do a good job and defer that fate as long as possible. He'd made the last leg of the trip on a small commercial carrier that seemed to specialize in transporting families with small children. He'd never been in close quarters with children for so long–after Fimbul he'd spent his time entirely with Fleet–and he decided he hadn't missed anything. He was glad the trip was over.

He looked around, feeling lost. Sandero was purely civilian. The main police facility was located close to the docks, so he went there first. At least they wore uniforms; it might not be so different.

"So you're Commander Ennis," said the chief, a stocky woman with bristly red hair. She handed back his ID. "What do you want me to do about it?"

"I want you to check your files for these people," he said, trying to keep his temper from showing. He handed her the datatab with the mutineers' information.

"Yeah? What'd they do, salute with the wrong hand?"

"They mutinied." He had the impression the chief was struggling between sympathy for the mutineers and interest in tracking down criminals.

"Hey, Ouzbiakan! Run this for matches, willya?" A dour-faced man with a black mustache took the tab and returned to his desk. The chief sat back in her chair. "Had any luck?" she asked Ennis. "They run off near here, or somethin'?"

"They stole a ship." The chief raised her eyebrows, looking impressed. "Some of them were seen one jump from here."

"Hey Chief! We got some!" Ouzbiakan gestured at his desk display. "Dunno if he wants 'em now, though. They're in the morgue."

Ennis moved quickly to the display. The police data had them listed as Unknowns 16 and 23. "Markus Wenig and Tia Selamat," he said, reading the names from the Fleet list. "What happened?"

"I remember them now. Fight over a big card game," grunted the chief. "They took some people with 'em, couple a nasty folk that'd been giving me a headache, so I'm not complaining."

"Any others?" Ennis asked. Ouzbiakan shook his head.

"We only got bookings and bodies in our system," the chief said, apologetically. "Just don't have the equipment for anything else, and if we did we don't have the people to run it. Wasn't Yace on that one?" she asked. "Where is she?"

Ouzbiakan jerked his thumb behind him. "On break."

"Hey Yace!"

Yace was a tall, slender woman with a milk-and-coffee complexion and serious brown eyes. The chief gave her a brief summary. "So how 'bout you take him down to Reilley-san's place an innerdouce him, eh?"

Yace was willing to help, but didn't know much. The owner of the club identified a few of the mutineers, but not Moire Cameron. He went about the station with a still of her, but nobody had seen her. The other mutineers had left a long time ago, nobody knew where or with whom.

Ennis left a mail-link with the police chief in case anything came up and took advantage of an opening on a mail ship to get back to Lightline. It took a week, and he spent most of his time trying to make sense of everything that had happened. Umbra was up to something, Toren was *definitely* up to something, but none of it made sense.

At Lightline he found a seat on another ship to Domenici leaving only a few hours after his mail ship arrived. Remembering Namur's warning, he wanted to keep on the move as much as he could.

While waiting, he went to the Fleet station to use the kiosk to check his mail-link. It wasn't a multiple transmission delivery link, which was the fastest and most expensive, but it had more than a single route. Fleet had a contract with a hub-based courier system that also did civilian mail, and Namur had arranged a nonmilitary link for him as well. He hadn't used it yet.

Nothing from the police chief at Sandero, but that was to be expected. A note in his personal box from Shabata, dated two weeks ago, wishing him luck and telling him she had been put on the list for promotion. *Hurry up or I might not be on* Canaveral *when you get back,* read the postscript.

He read it with conflicting emotions. Shabata was due for promotion, and he suspected she'd do well. She might even get command of one of the new corvettes that were coming out. It was kind of her to imply he might be able to return, even though she must know better.

He was on semipermanent loan to Intelligence until he either found a way to make Toren stop chasing Moire Cameron or somebody shot him. His promotion cutoff date would have passed by then. There was no chance he'd be given another ship post by that point.

Ennis shook his head, banishing his self-pity, and replied to Shabata's message with good wishes. There was nothing he could do about it except follow orders.

There was one message in the general box, routed by his name from an on-station address. He opened it, curious. It was only one line.

"New sketch, same subject. Harrington."

His first reaction was it had to be a trap. Namur had said Toren would know, but this was incredibly fast. Then it occurred to him that *not* responding might trigger suspicion. He could just reply as if he were about to leave—which he was—and get on the ship to Domenici. Maybe leave some fake clues about where he was going for fun.

But when he sent the message from a station kiosk there was an immediate reply. A voice that he recognized as Harrington's greeted him.

"What a delightful coincidence. Are you making a prolonged stay? I am afraid the amenities of Lightline are rather sparse, or perhaps only known to the locals."

Yes, it was Harrington all right. "I'm just about to ship out."

"What a pity. I thought you might be interested in a new view on your mysterious web pilot, but perhaps you have already found her."

Damn him. Ennis weighed the risks of the still-possible trap and missing out on information on Cameron's location, and sighed. He checked the translucent gun, making sure of the settings, and tucked it away for quick access.

"Where are you? I have a few hours before I leave."

Harrington gave a level number. "Just follow the corridor that goes past the med station. You can't miss me."

The kiosk had a station map available, and Ennis brought it up to get his bearings before heading out. The station had a lot of construction going on–several sections on the map were flashing red, inaccessible. Lightline was apparently trying to improve its rough image by remodeling. Judging from what he'd seen so far, they were wasting their time.

The central corridors of the level met at a large open space, set up as a sort of community area. Harrington was seated on a railing that ran along one side. Otherwise, the area was empty. He had his datapad open as if he were sketching the discordant attempts at sculpture in the middle. He looked up when Ennis approached.

"How did you know I was here?" Ennis asked.

"I didn't," Harrington replied, returning his gaze to the datapad. "After seeing our mutual acquaintance again, I got word through various channels that an officer from *Canaveral* was being sent about the Fleet to advise on preventing similar problems. Once I discovered the identity of the officer, it was simply a matter of setting a databot wherever I made port. This isn't my first attempt."

"I haven't been away from *Canaveral* that long, though. How did you find me so quickly?"

"The Fringe isn't as large as it appears in a map. The population is sparse and located in concentrated areas," Harrington said blithely.

Ennis was not completely convinced. The reporter must have had some idea of where to start looking. Still, it was a useful piece of information. If Harrington knew, Toren probably did as well.

"I'm hunting the mutineers," he replied. Harrington already knew about them, and could guess the truth without much difficulty. "Where is she?"

Harrington smiled. "I have no idea where she is now, but I know where she was recently. She appears to have found some help." He tapped the datapad, then showed it to Ennis.

It was a shock to see her face again. He studied the sketch carefully, searching for details. She was different–not the weary, despondent figure in the previous sketch. Wearing a full hood about her head, she was looking back over her shoulder, alert and wary. A young man was beside her, facing the other way. He seemed unaware of any danger, intent and interested in something else. And there was something about him....

"He looks like her," Ennis said when he figured it out.

"The resemblance is pronounced," agreed Harrington. "Had I missed her I would still have noticed him. A relative she contacted, perhaps?"

Considering her jump in time, it would have to be a distant one. He looked too young to have been around when she left Earth with the exploration ship. How had she known about him? *She looks so much more...alive.*

"Where were they? How long ago did you see her?"

Harrington hesitated, looked at him in a calculating fashion. "Angelos. Two months ago."

His heart sank. That was a long way away, and a long time ago.

"I can save you the trip," Harrington said, in an offhand way. "For a consideration, of course."

"What do you mean?"

"I made inquiries at Angelos. About her, and the ship she left on. Information that I might be willing to share."

What did he have that Harrington wanted? It wouldn't be money, or...*information. He wants to know about Moire Cameron.*

"Why didn't you follow her yourself?" Ennis asked, skeptical. "You've had plenty of time."

"Other projects demanded my attention." Harrington shrugged. "My employers have this quaint notion I should do what they want on occasion."

"I can't tell you anything," he said shortly. "You know that."

Harrington sighed. "All too well. Credit me with some intelligence. All I ask is permission to accompany you on your investigations. In return I will give you not only the information I have, but any information I discover en route." He gave Ennis a guileless look. "What could be simpler?"

His suspicions flared anew. What did he really know about Harrington? Could he be connected to Toren somehow? No, Shabata knew him well enough to trust him even though he was a reporter, so he was probably not working for Toren. That didn't mean he should encourage him to stick around.

"Fleet would not be happy with that." Neither would he. The reporter had an uncanny knack for finding Cameron, and the only good thing about it was he'd communicated his information to Fleet. There was no reason to help him find out more. And why was he interested in Cameron in the first place?

"It is only fair to warn you that she does not frequent Fleet outposts," Harrington pointed out. "Quite the opposite. And there is nothing Fleet can do to prevent me from traveling on the same commercial transportation you use. Unless they have provided you and your team with a ship?"

Right. My team. But Harrington had given him an idea. The reporter knew how to get transportation on all sorts of unlikely ships; he'd told them as much on Andris Station. Now that Toren was going to be hunting him he needed to move fast and with as little notice as possible. Namur *had* told him to use his initiative.

Harrington didn't know what they could be getting into. Ennis didn't want to have an untrained civilian following him around, even if he was useful–it made it more dangerous for everybody.

"This could be dangerous. More dangerous than usual around here," he amended, seeing Harrington's amused look. What could he tell him that was both convincing and unconnected to Cameron? "One of the mutineers has been identified as an Armed Action Committee bombsmith. There could be others, and they could be making plans out here. They will definitely be violent if they know they've been found."

"I see." Harrington was thoughtful. "A pity that news tends to occur in dangerous places, but there's no help for it these days. I hear there is a war on. I appreciate your concern, however." He closed the datapad and stood. "Do we have an agreement, Commander Ennis?" He extended his hand. Ennis shook it reluctantly.

"We have an agreement, Mr. Harrington."

CHAPTER 19
MILITANT ECONOMISTS

When Moire returned to the bridge after visiting the galley, Harvey was still at the communications panel.

"That's an awfully weak signal, when it's so close," he said when he saw her. "They don't seem to be listening, either. I tried contacting them, but no reply."

"No point in continuing then. Probably just a recording." Moire didn't want to broadcast any signals that might be picked up by unfriendlies, crab or human. The possibility of *more* pirates was remote–they would concentrate on known routes, not out here where ships never went except by accident. She wondered how the other ship had gotten out here. They must have been very, very lost.

It would be useful to investigate the signal, even if nobody was alive on the other end. Perhaps they could get some repair parts, or additional supplies. She touched the control bracelet to contact Gren.

"What is it?" He sounded tired and irritable.

"We're picking up a distress signal. I'm thinking we might be able to help each other. It's not far ahead but I'll need to use the realspace engines to get there. Will that affect you?"

Gren was silent for a moment. "Nah, I'm fine. On the other side of the node. But the others will have to get behind the shielding. How long would it take?"

"Five or six hours."

"I'll have them work on the jack, then. Wait a few minutes; they'll signal when they are clear."

Moire looked at Harvey. He was bright-eyed and interested for a change. Almost hopeful. "I'll need you topside," she said. "Can you run the scan board?"

"Used to do it all the time, years ago," he said. "You think they might still be alive?"

"Could be. And if they aren't, I don't think they'll mind if we do some salvage."

She pushed off and up to the realspace bridge gangway, grabbing the rails to pull herself up. Harvey followed behind. The air was full of little pieces of junk–chewstick butts, mummified crusts of food, and other assorted garbage. Moire batted a crumpled piece of plastic printout away from her face.

"Let me guess. Nobody cleaned up here much."

Harvey pushed off too hard from the gangway and had to wrap himself around a pipe to avoid crashing into the ceiling. "Tidiness wasn't something Ramutis worried about much," he gasped. "God rest her soul, we all have faults."

The realspace bridge was tight for space. Zero-g helped here, too. Moire swam over to the controls, glad to see the seat had a crash belt. She strapped herself in. At least she wouldn't keep drifting while she tried to maneuver the ship.

"All quiet," reported Harvey at the scan and communications station. "Let's see if we can find anything else out there."

Moire found the toggle for the viewport shields and switched them open. They groaned and jerked, but finally moved up enough to reveal a starfield with no obvious landmarks. Moire shut them again. They weren't much use so far out, and it was safer to keep them closed. She'd wait until they were in visual range of the ship.

A click sounded in her ear, and then Freddie's voice. "All of us are out of the engine area now. Excepting Gren, of course. You are going to rescue these people as well, O Captain? You are needing something to do while you wait?"

Moire smiled. Freddie was sounding more cheerful too. "Exactly. We need more crew, don't you think?" He chuckled and signed off.

She turned her attention to the realspace controls and punched the startup sequence. The next few hours were uneventful. Harvey fell asleep, drifting by the scan board and gently snoring. Moire let him sleep until they got within scan range. He was old enough to need the extra rest.

"Hey, Harvey. Wake up. We're close enough to pick them up now. Got anything?"

Harvey jerked awake, mumbling, and in a few minutes was setting up the scanner board. He started swearing under his breath, searching the displays while running a hand over his head in a nervous, jerky way.

"I don't understand it. It's been too long, I must have forgotten something. Or maybe it's not working right, I don't know!" He slammed his hand against the board, then quickly grabbed the edge of the console to stay in place. He turned to Moire, his face pleading. "I'm getting about fifteen ship signals, and I recognize one of the names! D'ya think it's just coughing up all the IDs it ever found? There can't be so many ships out here and nobody saying a word to us. Are you sure we're where you said?"

Moire checked the range to the distress signal. "What does the scan say?”

He turned to another section of the board and busied himself for a few minutes, and started swearing again. “Now this damn thing is on the blink too. I got a whole bunch of mass objects dead ahead. On your scope, now. Asteroid field, maybe? But why the ship IDs?”

I don't think two different devices would have the same error. Moire slapped the toggle to open the viewport and ramped down their speed. She glanced at her scope, checking the distances.

The closest of the objects should be within range soon. “Harvey. Do a seek on one of them.”

Harvey fiddled at the controls. His constant muttering went silent, and Moire looked up. His face was ashen.

“Go on. Take a look,” he grated.

Her board had a scope with an inner display, for multiple signals. Now in addition to the full field scope output it was showing an image of a ship.

“What about the others?” she asked, after she had overcome her own amazement.

He concentrated. “Same thing. They really are ships. Is this where the pirates put them after...but that don't make any sense. Ships are too valuable to just leave like that.”

They were close enough to the first ship now to see it faintly reflecting the starlight. Moire nudged *Ayesha* around it and gasped. “Oh boy. Look at that.” The entire lower-rear section was missing, and struts and girders splayed from the edges, twisted and frayed.

Harvey looked out the viewport, somber. “Reactor must have gone. Poor devils.” He went back to his console, glancing at a display. “It's still pretty hot, too. Probably don't want to salvage that one.”

Moire nodded. Their best chance of getting help was the ship that was sending the signal. Nobody could have flown the first ship; it had to have drifted there on its own. But what had brought the rest?

They passed two more ships in the next few hours, one after the other, and then a clump of three. A few had obvious damage, but all were unresponsive to their signals.

“Will ya look at that,” Harvey said, shaking his head in amazement. “I never seen so many. That’s an old one, there,” he added, nodding as they passed a ship with a modular style of construction. “Won’t find much useful, except maybe supplies. Looks like there’s quite a collection still ahead. Closer we get, the more I’m picking up. They go out for a thousand klicks or more.”

“The ship sending the distress signal should be next,” Moire said, watching the scope. “Keep an eye out.”

There. It was out on its own, a big merchant vessel. It looked intact, and her spirits rose. She flew slowly around it. “Ah, damn. Looks like their cargo hold exploded."

"That don't mean they aren't still in there, or that the rest of it don't work. It looks like the rest is pretty much intact. If they were hurt too bad, or the crew didn't make it, maybe the engine is OK. We could take that one home."

Moire didn't say anything, unwilling to dampen his enthusiasm. She doubted they could make the ship run again, at least in the time they had available. It would be easier to fix *Ayesha*. Anything severe enough to blow out a section of hull had probably done significant damage to the control systems.

"Right. Let's find a door, shall we?"

Harvey snorted. "That hole isn't big enough for you?"

Moire swept the scope at higher focus. "That's going to be full of chunks of sharp metal and access to the rest of the ship may be blocked. Bad idea when you are running around in an EVA suit."

She wanted a hatch on the lower section of the ship, closer to the gravity node and engines. She found one midway instead.

"Get me the visual feed for our topside airlock," she said. She had never docked a ship this big. It would be easier if the airlock was close to the bridge. "And tell the others to get the suits ready."

She concentrated on the visual feed, only hearing Harvey's uncomfortable mumbling on the comm as a distant noise. "There. That ought to be good enough to grab to." She spun her chair around, activating the "all-channel" function on the control bracelet. "Everybody there?"

A chorus of voices answered her. "I thought you said there was one ship," Alan asked, justifiably confused. "But Felden is saying there are lots."

"I don't know how many ships are here. More than a hundred, if the scope is right." A stunned pause followed this information. "We're close enough to dock now. Who's going with me?" Another silence, this one awkward.

"Um, we got only two EVA suits," said Yolanda. "And...and we had to take some parts off a one to make the other work right."

Moire hid her face in her hands. *Sometimes I really wonder how they survived this long.* "Okaaay. So we only have one suit. Great. I'll look for more when I'm inside."

"You're not going," Gren said swiftly. "Anything happens to you, we are all dead."

"But—" This captain gig was not working. All the responsibility and none of the fun.

"We need someone who knows what to look for," Gren interrupted, "and is less essential. You're the only pilot on this ship."

If they puncture the only suit, we're dead anyway regardless of who's in it. "That lets you out too, Gren," Moire said, feeling annoyed. "You're the only engineer."

"I'll go," said Montero, surprising her. "I know what to look for. Besides, I know how to force the hatch," he said, sounding smug.

She only agreed when Gren assured her privately that Montero was capable of the job. She still didn't like it.

Moire slouched in the realspace bridge, keeping an impatient eye on the visual feeds while Montero cycled out the airlock. All exterior, unfortunately. The only vid they had was Tenna's cheap personal unit, and it didn't broadcast.

It didn't take Montero long to extend the airlock gantry out, latch an emergency cable, and force the hatch door open. The ship had no atmosphere, dimming hopes for finding any survivors. It also had no gravity, making it hard to get around.

She hated having to rely so heavily on someone else's verbal descriptions to understand what was going on. *I should be out there, not him.* Montero was not the best person to send on a solo mission. She could only hope he wouldn't get distracted and forget to come back.

"Ooh, this is real fancy for a cargo ship, " Montero's voice came over the comm, scratchy with interference. "This must be the main hatch. They got a titleplate and insignia on the wall and everything. Lessee...says the name is *Westeran Pride*, Oglala shipping line. I'm going to find a way down." After a moment of silence she heard a gasp, more a sharp intake of breath, and then nothing. "What is it?" Moire said sharply, leaning forward. They might have to risk going in in shipsuits if he was hurt.

"One of the crew," Montero said in a shaky voice. "Just floating there, my light picked it up. I thought they moved."

"Carlos, they've been dead for a long time unless they figured out how to manage without air."

"They're all dried up," he whispered. "I hope they died right away." More silence, except for his breathing as he moved. "Think I've found the node section, but the hatch is closed. Have to open it up."

Moire spun her chair around. *The suspense is killing me.* Maybe she should play with the scan board, learn how to work it. Just to have something useful to do.

Montero was not saying anything now, just grunts as he wrestled with the hatch. "Must've...shut automatic when the hull went," he managed after a moment. "Readout on the door says there's a little pressure on the other side, but not much."

"You'll want to check the main field assembly," Gren's voice came over the common link. "On a ship that size, it should have an access port just inside the shield wall entrance."

"Boy, this is big. My light doesn't even go all the way. Where's the shield wall again? Oh, I don't like that."

"What?" Moire and Gren yelled in chorus. *Why does he keep saying things like that when he knows we can't see anything?* Moire fumed. *Does he want to give me a heart attack?*

"Shield wall door is loose. And the latch is missing."

"That's not a good sign," said Gren. "You got a radiation gauge on that suit?"

"I don't think it's working," Montero said calmly, as if it didn't matter. "I'm gonna take a quick peek." He paused. "It's all melted, Gren. Nothing but slag in there. I'm getting out."

He took his time getting back, to Moire's frustration, but she forgave him when she saw the gear he'd found. *Westeran Pride* had been a well-maintained ship. He'd brought back two EVA suits and some medical supplies.

The crew had gathered in the galley to hear his report. Gren was there, his eyes bloodshot with fatigue. "I have some news myself," he said when Montero finished. "It looks like we can fix the main node, especially if we can salvage a few parts from these ships. That's the good news. The bad news is the node is so badly misaligned it won't work when we fix it. We'd need a major piece of hydraulics to move it, like in a repair station. I don't think we can do it."

The others were quiet. They were exhausted too, and trying desperately to keep their hope. She could see it flicker in their eyes.

"OK, so we either find a ship that works or we can fix easily. Looks like we have lots of options. According to Felden, we have enough supplies on this ship for several months, especially if we get into the cargo. We have more suits now, so we can get people out there to look and find even more supplies if we need to. I don't think it will be necessary. We'll beat this yet. Yes, we are stuck, but we are stuck in what appears to be the junkyard of the galaxy. Freddie probably doesn't want to leave."

Everybody laughed, even Freddie.

"So why are all these ships here, then?" wondered Harvey. "Was it one big accident? But nobody goes this way...."

It was a good question, and she'd wondered about it herself, until she remembered what had happened in the last few minutes *Ayesha* was in drive. "I think all these ships failed in webspace. There is the nastiest gravitational anomaly I've encountered near here; it snagged us so hard I couldn't get us loose. They don't have much of an effect in normal space so once the bubble pops the ships just drift until they all come together in this...sargasso of wrecks."

"Could be some valuable cargo in 'em," Yolanda said. Her face had a thoughtful, speculative expression. "That ship Harvey recognized—they carried more than the manifests listed, ya know. Good stuff." She nodded approvingly. Good stuff to Yolanda meant illegal, as Moire had found out.

Davies had evidently tolerated a little private smuggling.

"Just remember we have to get back to civilization for it to be valuable." *And may I be forgiven for calling the Fringe civilization.* "Anybody got anything else to report? Michel, how's Fortin doing?"

"She is talking, but it makes her tired," he said. "I put a fluid pump on her like the diagnostic said, and she started waking up more often. I think...I think she's getting better. I found a brace for my arm, so I can use it a little."

Poor kid, he wanted so much to help, and there was little he could do except care for Marie Fortin and bring food to the others.

"Now for Phase Two. Gren, you have stuff you need for repairs, right?" He nodded, wearily. "Make a list. As detailed as you can, and with hints where they might find it. Make that list and then rack out. That goes for you too, Montero. I'm going to scout around and find another likely ship for looting, and then I'm going to get some sleep myself. Who's going to be going outside this time?" She looked about the galley. Harvey raised his hand, fierce and determined. Yolanda twitched, hesitated, then raised hers.

"Alan, why don't you go too?" Montero said. "You know what some of that stuff looks like, and they might need someone strong."

Alan looked at her, uncertain. Moire's first instinct was to object. You needed a cool head and calm nerves out in an EVA suit, and she doubted Alan had ever been in one. Harvey and Yolanda weren't exactly the ideal candidates either, though, and if she tried to exclude Alan it would look like she was playing favorites.

She tried to think of some reason to stop him and failed. They would just have to watch out for each other, and before any of the three left the ship she was going to do a basic training session on the EVA suits. She nodded, reluctantly. "Yes, Alan, you too. If we need you back here, I will call you," she added, seeing the unspoken question in his eyes.

Leaving the galley, Moire went back to the realspace bridge. She set the ship in motion again, noting the location of *Westeran Pride* in case they wanted to get back to it again and the transmission had stopped. Instead of moving deeper, she cut along parallel to the field of ships. If she was right about her theory, the most recent wrecks would be on the outer perimeter. They wanted the most current ships they could find.

Too many of the ships were visibly damaged, or smaller and unlikely to have the parts they needed. She settled on slightly battered ship about the same size as *Ayesha* and brought it up to dock. It was near a cluster of ships. Curious, she fiddled with the scope to see if any of them would be a good next target. One looked quite promising–sleek and powerful, not like the working freighters and small transports she'd seen so far. It looked intact as far as she could see, but there was something dark visible to one side of it.

She increased the magnification of the scope, and went cold when she

recognized what the dark object was.
It was a crab ship.

CHAPTER 20
A SLAVE TO DUTY

The crew was already closing the holds when Ennis reached the small, short-run transport to Bendit. Harrington had found the ship the same day. He was cutting it a little fine by boarding now, but he didn't want to give Harrington the opportunity to send messages once he was actually on board.

He still wasn't sure if he trusted the reporter completely. He had been relying on Shabata's opinion of him at first, but it was doubtful they'd ever had competing interests to put that to the test. Then he remembered Pol Namur's fanatical attention to detail with regard to anything Toren did or was associated with. Namur had read the full investigation report, and Harrington, as a key witness proving the mutineers had survived, was definitely mentioned. If there had been any hint of a Toren connection, Namur would have told him.

Not Toren–but someone else? Perhaps, but was it anything he needed to worry about? He had to go with Harrington for now to get on Cameron's trail. If he saw anything that made him suspicious after that, he could head out on his own.

Ennis presented his passage chit to the crewmember at the open hatch and was waved inside. Following the signs for the passenger section, he found himself in a small commons area. This ship only carried passengers as a sideline; ten or fifteen at most. The cabins were tiny and had few amenities. He felt right at home.

Most of the other passengers were in their cabins. Harrington was in the common area, writing in his datapad.

"I was beginning to wonder if you had been able to get a berth," he said as Ennis approached. "An unexpectedly popular flight. The others are on a different ship?" He looked up, and got a better view of what Ennis was wearing. "Well. This is a change."

It had been a hard decision, but Ennis worried that his uniform made him too easy to track when he was on his own. Brand new clothes would be noticeable too. Fortunately he'd found a charity trade-up shop and was able to find what he was looking for.

"I obtained a partial itinerary for the ship when I was at Angelos,"

Harrington said, his voice pitched so softly Ennis could barely hear him. Ennis took out his own, smaller datapad and unfolded the optic port.

"I see what you mean," he said when Harrington transferred the data. "Even they don't know exactly where they'll be sometimes."

That was clever on Cameron's part. If the route was random enough she might think it safe to stay with that ship. That would certainly make his job easier. Maybe he'd be able to finish early enough to make Fleet change its mind before...no. He wasn't going to hope, because it would hurt too much when it didn't work out.

The flight took several days, during which he alternately slept and dodged Harrington's delicate questions as best he could.

When they reached Bendit Harrington went to a data terminal as soon as they left the ship.

"What are you looking for?" Ennis asked.

"A number of things. The obvious, such as the name of the ship, and some more specialized databots that can look for notable deviations from the norm. It will take an hour or so." He finished his entries and gave Ennis a bright, inquisitive look. "What shall we do next?"

Ennis caught sight of a sign saying "Port Master" and started heading that direction. The station was busy, and they had to weave their way through the crowd of people.

"You think they might know something?" Harrington asked, indicating the sign.

"People notice a lot of things they don't bother to file," Ennis answered. "Hard to search for that." Harrington looked amused, but it might be because he already knew. A successful reporter would.

The station was really crowded. Was this normal, or was something special going on? He started to ask Harrington, but stopped short. He wasn't sure what had caught his eye at first, then he saw them. Two people, a man and a woman, to all appearances ordinary and unremarkable. They were scanning the crowd, looking for something. Or someone.

The hairs on the back of his neck rose. They had an ease and confidence that spoke of skill, of training. Not the kind of training common on a station. Tendo Berens had moved like that, when he thought no one was watching.

Ennis moved into a wide shop doorway and crouched down, as if he were rooting about in his duffel bag. He watched from the corner of his eye as the two moved by, still searching the crowd.

"Forget something?" Harrington had turned back and was looking down at him. Ennis was relieved. The two strangers wouldn't have seen Harrington's face either.

"Just checking." The two strangers were well away from them now, and he stood. He had no evidence they were Toren agents or that they were looking for him, but the timing was right. He couldn't take chances.

Harrington was looking at him with a crease between his eyebrows. "Is something wrong?"

"I'm not sure." The eyebrows went up. "Do you know how to use a gun?"

There was no amusement at all in Harrington's expression now. "Will it be necessary?"

"That depends on your interest in survival," Ennis said shortly. "I think we are being followed."

"Precisely what is going on here, Commander–?"

Ennis's furious glare stopped him midsentence. "Just the name, please. I warned you I couldn't tell you anything," he snarled. "I also warned you it would be dangerous. You can leave whenever you like." He picked up his duffel and continued walking.

The port master's office turned out to be a useful stop. The clerk was quite familiar with *Ayesha,* and willing to talk.

"Oh yeah, they come here regular. You missed 'em this time, though. Came through about four weeks ago. Probably come back in a few months, if your cargo can wait that long. First mate told me they have a new pilot, guess she's pretty good. Should speed things up. When it's just the captain flying, well, it can take a while!" The clerk shrugged his shoulders.

Ennis and Harrington exchanged glances. "Looks like she was still with the ship, at all events," said the reporter as they left the office.

"We're going about this the wrong way," Ennis said, pulling out his datapad. "They have a route. We should get ahead of them instead of trying to follow." He looked at the list. Now that he knew how fast the ship traveled, it should be possible to estimate the dates for rest of the stops.

If *Ayesha* had left Bendit four weeks ago, they should be near the end of the "miscellaneous" phase and back on the regular route soon. And the first regular stop....

"Ever hear of a station called Bone?" he asked.

Harrington looked thoughtful. "It is a planet, I believe, and not a station. Is that our destination?"

"Yes." Ennis worked his way through the crowd to a data kiosk and pulled up a transport schedule. Only one ship had Bone on its itinerary, and it wouldn't be getting there for nearly a month. "Hmm. Maybe we should try the next on the list. Pykko has several ships heading that way."

"Perhaps." Harrington took out his datapad. "You may be looking for the wrong thing, you know. Bone does not have a large population, so regular shipping will be sparse. However, it *is* a bio-positive planet."

Ennis hadn't known there were any bio-positive planets out on the Fringe. They usually were prime colony sites, and well known. "What does that mean?"

"It means we need to find a xenobiologist," said Harrington, and he busied himself at the terminal.

Ennis peered out a viewport at the planet below, waiting for the dropship to disengage from the research ship. The main group of researchers had already gone down. "They don't have a station?" he asked, disbelieving.

"Nope," said one of the researchers. She was a planetary weather specialist, tagging along with the main xenobiology team. "This is the real Fringe. Used to be like that at Amber, too, until it got built up. If you don't have your own vacuum-to-atmosphere transport you have to wait for the shuttle, and I do mean wait."

Harrington returned from the back section and took his seat just as the dropship pulled away. "Do you think this will be adequate for the dangers that await us?" He held out a small, stubby gun.

"Where did you get that?"

He tilted his head toward the back of the dropship. "One of the researchers. He has another, larger one that he prefers. It appears the region they are headed for is quite dangerous."

"Local fauna?"

"Human. There is controversy over the fate of Bone, and some have resorted to violence to make their point."

The xenobiology expedition the reporter had found required another jump to connect with it from Lightline, but it was going to Bone. The expedition had been willing to let them come along in exchange for their help loading and unloading equipment after they recognized Harrington. They could even catch a ride back with the main ship if they wanted to.

"These other people in your team—how are they traveling?" Harrington asked innocently. Ennis wasn't fooled. Harrington must have figured out by now he was on his own.

"They'll manage. They always do."

Harrington's mouth quirked. "It must be a testament to your leadership. They seem to know where to go without a word from you!"

"It's rather convenient," Ennis agreed. The planet got slowly closer, and he could see more of the dark belt around the equator. "I hope we're in time," he said quietly. "If we're right about the schedule they should be showing up any day now, if they haven't already."

"Quite. The ship seems to have a reputation for erratic scheduling."

After they got down to the base camp and finished the unloading, Harrington scouted out a ride to the main settlement. Ennis got out of the chaos of setting up the camp and stood about gawking at the scenery. The twisted foliage, he'd heard from the xenobiologists, was the end result of vicious vegetable competition. The plants would actually try to uproot their neighbors and then incorporate their nutrients. It all happened very slowly, but he could see it in the way ropy tendrils wound around the bases of other plants.

Harrington arranged transport to Waylands that same day. They'd been told Waylands was the main trading and communication center for the planet, and Ennis hoped to find the information he needed there.

When they landed, they stumbled through the knifing cold into the settlement proper.

"Try the restaurant," said the pilot, when Ennis asked who would know about shipping schedules. "I know it sounds strange, but that's where everything happens. Or they know about it."

"I wouldn't object to a restaurant," said Ennis.

"Don't get your hopes up," cautioned Harrington as they walked down the chilly corridors in the direction the pilot had indicated. "The emphasis tends to be on quantity over quality in places such as this."

I'd say the emphasis is on cost, thought Ennis, looking at the prices when they entered. How could people afford to eat here?

The restaurant was popular, though, judging from the number of people coming and going, greeting the dark-haired woman who seemed to run the place and stopping to chat.

When she brought their order, she remarked in a friendly fashion that she had not seen them before. "Are you then with the new research camp in the Belt?"

"We came in with them," said Ennis.

"Can you tell me when *Ayesha* is expected?" asked Harrington.

All friendliness departed with sudden swiftness from the woman's face. "It is anyhow late," she said shortly, and left.

The coldness seemed to spread to the people seated at the tables nearby. They were now looking at them both, unsmiling.

"So whaddya want with *Ayesha,* anyway?" a tall, rangy woman asked.

"We just want to know when it is supposed to show up. What's wrong with that?" Ennis spread his hands, trying to look bewildered. He certainly felt that way.

"And I just want to know why. You got stuff to ship already when you only just landed in the Belt?" The woman was frankly skeptical.

Good point. So why would I want to find the ship if I don't have cargo? "I'm looking for someone on the ship," he said finally.

She raised an eyebrow. "Yeah, I know. At least you're honest—took the other bunch hours to get to the point."

She knows? "What other bunch?"

"Same deal," said the woman, leaning forward. "Strangers, come blazing in here asking all kinds of nosy questions. Well, I'm telling you what I told them. *Ayesha* is late. I don't know where it is. Now get back to whatever hole you crawled out of and leave us alone!”

Moire jerked awake, breathing hard and struggling, the echoes of a nightmare subsiding in her mind. The blanket was tangled about her shoulders, trapping her arms. No wonder she had dreamed of being captured.

When she worked her arms free it took her a moment to find the line about her waist and pull herself back to the controls. She'd tied it to keep her from drifting away while she slept. The communications board was clear, and so was the scanner.

She'd had a hard time sleeping at all after seeing the crab ship, and she still hadn't mentioned it to anyone. What could they do? *Ayesha* didn't have any weapons. Besides, the crab ship hadn't moved an inch since they showed up, so it was probably just as much of a wreck as the rest. It also didn't look like a warship to her. It was bigger than a fighter, and the surface didn't have many spines, either. Maybe it was a crab freighter. They had to have something like that, didn't they?

The ship itself wasn't really the problem, though. They must be near crab space or the ship wouldn't be here. If there was one ship, there could be more. That was why she'd shut off the distress signal, also without telling anyone. It probably wouldn't make a difference–nobody seemed to have found this place before, human or crab. The chances of another human ship coming within range of any sublight signal they sent were remote, and she *really* didn't want the crabs finding them.

Moire hardly ever left the realspace bridge now. When she wasn't keeping the ship in trim or moving it to a new location she wanted to be watching the boards, just in case. They were looking through their third ship now. The second one had been disappointing–too much internal damage, making it hard to search.

The captain's earring chirped. *Already? They only just got inside.*

“Get Gren on the line.” It was Montero, and he sounded breathless. “I think we found something.”

She punched his code, using the override. “Yeah?”

“It's an ore ship, Gren,” said Montero immediately. “One of the new ones. For rock planets that don't have atmosphere, that sort of thing.”

“So? What the hell do I want with a bunch of rocks?”

“You don't understand. It's built to *land,* Gren. It's got hydraulics. *Big* hydraulics. Mounted on the outer hull.” Montero paused. “You could use them to align the node, maybe.”

The next three weeks went by in a blur of fatigue and aching muscles. Gren returned from his own inspection convinced and inspired, and immediately got to work. Since their scavenging had found enough EVA suits for nearly half the crew, even Moire joined in. It was better than sitting around on the bridge, worrying.

First they had to fasten the two ships together with a brace. Gren severely modified the hydraulic to move the gravitic node on *Ayesha*. Then they discovered they would have to shift the hydraulic position, and everyone got snappish with frustration.

The only one of them who didn't lose his temper was Freddie. With every harried request for some esoteric connector or small component that he was able to scavenge from his amazing piles of junk, his mood improved. "Now, aren't you glad I didn't throw that away?" he'd ask Gren, grinning widely, and Gren would snatch the part and leave, grumbling.

Finally everything was connected and ready for the realignment. Part of the problem was getting a landing hydraulic to move in small, precise increments. Gren had figured out a rough equivalent and patched it in to some jury-rigged controls, but it wasn't the same as something built-in. Montero was actually running the controls. Besides his usual fogginess he was also getting tired and making mistakes. Moire was just about to order him to drop it and get someone else to take his place.

"No, *no!* Other way!" Gren shouted, his voice raw and ragged. "Just a quick pulse. Two seconds, thirty percent power."

Ayesha shuddered faintly. That had been the hardest part for her so far, feeling it shake. Worrying about it staying together. So far the brace had worked.

Deciding she had to step in, Moire became aware of a silence that stretched into minutes. She restrained herself from calling to check. They'd say something if there was a problem.

"I'm running a diagnostic," Gren said a moment later. "Damn, that's close. I gotta shift the attachment position. Be another three-four hours."

The four hours stretched into five, then six. "OK, gimmie three pulses, one second each, ten percent power."

She barely felt the vibrations this time. Gren asked for another set of pulses. A pause, then he came on the line. "I think we're ready for the ship codes, Roberts. The diagnostic looks good."

Moire had taken the ship code datatab from the safe some time ago. She pulled herself down the realspace bridge gangway to the main bridge, and found the wall panel for the main controls. Opening the cover, she inserted the ship code into the slot.

"Whenever you're ready, Gren."

She waited, minutes ticking by. How long did it take a main node to start up from scratch?

When it happened, she didn't hear anything. Slowly, gently, her feet moved down to the floor. Touched the floor. And then she had to use her muscles to stand against the pull.

Her general commlink was going wild with cheering and yelling. She sat down, suddenly shaky with relief. Maybe they would get out of this.

She made sure everyone was fully rested and all usable supplies had been scrounged from the ore hauler before starting on the trip to Mullery, the station she'd picked as their destination. It was a good week's worth of solid travel from the sargasso of dead ships, assuming nothing went wrong.

When she started up the drive, Gren and Montero watching the node readouts and engine levels like hawks, she knew it was going to be a long trip. The node was rough and ragged and she had to concentrate even harder than before on keeping the alignment locked on.

Eventually she had to drop out and rest. Her arms felt like rubber each time, so weak she couldn't hold her own coffee mug in the now full gravity of the ship. She made the hops as long as she could before stopping. They were now only three days from their destination.

"I need to talk to you before you start up again," Gren said over the comm. "I'll be there in a minute."

At least the node worked; she should be grateful for that. Moire heard the steps of someone approaching the bridge and looked up. It was nice being able to hear things like that again. Going from zero to a full g had been painful and it was awkward near the hull without the trim nodes to correct the field, but she wasn't complaining.

Gren appeared at the entrance to the pilot's pit and came down the stairs. He looked stunned.

"Everything OK?" she asked.

He shook his head. "Turns out we stressed the Linzer elements when we aligned the node. There's a measurable variation, and it's getting worse."

Moire went cold. "We can still go into drive, though. Right?" *Please?*

He swallowed. "We can go into drive. They can handle that. Dropping out's the problem. One more cycle and they'll blow."

She absorbed this for a moment. "We can't fix them?"

Gren shook his head again. "We'd have to replace the whole unit. Usually they don't fail. I should have gotten some backups when we had all those ships there, but I just didn't think. I didn't know there was a problem." Now he really looked gloomy.

"We are still three days away from Mullery," Moire said, grimacing. "There is no way I can stay awake that long, not with the node like it is." She got up and climbed the pit stairs. She was still going to have to do it, or they would die.

"What are you going to do?" asked Gren. "Maybe one of us could help...." His voice trailed off as he looked at Moire, then at the pit.

"I am going to pay Madele Fortin a visit."

He frowned, puzzled. "She couldn't sit up for five minutes. How can she help with the piloting?"

"She's a medic, right?" Moire asked. "She'll have something to keep me awake. I just hope she has enough for three days."

Harvey Felden grudgingly allowed her to wake Madele, but he glowered at her all the time she was there. Seeing the change in Madele Fortin was a shock. She had been so large and full of life it was easy to forget her age, but now she looked frail and thin.

It took her a moment to wake up enough to understand, but she directed Moire to two different medications, warning her they were less than ideal—they were intended to counteract an overdose of the muscle relaxant Captain Davies had used—but they would work as emergency stimulants.

Moire returned to the bridge slowly, staring at the small box she held with the brightly colored pills. *Not until I need them.* She'd done the basic alignment before Gren called, so she only needed to engage the drive.

She put her hand on the drive lever, then let go. Her hand was slick with sweat. *You have to do this. The other choice is to stay here and rot.* That almost seemed like a reasonable choice, compared to what she knew could happen. She put her hand back on the lever. Clenching her teeth, she pulled it down.

The drive engaged, rough and hard. She struggled for a long moment to regain her alignment, cursing, finally pulling it back. She tried not to think about doing that for three days.

She lasted nearly eighteen hours before she finally took the first stimulant. Her heart pounded, slow and powerful, and she wondered if the drugs were damaging it. Maybe they could grow her a new one. It was amazing what they could do these days.

The second stimulant wasn't as effective as the first. Madele had warned her about that, too. There wasn't anything that could be done except take more.

By the start of the third day she was taking a stimulant every four hours, and she was starting to see things she knew weren't there. Shadows moved in the edges of the bridge, at the corners of her eyes. Colors shifted unexpectedly, and she heard echoes but not the sounds that made them.

The shadows slowly started to take shapes. The shapes of people. At first she thought it was Harvey—he'd been checking up on her, bringing her food and anything else she needed. But he was only one person. One by one, the crew of *Bon Accord* emerged from the darkness and stood around the pilot's pit, staring at her.

"I had to do it," she said, startling herself with the rasp of her voice in the silence. "You ordered me to, Etienne. You said I had to get the ship back. You wouldn't *let* me help you!" She was crying, pleading with the silent figures that watched her with calm, remote, unmoving faces. "Please say you understand!"

Even as she raged she kept the legs steady on her target. Just like on *Bon*

Accord, surrounded by the dead and bloody bodies of the crew. Her friends. Her lover.

Just how long she had been in this state was unclear; time seemed suspended. When the visions began to fade she found she wanted them back desperately. Etienne was the last to go. She stared at his image, tears streaming down her face, trying to memorize every feature before he vanished. Again.

None of them had moved–but it almost seemed like he looked down before he faded away.

She glanced down at the console. There were numbers on a display that were changing. She should be doing something now, shouldn't she?

Now she remembered. That was the dropout time display. The comp readout of the gravity profile was nearly even, too. Fear sharpened her drug-fogged mind, waking her up. She had almost forgotten to do the dropout. Five seconds, four, three. She reached up for the switch. Two. One.

The dropout was even more rough than the start; she could feel the ragged nature of the gravity bubble as it went. She wanted to collapse right there, but she couldn't. She wasn't finished. Her legs were too weak to climb the stairs so she crawled, pulling herself up one painful step at a time.

There were people again, but it wasn't the dead ones. At least she didn't think so. Was Felden dead? She couldn't remember that, either. Maybe she was dead now, too. She grabbed the edge of the communications console, trying to remember the right switch. Trying to reach it.

A hand came and got it for her. That was considerate. She liked these ghosts better. They did things. A signal code from a station beacon blinked on the board. "And it's even the right one," she said, feeling pleased.

She let go of the console and collapsed.

CHAPTER 21
TRUTH AND CONSEQUENCES

I don't like the sound of "the other bunch", Ennis thought as they left the restaurant. They needed to know more and nobody wanted to talk to them. It was going to be even harder to keep out of sight here, too, with such a small settlement. He was assuming it was Toren, but who else would be interested in the whereabouts of a dubious tramp freighter?

"You guys coming back, or what?" It was the pilot of the ship they'd taken from the Belt. He was pulling on thick gloves. "I'm leaving now."

"When does the Foundation ship leave?" Ennis asked.

"Two-three days." The pilot shrugged. "You'll have to get your own way out, though. I'm not coming back here before then."

Harrington glanced at him, and Ennis shook his head. They had to wait until *Ayesha* showed up. If it didn't, he wasn't sure what he would do next anyway.

They waited a day without any news, then two. Ennis was sitting in Mammachandra's wondering if perhaps that was best for everyone. It was all very well for Namur to tell him to bring her back alive. Cameron wasn't going to cooperate, not with the consequences of her involvement in the mutiny hanging over her head, but if he didn't succeed his days in Fleet were numbered. How was he going to do it?

She'd escaped from Toren despite all their resources. That didn't bode well for his chances of success. He suspected Toren had underestimated her abilities. She was an explorer. Improvisation and survival were instinctive to her.

Survival—that might be the key. The one thing he could offer her that would make her willing to come back. Even military prison would be better than what Toren had planned. *At least she would be alive.*

"You have a gloomy countenance," said Harrington, taking a seat opposite him. "Not bad news, I hope?"

"No news of any kind," Ennis answered, shaking off his mood. "Did you have any luck?"

"Not a bit. One has the sense that those who do know anything about her are unwilling to talk. It is most curious."

A man came in the restaurant, and when he removed his oxygen booster

Ennis recognized him. He'd seen him at the research station. Eng, a xenobiologist.

Eng was glancing about the room, and when he saw them, he came over.

"I didn't know you were here," he said, smiling and extending his hand to Harrington. "The *Cosmographica* article turned out pretty well, even though they cut out the part about George's adventures. I suppose they weren't suitable for a family publication, were they? But what are you doing here? All the wildlife is in the Belt."

"A different topic this time," Harrington said as he shook hands. "I'm looking for someone, and the locals are most uncooperative."

Eng looked interested. "That's strange. They're usually rather friendly. Who are you looking for?"

"She goes by a variety of names," Harrington said dryly. Ennis took out his datapad and pulled up a still of Cameron.

Eng looked at the still and his eyebrows shot up. He looked at them both, puzzled. "Yeah, I've seen her. Not for a while, though, and I wondered where she was. I heard she left on a freighter four months ago. Why are you looking for her?"

"How long was she here?" Ennis asked.

"Not too long—maybe a month or two. She worked for the local delivery service. You could ask there; maybe they know something. End of the north cross-corridor, big double doors. Lorai Grimaldi runs the place. If you stop by the station before you leave, I can tell you some more stories," he said, grinning, as they left.

"A fortunate encounter," Harrington commented. "Very observant, these researchers."

Ennis scanned the walls as they walked, looking for the north cross-corridor. He saw the paint-penned marking first: "All-Planet Delivery." Why had Moire Cameron stayed here for so long? Maybe she thought it was safe—it certainly was far away from anyone who might be looking for her. But then why did she leave?

The double doors opened into a big, high-ceilinged depot with two beat-up shuttles parked inside. No one was immediately visible, but Ennis could hear a voice on the far side. They started walking toward it.

"...Nah, the first ones went back up. I don't know if the new ones are with them, or someone else...still in orbit. I got a good view the last time I went up. If those aren't gun ports I'll kiss a nerya...yes, I'm sure...I don't know, but if you come up with any good ideas let me know."

A silence, then a woman walked around one of the shuttles. She stopped short when she saw them, a sour expression on her leathery face. It was the same tall woman who had been in the restaurant.

"What do you want? If it's passage off-planet I'll be happy to help, otherwise, suck vacuum."

"I was just curious," Ennis said, holding up a hand. "You mentioned some other nosy strangers. Mind telling me who they are?"

"Ya know, they didn't say. But I saw the circle-tee on some of their gear so I'm guessing if they aren't Toren, Toren hired 'em." Lorai Grimaldi gave him a hard look. "You're not with them?"

"No." Her head jerked back slightly at his emphatic denial, and she got a thoughtful expression in her eyes. "When did they show up?"

"Dunno exactly. They came dirtside ten days ago, but who knows how long they were in-system? We don't have a detection net."

So it was possible they had been told about him, but not certain. "And they're all up there now? In a ship that's armed?"

She narrowed her eyes. "Yeah. Far as I know. Strangers stick out here, if you know what I mean." She smiled without humor.

"Is this the person they're looking for?" He showed her his datapad screen.

"That's not the picture they had, but it's the same person. Satisfied?" Grimaldi glared at him. "What did she do to you? The other bunch of yahoos said she was a thief. Strange, she never stole a damned thing from any of us. I even loaned her money and she paid it all back. What's your story?"

"She's in danger from the other people looking for her," he said, surprising himself. He felt an odd urge to trust Grimaldi. She was only trying to protect Moire Cameron. "I want to find her before they do."

"Huh. She said there'd be people after her, and she didn't say nothing about liking any of them. She just ran, and she ain't the running type."

"I know."

She gave him a long, considering look. "Look, it's the truth. *Ayesha's* late, and we aren't happy about it. Maybe it'll show up—it's been late before. Maybe she won't be on it when it does. But it might not show up at all." She wasn't sounding so hostile now. She was sounding worried.

"When we asked at Bendit they said *Ayesha* had left six weeks ago," Harrington said.

"You know she was on it then?"

Harrington nodded. Grimaldi rubbed her chin.

"They want her alive, you know," Ennis said. "They won't blow up the ship."

She grimaced and looked out at the depot doors. "They may try to stop it, though. Fire a few shots. That ship is falling apart and it wouldn't take much to pop it without meaning to."

Yes, they might do that. Now he knew why she was so worried, and now he was too. The ship could show up at any time.

"We have to get rid of them," Ennis said immediately.

Harrington and Grimaldi looked at him, Harrington with an expression of bright, curious interest. "But of course. We *could* simply ask them to leave, but I doubt they would be willing. Really, the easiest thing would be for you to remember where you parked a battleship for convenient retrieval. Or had you something more subtle in mind? Recall that I am only a reporter and unused to such bloodthirsty activity."

"Which is why you are usually found near a conflict," Ennis replied. "Shabata was right about you." Harrington's look of amusement deepened.

"So you're gonna get 'em to pack up, huh? I don't think they will until they get what they came for." Now Grimaldi was looking interested. Not friendly, but interested.

"Exactly." Ennis said. "What kind of communication system do you have here?"

It was an effort to keep his face from revealing his astonishment when they showed him. Ground-based booster transmitters? They'd had a better system on Fimbul. *Steal only the best,* as Penderhest liked to say. Still, it had enough for him to work with, especially after the restaurant owner unearthed a field comm for him to borrow from her store. He had to pay a deposit, of course. The locals were more helpful now, but not to the extent of handing out free equipment.

The store also provided Harrington and him with badly needed thermal gear.

"Not that I presume to question your methods," Harrington said, his eyebrows quirked, "but is it necessary to conduct this subterfuge in an unsealed and unheated shed?" His voice was muffled by the oxygen booster over his face.

Ennis placed the field comm on the remains of an empty crate. The shed had been abandoned for years, but was within a reasonable walk from Waylands.

"First, the signal has to come from somewhere believable. Nobody plans intrigue at Mammachandra's."

"I believe we were, rather successfully, too, once they knew what we intended to do."

"Yes, but not Toren's kind of intrigue. They tend to be more...professional," Ennis said grimly, remembering Tendo Berens. "That was my second reason. I want to keep this away from the locals. They carry guns but they aren't really killers at heart."

Taking the specialized scrambler unit he'd gotten from Umbra out of its case, he began to attach it to the auxiliary outputs of the field unit. Harrington watched him in silence.

"You were not surprised to hear the name," Harrington said finally. "Did you know Toren would be looking for her?"

"I've run in to them before," Ennis said, grimacing in exasperation as the unit came loose and fell. The cold was making his fingers stiff and clumsy. "Which reminds me. How do you keep managing to find her? Once could be a coincidence, but we both know she's trying to hide." Ennis watched carefully from the corner of his eye for Harrington's reaction. There wasn't one.

"Quite. Yes, I was looking for her. The number of pilots who stick exclusively to the Fringe is not immense. It wasn't that difficult, if one knew the proper things to search for."

Oh well, it had been worth a try. He supposed reporters had to be nosy by profession, but he still wanted to know why he had fixated on Cameron.

On the third attempt Ennis got the unit connected and powered up. He was beginning to worry he'd have to modify the field comm and risk losing his deposit.

"How are you going to use this to convince them to leave? Make noises like an entire carrier group?"

Ennis gave a taut smile. "One thing I learned in my shady past—never waste ammunition if you can't hit the target. This is just test bait, this time. I want to do this right." He had to get that ship away, and he probably only had one chance.

The compression scrambler was a useful device for sending secure messages in remote locations, allowing the signal to ride on a regular transmission. It wasn't the best option for field operations—it only had a few compression algorithms, and it was difficult to change the scrambler. They'd warned him about the danger of leaving it on the default minimal security setting, so that's what he was doing. It would be believable when the transmission was picked up.

"Will Toren be able to listen in on your special device?" Harrington asked.

Ennis pointed to the small blue logo on the side. "They made it. Nobody else on this planet should be able to listen in, so all that remains to be seen is if Toren is scanning. They don't have much else to do up there so they probably are."

Harrington nodded in approval. "Neat and tidy. But even if they hear you, why will they come down to check?"

"Because I know things I shouldn't." Would Harrington ask about them? Ennis took the cheap plastic carrybag and handed it to Harrington. "See if you can get that locker open over there without disturbing the dust too much, and put this in." It had taken him some thought to find things that Moire might find valuable. Money, of course. With a pang, he included the copy of the explorer book. The book tab would have the information that it had been borrowed from *Canaveral*, and that would add an extra degree of verisimilitude.

Harrington delicately shifted the dented metal locker door open and stuffed the carrybag inside, then left the door slightly ajar. He made as if to scuff his footprints away.

"Leave them. They'll expect to see something."

Harrington nodded. "Of course. You have experience at this, I see."

Ennis started up the comm unit, repressing the impulse to snap at Harrington. If the reporter had known about his past on Fimbul he would not have made the comment, but it still rankled.

He set the comm for three repeats, as if he were transmitting to a storage receiver somewhere on-planet, and started it up.

"Found out about a stash location Cameron used. Old shed north of the Yellow tunnel exit. I'm going to wait for prime cycle to end and the yokels to go to sleep. Did you find the person you were looking for? Remember to keep it quiet–they don't know who we are and we want to keep it that way." He shut off the comm and disconnected the scrambler.

"Oh, very good," said Harrington. "Quite cryptic. I assume Cameron is one of the names our mysterious friend is using?"

Ennis nodded. "Her real name. Not many people know it." He looked about the shed. There simply wasn't any place to hide that wasn't likely to be searched as well. "Let's get to the roof."

Harrington groaned. "If it wasn't for the heater elements in these suits...."

"That reminds me." Ennis searched his pockets and brought out the small, flat IR viewer. He held it up and looked at Harrington. "You've got a heat leak. Take some of that packing material with you," he said, pointing. "They will probably scan before they come in."

It was a long wait on the cold shed roof, and Ennis regretted it more than once. It was too close to what Fimbul had been like–cold, not enough air, and dangerous. An hour ticked by. It was fully dark now, and getting colder. Even with the heated gear they couldn't stay out much longer.

"Do you think they just weren't listening?" whispered Harrington.

Ennis shook his head, then pointed. Darker shapes were moving in the shadows, moving fast. There was no point in concealment out here, everything was open. As they got closer he could see long, angular objects in their hands. Harrington stiffened beside him.

Two waited outside the shed, two went inside. Ennis could just see one stationed farther out. There were faint sounds inside the shed now, metal on metal, crates being shifted. Good. They were bound to find it. Mere moments later the two inside came out with the plastic carryall.

With the same speed that they came, they left. The last one stopped and turned, raising a weapon and aiming. A blaze of flame erupted from the nozzle.

As soon as he'd seen the muzzle flash Ennis had pushed off the roof, dragging Harrington with him. He rolled as he hit the ground, shielding his face from the shards of sharp metal debris as the shed disintegrated. When Harrington tried to get up, he pushed him back down. "If they notice us now we're really dead!" he whispered. "Don't move!"

He stayed motionless until the inhabitants of Waylands came out to investigate and they could blend with the crowd. Then he made a direct line for the nearest door to take stock of their situation at Mammachandra's.

The field comm was a complete loss. Harrington poked a finger through one of the larger holes in his heated suit and sighed. "This is becoming a rather expensive story."

The other occupants of Mammachandra's were studiously ignoring them, but in a friendly, I-didn't-see-anything-officer way.

Ennis was thinking about his own expense report and had no sympathy. "You can leave any time."

Harrington gave him a long, thoughtful look. "I think you need to be a little more forthcoming," he said finally. "It is not merely a matter of my professional curiosity now, but personal survival."

Ennis nodded, feeling a twinge of guilt. He hadn't expected Toren to be quite so thorough about removing evidence. He'd been so busy suspecting Harrington's loyalty he hadn't considered he might be giving the reporter a new and unsuspected enemy. He owed him that much information, he supposed.

"All right, but I need your word you won't release what I tell you until it's safe. People's lives are in danger, and not just ours." Especially Moire Cameron. "I could use your help for the next part. It would be more believable if they hear a real conversation, I think."

"I would be delighted to assist. What is my role?"

"My long-suffering associate. You should find it no difficulty at all." He outlined the gist of the planned information, and they picked up their damaged gear. The locals were still willing to assist them, strangely. Maybe the destroyed shed had proved the danger was real.

Lorai left at a jog-trot, grinning. Some of the locals were *enjoying* the danger, if they got to do something about it.

"You think this is the right time? So soon?" Harrington inquired.

Ennis shrugged. "Of course I would call to complain after my target has been taken out, wouldn't you think?"

A big, bearded man showed them silently to the small room in back of the restaurant that held the communication gear. Ennis brought out the scrambler. "Thank you for your help," he said.

The big man gave him an enigmatic look. "You make these people leave, it is all the thanks I need. Maybe you think again about this chasing, eh?" He picked up a commlink. "You are ready, Lorai?"

"Ready as I'll ever be, Jens." Lorai's voice was thin and strained over the link. "OK, it's on."

Harrington took the link and stood out in the hall, where it wouldn't pick up Ennis's conversation in the background. It had taken them some work, but the signal from the commlink was being passed through the scrambler and then to Lorai's shuttle, currently in flight. This was all to make it look like two secure communications were taking place from different locations. It was a trick he'd learned from Penderhest that he'd never had a chance to try before.

Ennis nodded at Harrington and opened his own link. "Are you there? Pick up, damn you! Where the hell have you been?"

"Out looking for Enderson, just like I told you," Harrington answered at the other end of the restaurant, adding a nasal twang to his voice. "Did you find anything useful?"

"No I *didn't* find anything useful. Damn shed caught fire before I got there. How the hell can anything burn here? There isn't any oxygen to speak of."

"Hmm. Think someone was there before you?"

"I don't know, I didn't see anybody. How'm I supposed to keep an eye on everything? I was just out for a few minutes to eat...," he let his voice drift off uneasily. "This is a waste of time. Even if it was her stuff, she isn't here. Marchesi sent me here on purpose to get me out of the way. He didn't want me at Valmik. We know she's going there after Sequoyah, so why do we even bother looking here?"

"Sequoyah? What's that? " said Harrington, right on cue.

"Never heard of it, but it's on the list after Criminy, and we know they got there. Maybe it's a code name or something. So, did you have any luck?"

"Not a bit. Enderson hadn't even heard of her."

Ennis cursed a bit for authenticity. "Right. Maybe they'll come get us from this hellhole soon. Damned if I can see what all the excitement is about. See ya when you get in."

They closed their respective commlinks. Ennis removed the scrambler. Minutes later, Lorai Grimaldi strode in.

"You are quick," Jens said.

"Yeah. I didn't want to give 'em a chance to blow me up like that shed." She gave Ennis a look. "Dunno what they got from it; all I heard was squeals and static."

"How can we tell if they leave?" Ennis asked.

Lorai grinned. "Just so happens the shielding on the station relay is bad. Picks up the pulse when the drive kicks in. If we've got a signal going at the time, you can tell."

Jens set up the test signal, and Ennis and Harrington went into the restaurant to wait. An hour later Lorai came out from the communications room. "Good job," she said, and clapped him on the shoulder as she left.

"They're gone."

Moire dozed, shifting in and out of consciousness. She was aware of a niggling feeling that something wasn't quite right. There seemed to be more room than she remembered. Had her bunk gotten bigger, or had she shrunk?

She had been on a ship, hadn't she? Which one? *I hope I didn't sleep through my shift. Davies hasn't called, though....* The memories floated back. Davies wasn't going to be calling anyone anymore. She'd flown *Ayesha* out of the sargasso, and...and then what?

Her eyes snapped open. She was lying on a bed, a real bed. Not a bunk. There was equipment mounted along one wall. Medical equipment.

Terror surged through her. She struggled to sit up, arms and legs thrashing weakly at the blankets covering her. She had to get out before someone came back. How had Toren found her? No time for that, she had to get out....

The door to the room was open. She paused, head swimming, still sitting on the bed. Toren had never left the door open before. She felt at her arms. They hadn't used restraints this time, either.

Now she could hear voices. One that she recognized. *Alan is here too?*

"Get back here! Am I going to have to sedate you again?" asked a different voice, sounding exasperated. Alan came running through the doorway, stopping when he saw her awake.

He smiled at her, a shaky, tentative smile. "You took so long to wake up...days and days. Everybody was worried."

"It was only two days, and I kept *telling* you she'd be all right!" A man in a medtech's tunic came in and tried to push Alan away from her, with no success. "Now get back in the other room, you are agitating the patient. Look at that heart rate!"

Moire felt her heart rate slow. Alan was evidently free to come or go as he wished. Now that she looked more carefully, the equipment was visibly old and used. "Where are the others?" she asked Alan. "Is everyone OK?"

He nodded. "They're on the ship. They are talking a lot about what to do. They want to ask you. Madele Fortin is here also. They made a picture of her insides!" he said, impressed.

On the ship, which meant they were still at Mullery. *Ayesha* would not travel the web again.

"You were lucky," the medtech told her, after giving Alan a strange look. "The medical ship had just finished up a visit. It was close to going into drive when you folks showed up yelling for help, but they came back and patched you up. Just a little endocrine repair, nothing too serious. By the way, your ovary replacements need to be updated. Where do you think you're going?" he asked as she started to stand up. "You can't leave yet.

You need a lot more rest, and–"

"I'll rest on the ship," she said. Even if it wasn't a Toren facility, it made her nervous. She held on to Alan's arm to steady herself as a wave of dizziness swept over her.

Shuffling past the still-protesting medtech, she wound her way out of the medical area and out into the main part of the station. It was on the small side, as such places went, and looked threadbare and grimy.

Even with Alan's help she was exhausted when she reached the ship.

"What, they let you out already?" Felden dropped the box he was holding when she dragged herself through the main hatch. "You don't look that well."

"Yeah, I decided to be useless here instead of there. Hospitals make me nervous." She reached her cabin and collapsed gratefully on her bunk. Alan sat on the floor next to her, looking at her as if he was afraid she would disappear.

Ten minutes later the crew started to show up. Gren was the first.

"The Linzer nodes are powder, but you probably guessed that," he said. "We don't need 'em for environmental gravity, though, so the ship is still livable. Thing is, the station here wants to buy it for extra space. It's more than we could get in salvage, since the web engines are gone. What do you think?" He stomped up to the bunk and held out up a datapad screen for her to see.

Moire had wondered if she could just pull the blanket over her head and ignore him, but she couldn't let his last comment pass. "What does it have to do with me? You're the owner of record, aren't you? Since Davies and Ramutis are dead?"

"But you're the captain," he said, eyes wide and innocent. Moire wasn't fooled.

"That was an emergency! You all railroaded me, anyway. Made me do it," she amended, seeing his look of confusion. She really had to be more careful about the anachronisms. "I said only to the next port, and here we are."

Yolanda Menehune stuck her head in. "Didja tell her yet?"

"Just getting to it," Gren said testily. "*If* you don't mind."

Now she did pull the blanket over her head. *They have some crazy plan, I just know it. I am not flying* Ayesha *again for all the money in the universe, I don't care how well they fix it.* "Why can't you let me die in peace?"

"We want ta go back there," Yolanda said. She was in the cabin now, next to Gren. "The cargo alone would be worth it."

"You're nuts," Moire said bluntly. "It would take a fortune to fix this pile of scrap, and I wouldn't fly it if you did. Besides, Gren wants to sell it to Mullery."

"We'd buy another ship," Gren said, sounding almost cheerful. "We wouldn't need one this size for what we want to do, and with the sale price and the crew shares we'd have enough. We want to salvage the ships there. There's got to be some we could get to work, and it wouldn't take more'n two or three to make a fortune for us."

If only her head weren't threatening to come unglued. She would have several strong reasons why this was a bad idea if she could just think. Gren and Yolanda started discussing which of the wrecks they'd seen that might be good candidates for salvage. She tried to ignore them, but the idea wouldn't go away.

It might actually be a good idea. She was starting to realize she was not going to find someone to take Sequoyah off her hands and keep it from Toren, because even Fleet couldn't stop Toren right now. She glanced at Alan, who was looking back and forth as people talked, his forehead wrinkled with confusion. Something had to be done for him, too.

If she had a ship of her own, maybe she could track down Alan's Controllers. The sargasso made a good place to hide out—the crew would have to keep the location secret to preserve their monopoly, and that would be to her advantage. It would give her time to plan.

"I'll think about it," she said, sighing. Yolanda gave a whoop. "But you have to find the ship, *and* another pilot, or it's all off. I'm not doing that run on drugs again."

CHAPTER 22
OTHER PEOPLE'S PROPERTY

It was time to start the final leg of the trip to the salvage field, and Moire took her last cup of coffee with her to the bridge. She was glad they'd had room to transfer *Ayesha's* luxury cargo to *Raven*. They still hadn't gotten everything stowed like she wanted, though. Everything was happening so fast–they'd found both the ship and the pilot she'd demanded in a few weeks. That was the trouble with ultimatums; sometimes people fulfilled them and then you had to live up to *your* end of the bargain.

Raven was quite different from *Ayesha*. Bigger than a courier but nearly as fast, and everything worked. According to Yolanda, it was the size that made it affordable. It couldn't haul much cargo, which was what most people wanted out on the Fringe, and the owner had been desperate for money.

Everything worked, all the equipment was intact, and not a single dangling cable anywhere. Montero and his repair crew had nothing to do until they showed up at the sargasso, and then they got busy. They'd hired some new heavy mechanics and a new assistant engineer, besides the pilot. Most of the original crew had signed on.

The bridge, combining realspace and web, was on the same level as the officers' quarters. The new pilot, Kilberton, was seated in the pit, and looked up when she came in. He had a serious, dark face and an earnest manner.

"Time for me to leave, Captain?"

She nodded. "I'll call you when we get there."

He conscientiously entered his log data and locked down the legs before pulling his ID and leaving the pit. "You have the conn, Captain."

"Conn is mine. Call Gren Forrest and have him come up here, will you?" She waited until he'd left the bridge before putting her ID in. They'd set the coordinate displays and other positioning devices to only respond to her, a precautionary measure to keep the location of the salvage site a secret.

Secrecy was also the reason she always took the shift before getting to the site. Kilberton was some kind of relation to Madele Fortin; Moire didn't remember all the details. He was careful and competent, lacking only experience. They probably could trust him. Besides, if he was any good at all he'd figure out they were always going to the same place.

On their first visit they'd found a ship that had suffered an oxygen recycle failure. The only problem had been repressurizing the ship and finding a way to bring *Raven* along. It had taken a week. They'd left that ship with some associates of Yolanda's to sell, and the earnest money had been enough to get more repair equipment with a crew bonus to boot.

Gren came tromping in to the bridge, and she looked up from the setup board. "Secure the door, will you?"

He grunted and complied, setting the lock. "One of those conversations, is it?"

"We aren't that far out now. I don't like leaving the bridge open." She locked the destination for the salvage field and set the proximity alert setting well in advance. They'd get quite a boost from the whatsit that created the gravitational anomaly and she wanted to know before it got dangerous. "I still think we should tell them."

Gren took a seat in the captain's chair, midway between the web pilot's pit and the realspace bridge. "You only saw the one crab ship, right? In all the hundreds of others? It would only worry them to know. Why would the crabs be hunting us where we don't go? Besides, we got guns now." Not a trace of worry on his brown face.

Moire snorted. "Two fifty-gauge cannons, regular ammunition, and I'm the only one who knows how to use them."

"So teach somebody. We're going to have some time when we get there, I think. Doubt we'll be so lucky twice in a row with the ship salvage."

She nodded thoughtfully. It was a good suggestion, and fit in with her other plans. Alan had already shown he knew how to shoot, and shipboard guns would be a natural progression. If anybody was curious, they could say they were preparing against possible pirates.

"Think you are going to need the scout ship much?" she asked.

"Nah. We have the scooters now if we need to get around outside. Why?"

"I was thinking of doing some more investigating." She wanted to start teaching Alan to fly as well. "Did you see anything interesting last time we were out?"

It hadn't taken long at all. With so many wrecked ships in the sargasso, they could be picky and start with the easy ones first, building up capital for some of the more expensive tools Gren wanted. Moire wanted more guns, and better ammunition for them. She also wanted to figure out what she could do about her problem, and running all over the galaxy wasn't leaving much time for that.

So here they were, selling ship number two already. Next time she'd insist they pick one that needed more work.

"Why aren't there stars all the way down?" Alan wanted to know, gazing out one of the observation windows.

"Because we're on a moon. All the other stations we've been on are in orbit." Cullen was one of the oldest stations in the Fringe proper; that might have something to do with it. It had fabrication facilities, shipyards, and other plants on the tiny moon's surface, but the station itself was strung about the inside of the crater and in tunnels beneath.

"There are lights over there! Is that the station too?" Alan pointed. His sleeve shifted, revealing the plastic cuff on his wrist, and he pulled it back up quickly. She wished again he would let her look at it. There had to be some way to take it off.

"I wouldn't be surprised," Moire said. She looked around. Either it was the local shift change, or Cullen had a lot of people. Possibly both. "Let's go. Remember the Game, OK? You need to keep your voice down." She couldn't stop him from asking questions now. Everything was fascinating to him, and when he got excited his voice got louder.

Alan came away from the window reluctantly. "Why aren't we with the others?" he asked in a careful whisper.

"They don't need our help to sell the ship." And she definitely didn't want to be noticed or remembered by anybody. What she really wanted to do was get some heavy-metal shells for the guns on *Raven*, but she'd probably have to send somebody else for that too. At least she could find out if they were available.

After looking in a number of shops she picked up a catalog at a second-hand and refurbished place that carried a few weapons. Alan tugged on her sleeve. "Why are those people all wearing the same clothes?" He'd remembered to keep his voice down, anyway.

She turned her head, and her stomach knotted. A cluster of station police officers were walking down the causeway towards them. "Uniforms, kid. They're cops. Police." She pretended to be scanning the catalog, waiting for them to go by.

They didn't. She looked up; they were standing in front of her. She forced her expression to one of puzzled inquiry.

"Come with us, please," said the woman in front, who seemed to be in charge.

Well. At least they were being polite. "Of course." She tilted her head at Alan, hoping he would take the hint and not create problems. "Go back and tell them I might be late, OK?"

One of the others stood to block Alan from leaving. "Him too."

Oh, this is not good. "What's wrong?"

The station cop showed no emotion. "They'll tell you at the station. All

I know is we're to bring you in."

What could have brought them attention? Anybody after her wouldn't be after Alan, and vice versa. Was there some problem with the ship, or the sale? Moire thought up and discarded a handful of other possibilities before they finally arrived at the station police offices and were taken to a back room.

Another cop was behind a desk, looking harassed. Standing in front of him was a thickset man wearing a tunic and full trousers. She remembered seeing that kind of outfit on Earth, in the brief time she was able to watch vidcasts. It seemed to be businesswear nowadays. She'd never seen it in the Fringe before.

The man at the desk glanced up at them. He was wearing different insignia than the cops who had brought them in, and his nametag read Murayama. "Who are you?"

He'd been the one who'd wanted them brought in, hadn't he? "Ren Roberts, captain of *Raven*. My son, Alan. Mind telling us what this is all about?"

Now he really looked at them, his eyes going back between her face and Alan's. Murayama frowned. "Are you sure these are the people you saw?" he asked the businessman.

"Yes of course...." Now the businessman was looking less assured. "A chance resemblance, I assure you. Look at his arm. That cuff is all the proof you need. Those are our location tags for our restricted, full-contract staff."

Uh oh. Someone had seen Alan's plastic cuff, and had known what it meant. This was looking like big trouble.

"Look, Mr. Raleigh, this is a pretty incredible story you've been telling me," Murayama said bluntly. "Are you asking me to believe she kidnapped him from your facility and he just *happened* to look like her? I don't recall hearing anything about contracts that prohibit all outside contact before. Sure that just isn't a fancy way of saying 'slave'? Maybe she was trying to rescue him."

Raleigh was starting to sweat. "Slavery is, of course, illegal. I'm sure I don't need to tell you that, Chief Murayama. This is a...an extremely secret project, and thus we require our...personnel in sensitive positions to refrain from...purely voluntary of course, but once signed.... I must insist he be returned to us."

Murayama was stone-faced. "You insist, do you. Did you read the sign above the door? You want a contract enforced, call a lawyer. We deal with crimes. Got that?"

"Kidnapping is a crime," Raleigh insisted, pointing a stubby finger at Moire. "She's done something to him, or he wouldn't have left. Protect him." His attempt at righteous indignation was not convincing to Moire, but Murayama was frowning.

"He's my son. We've been shipping together; just got in to Cullen, in fact. When do you claim he signed this damn contract of yours? Let's see it."

"He can't be her son," Raleigh protested. He sounded genuinely puzzled. "The contracts are completely confidential. Nobody outside the company can see them."

Murayama looked at Raleigh in awe. "Not even a lawyer would defend a contract that can't be seen. Maybe we should take a look at this facility of yours, huh? I'm getting a funny feeling about it."

Moire saw the flash of fear and took the offensive. "The proof of your accusation boils down to my son's choice of personal decoration. You say I kidnapped him. I say you need to prove it. What kind of facility is this, anyway? What are you doing to these people?"

"I...that is, no charges need to be...as long as he returns...."

"He's not your property!" Moire snarled. She was afraid, but so was Raleigh. He seemed to be floundering and out of his depth. She suspected the police call had been an impulse not fully thought out. He hadn't counted on her fighting back.

Alan hadn't said a word since they'd entered the police offices. She glanced back at him. His eyes were wide with fear, and his breathing was quick and shallow. She smiled reassuringly at him, but it didn't seem to help.

Murayama sank his face in his hands, then scrubbed his eyes wearily. "I don't believe this job some days. All right, show me your ID," he said to Moire and Alan. "We'll just do a check to make sure its you."

"I'm not carrying my ID," Moire said with forced calm. "Neither is my son."

Murayama gave her a skeptical look. "Really. You must not be aware that you are required to carry ID on Cullen, one hundred ED fine for noncompliance. We had a lot of people trying to skip checks that way." He leaned back in his chair, looking thoughtful. "There is another option. We can do a direct comparison."

"Why should I have to prove anything? He's the one making wild accusations; why shouldn't he prove them?"

Murayama spread his hands. "I understand, but he's made one accusation I can't ignore. I notice he hasn't been saying much one way or the other," he said, indicating Alan. "Makes people like me suspicious."

Moire really didn't want Alan demonstrating his unique worldview right now, especially when he was terrified. "He doesn't talk much." Big lie.

"Or maybe you drugged him," Murayama said. "What do I know? One of you two has to come up with some proof."

"Fine. Do your test," Moire said recklessly. It was a gamble all around, she reflected as a station tech came to take cell samples from her and Alan.

Raleigh fumed in the background. She didn't dare let him contact this alleged facility of his; they probably did have proof Alan came from there and that would really sink them. She had some time while they ran the tests, anyway.

She had her commlink. The real problem was getting Alan away safely. She might be able to get him out of the room, but they were in the back of the offices and he'd have to get by any number of alert cops to get to the exit. Maybe she could pretend to collapse?

"Results, sir," the tech handed Murayama a slip of plastic printout. *Oh yeah. Tests don't take four days anymore. Damn it to hell.* Murayama looked at it, his eyebrows lifting. *I think your luck just ran out, Cameron.*

"Yes. Not really a surprise, is it? My apologies for the inconvenience, Captain Roberts. You can see the clerk at the front desk about paying your fines." He looked up. Moire was frozen with confusion. "Your lack of ID? You do still have to pay."

"What? That can't be right, your technician must have gotten the samples contaminated!" Raleigh was purple, leaning over the desk and trying to snatch the printout from Murayama's hand.

"I assure you, Mr. Raleigh, our evidence technician does not make mistakes of that order." Murayama's voice was cold. "Now, let's discuss this facility of yours."

"You bribed him!" Raleigh screamed at Moire as she moved slowly to the door. "When Toren hears about this...." He seemed as much frightened as angry.

"*What* did you say?" Murayama's face was dark with fury, and he gestured to his deputy.

Moire forced herself to move. She felt foggy, as if everything was happening far away. The clerk at the desk was talking to her. She had to pay the fines, or they would be looking for her again. She handed the clerk a paychip and walked away. She had to get out, back to the ship. Alan was close beside her, that was good. She didn't want him to get lost.

She made it all the way to the ramp to the main causeway before her legs gave out. She fell clumsily, grabbing the rail and sitting down hard. Alan crouched beside her.

"What's wrong? Why aren't you talking to me?" He looked worried.

His face. Everybody saw it but me. Somewhere in the back of her mind a voice was screaming get up, get out of here, but she couldn't move.

"Please tell me! What is wrong? Are you hurt again?" There was terror in his voice. "Moire!"

"No," she whispered. "Don't say that name. Not here." She reached out her hands and cupped his face. Her son's face. His eyes were wide with confusion. *All this time we were telling the truth, and we didn't even know it.* But how could it be the truth? She didn't have any children, not even preserved embryos. Her ovaries had been removed and stored before the accident, so even Toren couldn't have....

Toren. He'd said Toren. She wrapped her arms around herself, feeling a sudden chill. Toren had taken over the NASA facilities at Houston before the terrorist nuke vaporized it. They must have taken the tissue storage containers. *But why? Why would they want them?*

"People are looking at us," Alan said softly. "I think we should go."

He was right, of course, and if even he had noticed.... "Help me up."

He lifted her effortlessly to her feet and she started walking, slowly at first. Then she started to run.

"Now, let me see if I understand you," Harrington said slowly. "She was on a ship lost eighty years ago, and somehow managed to get back alive and apparently the same age as when she left? Are you certain this is the same person?"

"Quite sure. For one thing, we ran a check on her when she was on *Canaveral*. She's not in the Index."

"I see."

Mammachandra walked by their table with someone's order and gave them a polite nod. The local opinion of them had changed since the Toren ship left. They were willing to talk now, but neither Ennis nor Harrington had learned anything new. Ennis had reluctantly concluded the locals really didn't know anything that could be of use.

They had waited ten days now, with still no sign of *Ayesha*. He was becoming more than a little worried. Lorai had said they'd never been that late before.

A shout came from the back, and Jens burst through the door. "Mahari! *Sie ist hier!* Anja is even now in orbit!"

Mammachandra clapped her hands together, astonished. "We were not expecting her for yet two days! Quick, you have told Lorai?" They disappeared in the back together, talking rapidly.

Anja, not Ayesha. Ennis caught his breath, cursing the similarity of the names. For a moment he had thought their wait was over.

"Their daughter," one of the miners told Ennis. "They only see her once a year or so. Don't expect much from either of 'em until she leaves."

"It seems to be a matter of general interest," observed Harrington. The regulars were discussing the news with great energy.

"Oh sure," the miner nodded. "It's the medical ship, ya know. If ya got somethin' the regular scanner can't figure out, ya gotta wait for them."

A few hours later, Lorai came in followed by a beautiful young woman in a medtech uniform. Anja Parvati had her mother's dignity but was still young enough to be embarrassed by the enthusiastic welcome of the crowd. She emerged from her father's bear hug red-faced, but grinning.

"Oh, I had a pretty boring time," she said, responding to someone's question. "The usual stuff. I heard one of the other medical ships got called back for an emergency, just when it was leaving Mullery. This ship was jumped by pirates, and they were shot up pretty bad, too. It was the ship that came here sometimes–you know, the one that's falling apart?"

People looked at Ennis and Harrington, then looked away, but Ennis hardly noticed. He felt like he'd been punched.

"Was anyone killed?" he asked hoarsely.

"Yeah," she said with regret, turning to him. "The captain–but there wasn't anything anybody could have done about that; advanced Type III. And a woman, I forget her name...."

"The pilot?" *No, not Moire. She can't be dead.*

Anja shook her head. "No, I think the pilot was still alive. I mean, they got back all right. I didn't hear all the details, though."

Alive. She's still alive. Lorai was standing in front of him, pushing him back down in his chair with a firm hand. He hadn't even realized he'd stood up.

"Relax. She's a tough one, didn't you know that? Take more'n a couple pirates to get her." She gave him a shrewd look. "Guess you'll be heading out to Mullery soon as you can, huh?" He nodded. "I can guess why she'd want to miss that other bunch, but what's her problem with you?" She didn't wait for an answer. "Well, when you see her ask her what she did with the Veri-tru micrometer. I can't find it anywhere."

CHAPTER 23
STRANGE ATTRACTORS

Raven had a small room off of the main galley area with a table and enough seats for the senior members of the crew. Moire wasn't sure if it had been intended as an officers' mess, but that's what they used it for. She'd called a meeting as soon as they'd pulled free of Cullen, while Kilberton was taking the ship out to departure range.

"We are going to lose money on the sale of that ship," Gren complained in a tone she recognized as his I-really-don't-like-this voice. "I'm not saying they're going to cheat us, but we could get a better price *and* not pay Milkrik a percentage. Why did we have to leave in such a hurry?" Yolanda nodded, frowning.

Moire glanced at the door. It was closed. "Because some old trouble came and found me there. That's what I want to talk to you about. I'm going to be bad for you to have around now. We need to split up."

The others at the table looked at her in shocked silence. Harvey Felden was the first to speak.

"Huh. Trouble? Seems you could give 'em some and have plenty to spare. What kind of trouble? Cullen's got the law and order routine down. Talk to the police?"

Moire snorted. "I got *brought in* by the police. The law isn't going to help me, not against these guys. It's Toren. They're after me and they want Alan too. They'll have me down as wanted everywhere in the Fringe, which will make it impossible to do business." She took a breath, trying to shake off a sudden wave of depression. She was getting tired of running. "Here's what I suggest. We go back to the salvage field. I'll show Kilberton the trick to get there, and we'll find a small web-capable ship that Alan and I can run. The two of us will take off from there. Is that agreeable?"

"I don't see why we have to change just because Toren wants to get you," Montero said, blinking. "What can they do?"

Gren shook his head. "She's right, Carlos. Toren's got pull and they don't mind using it. If they had the police bring you in I'm surprised you got away."

Moire smiled. "They didn't have time to cook all the evidence right, and the officer was honest. We can't count on that happening again."

"What do they want from you?" asked Madele Fortin. "Can you just give it to them?" She wasn't as forceful as she had been before getting shot, but she was getting better every day.

"They want information, and a guarantee that nobody else gets it. My survival after that would not be a priority," she said dryly. Madele drew in her breath.

"You wanna dodge the law, right?" asked Yolanda suddenly. "'Cuz there are places that don't have much. Places we could still sell the salvaged ships," she said with exaggerated slowness, emphasizing each word as she looked intently at Moire. "Maybe they aren't so nice, OK? The people are dangerous, but they got plenty of money. Don't think Toren would like to show up there, either."

"You mean black market, right? I don't think the crew will go for that." Moire looked around the table, but she didn't see much agreement. Even Madele was nodding thoughtfully.

Gren cleared his throat. "You must have figured out by now Yolanda knows a lot about places like that," he said with a straight face. "She's always done some business that wasn't completely legal, and sometimes we, er, helped out a bit. You missed out on our usual visit to Kulvar; that would have given you a different perspective. I don't think many would have a problem with it. We'd still be doing legal salvage, just selling it somewhere different. It isn't like we'd be doing anything like murder or kindersex or slavery."

That was the trouble with being out of sync. Nobody was laughing like he had made a joke, just nodding in agreement. Now that she thought about it, the cop back on Cullen had mentioned slavery too. Was it really that much of a problem?

She was beginning to think she had underestimated the loyalty of her crew. The earnings from the salvage operation were enormous by Fringe standards, but they hadn't jumped at the offer to have Kilberton take over, which would have gotten them the same money. They wanted *her*.

You don't have to run this time. You don't have to fight alone. It was tempting, very tempting. She didn't want to leave. They were Fringers, they understood resisting authority at an instinctive level. If they knew there was even more money and rebellion she could offer them, her plans could expand considerably.

She almost told them right then about Sequoyah, just to get it over with. Somebody else had to know. The impulse faded when she thought about it longer. First she needed to make sure of *all* of the crew.

After the meeting she made a general broadcast announcement. Following further discussion with Yolanda and Gren, she lined up the ship to head for Kulvar. While it was definitely a criminal outpost, there was enough legitimate shipping that anybody who wanted to leave could do so.

The crew reaction came trickling in as the trip progressed. Some of the responses surprised her.

Moire eased the legs off a fraction and checked the proximity readout. Still a bit longer before dropout.

"Gren tells me you want to stay on," she said to Kilberton, who was watching her work. "You know that people will think we're criminals, right?"

He nodded. His dark face was hard to read and the heavy brows always made him look serious.

"My cousin says you are honest," he said. "One cannot be responsible for the opinions of others. You deal with dishonest people because you have no choice."

"Yeah, but *you* have a choice. I'm glad you are staying, but don't be a martyr. Let me know when it's too much for you and we'll find you a way out."

"As you are doing for these others," Kilberton said. "But why does Harvey Felden leave here? He told me he was staying."

The proximity meter beeped, and she dropped out of webspace. "He's going back to Cullen with them to get the money and pay them their ship shares. We'll pick him up later." She tilted her head toward the realspace bridge. "Take us in."

"Yes, Captain."

She stepped out of the pit and headed for her quarters. The other reason they wanted to stop here was to get her some good fake ID. Even though they were sticking to the shady side of the Fringe, she didn't want to have to deal with the cops at such a disadvantage again. Besides, if Harvey was going to sign off on the ship sale with the agents on Cullen he would need a witnessed signing authority from her, which would again require her to have believable ID.

When they docked, Yolanda accompanied Moire and Alan into the station.

"This doesn't look too bad," Moire said, looking at the main causeway. The people seemed ordinary for the Fringe; the shops and station worn but decent. Not the seedy criminal outpost that she'd been expecting.

Yolanda curled her lip with contempt. "This is Topside. We're headed for Downunder. Stationmaster is a drunken idiot and her deputy is bought, body and soul. Long as Topside looks OK she don't even notice what goes on anywhere else."

She led them through a series of dropdowns, the simple, one-level elevators that were used frequently in stations. As they left the last one Moire saw a group of toughs hanging about the entrance to the level. She caught the glint of weaponry on more than one of them.

One of the toughs slouched toward them. The others stood straighter, watching them with predatory interest. Yolanda pulled a chain hanging about her neck and fished up a metal pendant with an inset of some kind.

"They got business," she said, jerking her thumb back at Moire and Alan. Her accent was thicker, more accented and choppy. "They're with me."

The tough held the pendant between two metal-laced fingers. The inset glowed, a flashing swirl of color, then darkened. "'Zat so. Looks like you still got credit, *hancha*. You don't got load, taking walks instead?" His expression was mocking as he glanced at Moire and Alan.

"Na, I got load," Yolanda sniffed. "Later, beb. You'll see. Think I just run hot stick?" The others sniggered, and the tough looked angry.

"Didn't see ya running much, thought you liked the Topside these days maybe."

Yolanda tilted her head slightly, back toward Moire. "She my main line yehsure. Getting' the good stuff takes some time, beb. We been busy."

The tough looked at Moire with a fraction more respect, and stood out of the way. Yolanda stalked past him without looking, and Moire and Alan followed.

The interior was cramped and dingy, trash in the corners and odd smells in the air. She recognized the scent of tobacco, which she hadn't encountered since she'd last left Beta C. It was illegal now but people were smoking it openly here.

Moire glanced at some of the inhabitants and was glad Alan was with her. These were definitely not Kulvar's good citizens. They were also wearing enough bodymods to make the mercenaries feel right at home—although she doubted the mercs would try the skull implants. Too dangerous even for them. She caught sight of one woman with bony spikes protruding through her transparent purple hair, and wondered how anyone could make a helmet for her.

"Kiyo isn't the cheapest, but he won't sell out. Least I never heard he did. And he's good," Yolanda added.

"We need the best we can get," Moire agreed. "I like people who stay bought, too."

Kiyo was located in a warren of narrow, winding passageways leading to tiny shops. The walls were covered with swirls of color, dulled with grime. Art, or graffiti? Moire couldn't tell. Kiyo's shop was at the end, and unlike most of the others was reasonably intact. The door even looked like it might seal.

Kiyo had a face like soft, worn leather. He didn't look at them, but heard their request in silence, his eyes on a desk display. "Where 'is a from?" he asked in a raspy voice when Moire finished.

"Where do you want it to say you're from?" translated Yolanda, seeing her baffled expression.

"Yeh. Just want tha docs, say Earth, mebbe. If ya tryin' ta stay out of sight of somethin', say Fringe."

"Someplace Fringe. Not Cullen." They might remember her on Cullen, might even have some sort of record. She didn't want anybody to start checking up on her there.

He nodded and rummaged in a drawer for supplies. Kiyo reached out and stuck a sticky patch on her face, another on Alan's, then pulled them off and carried them to a grey box with part of its cover missing. Giving the machine an expert whack, he fed the plastic patches in, one by one, to a narrow slot in its side. Next he did a thermal pattern of their faces, and a regular 360 still from a vid. He pursed his lips as he stared at his desk display, marking something on the screen with his stylus now and then.

The grey box beeped and he inserted a datatab in a slot on the side. Glancing repeatedly at his desk display, he tapped in information on a panel on the box. He pulled out the tab and inserted another one, repeating the process.

"There ya go," he said after a few more steps. He placed the new ID tabs before them, and the plastic patches he'd used for the DNA samples. "Now I remove data." He hit buttons on the grey box and the other devices, and the displays cleared. "I don't keep nothin'." He held out his hand, and Moire gave him a paychip with a huge sum of money on it. He checked the value, not with the display but with a reader, then nodded. "Bye."

"One more thing," Moire said hastily. "Know how to get this off?" She held up Alan's arm so the cuff showed. Alan twitched his arm away, looking worried.

Kiyo flicked a glance briefly, then looked away. "I don't do that. You want Savarinsen. Not if she's drunk, though. Can't trust her then." He waved a hand, indicating they should leave. He seemed uncomfortable.

Yolanda grumbled but led them to the mysterious Savarinsen. She ran a shop full of strange equipment, none of which Moire recognized. They looked dangerous. She didn't seem drunk, so Moire showed her Alan's cuff.

"Ohh, yeah. Haven't seen that version before but I know the type," she drawled. "Won't be comfortable, but I can get it off."

"I don't want...," Alan gave Moire a despairing look. "It *hurts* you if you try to move it."

"She knows how to take it off without it hurting," Moire said softly, hoping desperately this was true. Savarinsen had recognized the device, so she probably did. "It's too dangerous to leave on. What if that man sees it again?"

Alan reluctantly let her hold out his arm and pull back his sleeve, but he flinched when Savarinsen tapped the cuff. She slicked down Alan's arm with a thick, white goo, making sure it went under the snugly fitting cuff. She then attached a loop of black metal connected by pair of tubes to a cylinder with frost along its outer edge.

"This is gonna get cold, now. But you can't move or it'll set it off."

Alan nodded. Frost began to form on the black metal loop, and then, slowly, on the plastic. Alan's face twisted, and he made small whimpering noises, but he didn't move.

The cuff cracked suddenly, giving off an acrid, chemical smell and pops of discharging energy. Savarinsen quickly disconnected the loop and grabbed the cuff in a large set of pliers with clear plastic handles. Moire took a wipe Savarinsen handed her and gently removed the paste from Alan's arm. Where the cuff had been it was solid, and his skin was cold.

Alan touched his wrist where the cuff had been, then stared at Savarinsen. He didn't seem to have any serious damage.

"That was a nasty one," Savarinsen said, shaking her head. "Don't want to know why you had it, beb, but they sure didn't like you. I'll get rid of it, if you like. Got a furnace next door. Gone like it never happened."

Moire scooped up the pieces and put them gingerly in an empty food carton from the floor. "Thanks, but I'll take it with me." Kiyo's paranoia had rubbed off on her and she didn't want to leave any evidence behind.

When they got back to the ship everybody who was leaving had piled their baggage outside the ship dock and was loading it on float-pallets. Harvey Felden was there too, with two small carrybags and a harassed expression on his lined face.

"You got everything you need?" Moire asked.

Harvey gave her a look. "Haven't lost anything since the last time you asked me. What is it with you? You're so twitchy it's making me nervous."

Moire glanced at the others milling about. Tenna and Michel were leaving, unwilling to deal with any more danger than they'd experienced already. She wasn't surprised about them. What was surprising was how many had chosen to stay. Did they really understand how dangerous it was?

"I'm not making it up, you know."

Harvey hunched his thin shoulders. "Yes, yes, I believe you."

It wasn't a convincing statement, but Moire let it be. "I'm surprised Freddie is going," she said after a few minutes of silence. "He seemed to really like it out there."

"He'd have to leave his junk piles," Harvey said with a wicked gleam in his eyes. "You wouldn't let him have 'em on *Raven,* even if there was room. He's going back to Mullery to open a repair shop, last I heard. I'm sure that mechanic had something to do with it. Freddie likes the ladies and she was real friendly."

Moire grinned. Yes, that made much more sense. "Maybe we can stop by and offload any junk we don't want with him."

The bags were loaded and everyone made their final farewells. Moire started worrying all over again. She pulled Harvey aside.

"Look–keep a low profile, OK? All of you. Try to make them understand they need to keep quiet and out of sight for a while. And when you come back, don't talk to anybody. If they know you're meeting up with me...."

"I get the point," he said dryly. "I'll do my damnedest, won't talk to strangers, wash my hands, and change my shipsuit liner at least once a week. Satisfied?" he glared.

Moire smiled in spite of herself. "It'll do."

Ennis hastily finished gathering his gear together and sealed his duffel, activating the lock just to be on the safe side. The crew didn't know he and Harrington were planning to skip out on them. It had seemed all right at first, but he'd found one of them rifling Harrington's gear and they'd been shaken down twice for more money. Time to leave.

"This may not be an improvement," Harrington said softly. "Kulvar is, shall we say, famous for being a haunt of the criminally inclined."

"Yeah, but we'll have more of a choice in how we get robbed," Ennis muttered. "Is it quiet out there?"

"I will go ahead and check."

He picked up his bag and headed for the dock hatch. He quickened his pace when he heard voices up ahead. Damn. Some of the crew were still awake and on the ship. Harrington sounded cool and calm as always, but with a layer of tense annoyance; the crew voices didn't sound happy. One he recognized, a huge man who went by the name of Pud.

He eased up closer, staying out of sight.

"You said you going all the way, right? So you gotta pay us for the next leg. You go, you stay, I don't care. But we came here jus' because–"

"You were heading here from the beginning, and we agreed on a price all the way to Pykko. You can now get other passengers to take our places and charge them as well."

Ennis sneaked a glance. Pud shoved Harrington up against the wall, hard. He had a knife in one hand. One of the others was starting to rip open Harrington's bag. Harrington was struggling, trying to reach his weapon, but Pud had effectively immobilized him with sheer bulk.

Ennis felt for his gun, feverishly searching for the power settings. He found the tiny switch and moved it until the nub glowed orange, indicating lowest energy burst.

"Get back!" he shouted, and pointed the gun at Pud's broad back. "Let him go!"

Pud turned, and the other crewmember snarled and snatched for her own weapon. Ennis fired. The range was too far to cause anything more than surface burns, but the shock of the energy blast was enough to let Harrington get free. Ennis grabbed Harrington's bag and ran after him out the hatch.

"Thank you," Harrington said, breathing deeply as they moved quickly away from the dock. "I think our decision to seek alternate transportation was a wise one, considering recent events. We might not have made it all the way as it was."

Ennis nodded. "I hope they don't file a complaint." It would be difficult and dangerous to explain his scan-resistant gun.

"You haven't heard much about Kulvar, have you?" Harrington asked, visibly amused. "I'm told corruption is an art form here. If those thugs made a complaint they would likely get a fine for not paying off the security chief first."

They wandered the station for what seemed like hours. None of the docked ships were going to Mullery.

"Yeah, we go there sometimes, but we don't do passengers," shrugged a crewman standing by a ship hatch, when they asked.

"At this rate, we may have to hire on to get there," said Ennis, frowning. Harrington nodded, looking thoughtful.

"What ships are hiring?" he asked the crewman.

"To Mullery? Mebbe *Sassbaby,* or *Tiamat.* Second level, though."

"What does that mean?" asked Ennis as they walked away.

"The lower the level, the more, er, criminally inclined. Our former ship is docked on the second level, so I am not encouraged."

The hiring was quite informal, from what Ennis could see. Someone would be sitting outside the docking hatch, usually on a crate, and holding a datapad. A few just had a textsheet posted by the hatch with the open positions and a code to call.

"Is it always like this? All the ships seem to be hiring," Ennis added.

"I doubt there is a ship in the Fringe that runs with a full crew," Harrington said. "There simply aren't enough people willing—and please note I said nothing about their capabilities. The captains usually are hoping to find someone trainable and with a minimum of chemical dependencies."

Sassbaby was docked toward the end of the second level.

"A pity," observed Harrington, looking at the textsheet. "They only want a third-shift engineer's mate and a cook."

"I've held a number of positions in Fleet, but cook was not one of them," Ennis said. "My engineering skills are not much better."

"Yes, I think something more manual and less intellectually demanding is called for," agreed Harrington. "Did you see where *Tiamat* is docked?"

They wandered back up the level. A small crowd was gathered about a woman with a datapad, but she wasn't talking to them. Instead, she was talking to a man with long black hair and brown skin, waving her hands with great animation.

"How many you need, eh? What you gonna do with 'em?"

"I *told* you, Liza. We're doing salvage. Just send any repair crew you don't want yourselves to *Raven*, OK? We'll probably be here a few days."

"Ahhh...." Liza raised her hands to heaven. "If you weren't my favorite ex-husband...."

"Favorite *living* ex-husband," the man said, his expression gloomy but his eyes twinkling.

A young man was standing beside him, not paying attention to the conversation. He turned to follow the older man when he left, and for a brief moment his eyes met Ennis's. Ennis felt a shock of recognition.

"It's him!" he whispered to Harrington, nudging him and indicating the two who were leaving. "From the other sketch!"

Harrington's gaze narrowed. "Yes," he drawled. "I do believe you are correct. But is *she* here as well?"

The young man was wearing a red metalmesh scarf, tied about one forearm like the mercenaries did. Ennis recognized that scarf; he'd seen it on *Canaveral*. Cameron had been wearing it.

He felt his pulse quicken. "She's here." Of course she wasn't at Mullery anymore. If he hadn't recognized the young man, she would have gotten away again. *Not this time,* he vowed. He was too close to his goal to fail now.

They detached themselves from the crowd and followed at a careful distance. A wild-eyed man came staggering from a hatch in front of Ennis, making him take a quick step to avoid him, but the man was followed by several others, loud and swaggering. He tried to break through, but the crowd was already thick and by the time they struggled free, the two had disappeared from view.

"What level do you think they were going to?" Harrington asked, grimacing with annoyance.

Ennis shook his head. "It doesn't matter. We just need to find what level *Raven* is on."

Moire watched Alan poke at his food. "Not hungry?" Usually he had polished his plate before she was halfway through. He hadn't said much either.

He shrugged. His face was troubled. "Why did Tenna do that?" he managed finally. "She put her arms all the way around me. I thought that was a happy thing. But she was sad. Crying."

"She likes you, so she gave you a hug. She has to leave you, so she's sad." Confusion wrinkled his face even more.

"Why does she have to leave?"

"Because we are going to be doing dangerous things, with dangerous people. She was afraid."

"But...."

Moire held up a hand. "You and I are part of why it is dangerous. Bad people are looking for us. She will be safer somewhere else."

He started eating again. "I wish she wasn't sad, though."

"She gave you a mail link, didn't she? Write to her. That will make her happy."

Alan brightened. "OK."

It was hard for her to know how much to tell him, how much he would understand. Sometimes it was easy to forget his real age. She still didn't know how she would explain the truth about them.

"So what's this about a *festine?*" she asked. "What is it?"

"Yolanda says it is people doing tricks, and music."

"You want to go, right?" He nodded enthusiastically. Alan loved music. "I suppose—but stick close to Yolanda and do what she tells you, OK?"

"You don't want to see the *festine* too?" he asked, sounding disappointed.

"No, not really. Besides, somebody ought to be at the ship." It would be better if he didn't go, but Yolanda should be able to keep him out of trouble. She hoped.

"I saw that man again," Alan said, apropos of nothing.

"Where? From Cullen?" Moire asked, suddenly worried. He didn't seem concerned, though, just mildly interested.

"No, from the book place. At...at Angelos."

She frowned, trying to remember. The bookseller hadn't set off any of her alarms. It should be OK. "Yep, people move around," she said. Especially in the Fringe. Sometimes she thought Gren had an ex-wife in every station. "I'm sure even criminals like to read now and then. He should do well opening a shop here. Let's go find Yolanda, hmm?"

"You're sure this is the right berth?" Ennis looked at the closed hatch, skeptical. There wasn't even a textsheet outside, and the display for the ship name was blank.

"According to the current station listing," Harrington said. He pressed the annunciator button. After a pause, he pressed it again. "It appears that no one is home. We could wait."

Ennis frowned. "There's no cover. They'd see us before we saw them. Let's try scouting ahead first. If we don't find her we can always come back."

"You are not concerned they may leave before then?"

"Of course I'm concerned," Ennis said, irritated. "It's a chance, but he said they'd be staying a few days."

Raven's berth was at an intermediate level between the first and second levels. He hadn't seen any sign of the two they had been following on the way, so it was a fair bet they had gone down from the second level rather than up.

"Let's head lower," Ennis suggested.

Third level had a visibly seedy look to it. There were fewer ship berths, and more businesses. And people. He tried to keep a hard, unwelcoming expression on his face, one that would encourage them to keep their distance. The people and the surroundings were painfully familiar, and he felt his temper rise. He'd done everything he could to escape this kind of place.

"My, my—what a nice assortment of illicit pharmaceuticals," said Harrington, fascinated. "I think they've come out with some new ones. The dope-laced tattoos are getting quite sophisticated. I see they are no longer restricted to foil inserts."

Ennis glanced over. "You're kidding. How do they dope tattoos? And why?" He recognized some of the metal foil designs—the mercenaries had them.

"If you are in a situation where dope might be hard to obtain, or would be dangerous to store, all that is needed is some kind of stimulus. Electricity, or heat. That releases the drug."

Yes, that made a lot of sense. Something to be aware of, should he ever get back to *Canaveral* and his old duties. He wondered if that was a possibility, even if his mission was successful. He couldn't help speculating now that he was so close, even as he reminded himself the chances were small. And he still had to find Cameron.

They followed the narrow causeway as best they could for the people crowding it. Ennis wondered if the station safety officer had ever been down here—the minimum space requirements had been ignored for some time, from the looks of it, and they had replaced the metal sheath and vents of the air shaft with wire mesh for better circulation. The shops and living quarters were crammed in every available corner, sometimes in multiple levels.

The walls and structures became more well-maintained as they walked farther in. This section seemed to be the weapons merchants; personal firearms, various kinds of metal or carbon-fiber blades, and even explosives.

He blinked in astonishment, recognizing a military-issue thermal grenade, extremely illegal anywhere outside of Fleet. He supposed he should be glad there was only one on display.

"...do you have heavies in that caliber?"

He stopped short, listening intently. He knew that voice. Slowly, carefully, he scanned the crowd. Nothing. Had he imagined it? How could he have missed her? Another careful look, but still nothing. Harrington, picking up his silent signal, was backing up, eying the crowd.

"I've already got regular ammo. Anybody else carry this?"

There. Crouched over a small open crate, wearing a dark red wrap jacket.

Her back was to them, her face upturned toward the shop owner.

It was suddenly hard to breathe. The sketch had been right. She did look different. Alive. Intent.

Beautiful.

Moire shook her head and stood, exchanging a few more words with the merchant before turning to leave.

She was standing directly in front of him before he could move. The crowd had thinned just at that moment and she glanced at him as she went by. He could see recognition, then shock, in her eyes, and she stopped. Her lips parted, whether in astonishment or to speak he couldn't tell.

He was frozen, staring at her. Then she suddenly darted to one side.

"Wait!" shouted Harrington, stepping into her path. She jerked, stumbled, and avoided his outstretched arms.

She sprinted away. Ennis followed.

CHAPTER 24
WHERE THE HEART IS

Of course it was too good to last. Damn, damn, damn! Moire ran, heart pounding as she dodged the people on the causeway. She should have listened to Alan. He tried to tell her.... *I saw that man again.* Not the bookseller, but the man in the black vest who had been so talkative. How was he connected to Ennis?

Ennis wasn't in uniform. Undercover, or the next thing to it. That meant she had no way of knowing how many of them there were. But of course one of them had to be Ennis, who she'd been so unreasoningly glad to see she'd nearly gotten caught right there. *That's the kind of sappy thinking that can get you killed, Cameron. You can bet he wasn't glad to see you.*

She had to shake them; get them lost or confused or slowed down. And then what? Back to the ship. Fleet couldn't know about *Raven* yet, she hadn't had it that long.

Moire risked a glance over her shoulder. Still chasing her, damn their eyes. She vaulted over a slow-moving pneumatic lift-pallet full of boxes, tossing some behind her for luck. The pallet driver shouted curses after her.

That stunt increased the distance between her and her pursuers, but not enough. She had to do something more. *There's always a way...think, dammit!*

At first Ennis wondered why nobody seemed to be even slightly interested in the chase going on in their midst, then he shook his head angrily. How could he have forgotten? If it wasn't your fight, you didn't get involved. That was the way you survived.

Of course, it worked both ways. The locals weren't interfering with them, but they weren't stopping Moire either.

Harrington shouted a warning. Ennis spun and flattened himself against a wall, just avoiding a mechanical lifter with a load of scrap metal lumbering out of a side corridor. As soon as there was space he squeezed past, but Moire was no longer in sight.

"Damn!"

"What's that?" Harrington pointed. A flash of dark red was moving away from them, the same dark red as the jacket she was wearing. The reporter ran after it.

Ennis followed, frowning. She wasn't moving very fast. Then he saw why. The jacket was clutched tightly in the hands of a grimy indigent, his face still showing his bemusement at his sudden and inexplicable good fortune.

Clever–but she had to be somewhere close; there wasn't anywhere to go. Ennis turned, searching. Strange motion caught his eye–a dark figure, hunched over and moving swiftly through the crowds. He called to Harrington and ran, not waiting to see if the reporter was following.

She'd seen him now and was no longer trying to stay out of sight. She turned down a passage that was a visible dead end, the metal mesh screening of the air shaft blocking her way.

She jumped and grabbed a ridge of one of the flimsy shelters, pulling herself up and then sprinted noisily across the sheet-metal roofs. Loose dust and crud fell as she ran, bringing out irate shop owners from inside. When she got to the mesh guarding the air shaft, she started to climb. Ennis saw a gap in the mesh at the top, just below the ceiling. Moire pulled herself through the gap to the other side of the mesh and started to climb down.

Looking quickly up and down the passage, he discarded his first idea of following her. The shop owners were armed, and looking annoyed. At him.

It wasn't a good idea anyway. It was too easy for her to elude them here, and he didn't need to chase her. He knew where she would be headed, sooner or later. He turned back toward the level exit. He just needed to get to her ship before she did.

Still no sign of Harrington. Ennis hoped nothing had happened to him, but he couldn't take the time to find out. He had to find Moire before she could leave the station. She would be even harder to locate now that she knew he was looking for her.

There were plenty of people moving past *Raven*'s dock when he got there. He must have gotten there before her; she couldn't have gone all the way from fourth level in the same time. Fourth level would be even worse than the one they'd been on.

She would have to use this passage to get to her ship. He needed a place to stay out of sight, yet be able to watch the dock. He took up his position behind the bulkhead of an emergency pressure door, watching the entrance from the lower levels.

Ennis waited impatiently. A gangly spacer wandered up to the dock entrance and pressed the annunciator, but nobody answered and eventually he wandered away again. *Still nobody on the ship. I wonder why?* It wasn't going to do them any good to ask for mechanics if they weren't there to hire them.

A woman walked by him in the crowd, coming from the upper level.

She was wearing a torn shirt over her shipsuit, the same kind of shirt Moire had been wearing. His eyes widened in shock. It *was* Moire. She must have climbed down the air shaft to trick him, then climbed back up. Had she seen him? He'd been turned away, watching the lower level entrance.

She was between him and the ship now, and he swore. If she got away now...he pulled out his gun, glancing to check that the settings were still for energy burst and low. The nub glowed a reassuring orange.

"Cameron! Stop!" He stood out away from the bulkhead, the gun pointing ahead. She darted a disbelieving glance over her shoulder and reached up to the dock security plate. He fired.

The gun jumped in his hand and Moire cried out, slumping and falling against the now-open dock entrance. She was clutching her side.

Ennis felt his heart constrict. No energy burst–but he had it set, he'd checked it!

He ran to the dock hatch, numb with terror. She lay slumped against the door, blood drenching her arm and side. He had to do something, but he didn't trust the station. That could get them both in to trouble. The shooting had drawn attention; people were stopping and looking their way. He needed to get them both out of sight.

Ennis reached under her shoulders and picked her up, half-lifting and half-carrying her through the dock entrance. The ship must have some medical supplies, enough to stabilize her until he could get reliable help.

Moire groaned, turning her head restlessly. "You shouldn't say the name," she mumbled. "First Alan, and now you...."

Still alive. He had to keep her that way.

Her side was on fire, and her left arm wasn't working properly. Ennis was dragging her into the ship, and pestering her about something. It didn't make any sense. If he wanted to kill her he should do it outside so it wouldn't make a mess for the others to clean up.

She closed her eyes, hoping he'd go away, but that only made him more agitated.

"Where is your medical kit?" Ennis said, loud and angry. He shook her.

"If you hadn't shot me you wouldn't need it," she complained, her words stumbling over each other. "Make up your mind...'s at the, the end there," nodding her head at the first corridor off the main passageway.

Ennis dragged her good arm over his shoulder and pulled, sending a wave of agony through her body. Her vision darkened, then cleared.

The medical station was small and narrow. Ennis was struggling to pull down the examination table while still keeping a grip on her.

"There." He shoved her down, grabbing her legs and swinging them up to the table. He turned his head, searching the station. "Medical kit, medical kit...got it." Moire lay on the exam table, feeling curiously detached as Ennis scrabbled through the kit, cursing. She could just drift off, it would be better for everybody, really. Almost everybody.

"Don't shoot Alan," she said when Ennis stood back up. "He wouldn't like it...besides, might get you first. Must have been his father, sure didn't get that from me...."

"I don't know what you are talking about," he said shortly, doing something to her side that would have made her scream if she'd had the energy to do it. The pain ebbed and a feeling of cool numbness spread. "There, the bloodglue is holding. Damn them...." He was holding a sliver of white, smeared with blood. "Ceramic needle. I knew that gun was a bad idea. Hold on, I'm going to have to cut your shipsuit to get at your arm. It went through."

How pale his face was. And the hand holding the needle was shaking. Maybe he didn't like the sight of blood. *Tough. I don't like the sight of my blood either.*

"That's a good shipsuit you ruined. Dammit, Ennis...." Her mind was clearing a little. She could see the butt of his weapon sticking out of his side pocket, where he must have jammed it in a hurry.

"It was set for energy burst. I don't know why it...." He pulled the tattered section of her shipsuit sleeve free and squeezed more bloodglue from the packet on the wounds. "What's this on your hand?" He turned up her palm. It was raw and bleeding, covered in scratches.

"Climbing up three levels of air shaft," Moire sighed, holding up the other hand. "It seemed like a good idea at the time."

He gave a laugh that was more like an explosive snort. Cleaning the blood off her forearm, he attached a fluid pack and then started bandaging her hands. "It worked too well for me. If I hadn't known you'd head back to your ship you would have gotten away."

Moire wiggled the fingers of her left hand experimentally as he was bandaging the right. The ceramic needle must have missed any bones. She could use it if she didn't let the agony get in the way.

When he finished she grasped his arm and struggled to sit up, ignoring his protests. She sagged forward, and he caught her. She leaned her head against his shoulder as if she was faint. It didn't take much effort to fake. Ennis made no attempt to move her away.

Yes, this is very comfortable. But it isn't going to last. Remember that. She forced her left hand to move to his pocket. Pulling quickly away, she braced herself against the wall and pointed the gun at him.

"Thanks for plugging the holes you made. Now get lost."

Ennis went completely still, staring at the gun. "This is not going to help."

"Even I can hit you at this range. Going back with you isn't going to help me either. I was involved in a mutiny—do they still do firing squads for that? That's if I'm lucky. If Toren gets me, they will suck my brains out my ears and *then* shoot me." She shook her head. "Next time, take better aim. Go find the others, that should take you a while. Does Fleet care what order you get us in?" A wave of pain made her wince, and she concentrated on holding the gun steady.

He closed his eyes. "I'm only supposed to find you. They want to know why Toren wants you so bad they compromised Fleet security. Do you realize we thought you were dead? We couldn't find the courier ship." He opened his eyes again, and they were blazing with anger. "Nobody knew you could fly it."

"I've been flying web for a long time."

"I know." His face was somber.

He knows. He knows what I am. "Then you know I can't go back." Relief flooded her, made her voice soft.

His face twisted. "You could make a quite convincing case of extenuating circumstances for your participation in the mutiny. Evidence you stopped it from getting worse. They won't execute you." He sighed. "And Toren...it's Umbra that wants to know about them. If anybody can keep Toren out, they can." His eyes searched her face. "You have to trust me. You want to survive, don't you? Please. It's hard when you're on your own. Help me."

The last words were so faint she barely heard them. She wasn't sure what he was trying to say but he sounded desperate. There was more going on than a Fleet investigation, and he wasn't going to go away. She would have to shoot him or give him the gun.

"All right," she said after a long moment. "There are some people I need to say good-bye to. Can you wait a bit?"

He nodded. She took a deep breath and handed him the gun. He adjusted something on the side and tucked it in his back waistband.

Moire pushed her hands against the table surface and stood up, gasping at the pain lancing up her palms. An idea started to take form.

"Madele has some painkillers somewhere." She moved stiffly to the pile of fiberboard boxes still stacked against the wall.

"Madele?"

"Our medic. We moved a lot of stuff from the old ship, and she still hasn't stowed it." The others had done the packing, which was what she was counting on. They wouldn't know what was important and what Madele, at least, would consider no longer needed.

There. She opened the box before Ennis could get a clear view of the label. "Oops, wrong one." The red tabs slid into her pocket. "Other box, maybe. Yep, this is it." She swallowed the pill quickly, feeling the quickening in her blood a few seconds later. *They are definitely going to have to grow me some new innards this time.*

"The others are still at a show on station, so it might be a while," she said, trying to keep her expression relaxed. The pain was throbbing through her now. "We kept some of the old cargo, too. Luxury goods. Have you ever had real coffee?"

Ennis followed Moire back down the main passage and down a level to the galley. She was moving slowly, but at least she was moving. The dart had cut through her rib muscles, but nothing too serious. He'd been lucky. He didn't like to think *how* lucky.

In the galley she opened a cupboard and started pulling out supplies one-handed. "How did you know my name?" she asked, adding water to a metal container with some controls on the side.

"I found a still in an old book. A picture of the crew of *Bon Accord*," Ennis answered.

She stopped pouring out some small, dark lumps from a foil bag into the machine and stared down at the counter for a moment. Then she shook her head, as if trying to wake up. "How did you find the book?" She pressed the top of the device she'd put the lumps in, and it made a brief grinding noise.

"Remember I said Toren sent someone to look for you? I overheard him interrogating one of the mercenaries, and I looked up some of the things he asked about." Ennis took a seat at one of the tables, keeping a careful eye on what Moire was doing. She could still try something to get away, and he didn't want to give her the chance. But she was only adjusting some settings on the equipment. "We took the gun from him. It's scan resistant."

It was capable of overriding its settings, he realized bitterly. It must have an automatic switch from energy to projectile, if the range was too great for the energy burst to have an effect.

"Toren knows you know? That must make things awkward."

He smiled sardonically. "Fleet wants me to stay away from their ships for a while. That's why I'm with Intelligence now. Toren doesn't know everything, but they know enough that they want to talk to me. I'm sure you know what that's like."

Moire gave him a quick grin. "My sympathies. And what did the other guy do to deserve this job?" Seeing his questioning look, she added, "the guy with the silver hair, who was with you down below."

"Neville Harrington. He's not Fleet, he's a reporter."

She laughed out loud. "A reporter...wouldn't Toren have a fit if they knew." She took out some cheap plastic mugs. "Will you take the pot to the table?" she asked, indicating the container.

He took a mug and the pot, while Moire put things away again. She took the remaining mug and sat down opposite him, pouring out a dark liquid with shaky care. She drank deeply, visibly relaxing with the first swallow.

Ennis took a sip. It was bitter, harsh—not like the synthetic he was used to. When he looked up, she had an amused expression on her face, watching him.

"It does take some getting used to," she said. "But now you can say you've tried it."

"True." He took another sip. It wasn't bad, except for the chemical aftertaste.

"What are you doing hanging out with a reporter?" she asked.

"He saw you at Thuban, and he knew where to look for you." He hesitated. "We saw someone who resembles you here. He'd seen him with you before."

"Yes, I know." She took another drink. Her face had a distant, empty expression. "He's my son."

Shock held him immobile for a moment. "I thought you didn't have any family."

"I thought so too." Her voice had an angry edge to it now. "It's a long story and I don't know all of it myself."

This didn't seem like a safe topic of conversation. Ennis was surprised to see that he'd finished his mug of coffee, and poured out some more.

"I have to ask—what is Sequoyah? Is it a planet?"

She nodded. "Found it on the last mission. We had to land somewhere—we got damaged on the way in. We thought we'd fixed things, but it was even worse on the way back. We...the ship...." She was staring into her coffee, seeing things that weren't there. "Etienne made me keep going. He wanted that information to make it back even if they didn't. So I did. We were all in suits then, no air to speak of, ship falling apart around us. That's what happened, in the end. The drive field failed. Out of webspace and back into relativity, and in a few minutes I went almost eighty years. I don't remember what happened after that."

Ennis felt a wash of cold. He'd heard of Einstein's Revenge, but it was usually just a few minutes off your chronometer that needed adjusting if the pilot was clumsy.

He tried to lift his mug, but it was strangely heavy. He was tired...when was the last time he'd gotten any sleep? Grimacing with effort, he tried again. His arm strained upward then dropped, the coffee spilling over the table. That wasn't fatigue. *She put something in the coffee.*

Ennis made a violent effort to stand, to pull out his gun, but it only made him fall clumsily over the table.

"You aren't...," he gasped. She was drinking the same thing he had, hadn't even made him take one cup instead of another. Why wasn't she affected?

She didn't seem triumphant, or mocking. Just sad. "That wasn't a painkiller I took. It was a stimulant. I put a muscle relaxant in the coffee. You probably won't even lose consciousness."

"You said...you trusted me." That's what hurt the worst now—not that she was getting away. Again. That she had lied, and he had believed her.

I *should have palmed some real painkillers along with the Solverlactin,* Moire thought. The temporary numbing effect of the bloodglue had worn off some time ago and it was getting harder to concentrate past the pain.

Ennis was sprawled on the table, and she didn't have the strength to move him. He still had enough control to give her a burning, angry look as he made his whispered accusation.

"I trust you, but I don't trust the people you work for," Moire replied, feeling defensive. She got up, wincing, crouching down closer to him. "Fleet wasn't able to stop Toren from getting on your ship, were they? I've got too many people depending on me. Like my son. If I leave now, they will still be in danger from Toren."

He just glared at her silently.

"I promise I'll go, someday. When I can do it without risking anybody's life but my own. Here," she said, fumbling in her pocket. "You'll know what it means. It belonged to someone I knew." She held up the NASA pin. "I'll come back for that."

Ennis closed his eyes, which she took for a positive sign. His eyes flew open when she put the pin in his shirt pocket, his hands spasming with motion for a brief moment, then subsiding.

Reaching awkwardly for her comm, she punched the general recall signal. All the crewmembers were carrying links, so that should get them. She called Alan directly.

"Come back now. I need your help."

"OK. Yolanda says it is over anyway."

In a few minutes he was there in person, Yolanda looking wide-eyed first at her, then at Ennis sprawled on the table.

"You know there's a trail of blood all the way from the hatch, right? Want me to get rid of the body?"

"He's still alive, and we're going to keep him that way. It's my blood."

Alan was pale, staring at her in horror. "Is he a pirate?"

Despite the pain, she had to laugh. "No. There was an accident. I'm all right, really." Alan started to argue, but she cut him off. "We don't have time. Yolanda, I need you to find someone on station."

She propped her head up on one hand, trying to think. Ennis was probably going to get in trouble for this. What had he been saying? Fleet wanted to know why Toren was after her. Maybe she could give him the information, and they'd let him off the hook.

"Bring me a datapad and some blank tabs before you go, OK?" She quickly described Harrington the reporter to Yolanda. "Just tell him Commander Ennis sent you, and he needs his help." Yolanda rolled her eyes and departed on her errand, reappearing a few minutes later with the datapad.

It hurt to transcribe, with her wounded hands. It hurt to remember, too. She put down everything she could think of, paying no attention to organization. She made a copy of the first set of data, the general information, then started adding more details.

Madele showed up not long after that, exclaiming in horror at the scene in the galley. At least she found something to take the edge off the pain, which helped.

When Yolanda called, Moire finished the last copy and struggled to her feet. "Let's get him out of here. They're coming." She tucked the datatab in the same pocket with the pin. It wasn't everything Fleet wanted, but it was better than nothing.

The rest of the arrangements were simple. Gren to the weapons locker for a rifle for Alan, and a float-pallet for Ennis. Then they just had to wait.

Moire glanced at the shadow near the hatch, where Alan was gripping his gun, looking sullen. He was upset because she had refused to give him ammunition. In the mood he was in it was a bad idea. He still looked dangerous; nobody in their right mind would put it to the test.

Where are they? Yolanda said they were almost there.

Ennis was lying on an empty crate they'd moved outside the hatch. The drug should be starting to wear off by now. He hadn't shown signs of recovering, but then he wouldn't. Sneaky devil.

Now she saw them. Yolanda standing well to the side, putting Harrington between her and Alan. The reporter was wary, but calm and self-possessed. He kept his hands in view.

"How would you prefer me to address you?" he asked. "You seem to have quite an assortment of names."

Polite of him. Moire smiled. "Only one name, but several aliases. I'm known here as Captain Roberts."

Harrington nodded. "I trust you have not done away with him, Captain?" Moire indicated the crate, and stepped back. Harrington approached with caution, casting a quick glance at Ennis, lying on the crate. "His indisposition...?"

"Temporary. If you're impatient, use one of these." She tossed him a packet with some stimulants, and he caught it smoothly. "Probably not a good idea to leave him like that, even with you to watch him. Not around here, anyway."

He examined the packet. "What is the datatab for?"

"I hear you're curious about me. It has some answers."

"Why?" He looked at her, dubious. "Why would you want to help me?"

"You're a reporter. My enemies don't want that information to get out at all. They will be your enemies too, if you publish it." She smiled again. "But exclusives don't come cheap."

She nodded at Alan and Yolanda, and they moved toward the hatch.

"Don't be looking for me, Mr. Harrington," she said before closing the door. "I'm going to be very hard to find for a while."

The yelling started shortly after Gren dogged the hatch. If only she could make it hard for *everyone,* including her crew, to find her.

Sequoyah. Her hidden world.

"I *thought* you were staying out of trouble!" Gren said through gritted teeth. "You could have been killed!"

"An' why didn't you entro that guy?" Yolanda wanted to know. "Ya don't do stuff like that on Kulvar–they trouble, they dead. Now he's gonna be gunning for us and his buddy too! You trying' ta get us all wiped?"

"He's Fleet," Moire managed to say. She was having trouble staying upright now. She sagged against a wall and glanced up. Everyone was staring at her in stunned silence.

Her temper snapped. "I was a mercenary on a Fleet carrier, got involved in a mutiny, oh and by the way you remember Toren wants me too? I *told* you I was trouble and you wouldn't listen! So let me go!"

Her face was wet, and she couldn't even wipe it off because of her bandaged hands. Gren caught her just as her knees started to buckle. Things got a little blurry for a while, and then she found herself in a chair in the room off the galley. The crew was all gathered there, except for Kilberton.

"Just give me a ship. I'll leave."

"It's too late for that," Gren said with a sigh. "We're already involved. Toren maybe we could handle, but not them and Fleet too. You can't just up and leave us with this mess. Look, we'll help if we can. You're our captain. But we need to know why we're fighting!"

"They just want me." Moire's voice broke, and she struggled to speak. "It's...something I know. Something I found."

And an order given over eighty years ago that she could not fulfill. Who could she tell? NASA was gone. Government, Fleet–it would just end up in Toren's hands. She looked at her somber crew, all staring at her and waiting for her to explain. Ordinary people just trying to survive, and she'd just made that job much, much harder.

Ordinary people, like the ones the crew of *Bon Accord* had wished to serve.

Moire sat up.

"Tell you what. I'll show you what all the fuss is about. It's hard to get to, harder than the sargasso. We can hide out afterward, split up–your decision. But I think...I think you will understand then what we are fighting for."

She'd give them Sequoyah. Reparation for the danger she'd put them in. Even if it put them in more danger it would be their choice, and it would satisfy Etienne's final order. And she would finally be free.

The End

ABOUT THE AUTHOR

Sabrina Chase was originally trained as a Mad Scientist, but due to a tragic lack of available lairs at the time of graduation fell into low company and started working in the software industry. She lives in the Pacific Northwest and is owned by two cats.

Further sordid details may or may not be available at her website, chaseadventures.com